HEIR

OF

TWISTED

LIES

TITLES BY LJ ANDREWS

THE BROKEN SOULS AND BONES SERIES

Broken Souls and Bones
Heir of Twisted Lies

THE EVER SEAS SERIES

The Ever King
The Ever Queen
The Mist Thief

THE BROKEN KINGDOMS SERIES

Curse of Shadows and Thorns
Court of Ice and Ash
Crown of Blood and Ruin
Night of Masks and Knives
Game of Hate and Lies
Dance of Kings and Thieves
Den of Blades and Briars
Reign of Stars and Fire
Song of Sorrows and Fate

HEIR
OF
TWISTED
LIES

LJ ANDREWS

ACE
NEW YORK

ACE
Published by Berkley
An imprint of Penguin Random House LLC
1745 Broadway, New York, NY 10019
penguinrandomhouse.com

Book design by Daniel Brount
Map illustration by Alexis Seabrook

ISBN: 9780593818701

An application to register this book for cataloging
has been submitted to the Library of Congress.

Printed in the United States of America
1st Printing

The authorized representative in the EU for product safety and compliance is
Penguin Random House Ireland, Morrison Chambers, 32 Nassau Street,
Dublin D02 YH68, Ireland, https://eu-contact.penguin.ie.

To anyone afraid to show their jagged edges.
You brighten the night for those who see
your darkness and love it anyway.

Heir of Twisted Lies contains dark themes and topics that might not be suitable for all readers, including: mental abuse, manipulation, graphic violence, explicit sexual content, loss of loved ones, gore, past torture of a child, torture, and body mutilation.

BROKEN SOULS
AND BONES RECAP

WELCOME BACK TO THE REALMS OF STÌGANDR. *HEIR OF Twisted Lies* is about to pick up right where *Broken Souls and Bones* ended, so here is a little refresher on how we ended up where we are.

Lyra Bien is an orphan, raised in a youth house after bloody raids slaughtered her family when she was a young girl. There, a woman from the clans of the Unfettered named Gammal teaches Lyra to hide the silver scars in her eyes, a sign she holds a rare magical craft called melding. After a time, Lyra is sent to serve House Jakobson. But years later, her fate takes a deadly turn.

When the silver scars in her eyes are discovered, Lyra is ripped from her quiet life in the small fishing village of Skalfirth by the silent, brutal Sentry, Roark Ashwood. Removed with her is her foster brother, Kael. Lyra is discovered to have the rare magical craft of a melder and brought into the stone walls of the royal fortress, Stonegate, to face the king of Jorvandal.

King Damir covets Lyra's craft since he recently lost his

melder, Fadey, to their enemy of Dravenmoor. The king uses Kael's life as a bargaining chip: if Lyra will use her craft to build up his armies by melding soul bones to the bodies of his warriors, her brother will live in the fortress unharmed. This melding process creates fierce, nearly indestructible armor around the Jorvan Stav Guard warriors, giving them the title of Berserkir. To save Kael, she agrees.

But making it all worse, Lyra's protection detail is none other than Roark Ashwood, the man who destroyed her life and stole her from her home.

While in Stonegate, Lyra learns about the different crafts of the three kingdoms—bone craft, soul craft, and blood craft. Melding, in a way, encompasses all of them, and her ability to create unstoppable Berserkir warriors is the reason Jorvandal's enemy, Dravenmoor, despises her.

The deeper Lyra falls into the lore of magical craft, the more she realizes the corruption behind the use of soul bones and melders. She's not alone in her disgust. Every time she melds a bone to a warrior, Lyra is tossed into a dark mirrored world and comes face-to-face with a spectral of the brutal Draven assassin, Skul Drek. He vows that for every soul bone she melds, he will take a life to replace it.

As attacks on Stonegate grow more frequent, Lyra is convinced there is more to King Damir's desire to meld his warriors. Along the way, Lyra befriends Prince Thane, King Damir's son, and Emi, a converted Draven-born bone crafter. She even reluctantly begins to admit that there is an unnerving bond forming with Roark.

Not only do they both feel a strange draw to each other, they also begin to realize that some of their forgotten pasts align. But it isn't only Roark she's drawn to. The more she's forced to meld, the more the shadow of Skul Drek seems to pull her in.

When Roark helps Lyra escape an attack, their hate for each other crosses a line to something else entirely, and romance begins to bloom . . . until Dravenmoor infiltrates the gates of Stonegate, along with Skul Drek. While Roark defends the walls, Lyra faces the assassin outside the mirrored land and finds herself fighting beside him against one of Damir's Berserkir warriors.

Skul Drek confesses to Lyra that King Damir is searching for the missing bones of a long-dead king who is known as the father of magical craft, the Wanderer. Damir plans to find the first king's bones and meld them to his own body. Doing so will make him unstoppable, for the soul of the Wanderer will reign over all magical craft.

To protect the bones, Lyra makes an alliance with the assassin, and when she is alone with Roark again, she confesses the truth. Instead of hating her for betraying the king and her people, Roark vows to help free her from Stonegate, for what Damir has planned will surely strain her melding craft to the point that she won't survive.

Before they can finalize their plans to escape, Lyra and Kael are summoned by the Jorvan queen. When they arrive, they find King Damir slaughtered and his bones melded. Kael is taken prisoner, a pawn to use against Lyra, and it is revealed that the queen staged a coup with the former melder Fadey, who falsified his own death and hid his identity. Fadey needs Lyra's stronger melding craft so he can claim the hidden Wanderer's bones for himself.

Lyra narrowly escapes and is desperate to find Kael. Before she can rescue her brother, Roark sees her fleeing the guards, framed for the death of King Damir. Desperate to protect her, Roark reveals his darkest secret: He is a split soul. His other half is Skul Drek. With his strength and darkness, he, along with Emi, takes Lyra from the gates of the fortress, leaving Prince Thane and Kael behind.

Lyra is distraught to learn that the man she'd fallen for not only lied about his identity, but also abandoned her brother to their new enemies.

With control over his dark soul restored, the past is no longer shadowed, and Roark and Lyra are both able to recall that a now-dead Draven prince, Nivek, rescued her as a child. But only at the behest of a young Roark, who, as a boy, insisted she was his soul bond. Such a connection is normally regarded as sacred to the Draven folk, but Roark finally recalls how his clan viewed his bond to a melder as deadly, forbidden, and treasonous.

Prince Nivek was killed for his involvement, and Roark's soul was split to sever his growing soul bond.

Before he can finish explaining his reasons for believing his soul bonded with Lyra, their camp is invaded by Draven Dark Watch warriors. Next, the vicious queen of Dravenmoor appears and orders her warriors to take them, for her second son—Prince Roark—is finally coming home.

HEIR
OF
TWISTED
LIES

1

LYRA

PRESSED AGAINST MY RIBS WAS A DAGGER STAINED WITH blood that had long since dried black.

Water lapped at the thick logs of the makeshift boat. The rails were uneven and the floorboards were roughly cut with cracks, leaving my feet soaked in the rimy water of the Black Fjords.

It felt like ages since I'd been tossed into the vessel and forced to cross the neck of the cove, toward the enemy border of Dravenmoor. In truth, we'd only sailed through the whole of one night. The upper forest of Jorvandal had been long ago blotted out with a velvet shroud of night, and now, in the pearly mists of dawn, nothing but unknowns lay ahead.

I hugged my knees against my chest but lifted my chin, staring at the warrior aiming the blade into my ribs. Four lanterns hung from separate posts on either side of the boat, and the amber light cast angry shadows over his features. From beneath the pelt of a brindle fox covering his head, he kept watch over me through the narrow slits of blue eyes, sharp and cold as a first frost.

"What are you staring at, Melder?"

It was the first word any of the surrounding warriors had spoken to me, and I could not find the strength nor desire to reply. Instead of looking away, I merely studied him. As though marking every scar, every line of his face, might help make sense of all this.

From beneath his pelt, more than one lock of golden hair fell over his shoulder. Nearly the same shade as Kael's.

My heart burned, a knife to the center.

Kael. My brother, my truest friend, remained trapped behind the impenetrable walls of the Stonegate royal keep in Jorvandal. Fadey, the once-dead melder, was alive. Along with the cruel Queen Ingir, Fadey had stolen Kael from me.

Panic, despair, and rage were cruel foes, the sort that drew their blades swift and deep. I felt them all lodged deep in the sinews of my heart, and I could not stop the sharp, jagged breaths from sliding over my lips.

I wanted to scream and bite. I yearned to turn the blade on the Dark Watcher eyeing me like I might lunge at any moment. I ached to curl inside myself, somewhere dark and distant, and never emerge lest a new reality take shape.

"If you're going to be sick, spew it over the side," the warrior grumbled.

Focus. Piece by piece, my resolve to not bend in front of the Dark Watch splintered beneath the weight of reality. I peeled my stare from the watcher and looked to the palish sky, recalling the moments that brought me here, shivering and seething among the Dark Watch army.

Damir, the Jorvan king, was dead, and blame for his murder was placed at my feet.

And now they had Kael.

I abandoned Kael.

No. I was *forced* to leave.

"Make ready to dock." Somewhere across the raft another warrior called out the command.

Darkly clad bodies rose, stretching arms overhead, cracking necks side to side, and readying more blades in sheaths and scabbards.

When I stood, my blood felt too cold in my veins, my feet had long gone numb, and I nearly crumbled when my knees bent. My long, dark braid had loosened from the winds, and no matter how I braced against the bite of it, the cold dug into the marrow of my bones.

A gentle hand curled around my wrist. Glassy, vibrant blue eyes locked with mine. Emi Nightlark, a woman I'd considered a friend—before everything fell apart—stepped beside me.

"They're going to try to keep you separated," she whispered. "Stay by me."

I didn't have a moment to puzzle out what she meant before both of us were shoved forward toward the rail of the boat.

"Get moving," the Dark Watcher snarled, his lip curled like a snapping wolf's. His contempt flicked between me and Emi, like the sight of us turned his insides.

Emi curled an arm around my waist and whirled on the man. "You'd be wise to stay your hands from the melder. You are being watched *very* closely."

As if the warrior could sense the sharpness of distant disdain, he looked over his shoulder.

On the far side of the boat, a man stalled while packing a leather satchel with rope and what seemed to be a bone-hilt knife. The commotion drew the molten gold of his eyes to the silver scars in mine—fire and starlight.

Him. He'd taken me from the Stonegate fortress, insisting my life was of more value than Kael's. He'd taken me.

Roark Ashwood. My hunter. My protector. My lover. My liar.

For a heated moment, Roark looked nowhere but at me, then he slowly tilted his regard toward the warrior. Shadows doused the fire of his eyes, a sharp reminder of the secrets and lies the man carried soul deep.

At my side, the warrior shifted uneasily and rested a hand on the amber pommel of his blade.

He cleared his throat and used his chin to gesture us forward. "Move, then."

Emi tightened her hold around my waist and leaned into me. "Keep Roark in your sights."

Truth be told, I wanted to flee from them all, even Emi. As his cousin, she'd kept Roark's secrets as well as he had. She'd deceived me and her own lover.

Pain and betrayal urged me to pull away, but something fiercer, something deeper than instinct, kept me at her side. Like the friendship forged behind the walls of Stonegate crafted a bond made of sturdier things than the mistrust between us now.

Then again, Emi was not the one who'd shattered my heart.

When my boots sank into the damp sand of the shoreline, I looked behind me. Back to him.

Roark shouldered the satchel, his jaw pulsing with tension so fiercely I was certain it ached, but he studied my every move, my every breath. Like the shadow he'd always been, he remained on the brink of attack, a villainous predator.

The Dark Watch of Dravenmoor had been subtly trying to separate us along the journey from the wood to the Black Fjords. What I knew of Roark Ashwood was that should he be pushed too far, blood would spill.

He seemed on the brink of bloodlust even now, and I hated how I felt the need to go to him, to soothe whatever fury burned under the surface. After it all, how was it that I still yearned to be near the man?

Once, I was taught folk could never truly know a heart until they saw the darkness kept inside. But there was more to it. No one ever mentioned that to love the darker edges of a heart would consume everything. And never did I anticipate that the dark heart I fell in love with would belong to a damn prince.

A vicious truth I'd discovered not even a full sunrise before.

Was he a gallant prince from fables and sagas, like the glittering lovers that Gammal read tales of to me in the youth house so many seasons ago? No. He was the sort of prince so vicious the heroes of lore would cower at his feet and name him the villain. A man hauntingly beautiful and more inclined to slit a throat than to touch it gently, save in rare moments with me.

With me, those fingers traced my skin with a sort of reverence. In those moments, he owned me—body, heart, and soul.

I tore my gaze away and looked forward to the path ahead. Somewhere during the journey, with nothing but my tumbling thoughts to lead, Roark's lies grew into a poison tainting those sweeter memories of us together. Every cruel omission of the truth stained the tenderness of his touch, the burn of his eyes, the taste of his kiss.

How much of it was true and how much of it was to gain the trust of the melder?

It would be wiser not to feel, not to desire.

There was no longer any existence where twisted lies were not tangled between us.

"Keep pace." A tall brute of a man waved the Dark Watch warriors forward. "We need to be off road before sunrise. Move your asses."

More than one warrior shoved past me and Emi, knocking our shoulders. I was pushed aside, proving who claimed their true ire.

More warriors filtered between us, and soon Emi was drawn into the rows of Dark Watchers, at least ten paces ahead. A touch of panic brightened her eyes when she looked back, and I thought she might've called my name before she was blocked by a taller warrior.

Alone. Among those who'd be glad to ram a blade into my spine.

I quickened my steps and followed the procession up a slope from the shore until the fjord was shielded by trees and thick branches, a militant wall caging me away from any chance of freedom.

"Where do you think you're going, Melder?" A lanky Dark Watcher slipped against my side.

Another warrior chuckled and strode up next to my other shoulder, trapping me between them. "Slow down. Let us get to know each other better. Perhaps find a good reason why you ought to keep breathing."

Panic was tight in my chest. I held no power here, but I would not be slaughtered while whimpering. "Do not touch me."

He merely widened his grin. "Ah, but we know you prefer Draven cock. Must be something about you if—"

"You will step back," I said through my teeth. Craft flooded my veins, heady and cold. A taste like swallowing the tides of the sea coated my tongue, and a hint of smoke and ash burned in my lungs. I clenched one fist, readying to strike should he reach for me again. "I have melded a man's mouth shut. I have broken a Berserkir until he met Salur. I will do it again."

Something like hate darkened one of the watchers's cerulean eyes. "Do it. Gods, I hope you do. Give us a reason to end you . . ."

His words died off. Roark stepped in front of me. His stance was one of ease, almost like he was irritated that he needed to intervene at all.

Roark raised his hands to gesture a simple but direct command. *We have the queen's word the melder enters the gates unharmed. Do you stand against your queen?*

The watcher swallowed. "I . . . I don't understand."

With an agitated twist to his mouth, Roark looked to me and waved one palm.

He wanted me to . . . translate for him? I blinked, then repeated his words to the watcher.

The man seemed befuddled for a breath. "She can speak for you?"

Strange how she picked up my words swiftly. Others rarely can, not since my own clan ripped out my voice.

Damn him. Heat flooded my cheeks as I repeated Roark's words, but I left out the reek of bitterness in his silent tone.

The watcher's brow furrowed, but after a moment he stepped back. "She needs to keep up" was all he said before he fell in line with the rest.

For a few heartbeats, even surrounded by Draven warriors, it felt like Roark and I were alone.

I studied my hands, unsettled by his nearness. I'd felt the warmth of his bare skin pressed against mine, the heat of his mouth on my flesh, and now I hardly knew how to be in his presence.

For a man who'd sworn such violent devotion, he seemed wholly unbothered by the threats of the warrior. Tomas Grisen, the sod whose jaw I once melded shut, had threatened me, and Roark had forced him to eat his own finger.

Unbidden, a bite of pain lanced through my heart. Perhaps, surrounded by his own folk, the formidable Sentry was beginning to recall why his clan despised melders.

We need to move, Roark gestured and opened an arm for me to take the first step.

I didn't speak, merely followed the Dark Watch procession. What was there to say? Fate would never be on our side.

Better to end whatever had only just begun before more lives were lost.

LYRA

Briars and nettles blanketed the forest floor. Night settled over the trees like a satin shroud. Evening mists entwined the thick oaks and evergreens like claws slicing through the earth. A heavy chill in the air lifted the hair on my arms and caused each puff of breath to billow like a cloud in front of my lips.

I hugged my middle. My thoughts were too wild, too frenzied, to think of something so inconsequential as the cold.

Roark kept a steady pace. His knuckles had gone white from grasping the handle of his bearded ax with such ferocity. Any notion of comfort among his clan had faded.

As though he sensed my study, Roark looked my way. A shudder lined his breath when he turned my palm up. The gentle brush of his fingers against my skin spoke words only meant for me. *I need you to remain close.*

I winced but kept my voice low. "You were the one who settled away from me on the boat at the fjord."

Roark closed his eyes for half a breath, then barreled on, almost frantic. *I cannot let on to the depth of my feelings for you. Not here. Last I confessed feelings for a melder, blood was spilled and my voice was lost.*

Damn the gods. He was playing a role, a vicious prince who brought the melder along as something more like a prize he'd won.

Signs of his unease were all at once clearer—the way his shoulders never relaxed, the way his eyes kept scanning the rows of warriors, waiting for attack. The way his breaths were sharp and uneven.

Roark Ashwood was silently reliving the horrors of his past.

And I hadn't even noticed.

Unable to stop it, I felt a knot of anger tighten in my lower belly, sharp as broken glass. Anger for the raids that destroyed both our houses. Anger for a boy who'd done nothing but confess he felt something for a girl, then lost his soul for it.

I tugged on the end of my braid. "I don't know how to be near you anymore."

Roark spoke swiftly against my palm. *Then find a way. I do not know how much longer I can keep my darker soul at bay should anyone else disrespect you. Stay close.*

He took a long stride, abruptly ending any protest or comment from me.

But I took note of the way he kept flexing and extending his fingers, the way his neck was corded in tension, the way every step forward was forced.

He was trying to keep the second, crueler part of his soul intact.

More than the royal title he'd hidden, he'd concealed the truth that he was the tormenter of the kingdoms from the folk of Stonegate. Skul Drek was a piece of his soul determined to slaughter any who used magical craft for their own greed and desires.

The scar where his darkened soul had torn from his body at Stonegate, giving up his first lie, was still weeping streams of blood. Dirt and mud coated his palms and cheeks, and there was darkness in his eyes.

I wasn't certain he even noticed the gore on his skin. He seemed wholly transfixed by those striding alongside us, closing us in. A true hunter. A true protector.

The lies began with our interactions at Skalfirth, when he played the role of thief near my cart, and they continued within the walls of Stonegate. Deception unraveled every thread of my life. From forcing me into the service of the Jorvan royal house, to the brutality of my magical craft, and now to the imprisonment of Kael.

Still, the desperation of his plea to remain close, to help him soothe the villainous pieces of his soul, dug into my bones.

I reached out and curled my hand around his last two fingers and pulsed my grip three times. A mirror to his gesture of claiming something—three taps.

This was a signal that I was here. With him. For now.

Roark's lips parted in a quick release of air; his shoulders slumped. Like he could, at last, breathe. Gods, I despised him. Perhaps it was more that I *wanted* to despise him. Perhaps I despised him because I couldn't.

My brow furrowed against the hot sting of tears. "I will remain close, but it does not mean I trust you. I merely distrust you the least."

Roark dipped his chin in a silent acknowledgment. I released his fingers and fell a pace behind.

Draven Dark Watch warriors surrounded us. Most were muttering to one another between sharp, angry glares aimed at me.

All my life, Draven folk were considered the wild clans, feral and bloodthirsty. The Dark Watch dressed in thicker furs than

Jorvans to protect against the bite of the north winds, and the kohl and dyes painted on their faces added a touch of ferocity absent in the Stav Guard of Stonegate.

A scuffle of boots, as though someone stumbled, drew my attention. Emi tugged the hem of her tunic free from a briar shrub. One of the Dark Watchers laughed at her misstep.

She flashed her teeth with a hiss in return and lifted her chin. The long waves of her pale golden hair were tinted with dirt and darkened from damp mist and sweat. The icy blue of her eyes locked me in a hard stare, and only then did I see the slightest tremble of her lip.

Roark's cousin was treated like an outsider as much as me, and I did not understand it.

Emi fell into step at my side. "Saw the watcher pestering you. They'll try to do worse if they can get you away from Roark."

"So I'm told," I said, low enough only she would hear. "But he seems to believe showing he cares at all is more dangerous than not."

"They killed Prince Nivek, a damn heir, over Roark's connection to you already," Emi said. "The raids nearly tore Dravenmoor apart; some tried to usurp Elisabet over the perception of betrayal from her house. You think our folk will risk such division again? They'd sooner just kill you to avoid it. If he is not yet revealing the depth of his feelings, it is only for your benefit. Do not waste his effort by being reckless and stubborn. Shout and rage later, but not here in the open with more blades aimed at your throat than there will be if ever Roark can get you safely holed away from the Dark Watch."

My skin lifted in disquiet the longer she spoke.

I took in the nearby watchers. Draven folk had strange eyes, bright like gemstones, and they all seemed to carve through the darkness. All seemed to be waiting, watching, for the best moment to strike.

I stood no real chance against the warriors, and if Roark spoke true, should he fight for me, which he would, there would be no second chance. They'd kill him, the way they killed his elder brother.

I looked at the ground. "I won't be reckless."

"Good. He remains the one who will stop at nothing to keep you alive."

"Not you any longer?"

"As your friend, I would die to protect you, but I very much doubt I will be around much longer to do so if I am returned to my father. Remember? Our last meet resulted in me trying to kill him."

"But he hurt *you*."

"And made certain much of the clan assumed I was the result of an unfaithful wife, not a true Draven. Who will they believe? The bone crafter who lived half her life among our enemies? Or my father, the late king's brother? Please find trust for Roark. Soon, he may be all you have."

A sharp, twisted knot gathered deep in my belly. Emi truly believed she was striding to her death.

A new sort of heat flooded my veins. "Then you stay close to me."

"Lyra, you can do nothing for me. I left my clan as a fugitive. There is no helping me, but you . . . you and Roark must find a way to stop—"

"Ready to cross the ravines!" a Dark Watcher shouted down the line.

Emi blew out a rough breath. She reached for my hand, squeezing. "Listen to me: Elisabet won't kill you, not right away. She'll want answers for what broke the control of Skul Drek."

Emi straightened when two Dark Watch warriors drew near. A hand fell to the small of my back. Roark. Unease carved into the sharp lines of his face.

Against my spine, his fingers moved, gently, carefully, gesturing his command. *Cross with me.*

I bit down on the inside of my cheek and peered over the stony cliffside of the ravine.

The Red Ravines were deep fissures lined with crimson-leaf aspen trees. From warm months to frosts, the bloody shade of the leaves never fell away, only deepened in color from vibrant fire red to rich burgundy.

Between the twisted trunks were sharp, stony ridges the shade of rusted iron. Specks of inky black jutted through the shade, and I knew more than one blade was made from the dark ore. Whether the soil had some element that stained everything from the rocks to the leaves red, I didn't know. Most lore on the ravines insisted that great claws from the gods' wolves carved the soil, digging so deep the land bled.

A single unsteady step, and one would fall to their death onto the jagged stones in the river below.

Where the Dark Watch led us revealed five bridges. But not secure, wide bridges. These were made of a rope below and a rope above. Already, Dark Watchers were striding out onto the taut strands.

They fastened blades, arrows, and bows to their belts, then held firmly to the line overhead and walked out over the gaping canyon.

I swallowed against a thick knot in my throat. "We're crossing? Like that?"

Roark regarded me with an unreadable expression as he spoke with one palm. *It is the only way forward unless we take open roads to the shore, where Jorvans may find us.*

Naturally the Dark Watch would avoid their enemies and take the most foolish, dangerous path to do so.

Before I could respond, a heavy hand fell on my shoulder, gripping me tightly and drawing me too close to the edge.

A Dark Watch warrior beamed through the gruesome streaks of kohl down his young features. "Melder, seems I'm to see to it that you cross the ravine. Hold tight, now. I'd truly hate to see you fall and snap your pretty neck."

ROARK

GUNTER BLACKVALE WAS GOING TO DIE.

Forget our history—friends since the time I could walk—too much time had passed and now the bastard was going to split into pieces on the ravine floor.

Upon the first touch of Lyra, I had the knife I kept sheathed above my ankle in hand. In three paces, I was at his back. And in the next breath, I had my blade pressed against the hollow of his throat.

Gunter had the gall to look stunned.

"What are you doing?" His brows tugged together, and his wild eyes were still the shade of lavender blooms, but now they were filled with a strange sort of wounded heat. "Get your knife off me. You were never as swift as me, and I'll prove that truth remains. What's with the look? Oh, are you taking some great offense I haven't addressed you formally? What a snob you are."

I didn't understand how the man could have grown so dense,

but—still with my blade under his chin—the fool bowed at the waist, his eyes rolled up to hold mine.

"Satisfied, *my prince*? Now, step back, so I can see her on the rope properly."

What in the two hells was he doing?

I removed the knife and shoved him away from Lyra, only content to leave her when Emi gripped her arm. Even though I knew Gunter would not understand my tirade, my hands spun and gestured my demands to stay away from Lyra and vows that his blood would spill should he touch her again.

I'd not wanted to reveal my affection for Lyra on the journey forward. No doubt the Dark Watch would still see our bond as something twisted and wretched. I'd planned to keep my indifference until I could safely lock her away inside the royal house and plot a way out of Dravenmoor.

But plans would need to alter course; I could no longer find a reason to care whether the darkness inside bled out.

Gunter watched every signal, one of his palms scratching the back of his neck where his bronze hair waved around his shoulders. "Listen, I've tried to learn some of this"—he waved a hand at my gestured words—"but frankly any ravagers who survive your blade don't really wish to speak much after. Seems you're a bit frightening to them. What's he saying, Nightlark?"

I spun on my cousin. Her fingers were still curled around Lyra's wrist, but the barest of grins teased her lips when she looked to Gunter. "He's describing all the painful ways your bones will be plucked from your flesh if you touch Lyra again."

Lyra did not look mortified, not like she had when I'd once demanded a reckless Stav kneel at her feet for her forgiveness. I dared not allow the slightest hope, but I could not deny there was a buried passion behind the silver scars in her eyes. Like she might want me to recite more gory promises to my own folk.

Gunter snorted. "Well, I'm going to need to touch her. I'm to tether her to me, after all. Or do you prefer she walks out there on her own with no previous experience? A little ruthless, wouldn't you say?"

My chest butted against his. *I will cross with her.*

After Emi translated, Gunter grinned. "Not what my orders are, you ass."

As though time hadn't created a divide between us, Gunter patted my cheek, the same as he often did when we were boys. Hard. Then took a step toward Lyra.

She lifted her chin. "I'm not going across the ravine with you."

Gunter let out a groan and pinched the bridge of his nose like we were all petulant young ones. "Fine. Suit yourself. I'm cold, my feet have ached since I stepped on a damn thorn before we ever found you, and I had a meet set with Sigrid and her naked body before the Watch was called away. I intend to keep it the moment we're inside the gates."

Gunter moved aside, waving his arms in a gesture for Lyra to go to me. "Just so you know, Melder, he always was terrible at balancing and rocked the entire tether. But please, choose him. Nightlark! Ahead of me. I'll keep watch on your back, it seems."

Emi shifted in disquiet but forced a grin when she faced me. "He wasn't horrid to me before I ran. He's not going to toss me off the side."

My fists clenched all the same.

Gunter took note. "What now? Going to eat me with your dark soul? Didn't even give me a chance to see it before you went off to bleed, and I'm still holding that against you."

Lyra's lips parted, and a heated flush filled her cheeks. "When he . . . went off to bleed? You mean when his own folk *tore* him apart?"

By the gods, I could not keep the smirk from my lips. Try to resent me for the secrets kept between us all she wanted, but Lyra Bien was not one to hide when she cared for someone. I took a bit of pleasure being on the receiving end of her defenses. It was another taste of hope.

I would have that woman in my arms, on my tongue, in my soul again.

Gunter chuckled, but there was little delight in the sound. "Yes, Melder. That's the day. Life-changing for many of us, you see." With a new shadow to his features, Gunter faced Emi. "Come, Nightlark. As cousin to the prince you're safe with me, for I still have a long-standing debt that must be paid to him for vital services rendered on my behalf once. Perhaps he has forgotten how fiercely we Dravens honor our debts."

One final narrow glare, and Gunter strode to one of the heavy ropes buried beneath vines of pale blossoms, still damp from the morning mists. Disquiet over Emi burned heady in my chest, but she would need to cross, and I would not leave Lyra.

I would simply try to stay as close to my cousin as possible.

"Are we truly doing this? The slope seems to go on for ages." Lyra cautiously peered over the edge of the ravine.

Had I not been so near I might've missed the subtle drum of her fingers against her sides, a show of the apprehension she fought to conceal.

I ran my knuckles down the back of her arm, waiting until she peered back at me. *I vowed not to let you fall.*

A vow made in Stonegate the day she met King Damir. A time before I loved her, a promise to keep her upright, bolstered against the burdens of her craft. I meant it then, and I meant it now.

Lyra's lips pinched. "Don't do that."

I arched a brow, a silent question, perhaps a bit of a taunt.

"Don't speak like . . . like we are the same as we once were."

We are not the same. I took a step nearer until my chest pressed to her back. One arm slipped around her body, my fingers slowly gesturing against the place just above her heart. *I will not pretend everything has not changed. But my vows never will. I will not let you fall. Ever.*

Her pulse was a storm beneath my palm. After a drawn pause, Lyra lifted her chin with the touch of defiance she wore like steel armor and strode to a thick, dark rope. "I'd rather get on with it, then. How do I do this?"

I approached a Dark Watcher and pointed at a tether rope entwined around his belt. The man had a scowl so deep it hid his eyes beneath his thick brows. Sweat carved through streaks of kohl and dirt on his cheeks, and his front two teeth were made of tarnished silver.

After another brisk point, the watcher relented and tossed the rope over to my outstretched hand.

"Better for the clan to hang her from it, my prince," he said in a grit-soaked rasp.

Heat from rage I'd kept buried prickled over my skin. Words I wanted to gesture and rant would fall on ignorance. I did nothing more than lean closer and clack my teeth, nearly biting the watcher's nose.

He jolted back, his vibrant violet eyes growing wide in stun.

A frigid breeze wrapped my limbs. The deledan soul—the darker edge of me—fought against the unseen chains I tightened to keep my depravity bound. For this fool, it seemed every piece of me wanted to make an exception.

I took a bit of pride in the way the watcher stepped back. His gaze bounced between mine and the dark coils of a crueler soul bleeding from my skin.

A warning.

A reminder.

I was not good. I was made of darkness.

Lyra watched with a sort of bemused hesitation, a collision of disquiet and delight.

Without a word, I made quick work of encircling her waist with the rope.

"It's . . . *he's* touching me."

I lifted my chin. All around Lyra's wrists were inky shadows, almost caressing her, clinging to her. A desire burned in my chest, screaming to draw her nearer, to devour her.

I finished securing the knot with a yank on the rope, then curled my fingers around the tether and tugged her against my chest. *Because all of me is consumed by you.*

Lyra's mouth tightened. I flashed a smug sort of grin and dipped my face closer. She aimed her regard to the sky, avoiding my nearness, and I could not stop the rough, breathy laugh that slipped up my throat. The stubborn, beautiful woman kept trying to avoid me and made it wholly obvious she wanted to do the opposite.

It's true, I gestured where she could read my hands.

Lyra huffed and took a step away. "We ought to keep going."

We would need to speak on the lies and secrets kept between us, but the way she shouldered away from me, it was clear she had no desire—perhaps no strength—to do so now.

I hurriedly secured the opposite end of the rope to my waist. Most watchers did not cross tethered to a partner, but I would not risk Lyra.

Emi had already stepped onto one of the taut ropes, carefully moving along, her hands gripping the top. Over his shoulder, Gunter flashed his white teeth behind the blue and black smudges on his face. "Wager I still best you in how swiftly we cross."

Ass. Gunter always boasted he was faster on the ropes when we were boys, but in truth, he always required his father to aid him.

I turned to Lyra, one hand raised. *Ready?*

"No." She stretched her throat to peer over the ledge once more without stepping nearer. "But I admit, I'm curious about the debt he mentioned. I cannot tell if he admires you or wishes to defeat you."

We were once close.

"Meaning you were friends."

I merely shrugged. *When Gunter discovered his cock for the first time, I guarded his door and saved him from his mother walking in before he'd explored long enough.*

Through all the pain and fear weighing on me since leaving the Jorvan fortress, I did not anticipate the laugh to take her so abruptly. A loud bark of a sound. Lyra quickly clapped a palm over her lips when more than one Dark Watcher looked our way.

It was the burning gaze twenty paces below us that brought me to pause. The Draven queen. I returned Elisabet's raised brow with a sharp glare.

I would do, say, and be anything if I could draw out such sounds from Lyra again and again.

In a moment of boldness, I pinched her chin between my fingers, drawing her face to mine, and slowly gestured: *Trust me.*

"I already did that once," she whispered.

Well, shit. What more could I say?

I led us to the edge, but when I turned to usher her onto the rope first, my insides plummeted.

Fillip, the Dark Watcher the queen had commanded to lead the caravan away from Jorvandal, raced toward us, a knife aimed at Lyra's back.

There was no time to think, only to fall into instinct.

Cold, fierce as the frosts on the fjords, enveloped my body. Darkness clouded my vision. Tension snapped—the sort that felt like teeth gnawing through my skin—and broke free of my chest, my throat, my soul.

In the murky shadows that billowed around my shoulders the air filled with Lyra's screams.

LYRA

SOMETHING HOOKED AROUND THE ROPE TIED TO MY WAIST and pulled me backward with such force, I tumbled to the ground.

I screamed when a man fell over the top of me, a Dark Watcher, his eyes wild like a blaze in the woods.

A knife was pressed to my throat as the hiss of his words loosed spittle against my cheek. "I will not have you in our borders. How the queen can stomach you near us, I do not understand. You are the cause of it all, the blood, the pain, the suffering. Dine in Salur, Melder!"

Short, jagged breaths lifted my chest; I fought the urge to scream again. Thoughts spun as the sharp sting of steel cut into my flesh.

Until the blade was ripped away.

Shadows, thick as a stormy midnight, encompassed my body. Familiar cold enrobed my shoulders, and glossy ribbons of darkness curled around my limbs. Through it all a pair of vicious copper-red eyes glared back at me.

Skul Drek.

Roark.

My hunter. My protector. My lover.

My liar.

In my time in the mirror realm, where I would go to meld the bones of the fallen, I'd grown accustomed to the sight of the phantom assassin. But to know, all this time, those otherworldly eyes belonged to the man who'd stolen my heart had changed it all.

Skul Drek slaughtered folk. He was wicked.

And he saved me.

More than once. The same as he was doing now.

Perhaps it would be wise to recoil, but instead I leaned in. The darkness cocooned me in a swirl of shadows, a taste of salt and smoke on my tongue. Protected. Shielded.

"Lyra!" Emi's voice was distant.

Through the mists, I could make out Gunter stepping off the rope, back on our side of the ravine, then handing Emi off. She sprinted forward.

Without hesitation, she reached through the billows of shadows that made up the darker soul and had her slender arms wrapped around my shoulders.

"Gods, I saw Fillip . . . I tried to call out, but he moved so swiftly . . ." Emi didn't finish, merely tightened her hold.

Little by little the dark coils of mists retreated. Through the fading remnants of his crueler soul Roark stepped through. The burn of gold in his eyes collided with the blaze of copper for a fleeting moment.

His jaw was taut, his fists curled. He spared one glance down to where I was wrapped in his cousin's embrace, then looked to the Dark Watcher.

Fillip backpedaled, the knife still in his hold. "What did you expect? This was bound to happen sooner or later. I'm merely doing every damn kingdom a favor by getting on with it."

Roark removed a knife from inside his boot.

"Don't!" I tried to go to him, but he was already out of reach.

"Stop this!" Elisabet pushed between Dark Watchers near the ledge, but her son never even glanced her way.

Roark reached Fillip as the man raised his own knife, but he was no match for the Sentry of Stonegate, the Death Bringer. The moment Fillip went to strike, Roark buried his knife in the side of the warrior's throat. No hesitation. No remorse.

I clapped a hand over my mouth and watched with a bit of horror as Roark twisted the blade and thrust it deeper into the man's flesh.

Fillip's eyes flew open. Blood fountained over his kohl-painted lips. His palms padded across Roark's chest as though seeking a ballast in death.

Roark's teeth were bared when he gave another fierce thrust of the blade until the tip of the point jutted out the opposite side of the man's neck.

In the next moment, Roark tore the weapon from Fillip's flesh, then stood by as the warrior crumpled at his feet.

Dead.

Roark wiped the blade of the knife clean on Fillip's unmoving body, then spun on his clan, malice written in every line of his face. His hands gestured frantically.

Emi, her fingers still entangled with mine, cleared her throat. "Your prince demands that you look at this fallen soul."

Roark's hand speak was brisk and rage filled; it was loud and suffocating. Voice or not, the same as he'd done as Sentry, he commanded terror-lined silence.

The man was a godsdamned force.

Emi barreled on, more boldness in her own tone. "His vow—

not a threat—is simple: touch the melder, and you meet the gods. No questions."

Elisabet's brilliant eyes darkened, but I did not think her frustration was entirely pointed at me. More like she was frustrated with her son and would have words with him later.

A Dark Watcher with a fox fur draped over his head stepped forward. "Why don't you tell our lost prince—"

"I do not need to tell him anything, Ofan," Emi snapped. "He speaks with his hands but has ears as he always did."

Ofan glared at Roark. "You are not king. Yet. Do not blame your exile on your clan. You would've rejoined us, lived among us, if only you'd done your duty and killed that." The warrior pointed at me, hand trembling. "Yet you slaughter your own folk to keep it breathing. After all that was lost, you chose the melder. King Vishon would be ashamed to call you a son."

If I'd not been so near to Roark, I would have missed his flinch at the vicious retort. Still, he did not step away; he did not look ashamed.

Roark grinned. *If I am a disappointment already, why not seal it by making my loyalty known?*

With slow, prowling steps, Roark returned to Fillip's corpse and soaked his palm in the fountain of blood still leaking from the man's neck.

"No. That is enough," Elisabet said through her teeth.

Her son ignored her. Blood on his fingers, his hands, Roark washed the whole of his face in Fillip's gore. Great gashes of sticky red over his frightening smile.

A few gasps and grumbles filtered through the Dark Watch. They were Draven, the wild, bloodthirsty folk. I did not understand why a bit of blood affected them so.

I tucked myself closer to Emi's side and watched Roark drag blood down his lips, through his hair, and across his chest, staining his tunic. It was a glimpse of the darker pieces of his heart bleeding through, the depravity that was meant to make up Skul Drek, and I could not look away.

Truth be told, if I had questions about whether I could love Roark Ashwood despite the lies and omitted truths, this moment proved the sharper, crueler pieces of him stirred my soul as much as the gentle.

I did not know what sort of fiend that made me.

"He is shaming Fillip," Emi whispered. "Draven folk hold a great deal of respect for the dead. They honor their souls and will often paint belongings in blood for their souls to visit loved ones."

"He is washing himself?"

"It is a sign of disrespect. To bathe in the blood of the fallen shows you revel in their death, you spurn any hope they will find peace. You invite their soul to you so you might torment them even as they dine in Salur. He is marking Fillip as his enemy for what he did to you."

Roark finished coating his skin in Fillip's blood and brazenly walked over the body, stepping on his remains like he was nothing but a fallen tree.

Gods, why must he be so grotesquely wonderful? He'd killed a man on my behalf in Stonegate; now he'd done it again.

I did not know if Roark's brutality would fill the cracks of mistrust in my heart entirely. But for a moment, I stepped nearer to him, stood straighter. A show of support for a man who killed without mercy.

My ally. My protector. My villain.

He raised his hands, still grinning, and spoke to the warriors. *Vishon made me. You all made me. But tell me, Ofan, will you kill me? Perhaps you have already killed a prince.*

Emi blinked a few times before finishing the translation. Elisabet shot a glance at Ofan.

The man faltered, his eyes narrowed at Roark. "I don't know what you mean."

Roark laughed. Raw, breathy, his voiceless laugh. *Let us hope that is true.*

Ofan's disdain fell back to me. "I'm merely saying what we're all thinking. The deledan rite was done to rid the land of melders, now we're embracing one. Fillip was loyal. Merely doing what you didn't have the damn stones to do."

He didn't wait for Roark to respond before shoving his way back into the crowd of the Dark Watch.

Elisabet blew out a rough breath. Near her side she cracked one knuckle, but after a moment, the queen stepped forward. "We keep going. All these . . . disputes will be dealt with in our courts."

She flashed a single glance at where Fillip's corpse remained and pushed to the front of the line.

Emi let her shoulders slump. "Remember how I told you I missed the wildness of Dravenmoor?"

I nodded, unable to tear my attention from Roark's profile.

"Well." Emi shouldered her satchel. "I think I spoke too soon."

Roark wheeled around to us. *I will be called to answer for this when we reach the gates. You two are never to be parted, understand?*

Emi shook her head. "You know he'll be searching for me the instant we return."

And his position does not surpass mine.

I could only assume they spoke of Emi's father.

"Listen." Gunter approached, one hand rubbing his chin as he cautiously peered at Fillip's body. "I know you don't think much of us anymore, and I'm trying not to be offended and such, but I'd like it if half the clan didn't end up slaughtered by your blades."

Roark glared at Gunter, waiting in dark silence for the man to continue.

"I'm only saying, when you're called into the úlfur to be rep-rimanded, I'll see to it they're both secure until you return."

"What is the úlfur?" I whispered to Emi.

"Draven council. Brutal warriors who live by their rituals and laws. They are the councilmen who oversaw Roark's soul rend to create the deledan—Skul Drek, I mean."

Liquid heat burned under my skin. I despised the lot of them without even meeting any.

"Believe it or not, my prince," Gunter went on, "some of us didn't stand for what was done to you."

Emi scoffed as though she didn't believe a word.

"A lot changed after you left, Nightlark. We grew up. Under-stood more." Gunter's words were firm, steady. "We've merely been waiting for the end of your sentence locked with some sod-ding prince and the damn Jorvan king."

My heart cracked a little thinking of Prince Thane. No mis-take, Roark felt a great deal more than he let on about his betrayal of the man. Yes, they were meant to be enemies, but they were brothers, as true as if they shared blood.

And Roark had abandoned his friend—his brother in all ways that mattered—to chaos and danger in Stonegate . . . to save me.

Unbidden, I gripped Roark's wrist. Tension flowed in his forearm, but at my touch, his breaths eased.

Gunter let out a heavy sigh. "Come on. You may have no choice but to trust me. Let me at least try to prove it'll be worth it."

After a moment of hesitation, Roark adjusted so his fingers slipped through mine, urging us forward to where the ropes to cross the ravine awaited.

5

ROARK

Most of the dark watch gave us a wide berth after Fillip met the gods.

The rope walkways swayed in the wind. Lyra had need of a pause twice before hurrying off the opposite end to the forest paths over Dravenmoor borders, her shoulders slumped in relief to be on solid ground.

Only when I dragged Lyra to a narrow, more isolated path did a blade stand in my way.

A young Dark Watcher swallowed thickly. "Can't be straying, Highness."

I grinned, hoping a great deal of Fillip's blood stained my teeth.

"You want to end up like Fillip, Henri?" Gunter knocked the watcher's blade away. "Where do you suppose they can run? We're in Dravenmoor, you sod. There's only forward lest the prince wishes to flee for the Night Ledges. I'd wager my own cock we'd catch them first."

"I'm to keep them in sight," argued Henri.

"Oh, are you, now?" Gunter flicked at a piece of a dried leaf on his arm. "You wish to force the man the Jorvans named Death Bringer, whose soul will likely eat yours out of sheer annoyance, to walk by your side?" Gunter chuckled darkly and leaned closer. "Who do you fear more, Henri, your Dark Watch commander or your damn prince?"

Henri hesitated but soon lowered his blade. "Keep close, the wood is—"

Does this fool think I have never traipsed these damn woods? My rough gesture cut him off.

Lyra cleared her throat and spoke. "He reminds you that he knows these trees."

Gunter laughed. "The amount of time we spent on these trails, we know them better than you, Henri. Set the fara on their scent. They won't run. Same as before, my prince, I'll watch Nightlark."

"You keep thinking I can't handle my own neck," Emi called from where she stood ten paces off.

I did not revel in the idea of Dark Watch fara wolves tracking our every step, but I would prefer it over traipsing about with a horde of warriors who wanted Lyra dead and were willing to disregard their queen's word to see it done.

I made no more effort to speak, merely led Lyra into the trees. The path was narrow but shadowed. Free of scrutiny.

"Where does this lead?" she whispered once the steps of the Dark Watch were more distant.

The back side of the palace.

"Are the wolves truly there?"

I tilted my head and slowed my pace for a breath, then another. I nodded. *Twenty paces away on every side. They won't harm us unless signaled.*

"Unless signaled." She scoffed. "Not exactly comforting after . . . what happened."

I tightened my hold on her palm. *We'll be fine.*

Lyra didn't protest, nor did she try to use the wretched truths between us to create distance. She clung to my arm, my hand, like I was her beacon in the night.

Forest winds were cold and fragrant, tinged with the sweet moss that grew on the banks of the small creeks that cracked the soil across the kingdom. Each draw of air filled my lungs like a frosted morning, clean and fresh.

Overhead tree branches intertwined like armies tangled in battle. Dark and formidable, the trees were places where young Dravens learned to hide, to sneak, and to trust the creatures of the forest.

More than once I let my fingertips brush the branches of hedges or leaves of satin ferns. Such a strange feeling—returning home but not truly belonging.

New aches burned in every muscle, from the base of my skull to the small of my back. Lyra was not safe here, no matter my title. Fillip was proof of that.

Pale dawn crested over the rocky peaks, extensions of the Night Ledges that formed a natural barrier around the heart of Dravenmoor. Last I'd laid eyes on these cliffs, my brother was dead and my soul was carved in two.

For a moment my steps slowed until every motion felt a great deal like leaden ore lined the soles of my feet.

Lyra glanced over her shoulder, her brows stitched close.

I didn't lift a hand to speak, didn't look away from the cliffs. Damn the gods, I was a fool. During the seasons as the Sentry of Stonegate, I'd lost count of the souls I'd sent to the hall of the gods in Salur. Skul Drek was feared by all. Enough blood marred my palms to name me a monster, but the sight of mountains from my childhood brought me to tremble.

"Roark." Lyra rested a hand on my forearm. "What is it?"

My scrutiny of the peaks broke, as though her nearness brought a bit of clarity. In the haunting gray of the early bell tolls, the silver scars in Lyra's eyes glittered like pieces of the fading moon. They drew me in, captured me, reminded me of why all of it had unfolded.

Still I said nothing, but I wasn't certain I needed to.

Lyra's face softened. She tucked a lock of her long hair behind her ear and stepped closer. "I imagine it is difficult to see home again after what happened."

I cleared my throat as though I might speak with my lost voice. *Last I stepped through these gates, I was told my brother was dead.*

Lyra dipped her chin. "What was he like?"

Nivek was good. Honorable. Nine seasons my elder, so I looked up to him all my life. He did not deserve to die.

"And you don't know who killed him?"

I shook my head. *I know my uncle informed the king and queen of Nivek's betrayal, but that was his duty as my father's brother.*

"It wasn't him?"

I can't say. I am told he was furious when he discovered the prince was killed without a trial. I did not see much from where I was hidden. Someone struck me from behind and I woke here, at the gates. If I find out the truth, their soul will be mine.

"Explains your questioning of the warrior."

I scoffed. *Someday I will know exactly what happened that night.*

"I hope you do." Her words were soft but sharp enough that they burned into my chest. "I wish he had not died because of me. But I can see that he must've loved you to take such a risk because you asked it of him."

I hesitated. *He died because he believed in soul bonds and respected them, the way the clan should.*

"You have based every decision of late on these supposed bonds." Lyra bit down on her bottom lip. "You and I have never had much choice in our lives; we should not let some bond of fate take a choice from us now."

What are you saying?

"I'm saying we are dangerous for each other. I'm saying truth matters to me. I'm saying . . . perhaps we both deserve a choice for once, and maybe we would be better off forgetting . . . what happened between us in Stonegate. Forced love is not what I desire."

Fear was talking. Fear, pain, and likely a bit of anger.

I drew closer, chest to chest, hip to hip, taking a bit of twisted delight in the way her lips parted, her eyes widened.

For a moment, I made no attempt to speak at all, merely held her close, studying the light in her eyes. My palm splayed over the small of her back, my fingers brushing across every divot of her spine.

With care, I lifted one hand and fashioned my words against her cheek. *You are my choice. Should I discard you at the command of kings or queens, that would rob me of my true choice.*

"But if you believe fate bonded us, then there is little—"

You misunderstand soul bonds, I said, pausing to run my thumb across the ridge of her cheek. *It does not force a love match, merely reveals the potential of a match in another soul. A bond can wither if left unattended. More must be done to make it truly unbreakable.*

Lyra kept a keen watch on my hands, as though she did not want to misunderstand a word, then lifted her chin to meet my study. "What more must be done?"

I shook my head, uncertain how to explain the sjeleven sealing ceremony and what it meant. *It's not important right now, but trust I know how to recognize the difference between a bond and what I feel in my heart, Lyra.*

"How can you tell the difference? I am questioning every damn thought I've ever had. You . . . kept this from me when you could've told me, even portions of it."

Her voice trembled. I held the side of her face, studying her, catching sight of the shadow of uncertainty in her eyes. The same look she had when I'd dragged her from the borders of Skalfirth. Gods, it felt like an eternity ago.

What I feel for you should not be possible because my soul is split.

"What does that have to do with it?"

One corner of my mouth curved up in a reluctant grin. *The curse was done to prevent me from being able to restore my soul bond.*

"But I saw the connections. I saw the bond," she said, her voice rough and low, almost reluctant to admit she had seen a connection between us.

As did I. Your sheer stubbornness captivated not only me, but every darkened, cruel, unfeeling piece of me. Something I do not believe has ever been done.

Lyra looked down. "I wouldn't say I captivated Skul Drek. I think I annoyed him . . . you."

A deledan is a split soul and meant to be a weapon, not meant to feel much more than duty. What I feel for you should not be possible. Despite everything, you took ownership of all of me, but I do not know if it is the same for you.

Lyra scrutinized me, as though scouring my words for more lies. At long last, her face fell, her shoulders slumped. She placed a palm over my heart. "I'm not certain I know you, Roark. Not as I thought I did."

A sharp pain dug into my chest, but I did not flinch, did not look away. How could I fault her? All the time she thought she spoke to the Sentry of Stonegate, all the fear she held when she melded and faced Skul Drek, instead she was speaking to a traitor and an enemy prince, a cruel soul sent to slaughter her.

I gave a brisk nod, then held out one hand for her to take and spoke with the other. *We need to keep moving.*

After a moment of hesitation, Lyra clasped my palm in hers. I would take it as my own small victory. I would take it all as proof her heart was not wholly closed against me. Any other alternative would simply not do.

The narrow path opened to a wider back road, both sides lined with ominous oaks. Blankets of leaves shielded us from the warmth of the morning sun. Thick roots jutted out from every knobby trunk like great sea serpents diving beneath the tides.

We took the final bend and, all at once, faced the front gates of the royal township of Dravenmoor.

Moss-coated dark stone walls in a poisonous shade of green. Every ten paces jagged iron spikes rose through the stone with skulls piked on the tops—ravens, wolves, even human skulls of those unfriendly with Dravenmoor who'd come too close to the gates.

Totems made of peeled twigs, toad bones, and raven blood hung from iron hooks at every spiked post, signals to those approaching that these lands were guarded by craft and blades.

Lyra's regard trailed down a long twine rope tied with numerous bones. Her fingers tangled together, and I did not think she even realized she was about to snap off her thumbs.

Fears would be dealt with, but not now. Not here.

Shoulders back, I guided us beyond the walls. Each step was a pace into a past version of my life long gone. Amid the gloom and mists were sod-topped roofs that rounded like knolls. Cottages dotted the outer edges of the trees. Small farms lined in black oak fences had totems hanging from their arched doorways much like those on the border gates.

The main caravan of the Dark Watch must've already entered the gates, for the heavy doors were open and raucous applause roared over the walls.

"Will Gunter truly watch over Emi?" Lyra asked, a shudder in her voice.

No mistake, I'd wondered the same. My cousin fled these gates after nearly murdering her father. Hateful as my uncle might've been to his daughter, for some, Emi's crime would always be the more grievous.

We should hurry was all I gestured before striding past the long wooden gates of farms and cottages that lined the outer walls.

Young ones leapt onto the tops of fence posts and waved, pleading for a token or bit of the wild honey warriors were known to bring back from the ravines.

Abandoned, cursed, and brutalized by these people, I'd often tried to twist memories of my homeland into something cruel and wretched. Now it seemed so ordinary. So . . . familiar.

I tightened my hold on Lyra's hand, forcing my attention forward, and quickened our steps toward the back side of the palace.

Slats made of stained blackwood coated the rooftops. Points and peaks reached toward the dawn like gnarled teeth seeking to bite a piece of the sky. There were not as many turrets and towers as at Stonegate, but the walls were sturdy, made of thick beams and heavy rock.

When we reached the rear gates, a whistle broke over the shouts of those greeting the Dark Watch. A deliberate tune, one meant to be used for a certain command.

I held out an arm, blocking Lyra from continuing. Deep, raw snarls rolled down the stone steps beyond the gates, and rumbling growls came from the trees on all sides like echoes of a nightmare.

Gods, no. In one swift movement, I shoved Lyra behind me and yanked a dagger from the sheath on my thigh.

Her eyes widened when she peered over my shoulder. A line of gray, wiry fur raised over large forelegs, and the whip of swishing tails behind clawed haunches came into view.

The fara wolves tracking us in the trees surrounded us from the sides, and ahead two more emerged from behind the palace walls. No less than a dozen. Too many wolves to calm alone. Too many to slaughter with the blade in my hand.

I rolled the dagger in my grip, point down. I could fight long enough for Lyra to run. She was swift and might make it beyond the gates, back through the wood. She might even be able to hide in the ravines until she could find her way to the Night Ledges.

The lead wolf snapped its jaws. I returned a narrow glance. She would live, even if I did not.

I patted Lyra's hip without turning around and gestured the word *Run* against her tunic.

She merely dug her fingernails deeper into my arms. "Roark, no."

Stubborn, foolish woman. Jaw tight, I relented my command for a moment when the first wolf padded its heavy paw down the steps. The familiar prickle of frigid craft rippled over my skin. The taste of smoke and ash coated my tongue. In the corners of my eyes, layers of shadows took form around us.

Even with Skul Drek's aid, I was not certain I could handle so many beasts before they attacked.

Lyra would run even if I had to shove her down the road myself. But as for me, this would be the final, brutal welcome of the banished Draven prince.

LYRA

DARKNESS CLOAKED MY SHOULDERS, CARESSING MY SKIN with a cold, velvet touch. Skul Drek did not take shape, more like his essence bled from Roark's body and encircled me.

Not himself.

The stubborn, relentless fool shoved me behind him, ensuring his darkness formed a strange barrier around me, then gripped his dagger with his other hand.

He was trying to force me to leave him, much the same as the first time the fara wolf came into the Phantom Forest.

One wolf was vastly different from twelve.

I crouched down and plucked a jagged stone from the ground. A pitiful weapon, but I'd lost any blade worth using. Instinct roared at me to run, to save my damn neck, but something deeper, something darker kept my stance planted at the side of Roark Ashwood.

If he fell, I fell.

The looming battle brightened his eyes to a fiery gold. A low

growl rolled from his throat, but when he seemed to realize I was
not moving, Roark whirled back to the line of wolves, blade out.

Fangs bared, fur raised, the pack prowled nearer, some drifting to the sides like the wolves were preparing to form a circle
around us to trap us in. One beast snapped its jaws my way. I
lifted the stone overhead, readying to throw, knowing in the
back of my mind that my worthless weapon would offer me one
potential shot against one damn wolf.

Roark could at least slash several before they tore out his
throat. Perhaps he might even get away from it all. Unbidden, the
thought drew a small grin. Perhaps he could find a way to finally
be free.

Tap. Tap. Tap.

I looked down. Roark had one palm on my hip. He kept
tapping in threes, pausing, then beginning again. Mine. A final
claim. Only then did I know that Roark could not see a way free
from the wolves. He wanted me to feel that his last thoughts were
of me.

No mistake, this had been his mother's plan all along. Draw
me beyond the gate, then tear me apart.

I didn't believe she anticipated such a fate for her son, but because the bastard refused to leave my side, he would fall too.

Tears burned over my lashes. Gods, I hated him for being
such a beautiful fiend. Deceit, manipulation, and bloodlust, yet
through it all my heart still yearned for more of him, for a bit
more time.

A sharp whistle broke over the low growls of the wolves. Both
ears on every beast pricked upward, and the tension in their
coats and haunches eased. From behind the line of fara, a man
emerged onto the grounds from an arched doorway of the palace.

He was clad in a fur-lined cloak, the way he moved was direct
and intimidating. The man's height was formidable, but the

contours of his shoulders and arms gave up that he was no
stranger to swinging a blade.

His eyes were a shade of rose, vibrant and eerie, and he kept
his long auburn hair shorn on the sides but braided down the
center of his skull. I could see the sneer, even beneath his beard.

"Seems the fara have some sliver of respect for you." He let out
a condescending chuckle. "Half expected them to attack at first
glance. Suppose it should be a consolation you still possess a
touch of your true blood." He paused, those strange eyes locking
on me. "Then again, I'm not certain you even remember what
your blood means."

Roark straightened. Based on the tension in his corded neck
and the pulse of his jaw, this man was not a welcome face.

Slowly, Roark raised one palm for a single word. *Uncle.*

All gods. Emi's father. Where was she? Gunter vowed to look
after her, after us both. But I had yet to see them.

Fists curled, my fingernails dug into the flesh of my palms,
and with every pump of my heart, I frantically scanned the
stairs, the gates, the trees, for any sign of Emi Nightlark.

Her father laughed with a touch of bitterness. "You'll need
your little pet to speak for you, boy. I've no idea what you're
saying."

*Speak to her in such a way again, and you will become feed for your
beasts.* Roark glanced at the wolves, unbothered by his uncle's in-
ability to understand him.

When he gave me a look, like I ought to translate his threat, I
shot him a glare. "I am not telling him that."

Roark had the audacity to smirk.

"I hear you come with more than just the melder," his uncle
said. "Where is my wife's daughter?"

Any levity in Roark's features faded. He took a step closer, standing between two fara wolves. As though it were the most natural thing to do, Roark rested a palm on top of one wolf's head.

The beast flinched for a breath, then seemed content to be touched. A truth that seemed wholly bothersome to Emi's father.

My cousin is under my protection, Virki, he said, lifting his hand from the wolf so he could use both to speak. *You are not permitted to go near her.*

I swallowed and translated in my own way. "You will stay away from Emi. She is not yours to harm anymore."

Virki's lip curled, as though my very voice made his hatred boil. "Harm *her*?" He pulled back the cloak, revealing a long, gnarled scar on one side of his throat. "Was it she who was harmed?"

Roark narrowed his eyes. *You gave her good reason. You won't touch her.*

This time, I repeated his every word.

"Think you can come here and command how I handle my household?" Virki's face flushed. "I've kept this kingdom alive after your betrayal." In three swift strides, Roark's uncle stepped forward, chest to chest, teeth bared, much the same as his wolves. "Do not mistake your place here, boy. Or you might meet the same fate as your brother."

A flash of darkness cut across Roark's eyes, but before he could make a move or response, the same door to the palace swung open.

"Virki." Elisabet, her hair tamer than it was at the ravines and shoulders now draped in a long cloak, stepped forward. "I see you've reacquainted yourself with your prince, though I am uncertain why you brought your pack."

"I don't much care for outsiders, my queen. Thought they deserved a test. The wolves calmed, as you can see."

Elisabet peered down her narrow nose. "I would hope you

would not be so foolish as to bring harm to royal blood of Dravenmoor."

Virki did not face the queen, simply held Roark's glare for another drawn breath. "Of course not. But I am uncertain why this woman still breathes at his side. Or has your son forgotten what happened to the last prince who protected the melder?"

"Our prince has much to answer for." Elisabet clasped her hands in front of her body. "And until we have those answers, I've offered my word. The woman remains untouched."

"You would shield her, Bet? After everything?"

"You must have forgotten how insistent the darker half of a soul can be."

"You allowed your own son to threaten you?"

Elisabet did not falter beneath Virki's scrutiny. Truth be told, the queen seemed to stand taller. "To prevent bloodshed, we made a compromise. I intend to see it through." With that, the queen looked to Roark. "The melder will be kept out of sight and under guard. Watcher Blackvale suggested these watchers to see to her."

Elisabet opened one arm, welcoming two new faces to her side.

A woman stepped forward. Her features were lovely and sharp. She stood taller than the queen, and her chestnut hair was shorn close to her scalp on one side, and on the other, it was intricately braided over her shoulder.

At her side was a man whose face was nearly a mirror to hers, save for his eyes, which burned in a vibrant shade of green while hers looked more like the coral shells that would wash up from the Green Fjord back home.

I was not certain I trusted Gunter Blackvale, but there was a touch of relief hearing that he'd suggested these new Dravens, until Emi's father laughed.

"Well thought, my queen."

Roark shifted in front of me, his attention on the two new-comers, and I did not think they were welcome.

"We will see to the melder, my prince," the man said, a sly sort of grin spreading beneath the russet stubble on his face. One fist pounded over his chest. "She will be unharmed when you find her, on my honor."

No. Roark gestured and shook his head, once, twice, three times, until the queen let out a sigh.

"Brynn and Auki will take her to a secure chamber. You will stand before the úlfur." The queen lowered her tone. "I kept her alive; now you keep your end of the bargain."

Roark would not have a chance to protest again.

With a quick clack of his teeth, Roark's uncle signaled his pack forward. I cried out when three fara wolves, tall enough that their heads reached my ribs, herded me away from the prince.

Roark made a move to reach me, but five more wolves circled him. In the next breath, darkness bled from the scar on his throat.

"Roark." Elisabet's voice rose over the chaos. "Control yourself or we'll put an arrow through her heart."

Roark spun around, looking to the balcony of an upper level of the royal house.

Shit.

Beneath cowls of fur and wool, a line of Draven archers aimed dark onyx arrows straight at me.

The man Elisabet called Auki drew me against his chest, a grin still written on his face. The woman took my other arm and guided me toward a narrower doorway on a side of the palace that was opposite the direction Roark was being led.

Frantic, I looked over my shoulder. Roark was made of dark rage. He looked nowhere but at me when he raised one hand and gestured, words only I would know: *They touch you, be ruthless.*

I swallowed and shouted, "Just like Tomas!"

Roark's mouth quirked in a bit of wickedness, the last sight I saw before the door slammed between us.

"Knew it'd be interesting when she showed her face," Auki murmured, guiding me toward a coiled stone staircase.

"Didn't think we'd ever get a chance to see her until Gunter showed up," said the woman.

"Who are you?" I snapped.

She chuckled and spun me around. "I am Brynn Oakbriar. Virki is quite pleased I'm the one to guard you, for you see, Melder, you stole my crown when you fell for the man I was sworn to wed."

ROARK

WHEN THE DOORS SNAPPED SHUT, SEPARATING ME FROM Lyra, I spun on the queen.

Elisabet would not understand my gestures, but when I pinned her with a sharp glare and a finger pointed at her face, the queen sniffed.

"The melder will not be harmed. I gave my word I would hear her, speak with her, before any fate is decided."

I took out the same knife I'd used to slice Fillip's neck and twirled it in my fingers, never breaking my watch on my mother.

A bit of a flush coated her cheeks before she shoved aside my blade. "You are the prince of Dravenmoor, the heir, whether you revel in the title or not. There are explanations you must proffer your folk, and actions for which you must answer. I make my moves with precision, son. When I say the melder will still be breathing, I speak true. Now, finish this meet and cease wasting time."

I did not trust a soul within these walls, but there was a ferociousness about the queen, a tremble in her words that struck me to the bone. A sort of unspoken vow that gave up the truth behind her words.

Perhaps the queen did not send Lyra to her death, but there remained an urgency in her command. Like it was only a matter of time before it all changed.

I opened my hand, a curl still on my lip, and waited for the queen to stride into the room first.

Archways made from shaved antlers and boar skulls topped every doorway, and every rafter was carved with runes and prayers to the gods. Heavy chairs with armrests that ended in claws or fangs surrounded a black oak table, oblong and large enough to seat twenty men shoulder to shoulder.

The instant my lungs filled with the scent of pine smoke in the inglenook and parchment from stacks of old sagas and histories, memories of days running among the seats, hiding from playmates in mock battles and sieges pummeled my mind. But the joyful remembrances soured with the unmanaged rage boiling in my blood. The need to lash out, to unfurl into the split creature I'd become, scorched beneath my skin like hot iron.

Before, when control over my rent soul was not mine, it felt like a mere prickle would flutter across my flesh. Like drawing too near a flame. Now, with the darkness unified with my own rage, I felt as though I were in a constant state of violence.

I crossed the council room in long strides until I reached the parchment. With no thought to the others filtering in behind me, I took hold of a raven feather quill and a stoppered inkwell. Without looking up, I slid into one of the seats, furiously penning my every damn thought.

I did not need to look to know my mother took a place beside me. The instant she settled in her chair, I shoved the parchment in front of her.

Elisabet held the name of Foxglen. Once, she'd explained that my grandfather said she was born with the most cunning of smiles, much like a fox in the glen. Innocent and lovely at first glance, but shrewd and sly in the next instant. The way her eyes gleamed like a storm on the sea, the way her dark rouged lips curled in one corner, I could see the foundation for her name. "What little you know."

She slid back the parchment. I scanned my words, trying to make sense of her reply.

You may think I hold love for this place, but I assure you, I will slit every throat I once knew if you sent Lyra to Brynn and Auki for vengeance. It is no less than you did to me.

Brynn had been my betrothed from infancy. Only a proven soul bond would disrupt an arranged vow in Dravenmoor.

Like Gunter, Brynn and her twin brother, Auki, had been my playmates. We'd always known Brynn and I would wed one day, much the same as Thane and Yrsa. I did not recall her being hateful or the jealous sort.

Then again, we'd been children. Brynn was hardly in her eleventh season when I was tossed away. I saw the delight in my uncle's eyes when she appeared, so my written threat was sound, I thought. Simple. Direct. A promise.

I crumpled the parchment in my grip, mouth tight, and waited until more seats were filled.

Virki, naturally, took the seat across from my mother. Truth be told, with what Emi reported that her father had done to her after I'd been exiled, I wasn't certain I cared if the creature beneath my skin destroyed my uncle's soul.

I recognized most faces, aged as they were. Sampson, a loyal warrior who'd been my father's second when the brother-in-law of King Hundur of Myrda challenged my father over rumors the Draven king had bedded his wife.

My father was once a king loved by his clan and feared by others. But if Myrdans had any understanding to the depth of soul bonds, Hundur's dead brother-in-law would never have challenged my father, for he would've known it was impossible for King Vishon to betray my mother by taking a mistress. Their bond wouldn't allow it.

Then again, it was the destruction of my parents' soul bond that left me with little trust for the queen.

Sampson removed the pelt of a white wolf from his head and looked across the table at me, a bit of sadness in his auburn eyes.

Next to him was Yanson, Gunter's father. The day I was torn apart, Yanson held down my shoulders on the slab of cold stone and murmured assurances into my ear when the blinding pain took hold and my screams faded to silence.

Yanson held a warning in his eyes, much the same as he'd always done when Gunter and I schemed our next trick inside the royal house.

"There is no sense delaying the purpose of this meet." The queen rose, leaning over her fingertips on the table. "Our prince has returned from his duty beyond enemy gates." Virki scoffed but did not interject. My mother did not pause to indulge him and kept her voice steady. "Fate has not gone as we thought, but the Norns rarely appease our desires. We are here to discuss the connection to the lost melder."

"And Fillip's death," a man five seats down the table said in a sort of growl. "He slaughtered a man without cause."

I leaned back in my chair, grinning. A wordless reply of how little guilt I harbored over Fillip's death.

The queen frowned. "Without cause, Ubbe? Fillip went against my word. As deep as his loss will be felt, there was cause."

Ubbe clenched a fist over the table but did not retort.

Virki slumped in his chair. "The more pressing matter is why *our* prince returns to us while the Jorvan prince he was commanded to slaughter still lives. Why does he step through the gates with a living melder, no less protective of her than before?"

My father's brother held none of the gentleness of Vishon Thornwood. Where my father was playful, Virki was brutal. Where Vishon spoke with diplomacy, Virki demanded blood.

I did not know if he played a hand in Nivek's death beyond his duty to report that the prince had smuggled the melder away, but I would not be held back if he'd been part of the slaughter.

"Roark." My mother drew my attention. "How do you answer?"

Her expression was unreadable save for the glimmer of something like pain behind her eyes.

I hesitated for a breath, a little petulant with a desire to be wholly uncooperative to the people in the room. The longer I delayed, the longer Lyra was left with unknowns.

I smoothed the wrinkled parchment and penned the reply.

You expect me to despise the prince who saved my life when you all left me for dead. I do not. You expect me to forget a bond for which my brother died. For a time, your curse worked and I had no memory. But it was restored. What more do you wish me to say?

The council would want to know of Fadey and of Damir's death. But if they knew Fadey desired Lyra for her power, if they knew what she could do with her craft, no mistake they would kill her and bring war to the gates of Jorvandal to finish Fadey.

The latter I did not mind, but Lyra's life was not a game to be played.

My mother read my words out loud to the úlfur. Upon the final line, she closed her eyes, as though anticipating the shouts that followed.

"You should not have had the choice to even care for the melder," Virki said, his voice harsh and sharp. "I want to know why the bond was restored."

I popped one shoulder in a disinterested shrug, then laced my fingers over my middle, feigning indifference.

"Kaysar?" Virki faced a tall man with long features and a shorn head inked in runes. "You have nothing to say? It is your daughter who he forsakes for this so-called bond."

Kaysar Fernclaw was a stoic man, thoughtful, quiet. The opposite of Brynn and Auki's mother, who was warm and boisterous. At least what I recalled of her.

Brynn's father studied me for a breath, like he could break beneath my skin and see every scornful thought. "If the soul bond is true, why would I submit my girl to a marriage where she is the interloper? She would be wed to the prince, but in truth be the mistress."

Guilt was there. A mere bite of it. I would not betray Lyra for anything, but the image Kaysar created was true. Should Brynn and I be forced to wed, my heart, my soul, would never be hers. I would always belong to another.

No one deserved such a life.

"Good gods, have you all lost your damn minds?" Virki sneered. "Or perhaps I should place blame at the feet of the soul render, our very own queen."

It was not often anyone spoke of the Draven queen's ability to split souls. Like her craft was something sacred . . . or feared.

But Virki did not hold his tongue as he barreled on. "Was this connection restored because commands were not properly issued as agreed by the council?"

The queen snapped her attention to my uncle. "Speak clearly, Virki. If you wish to accuse me of treason, say it loudly and stand by it."

"I merely wish to understand why our *weapon*"—he glared at me—"for that is what your soul was meant to be, boy. Why did it not scorch the Stonegate fortress from the inside out? I do not speak for myself alone when I say the thought of the melder remaining within our gates disgusts me."

"But if the melder remains with us, her craft cannot be used for the Jorvans," Yanson insisted.

"Her craft should not exist for anyone to use."

"Can the girl help what the gods placed in her blood?" Yanson sat back in his seat. "I know you tend to place blame on the innocent for the craft the gods gave them, Virki—"

"Careful how you speak, Yanson," my uncle interjected.

Yanson hinted not only at Lyra, but at Emi. He spoke of how Emi's own father discarded his wife, his damn soul bond, all from hatred that their daughter had been cursed with bone craft instead of soul.

I was too young to recall most of it, but Virki corrupted his own thoughts into believing the woman who was sealed to his soul would betray him with some faceless Jorvan.

If one half of a soul pairing harmed the one to which they were bonded, it would darken a piece of their soul. Irreparable. It was punished in Dravenmoor.

Virki escaped punishment by using Emi's rare bone craft as proof enough to cast doubt on his wife's loyalty. He was allowed to exile his wife to the wilds, and there she died. Alone.

He might not have killed her with his own hands, but to me, what he'd done was unforgivable.

A sealed bond of souls was to be cherished and protected, even with one's life.

After he banished his wife, Virki had grown crueler. Another sign his soul was stained.

Yanson frowned. "All I'm saying is that we must decide if a woman is to meet the gods because of the power they gave her."

"Perhaps you have forgotten raids and battles were had all to hunt this woman. Do you not recall the bloodshed? The chaos?"

"I have not forgotten any of it," Yanson said. "Nor have I forgotten the way our warriors planned to slaughter a child at first sight."

"You know we tried different tactics before the raids, Yanson. Plans changed," Sampson said. "Better to send the girl to Salur than have the Jorvans corrupt her craft until they overtake everything."

"Yet here we are," Virki said, voice rough. "On the cusp of war with the Jorvans again now that they know their beloved Death Bringer always belonged to us, and their precious melder lives beyond our gates. Still, we sit here bickering on whether we should let the source of such strife live another day. The woman is a threat to our land, our clan, and our very lives."

My fist curled over my knee and I took up the quill once more, briskly writing a response.

There is no decision to be made. Lyra will not be harmed.

Virki scanned the response and chuckled. "The woman is the first female melder in centuries. Jorvans will fight to get her back. From what ravagers have said, she is stronger than any melders before her. And we know why. Are we choosing to disregard prophecies of old?"

My gut twisted. True enough, a traveling seer woman had

visited the clan when I was a boy. She spoke of death and shattered kingdoms at the hands of the new melder. Since those words were spoken, Virki would never view Lyra as anything but a curse from the gods.

My whole clan would do the same unless they took the time to *see* that Lyra's craft was not vicious like Fadey's use of it. She did not seek power.

Virki drummed his fingers over the table. "We are simply letting her live because our prince wants a hole to stick his cock?"

I shot to my feet and was not alone. More than one man stood, ready to dive between my uncle and my blade. Yanson tugged Virki away from the coil of darkness I had not even realized billowed off my shoulders.

The queen stood. "Enough!"

I slammed one fist over the wood, silencing my mother and drawing every eye my way. In haste, I wrote on the parchment, my throat burning from the silent rage I yearned to shout in their faces.

When I slid the parchment to my mother, she scanned the words first, then proffered me a look of annoyance, as though she wished I could keep as silent as my voice.

Still, the queen read every word to the council. "'We are here again when it could have been avoided from the start if the first threads of a soul bond had been honored. Do not make the same mistake twice. I am not a frightened boy any longer, and if you think I value any of your lives more than hers, you will soon realize just how mistaken you are.'"

For a moment there was silence, heady and potent.

"You would truly kill your own blood, your own folk, for the melder, my prince?" Yanson asked as though he already knew the response.

I plucked the parchment from my mother's hands and promptly responded.

"'I proved as much at the ravines. I will not hesitate,'" she read, voice flat.

"Then perhaps," Virki said, rising to his feet, "you have no place in our clan or as our prince."

"Enough, Virki." Yanson gripped the pommel of his blade. "The prince suffered long enough for Dravenmoor. Why the bond to the woman was restored, only the gods know. What causes me more concern is your swift rush to slaughter anyone who does not stand with you."

My uncle squared himself to Yanson and shouted, "Our king, my brother, gave his life to keep this clan safe. To protect us from the dark fate of this melder!"

"Enough!" The queen's voice rattled against the walls, silencing the room. Only when the men of the úlfur looked to my mother did she go on. "Lives were lost across the kingdoms over melding craft. I despise the use of melders in Jorvandal as much as anyone, but for all that I lost during those raids, never did I blame a child for her unfortunate lot in life."

"You sympathize with her, Bet?" Virki tilted his head.

"I do not desire to lose anyone else. Yanson is right: she is behind our walls and out of Jorvandal's grasp. Our prince is protective because of their connection, even if it's not a sealed bond. I will not kill her simply because we despise the way others manipulate her craft. Nor would our king if he was here. Vishon's command was to bring the girl to Dravenmoor, and you know this, Virki."

"Commands changed that night."

My mother's mouth tightened. "Yes. I suppose the raids changed many things. And I suppose I am changing them all again. For now, no one is to touch the melder. Not until we determine if the woman has committed crimes worthy of death."

"Crafting soul bones is not enough?" Virki fumed.

"For all I know, she was forced. I plan to find out before I rule on her fate. Now, leave me and the prince. I have much to say to my son regarding his . . . *conduct*."

With a touch of reluctance, the council slowly made their way out of the chamber, closing the heavy doors at their backs.

Elisabet leaned forward, her voice sharp as broken steel. "If you continue to threaten your own folk, I will not have the power to defend what you have done any longer."

I pressed a hand to my chest and mouthed, *Me?* Eyes narrowed, I pointed back to her, shaking my head, and formed the word *You*.

Her jaw tightened when she leaned closer. "You do not know what I have done for you and your precious melder."

Gods, I'd had enough.

The fury, the betrayal, the seasons of silent hatred for a fate I did not choose bled to the surface. Frigid shadows spilled from every pore. Flames from sconces on the walls dimmed to dripping ink on rotted wood.

The last sight was my mother's wide eyes before my darkness swallowed her whole and I lost myself.

SKUL DREK

WHERE WAS MY MELDER?

Want. Need. Desire. *Mine.* Now, where was my melder?

In the shadows, the line of a molten tether shimmered and led to somewhere in the distance. Golden heat tied us, bound us. She brightened the night and guided me home.

Alive. Fierce.

I took a step forward. I wanted to see my melder.

"What have you done?"

A frigid wash of unease rippled over my senses, drawing me to look back to the darkness, away from the golden bond.

Ah. The queenie.

My former captor was on her knees, a brilliant shade of gold tinged in crimson surrounding her.

I lowered to one knee, and billows of darkness pulsed until cold walls faded to nothing but night. Anger, hate, pain—all of it thickened the shadows here, where souls lived.

The queenie lifted her eyes, bright as starlight, and studied every edge of every feature before speaking.

"Why am I here?"

Why, indeed?

Shadows blotted out most thoughts. Instinct reigned here. But I could recall why I dragged her soul to meet mine. "It is time for you to converse with the monster you created." Arms open at my sides, I allowed the queenie to take in her masterpiece. "Soul Render."

"I never desired to use my craft on my own family. Certainly not twice."

Twice. Why did the word settle heavy like rotted logs in my shadowed mind? I am he, we are we. Still, shared thoughts beyond the shadows were trying, at times, to draw to the surface. Then, I grinned. "Ah, yes. Long live the king. Your first creature."

The queenie's eyes shed two golden tears onto the glow of her cheeks. "Do you think I wanted to rend my husband's soul?"

"Want means nothing. What was done is done. Now shoulder the weight of it."

"You do not know how many lives were lost, how corrupt our enemies had become. We needed a way to protect the souls of the fallen from their soul bones. The king truly believed to split his soul was the only way to protect them."

Anger. Hate. Shame. It burned through me in layers of cold, blackened mists. Teeth bared, I pressed the ice of my brow to the heat of hers. "And once you created him, I wonder, did you take pleasure in learning you could control his every move, the way you did mine, queenie?"

Her eyes followed my long fingers, watching me pluck the burning tether no longer owned by the queenie.

"I did not want this. I never wanted to harm your father or *my son.* You are all I have left."

"Yet you have anger knowing that the bonds that tied us together have snapped, and your creature no longer answers to you. A thing your first creation never managed to do. He could not break free of you before you ended him."

Her breath hitched. "Do not mock me. Whatever light still lived in my soul died when your father and I made that impossible choice."

"You killed your bond when he fought back, is that it? Decided to make another?" One fist pounded against the shadows where a heart might be in my chest. "Thought you'd have better luck controlling this soul, was that why you slit his throat?"

"Cease talking of this!" The queenie covered her ears, shoulders heaving.

For a time no words were spoken between us.

"You slaughtered your first bond to create your monster son. Now you lost control of even him. What a waste of souls you've caused."

The queenie scrambled off her knees. "You do not know the things of which you speak! My soul died that day."

The outburst was . . . surprising. Thoughts stirred of a time long gone. A kingly death. A curse. A desperate need to keep a boyish prince breathing.

Bits and pieces were forgotten, but there were memories of shouts, of pain, of tears, of queenly sobs.

"Where is my melder?" I spoke in a sort of jagged snarl. "I have need of her. I must take her away."

"Why?" She spoke softly. "You are keeping truths from us. What drove you from Jorvandal so violently?"

Memories of plans, of schemes with my melder. The Thief King sought the Wanderer's bones, sought to take his soul, sought to rule over all.

He planned to force her to steal the souls until she met the gods.

No. The Thief King was now gone to Salur. I'd felt his soul not so long ago, corrupted and bitter, but there all the same. I closed my eyes, pulling back mottled shadows, hazy memories.

The dark melder hurt *my* melder.

My eyes flashed. "If I speak true, you'll darken her soul the way you did your king's."

"Someday I hope you come to believe differently about the day your father died." The queenie shook her head. "I could've killed the melder already, yet I have kept my word. We know what the Jorvan king seeks beyond those wretched Berserkirs he crafts. You know we've understood for seasons he desires bones he believes are from the Wanderer. Now, what happened?"

A long growl slipped from my throat. Stolen souls corrupted the living. The Thief King reveled in the power of it. Undead warriors, unable to control the madness of corrupted souls.

I held no sadness knowing the Thief King was gone.

But worse was rising. And they wanted my melder, lest we find the lost bones first. Destroy the bones. Let the first king rest.

"Roark."

A name, familiar and painful.

I am he, we are we.

The queenie stepped nearer to me, her voice soft. "Tell me. I vow the truth will remain between us, but tell me so I might . . . help us all."

"Speak true, queenie?"

"I have never lied to you, despite what you think. I never will."

I hummed, uncertain if I could even recall if she spoke true, but darkness was crafted at her hand. She lost control and sought it back.

"I will vow. Soul to soul." The queenie stepped closer, palm outstretched.

"What will you vow?"

"What do you desire?"

Simple. "My melder's soul to remain bright."

"You wish the girl to live."

I dipped my chin, so it faded in the shadows coiled around me.

"Then should you confide in me, I vow to do all I can to keep her alive, and she will not fall to Salur from my hand or word."

No promises could be made of the hands of others, but . . . one could be stayed. "Soul to soul?"

The queenie nodded. "I break it, and my soul is yours to send to the molten hell if you wish."

Soul vows were sealed by craft. The queenie, should she deceive me, would become a walking shell, for I would destroy the soul inside.

Such a vow was no small act.

I held out my darkened palm, pressing it to the top of the queenie's. "Speak your words."

She swallowed. "I vow to do all in my power to protect the melder—"

"Her name," I said through the edges of my teeth. With two melders running amok, clarity would be needed.

The queenie swallowed. "I vow to do all in my power to protect Lyra of House Bien. Should I break such a vow or fail, I offer my soul as payment."

Brilliant skeins of light coiled around our wrists and fingers and up the length of our arms before fading into each chest.

When the heat from the vow had settled, I looked to the Soul Render. "Thief kings use their melders to hunt for the Wanderer."

"We already know this."

"Perhaps, but you do not understand all the schemes and tricks behind the Thief King's walls."

She looked back at me. "Did Damir truly find powerful bones? Is the woman truly as formidable as foretold?"

"What you heard from the seer's words long before is true, Soul Render. She is strong, she's hunted, and if wars begin, no doubt lands will be destroyed."

She blew out a long breath, and a bit of frosted air billowed from her painted lips. "Tell me what happened in Stonegate."

Little by little, I retold tales of my melder's gifts, her strength, her fears, and the rise of a dark melder.

By the end of it, the queenie paced in front of me. "Damir is dead. Fadey, gods, he's alive and hunts the woman to meld her bones to him?"

"Because my melder can come here, where the souls speak."

"So he thinks that by absorbing her craft, he will be able to see more clearly where the Wanderer's scattered bones are hidden?"

I gave a slow dip of my chin. "My melder is strong. The dark one believes she is who he needs to unite the power in the bones of the first king."

"*Dammit*. It is graver than I imagined." She whirled on me. "Should he restore the Wanderer, Fadey would control all craft. We all will be forced to bow to him."

"This I know. As does my melder."

"She does not seek the same power?"

"She seeks *peace*."

For a long moment, the queenie said nothing. "Then I may be able to help you. Lore says four pieces of the Wanderer were scattered, to honor the souls of his family he betrayed."

Three young ones and his god-queen. "This I know."

"I might know where something, possibly one of the remnant bones, was hidden. Once, it was believed each remnant had connections to the kingdoms or craft, Dravenmoor included."

Cold brushed across my shadowed face when the darkness thickened, as though the world of souls responded to the untamable need to know more—anything—about the first soul of craft.

Darkness lived in those bones. Not only the strength of all, but the corruption and greed of the first king. The dark melder could never be allowed to find them.

"Where is the bone of which you speak?" The sound was rough, raw, like a thousand screams had escaped my throat.

Brilliant eyes locked with mine, a collision of ferocious tides and the blaze of an inferno. "Even if I tell you, understand, our clan will not allow you to leave with the melder. To them, she is a risk should the Jorvans find her again."

"Are we to do nothing?"

"No. We merely need time to think of how you can hunt the bones yourselves, I suppose. The council will want her hidden. Frankly, when news of Damir's death reaches our walls, most on the úlfur will likely wish to chain her out of sight or put a blade through her heart."

"Keep her soul bright, queenie. That was the vow."

"And I will do my part, but you must do yours. There is a way to protect her within our gates that could give you time to plan your next steps."

"Meaning?"

She staggered, the brilliance of her soul fading. Time for conversing was drawing to an end. Craft drained the soul. Too long and the pull against our bond of blood grew weak.

Her words came out in a rush. "What is a custom that we revere as sacred? One that makes her Draven by law?"

A wash of ice crept across my shadowed flesh. "I do not know if my melder would desire such a thing."

"That is a problem for you to solve, then. It is not a perfect solution, but it can buy you time."

"You fought against her and now say these things? You tell me this to keep her alive without trouble?"

"Perhaps you will come to realize that you do not know everything about me. I am keeping my vow, not only one with you, but also one I made long ago to keep a king's son alive." The queenie looked over her shoulder. "Time is growing short. I feel myself falling away. Do not leave the melder alone for much longer."

My teeth clicked once, twice. I towered over her. "The First King, then. Where is the piece of his bones, queenie?"

The Soul Render had grown diaphanous, nothing more than a gilded mist. But before the shadows devoured her she spoke, soft and harsh. "Beyond the Night Ledges. In Unfettered Territory."

9

LYRA

SILENCE THICKENED IN THE CORRIDOR UNTIL THE PRESSURE of it knocked against my skull. Brynn stood at one shoulder, Auki at my other.

Brynn told me I'd stolen a crown from her grasp, then said nothing more. Together, they'd dragged me deeper into the royal house in silence.

Unlike Stonegate, there weren't endless stairwells and doorways here. Instead, long passages encased a large center courtyard. Rows of willows, natural creeks, and full shrubs with green blossoms were visible through the narrow, bubbled glass windows.

The grounds might've been lovely and serene save for the pairs of Dark Watch warriors striding down the dirt paths and the two Dravens forcing me farther from the protection of their prince.

When we rounded the corner, I let out a rough breath. Gunter Blackvale leaned against the post of an arched doorway, one knee bent so his boot pressed flat against the wall. He didn't look up to acknowledge our presence, seemingly wholly invested in using his knife to peel around the beds of his fingernails.

Auki cleared his throat, and Gunter lifted his chin. A grin flashed over his sharp features, still lined in kohl and painted runes. "Ah, found the melder."

I shook off Brynn's hold and took a step toward Gunter. Foolish of me, no mistake, but he'd sworn to Roark that he'd see to it I was safe during the council, and I had little choice but to trust the man.

"Come on, then, best to get you behind closed doors and away from all us frightening Draven folk." Gunter winked and nudged the door open with his toe.

"It is not Draven blood I fear." I kept my back to the wall and slid past Gunter, attention focused on the blade now sheathed on his belt.

"Clearly," Auki said, shoving between both of us. "Since she's bedding the prince."

Heat flushed my face. His sister had practically declared me her rival, and he spoke his assumptions so blithely.

Strange, but laughter followed.

Even Brynn fought a smile.

I shook away the odd interaction and stepped into the room. My heart fell to my stomach in such relief, I nearly stumbled over my first step. "Emi!"

Seated on a wooden chair, a book made of blue leather on her lap, Emi jolted at my shout. Her face had been scrubbed of the dirt and sweat from the wood, and her pale hair was free down her back.

"Lyra!" Emi scrambled from the chair, the book falling to the floorboards, and rushed across the room. In the next heartbeat her arms were choking off my air from her embrace. "Gods,

Gunter hid me away the instant he saw the fara pack, and I-I-I
didn't know . . ."

Her voice cracked and faded against my shoulder.

"Are you all right?" The pain of deceit and anger from Emi's
secrets faded in the face of her emotions.

She pulled back and proffered a small smile. "I'm fine. I'm a
little cleaner, and Gunter saw to it I had a bit of pheasant."

"Don't know why you're so damn surprised." Gunter sealed
the latch over the door, locking us into the room. "Said I'd look
after you lot"—he opened his arms, a snide sort of grin on his
face—"so here I am. Looking after you."

My grip slid to Emi's wrist, a bolster for her or me, I didn't
know. "Then why send them?"

Gunter's attention shifted to Brynn and Auki when I used my
chin to point their way. "Brynn and Auki tend to the wolf packs
of the Dark Watch, including Virki's. They were nearby and eager
to join in the fun."

Emi stiffened at the mention of her father.

Auki went to a small table with a wooden ewer and horn and
poured himself a drink the color of sea-foam. "The queen didn't
speak the exact truth. She summoned us. Not Gunter."

"Makes a bit of sense. Your queen wishes me dead."

Auki peered at Gunter over the rim of his horn, his brow furrowed. "Why does she think we're all going to slit her up? She was
skittish the whole way here."

They couldn't be so thick in their heads.

"It's not a coincidence my aunt asked Brynn," Emi said over
my shoulder.

"Exactly," I blurted before I could think to stop. "What you
told me about you and Roark is enough motivation to want me
dead."

Brynn sat in one of the wooden chairs tucked in a corner.

"You think I want you dead because my arranged betrothal from childhood is broken?"

"You said I stole your crown."

"Well, didn't you?" Brynn was a strong woman, beautiful and frightening. But when she smiled, her entire countenance softened like the calm of dawn. "Dravenmoor is on the brink of war. By all means, Melder, take the damn crown. I don't want it."

What sort of game was this?

"I think we'll need to speak a little plainer," Gunter said, low and like he was trying to whisper but wanted me to hear all the same. "She doesn't trust a word from our mouths."

"Why should she?" Emi snapped. "Our clan has wanted to kill her all her life."

"True enough." Gunter leaned against the wall, arms folded over his chest. "But I'd still like a bit of credit for not even attempting to kill you, Melder. A mark of good faith, don't you think?"

"Same for me," Auki said through a long gulp from his horn.

Much like my first interactions with Prince Thane, when I was certain King Damir would slaughter Kael and bind me in an iron cage, my head reeled at the oddities of their words, their actions.

I turned back toward Brynn—Roark's betrothed.

Desire for power rotted the corridors of Stonegate. Even in my old town Skalfirth, I'd witnessed more than one hopeful father step into Jarl Jakobson's hall, attempting to marry daughters to his heir, Mikkal.

True, Brynn had not drawn her blade, but doors were closed and fewer eyes were watching now.

She held my scrutiny with a touch of her own before she spoke. "Our father was a trusted adviser and friend to King Vishon. Naturally, our houses would arrange a bond. My betrothal was decided three days after my birth. The prince had not even met a full season of life."

"You speak as though it was nothing to you, yet you made your position known straightaway."

"I simply thought that by telling you, it would explain why Virki Wolfstone was so delighted at the sight of us. By sending you with us, Elisabet was appeasing the bloodlust many Dravens hold for your craft. They will think we are mistreating you."

"A little brilliant if you think about it. I'll accept praise for being part of the scheme whenever you wish to give it," Gunter said, still picking at his fingernails.

They spoke almost . . . playfully. I didn't understand any of it.

"So"—I cleared my throat and unfurled my fists—"you don't desire him?"

Brynn's lips curled with a new sort of cunning. "I didn't, until I saw how damn stunning that man has become. Gods, did you see the size of him? The pure feral rage in his eyes? His *hands*." Brynn hummed in delight until her brother strode past and shoved her shoulder, laughing.

Something bitter knotted in my chest, something like jealousy. The hands of Roark Ashwood had been mine not so long ago, and for the first time I would admit—to myself alone—that I did not want those damn hands to touch anyone but me.

Now Brynn laughed. "Stop looking at me like you want to pluck out my eyes. I'm not going to seduce the prince away from you."

"But you do desire him."

"In truth, woman to woman, I just desire *someone*." Brynn slouched in the chair. "Do you know how difficult it is to find a proper man to bed you when you were playmates with most of them? They start to see you as one of the men, not a lover with, frankly, unmet needs."

"Ahh, stop." Auki flinched, waving one hand. "You have never been bedded, and if I find out any bastard has ever tried, he will lose his hands."

Brynn snorted and Gunter made a sensual sort of gesture at her until her brother rammed his fist into Gunter's chest.

Emi took in her fellow Dravens, a little befuddled, like she'd expected viciousness and instead was met with . . . this.

At long last, Brynn sobered. "I was eleven when Roark was exiled, Melder. We knew of our betrothal, but our souls never fashioned a bond. Such things tend to make themselves clear."

"How?"

Brynn lifted one shoulder. "I hear it's different for everyone who is fortunate to find the other half of their soul. But it's a feeling, a draw to them, a love so deep you cannot fathom a world without them."

I hugged my own middle against the rush of heat in my belly. Roark Ashwood had pulled me into his maelstrom of darkness from the moment I met his eyes in the great hall in Skalfirth.

"But not everyone finds a sjeleven," Brynn explained. "You know what that is, right?"

I nodded briskly. "Most clans have some version of mates of the soul."

"Good. The prince and I made a vow as young ones that should either of us find a soul bond, then we would be free to seal it if desired."

"Seal it?"

"It completes a bond," Gunter offered. "It's a powerful ceremony and only done to those whose souls connect."

A shadow coated Brynn's features. "I was young but understood well enough my prince, *my friend*, was torn in two because his soul had the misfortune of craving the forbidden."

Angry tears burned behind my eyes. From exhaustion, from

resentment, from knowing that Roark's belief that his soul brightened when it came near mine had destroyed his life. "And? Now what do you say?"

"I say I'm glad to see him again," said Brynn. "I always told myself I would defend his bond should he find one, but I won't mince words—I don't trust you. You seem to resist him, and after all he has sacrificed by going beyond the gates of the Jorvan keep, I don't care for it."

"The man I fell in . . . the man I knew was a warrior loyal to the Jorvan prince. Not a prince himself and not Skul Drek. Two sunrises ago, everything I thought I knew unraveled. Forgive me if I seem untrusting of everyone, it is only because I am." Each word slid through my teeth, sharp and lined with venom.

"Do you want me to sympathize with you and your broken heart, Melder?" Brynn tilted her head to one side. "It pales in comparison to him losing his freedom, his soul, and nearly his life."

"You think I don't understand all that?" A tear fell onto my cheek and I furiously swiped it away. "Do you think I don't know exactly what he has lost because he keeps *choosing* me? I hold that truth heavy in my heart. But Dravens are not the only ones who've suffered losses. My family was slaughtered during the raids; my brother is trapped at Stonegate, likely being tortured because of me; and I am here, a captive of the clan who would revel in my death."

For a long moment no one spoke. When it felt as though the silence would crush me into the floorboards, Gunter finally broke.

"Fair enough." He shoved off the wall and strode across the room, pausing two paces away. "You may not trust us because we are Draven—no, don't deny it." He held up a palm when I began to protest. "We don't trust Jorvans and Myrdans because of their blood either. But what you can trust is that the souls in this room are loyal to Roark Ashwood. If he says he is bonded to you, then we honor that and will do all we can to defend you like we will defend him."

Bitterness was there, an urge to see them all as ruthless for allowing such brutality to befall their supposed playmate. But in truth, they'd all been young ones. Likely frightened, confused, and mourning losses from their clan as much as the rest of the kingdoms.

Gunter had protected Emi as he had vowed.

Brynn was expected to despise me, to want to be rid of the woman standing in the way of her royal title, but she had led me here. Safe.

My heart ached and I did not know when it might stop. Fadey knew he had everything to leverage against me. He had Kael, and no doubt he'd turned Thane and Yrsa against us by now. Hilda and Edvin were taken to Stonegate because they had the misfortune of living in the same village as me when I was taken. What would become of them and their families? Fadey could torture anyone I'd ever cared for.

I had little I could use to threaten Fadey.

Unless we found the bones of the Wanderer.

Battles were brewing and my army was made of a few people who had been raised to seek out my destruction.

Pride, fear, resentment—I needed to place them all to the side. I would never reach Kael without a bit of trust for Emi and Roark. To secure even a tentative alliance with a few more Dravens filled with loyalty complexes might not be so wretched.

I let my shoulders relax for the first time since the Dark Watch ambushed us in the wood.

The moment I parted my lips to offer a bit of reluctant trust, glass cracked and shattered. The hiss of an arrow sliced across the room. I had no time to think before screams rattled the chamber walls.

10

LYRA

BRYNN WAS ON HER KNEES, CURSING THE GODS AND IN-specting her brother's wound. The arrow narrowly missed my throat and rammed into the meat of Auki's upper thigh.

He gritted his teeth, back against the wall, but still reached for the blade at his waist.

Gunter rushed to my side and pushed one palm on my head and another on Emi's, forcing us to hunch over. "Stay down."

The words had barely crossed his lips before a second arrow cut through the shattered window. Gunter fell over the top of us, the point narrowly missing him.

"Damn the gods," Auki said in a low growl. He cried out when he snapped the end of the arrow, point still stuck in his leg, and eased away from the wall,

"It would appear our folk are too impatient to see if we've sent the melder to Salur," Gunter said with a touch of bitterness.

Fear thickened in my throat, but not for me. Drawn to the

forefront of my mind was the fear that if Dravens were attacking me, what had they done to Roark?

Brynn crouched next to the window, her head tilted to peer through the edge of the broken glass without stepping into the open. "Best guess, a single archer in the oak. They'll send more assailants before the queen intervenes."

I had few doubts the queen was the one who sent them.

The familiar roar from craft echoed in my skull and sparked in my fingertips. By my side, Gunter crouched on one knee, but a flicker of gold filament gathered around the dagger sheathed at his waist. Threads of light billowed as though underwater.

"Gunter," I whispered in a low hiss. "Is your blade made of bone?"

He glanced down at the dagger, then swiftly nodded. "Bear."

"May I use it?"

His brow furrowed. "Seeing how the only ones who stand a chance at getting stabbed by the melder are us, I think not."

"I have no plans to stab any of you." I kept steady and held out my palm.

Gunter hesitated but slowly tugged the blade free of its strap. "That accurate of a knife thrower?"

I didn't respond, merely palmed the hilt of the dagger. The edge curved slightly, and the pale blade was etched with runes and onyx stones. A fine dagger, but the intricacies of the design were soon swallowed by the glow of melding threads.

"Lyra," Emi warned and tried to reach for me when I rose and went toward the window.

"Don't be a fool, Melder," Brynn snapped.

I didn't stop. Unseen by them, fibers of craft curled and tangled around my fingers and the dagger, then stretched for nearby bones—Brynn, Emi, Auki—as I strode past them on my way to the window.

Halfway across the courtyard, a glimmering shape broke through the shroud of branches and thick satin leaves. The archer was perched there. Every motion he made broke through the shadows, a gilded mirror only I could make out.

Threads unraveled at the edges of his form, beckoning the craft from the blade to stitch into his bones.

In the corner of the courtyard, another shape shifted. Better concealed, and more difficult to make out his gleaming figure.

"There are two archers." My voice was flat, almost empty. "For now."

One long breath through my nose and my fear quieted. I reeled back my arm, and the brush of crafted threads flailed off the bone of the dagger, almost frenzied to meld to the man in the trees.

Once I'd fired bone-tipped arrows into a horde of ravagers at Stonegate. This was the same. My craft's desire to thread and stitch bone to bone could do more than build the monstrous Berserkirs; it was deadly in other ways.

"Melder." Brynn shifted to reach me and pull me out of the line of fire.

She didn't get the chance. I threw the blade. Palm open, I guided one of the golden threads toward the glow of bones from the unsuspecting archer in the tree.

When the filaments from the man's body securely stitched to the tendrils on the blade, craft yanked the strings and rammed the point into his chest.

I didn't move, didn't blink, and merely watched the archer curl forward and topple from the branch. Dead.

"I need another bone blade." I dropped to a crouch, out of sight. "Does anyone have one?"

Brynn blinked, then unsheathed a small knife from a strap on the inside of her arm in a frenzy. "How . . . how did you do that?"

"Melded bone to bone." I stood again, craft circling the hilt of the new weapon.

Before I could raise my hand, an arrow shot past me, nicking my side. I cried out at the burn of split skin and took cover against the wall, holding the knife to my breast until my pulse slowed. One more archer. I only needed to meld a blade to one more archer.

But for how long? How many more Dravens would think it better for the whole of the realms if I was dead?

My chest tightened as the light from the approaching dawn faded. Inky skeins of darkness peeled back the smooth wood rafters, leaving porous logs with rotted bark and swampy mists around every bloom in the courtyard.

Gilded figures surrounded me in the chamber. Emi crouched beside Gunter's larger form. Brynn was three paces away, still signaling me to move. Auki was swiftly pulling one of the arrows from the wall, and the wound in his leg glowed more red than gold.

Once, the cold wastes of the mirror frightened me.

Now it set my heart on fire.

With caution, I peered around the edge of the darkened window. A thick, taut rope of light split across my middle, every strand like roots of a tree overtaking me. I followed the strands to where they stopped.

One corner of my mouth tilted.

There, standing beside the fading glow of the archer I'd killed, was Skul Drek.

Roark.

"You're here." In the mirror, even my cry sounded hushed, almost dark.

The sharp copper eyes of Skul Drek glared up at me from beneath his misty cowl. His vicious teeth flashed in the shadows.

Movement was strange in the mirror world. One moment I would be still, and the next I would be tossed to a new location. I let out a gasp of stun when, all at once, my phantom was pressed against me.

The cold darkness of his body caged me to the wall. One long slate fingertip traced the edge of my jaw. Never had he touched me in such a way. Part of me still feared Skul Drek, but knowing his heart lived in Roark Ashwood, knowing his viciousness belonged to me, I tilted my head, leaning into his touch. Solid. Frigid. Gentle.

"Liars live within the clan of the Soul Render queen." Skul Drek dragged his finger across the curve of my bottom lip. "They're not to darken your soul."

"I don't want them to. Where are you?" I pressed a palm to the center of his misty chest, hoping he understood.

His dark lips curled. "We hunt you."

Roark was coming.

Skul Drek's icy palm held the side of my face, urging me to meet his vicious eyes. "Blood spills for those who would darken you. Their souls will rot."

I swallowed and held out the bone blade, pointing at the unmoving gleam of the dead archer. "I killed one already, but the other is hidden better and is harder to see with the threads of craft. I'm not certain—"

My words faded when Skul Drek promptly stepped away from me. "Where?"

I hesitated. "The far corner, near the pond. He's in the tree, but well concealed."

My head spun when the mirror shifted once more and Skul Drek was gone. For a fleeting moment, I caught sight of the gilded strands of the second archer's bones, but soon darkness enveloped the light.

Behind the man in the tree, Skul Drek's glare broke through the shadows.

Darkness thrashed and split into black ropes. My stomach flipped when the Draven archer cried out in agony. His body shuddered, but I could not make out what was happening. Another breath, another moment, and Skul Drek appeared to step through the man. In his grasp was a spool of icy white light.

With his gaze on me in the window, I watched as he coated the beam in his shadows until nothing remained but the pitch of night.

"I will end them before they touch you." The scrape of his venomous voice filled my thoughts, my heart.

By the gods, he'd . . . he'd claimed the archer's soul.

Somewhere beyond the mirror a warm grip curled around my wrist. Little by little, the rotted wood and walls became healthy and polished once more. Floorboards were not chipped and splintered, but smooth and level.

I blinked, knees weak, and leaned into strong arms when they encircled my waist.

My cheek pressed to a tunic that smelled of smoke and blood and the oakmoss on his skin. Chin tilted, I found a bit of steadiness in his golden eyes.

Around Roark's shoulders were wisps of shadows. Gold flickered with inky black, and the final pieces of the cold mirror realm disappeared.

Still coated in gore from Fillip, Roark looked like a beautiful villain—feral, wild, and maddeningly possessive. His jaw was set, and he touched me with the gentle ferocity I'd come to adore in Stonegate.

Like he wanted to mark me, claim me.

My body sank into him like I might want to let him.

To fall into the trance of Skul Drek always left my limbs weak as straw and my thoughts in a fog. Somewhere through the haze, I lifted a palm to the rough stubble on Roark's jaw.

"You came." In every way, Roark had been here for me. Protector. Hunter. Mine.

A muscle ticced in his cheek. His fingers brushed along my face. *Always.*

11

LYRA

ROARK TRAPPED MY FACE IN HIS PALMS, TILTING MY HEAD side to side, inspecting for wounds.

"Auki is the one who is injured," I whispered, my voice haggard from the exertion of using craft and falling into the cold of the mirror.

With a frown, Roark covered the bleeding gash on my waist.

I rolled my eyes. "It's a scratch. Auki has an arrow in his leg."

"Do you hear me whimpering?" Auki huffed, fighting a wince when Gunter and Emi gingerly wrapped the leg, avoiding the arrow shaft. "I'll be as right as I ever was in a few moments."

Brynn snorted. "He'll be sobbing once he's alone."

Auki cursed his sister under his breath, but it was cut short when Gunter, all at once, ripped the point of the arrow from his flesh. Auki shouted, spitting out cruel words toward Gunter while Emi made quick work of wrapping the wound.

"Told you." Brynn chuckled, but her grin faded when she looked at Roark. "I made you a vow to protect your bond, and I'll keep it."

In truth, their prince seemed more unsettled than anyone. He studied Brynn, and there was nothing warm or welcoming in the tension of his jaw, the way his fists curled at his sides.

She tilted her head. "What? Think I've been pining for you all this time?"

"He is stunning." Gunter winked. "In desperate need of a wash, of course, but beneath all the blood and grime, he's a sight any woman would be blessed to behold. Said so yourself, Brynnie."

"I stand by my words, but perhaps instead of gawking at the prince we ought to turn our attention to the fact that we were nearly impaled by damn arrows moments ago."

I bit down on the inside of my cheek to hide the tug of a grin. The longer we spoke, the more I enjoyed Brynn Oakbriar. Even if acceptance came with a touch of reluctance.

Roark's frown only deepened when Brynn drew nearer. He stepped in front of me.

Brynn sighed. "I'm not going to harm her."

"Told you, he's forgotten how deep Draven vows run." Gunter took a seat in one of the chairs beside Emi and Auki. "Said the same damn thing at the ravines, and you'd have thought I threatened to cut off his cock the way he bared his teeth at me."

The smile couldn't be helped any longer. I covered my lips with my palm.

"Roark," Auki said through a wince when he adjusted his leg. "We've waited for your return for seasons. We're not here to drive you away or betray you." He rubbed the back of his neck uneasily. "We understand why Nivek was killed, and we want to find the bastards the same as you. No one was ever caught, you know? Nivek deserved to have his voice heard before meeting the gods. What was done doesn't sit right. Never did. Not with a lot of folk."

"You might want to decide swiftly if we're worthy of being at the melder's side." Gunter peered out the window. "My father just found poor Máhtte. Gods, did you eat his soul? You'll be called back to the úlfur, I'm certain."

I followed Roark to the window. True enough, a tall man with the same shade of wild hair as Gunter helped steady the second archer. I did not know what was more horrifying, the dead archer bleeding over the briars or the second, whose eyes were dim, his movements more instinct than conscious thought.

Soulless. A shell of blood and bones and a beating heart.

Nothing more.

I want to know who sent them, Roark gestured. *The úlfur council just agreed you were to be untouched.*

Hot rage laced the movements of his hands. I did not know what to say. If the council agreed to stay my death a little longer, clearly the vote was not enough to guarantee my safety here.

"We'll learn who sent the archers," Emi said to her cousin.

"Until then, it might be wise to keep us close to the melder," Brynn said.

"I do have a name," I said, my voice rough.

Brynn smirked. "Apologies. *Lyra*. But by keeping you close with us, it will show that we stand with our prince and you. It might help soothe some of the unease in the clan."

"Or put blades at your throats." Emi folded her arms.

"We'll do the same for you, Nightlark," Auki said with a grimace and placed a palm over his wound. "Virki will not let you live here in peace on your own."

"Why?" I asked at long last. "Why risk all this for me, for Roark, when so many believe he has turned his back on your clan because of me?"

Brynn glanced at her brother, who tipped back a new horn. Gunter had taken an interest in tracing a finger over the carvings in the back of one chair.

"Because something is brewing here, something dangerous,"

Brynn said. "We want to know why Prince Nivek was slaughtered without facing our úlfur council. We want to know why you are the melder who brought every kingdom to battle. Not all is as it seems, but we must choose a side. We choose our prince, and that means you."

Roark waved a hand, drawing every eye. He shook his head, gestured at me, then pounded a fist to his chest three times. A signal that I was his to protect, but more that I was simply his.

"We know you'll protect Lyra, but you can't be everywhere at once, Roark," Emi said.

His lip curled and he dragged two fingers down the taut skin of his scar.

"If you keep yourself divided constantly, you know how difficult it is to reunite," his cousin warned.

My lips parted and I reeled on him. "What? If you keep splitting, there's a chance you can't be whole?"

I will never be whole. It is the nature of the deledan curse.

His words were silent, but I could feel the pain as he said them, like the notion he would always have a fracture within himself weighed heavy on his heart.

Emi frowned. "But it becomes harder to return to you."

Roark's brows pulled together. *Only if I remain split for a great deal of time. No one knows how long. Could take seasons.*

Gods, I wanted to shield the man or strike him. "You will not risk it to find out."

A touch of something smug, like he'd won some grand victory, played at the corner of his lips. *Worried for me?*

I frowned and folded my arms over my chest. "I recant. Remain divided. I think I prefer your darker side. *He* listens to me."

Roark chuckled, the rare rumble and rasp of his laugh. Gods, how I'd missed the sound. *Why are you surprised my depravity worships you?*

Low in my belly a shock of heat spread at the notion of Roark Ashwood's cruelest, most bloodthirsty pieces bending the knee for me. The thought of experiencing him in such a way—no lies, no secrets between us—was a sensual thrill I would keep locked away for my own pleasure.

By the molten hell, what was I doing?

Lives were at risk, and here I was imagining what the hands of this man could do . . . and perhaps the same of another piece of him.

Auki broke the silence. "What do you want us to do, my prince?"

Find out who sent the archers.

"Consider it done." Gunter flicked his fingers off his brow in a mock salute when Emi spoke for their prince. "Any idea on how to ensure that more assassins do not make an attempt on our lovely melder?"

Roark ran a palm over his chin, his exhaustion bleeding through. *I have a thought, but I must speak to Lyra. Alone.*

When Emi did not move to repeat Roark's gestures, I cleared my throat and spoke on his behalf. "He wishes to speak to me privately."

Gunter flicked his brows. "I'm sure he does."

I wanted to correct his insinuations. To talk, to finally bare our souls, was long overdue for me and Roark Ashwood. But Gunter was already across the room with Auki.

Brynn glanced our way, then to Emi. "Nightlark. You'll stay in my chambers. Òlmr never took a liking to Virki."

I did not know if it was wise for Emi to leave, but she wore a grin when she gave my hand a reassuring squeeze and followed Brynn.

Alone, the silence was thick, almost crushing. My finger traced the smooth wood on the back of a chair, uncertain what to say. "Who is Òlmr?"

Roark stepped against me, chest to chest. *Oakbriar's fara. I am told they have a fierce bond. If commanded, Òlmr will see to it that no one gets close to Emi.* He lifted his fingers to my cheek, speaking gently, tenderly. *Will you speak with me?*

The petulant side of me desired to turn away, to proffer a sliver of pain the same as I carried.

But the draw to him, the pull that never faded, had me leaning in to his touch. Gods, I was furious, frightened, and weary. But I could not deny my craving for this man was wretchedly vibrant, a near impulse to be closer, to fall into the safety those arms once provided.

I lifted my chin. "We both have much to say."

Roark slipped his fingers through mine and lifted my knuckles to his lips, kissing me there. Then he took us from the room, deeper into the Dravenmoor royal house.

ROARK

I COULD RECALL EVERY MOMENT IN THE SHADOWS WHERE my darker soul resided, a thing I'd never been able to do well before. Now every word spoken between my soul and the queen's was in my mind, as though I'd been in two places at once.

Strange, a little unsettling, but there was a power that came from knowing my own brutality was now mine to control.

I glanced at Lyra. I would need to tell her everything.

The trouble with recalling the words spoken with the queen was that I knew what she'd insinuated as a solution to keep Lyra safe while we plotted how to hunt the bones. Somewhere low in my gut was a tangle of barbs. After all that had happened between us, no mistake, Lyra Bien would not be pleased with the proposition. Then again, she trusted me in the ravines, and she'd gone toward my darkness when the archers attacked.

Her hand was nestled tightly in my palm, her body close, as we strode to the east wing of the royal house. Tapestries of fara wolves and black willows lined the corridor. A divot in one wall drew a reluctant grin at the memory.

I'd thrown a pigskin ball at Gunter, and the sod had been distracted by movement in the courtyard and missed the throw. Instead, our ball struck a favored clay basin of my mother's. It shattered against the wall and left a small divot in the wood from the force.

I turned away from the mark. Haunts lived in these corridors. Memories of a life long gone, a time when all I feared was whether playmates would make a fool of me on the sparring field.

We rounded the corner, and I came to a halt, my breath trapped in my chest.

"What is it?" Lyra squeezed my palm, on instinct or with purpose, I didn't know.

I didn't respond for a few heartbeats, lost to the onslaught of pain.

The door was carved in the shape of a kvistr tree, a towering, rare oak with lavender leaves that only grew along the ridges of Dravenmoor. Lore of the land insisted the shade of the branches would deepen to satin black in the presence of royal blood. A signal the gods approved of the royal house.

As a boy, my mother would whisper tales of the days she and my father took Nivek and me as babes to the tallest kvistr. Doubtless she took liberties with how rich the shade of leaves appeared, but she'd insisted that the purple had deepened to a pure pitch, that there was never a doubt her sons were the pride of the gods.

A thick board locked the door from the corridor. How long had it gone unopened? Since that night? No mistake, to enter was too painful, too raw.

"Roark?"

I tore my attention from the door and moved down the corridor, one hand giving a simple response. *My brother's chamber.*

Lyra looked over her shoulder but remained silent until we reached another door. It was arched much the same, but carved along the edges were blades and round shields with runes cer the center.

The second prince was always the hope of the Dark Watch. Nivek was to claim the throne, and I was to one day lead our armies.

How cruelly the Norns of fate had twisted our tales.

Walking into the second chamber felt a great deal like stepping through a door to the past. Against the wall was a large bed that I'd always felt swallowed me whole with its size. Shelves held small daggers, runes on wooden pieces, and strange colorful stones I'd loved to collect near the river.

Wooden drawers were covered in a layer of dust, untouched. A few larger axes and swords were stacked in the corner, along with folded trousers, boots, and tunics meant for a man.

For the days my clan anticipated my return from Stonegate. No doubt they'd hoped I would return with the melder's head, not my heart in her hands.

Dark shades were drawn, and I made quick work of lighting several tallow candles along a table. To let in the natural light by opening the shades would offer anyone who wanted Lyra dead a chance to retaliate, much like the bastards in the courtyard.

"What is this?" Lyra's tone held a laugh. Near a small stool tucked under a narrow desk topped in quills and charcoal sticks, she touched a few rice parchment sheets.

Skin prickled on the back of my neck.

Lyra lifted one piece of parchment, revealing a childish drawing of a black willow, a warrior with a too-large battle-ax, and a fara wolf with fangs coated in blood.

The grass beneath the oblong boots appeared like spikes more than anything, and the sun was horridly twisted in the corner of the sheet. I'd drawn a bleeding face in the golden sphere, attempting to show the gods' pleasure.

Lyra's eyes gleamed, the candlelight catching the silver scars through each center. "Is this meant to be you?"

I leaned against the wall, intent on concealing the disquiet of having her in this space, a place so familiar and so disconcerting all at once. *Do you not see the resemblance?*

"I see you were always inclined to swing a blade. Did you have a fara?"

Her finger tapped the sticklike wolf.

I shook my head. *Fara wolves are often bonded to a Draven in their fifteenth season.*

Her face fell in a touch of sadness, but she nodded. "Perhaps you can bond with one now."

I cared only for one bond.

When Lyra turned, I crossed the room, my chest to her back. A shudder rolled through her shoulders. Her breaths quickened. She didn't move away.

My fingers pinched the end of her braid, stroking the long waves, damp and dirty from the journey. Gods, I wanted to breathe her in. But there was more to discuss, more plans to make.

And my clothes, my skin, nearly every surface of me was coated in gore and sweat and the reek of days without a bit of soap.

I spoke by lifting one of her palms and tracing my fingers over her skin. *Do you wish to wash?*

"If that is some subtle way of telling me I smell, Roark Ashwood, I do hope you take a moment to look at yourself."

I grinned, went to the heavy door at the back of the room, and opened an arm to usher her inside. *One thing Draven folk do well is their washrooms.*

Lyra hesitated. "I might cry if I could wash, but . . . alone."

I hid the jolt of disappointment through a nod. No mistake, I desired to be anywhere she was, and if fewer clothes were between us, all the better. But I would not touch her again until every secret, every truth was brought to light.

If what I intended to happen was to be successful, trust would be needed.

There is more than one chamber, I replied.

Lyra slid past me into a narrow corridor made of marble stones. We strode in silence until we reached another doorway. She released a long sigh when a wall of damp, steamy air struck our faces.

The bath chambers were concealed well from the main house. Certain rooms would be left empty for the royals, others for the úlfur and high-ranking Dark Watch.

Incense and heat dug into my skin, my lungs, and for a moment, it felt peaceful.

Near an opening at the end of the royal bathing rooms, I paused, resting a hand on the small of Lyra's back before leading her inside. Damp stones arched overhead, and fragrant oils and herbs burned through the humid air.

Lyra's lips parted with a delighted sort of smile when she took in the room. It was small and round; every wall was covered in stone shelves with folded linens. In the center was a blue pool, clear as crystal.

"How is it heated?" Lyra knelt and touched the surface of the water.

The royal house is built beside natural hot springs, I explained. *Long ago, folk figured how to channel some of the springs to use as bathhouses.* I moved toward one wall, where a spigot with a latch over the mouth stuck out from the wall. With a simple twist, I opened the spout, allowing in more steam. *You can heat the room as you please.*

Lyra's shoulders slouched in a bit of relief. "By the gods, I think I will choose to remain, even if the whole of the palace wishes to slit my throat, if it means I have a washroom like this every day."

I stepped out of the room, pausing until she looked to my hands. *I will use the next chamber over. Then we will talk?*

"I only wish to speak if there are no more lies, no secrets."

I will tell you everything I know.

Her eyes were wet when she looked at me again. "You stole my heart, then you broke it. Perhaps it is not fair of me to blame you when I know much was out of your control, but whatever had grown between us now feels cracked. We will talk, but I do not know what happens next."

Give me a blade to the belly, an arrow to the chest. Give it all over, knowing I hurt Lyra Bien.

With a dip to my chin, I left her in the wash chamber and went to my own. Salts, oils, and soap chips were aligned in baskets for use. I sank into the pool and scrubbed Fillip's blood off my body until my skin burned.

Once finished, I found Lyra back in my old bedchamber, hugging one of the bed pillows. The woman was here to torture me, no doubt. She was dressed in one of my tunics. The hem struck just above her knees, and one sleeve slipped off her shoulder. Her damp hair was loose and long down her back, and I had to clench my damn fist to keep from curling my fingers around the locks.

I made a sound in my throat, drawing her attention. Cheeks flushed, she tugged at the hem of the tunic. "I did not have anything else to wear, and after the journey, I think that dress ought to be burned."

I smiled and stepped against her, a curl to my lip. *It suits you.*

Lyra nudged her palm against my chest, pushing me back. "I said we'd speak plainly. Can you do so without all your honeyed words muddling my thoughts?"

I do not have a voice.

With a scoff, she shook her head. "You have voice aplenty. And you are trying to seduce or soften me toward you. Stop it."

I refuse. And I'm a prince, so you cannot command me.

For a moment, I thought she might get angry, or at the least, agitated. Instead, Lyra's lips parted in feigned stun and . . . she laughed. "Oh, forgive me"—Lyra bent at the waist in a mock bow—"Prince Ashwood."

This almost felt normal, like nothing had happened to drive a cruel, bloody wall between us.

But our lives were never destined to be normal.

My smile faded and I spoke with one hand. *There are things I must tell you. And I'm almost certain you're about to get angrier with me.*

"Not a promising start." Lyra sat on the corner of the bed, releasing the pillow she embraced, and folded her hands in her lap. "What happened with the council?"

I made it clear I was no longer their creature.

The word pinched her face. "You are not a creature."

I dragged a dusty chair to the place in front of her and sat, leaning forward with my elbows on my knees. My hands formed the words in the space between us. *Did you not once think the same?*

"Only because I did not know my craft, nor understand why I was pulled into the darkness." A new gleam of fire burned in her silver scars. "Or do you not recall the night I confessed all my truths *to you*? I admitted I was captivated by the assassin of Dravenmoor. In that moment, why did you not tell me the truth?"

I wanted to. Each gesture was brisk, a sign of the shouts, the anger, the hate for what I was. A voice she could not hear, but one I hoped she could feel. I shook my head and slowed my hands. *Perhaps I ought to have tried. I was certain I did not have full control, and feared . . .*

When my words stalled, Lyra's face softened. "Feared what?"

I feared my clan would come for you directly if they knew I'd con-fessed the great Draven scheme to the melder. They would know the chains keeping me under their command had severed. I shook my head and shot to my feet, pacing as I spoke. *Not that any of it mattered. They have come for you, and now we are here.*

Lyra's chin dropped. "Could you truly not sense that your soul was not so divided anymore?"

How could I explain any of it? From living a life knowing a piece of my existence could be commanded to slaughter souls, leaving folk helpless to the blades of the Dark Watch, to sensing the severed pieces being stitched together, little by little, the lon-ger I was near this woman.

I lowered to one knee in front of her, hesitated for a breath, then took her palm in mine.

She did not pull away.

Against her hand, I gestured, *I knew I felt whole near you, and I did not understand it. All my life I was told that a soul rend left the split soul under the control of the render until the end.*

Her fingers curled around mine. "A soul render. Are there many folk with such craft here?"

I shook my head. *Only the queen.*

Lyra blanched. "Your mother controlled you?"

Elisabet of Dravenmoor no longer made much sense to me. Not after our interaction and the conflicting emotions of icy in-difference and passionate devotion when speaking of her family.

She did. I held Lyra's gaze. *And I was not the first.*

She tugged on the ends of her hair, glancing toward the win-dow. "Emi mentioned you were not the first Skul Drek, but I did not realize the same person controlled them all. Who else?"

There are sagas and records of split souls over the centuries, but the only other one done at the hands of my mother was my father.

"The king? And you knew this?"

I didn't for much of my time in Stonegate, but the more control I regained of my soul, the more memories were restored.

She nodded. "You know it was the same for me as well."

Much like mine, Lyra's memories of the raids and her past were shadowed. Hers were darkened by Nivek's craft, mine because of the curse of a divided soul.

Now I remember knowing my father protected the fallen souls in a world we could not see with our eyes. I rose and took a place beside her on the bed. *Since the first Jorvan king used soul bones for corruption, Draven folk have used soul craft to stop them. Most attempts came through forced bonds, usually during battles. Some soul craft can bind souls to souls. They are called soul weavers.*

"How?"

I wore a grin with little humor in it. *Bring a man to the brink of death, and he will give nearly anything to live a little longer.*

"And these soul weaver bonds would keep them alive?"

For a moment. Forced bonds are not favored; they're dangerous. To possess or overtake another soul is against Draven law. But it was an evil the clan believed necessary at the time. Most would command the bonded Jorvans to slaughter their own folk. Then soul weavers would release their souls, letting them die as they should've before.

"I've never heard of such a thing."

Jorvans retaliated, I went on. *To avoid soul weavers, they learned that by creating Berserkirs, not only would they have impenetrable warriors, but weavers could not bond with so many souls melded to one Berserkir.*

Lyra drew her knees against her chest. "I think I understand. Because of the Berserkirs, Dravens needed to find a way to protect the souls of the fallen from being used. And they believed the answer was to split souls, even knowing the risks. It's written plainly in *Tales of the Wanderer* what happens when a soul is split. Blood is claimed."

Yes. I patted my neck over the scar that robbed me of my voice. *It requires sacrificing something through the blood spilled to divide the soul.*

"Did your mother know that using her craft in such a way was the answer? Or was it always a risk?"

Berserkirs were crafted before my father was king, but for seasons, Dravens scoured lore to find the answer and read about other divided souls. It was only after my father was king that they determined splitting souls again was a necessary risk.

"How convenient his wife was a soul render."

I scoffed softly. *I'm told some took it as a sign from the Norns.*

"Why the king? Why not others?"

I once thought it was that because my mother and father had a soul bond, it was believed there would be less risk. But I am not sure any longer, for it shattered the bond. I cracked one knuckle before going on. *I remember being told by my brother that our clan insisted on taking such a risk because we had to protect the strongest souls.*

"You mean the Wanderer specifically." Lyra's voice was soft, but a bit of a thrill lived in her tone. As though she could not help but revel in the idea of learning more about a past we'd only begun to recall. "Skul Drek was the one who told me Damir was hunting the bones, which means you knew."

I nodded. *When you were lost after the raids, I was placed in Stonegate to await any hint you still lived. It was believed so fiercely that should you aid in the hunt of the bones, Damir would find them.*

Lyra's chin trembled. It seemed as though she held back words, likely the truth that I was placed in the Jorvan royal keep to kill her.

She cleared her throat and looked down at her fingernails. "When did the Dravens learn the truth about the Wanderer's bones?"

I was only a boy. I stilled my hands for a moment. The truth would be another layer of mistrust for Lyra. Or perhaps it might give her clarity to every thread of wretched fate that tore apart both our lives. *A seer woman from the Unfettered clans left the Night Ledges to speak to my father after she saw something horrid in the future of all clans.*

"She would've risked her life to do so."

I nodded. *I was eight seasons when she came. My folk listened to her tale of the hunt for the Wanderer's bones, but she told them more. She spoke of you.*

"Me? She saw me?"

I took hold of her hand again, using her open palm to form my words. *I was told she spoke of a melder, a girl, hidden in the lands. A melder as strong as the god-queen.*

Lyra's eyes narrowed when I did not go on. "I feel like you're not telling me everything. I swear it, Roark, if you keep secrets from me—"

Her words faded to a sharp gasp when I gripped her chin between my thumb and fingers, drawing her mouth close to mine. A slight movement to one side and I would taste those lips again.

I raised one hand to her cheek, speaking slowly, carefully. *There is more. The seer told my folk that this melder would destroy the lands.*

Lyra swallowed, her breaths deepened. "The raids."

My thumb brushed over the edge of her chin. *The raids are not on you, and they were not the destruction of which she spoke. They were done to prevent it.*

"No." Lyra pulled back enough to drag her fingers through her hair. "I am not as powerful as a legendary queen."

I tugged on her wrist. *The seer knew your potential strength. And you are stronger than Fadey.*

"Yes, and he wants my damn bones because he believes the same."

Fadey was a mystery in many ways. I could not shake the unease that there was more to his desire for Lyra.

I spoke gently over her palm. *The seer cared for you.*

"What do you mean?"

I swallowed. *You knew her. She was with you as an Unfettered servant.*

"No." Lyra's face pinched. "Gammal?"

Lyra had mentioned the old woman who'd cared for her before she was taken to work in the household of Jarl Jakobson. A woman who'd given an orphaned child a bit of kindness.

I nodded. *After she left her meet with my father, Gammal sent word that she would not be returning straightaway to the Unfettered lands over the Night Ledges. She insisted that if ever there came a time when we had need of her, we call upon her.*

"But Unfettered Folk don't have craft. Gammal told me."

I don't know much about their clans. But whatever her gifts were, they convinced my mother and father that she spoke true. The words were not spoken as hatred for you, merely to warn folk what was coming.

"Gammal." Lyra bit down on her bottom lip as small, jagged gasps rolled from her chest. "She . . . she told me to keep hidden, taught me to use the dyes. She taught me all I knew of craft. Gods. All that death during the raids came from the fear of one woman's word."

Lyra shot to her feet and paced in a bit of frenzy.

I followed her panicked steps, slid one arm around her waist, and pulled her back to my chest. I moved my words against the place over her heart. *It was a game of power, Lyra. Dravens wanted you dead, Myrdans wanted to study your blood, and Jorvans wanted you to find the bones of the first king. It was not on you.*

She spun around, her eyes bouncing between mine. "So after Gammal's predictions about my craft, your mother and father took drastic steps to protect the soul bones by splitting the king's soul?"

Yes. There was no need to mince words. *The clan believed that with the Jorvans' hunt aimed at the Wanderer, we had to do something equally monstrous.*

"So your father became a divided soul. Your brother was assassinated. You lost your clan and your voice." Lyra stood at my shoulder, a shadow over her features. "Why do you defend me, Roark? All my existence has ever done is cause you pain."

I lifted her hand and pressed her palm to the steady thrum of my heart. *Because this lives for you.*

She blinked, and a single tear fell from her lashes. Her fingers curled around my tunic. "Will you tell me of your father and how such a burden is now yours?"

I did. I spoke slowly, at times even tore bits of parchment to be certain not a word was missed, despite Lyra insisting she had no trouble.

The tale was gruesome, and I despised the whole of it. I told her how Vishon was torn in two by the soul render, a rite so vicious it destroyed the vows of his sjeleven bond with my mother.

I did not have a sealed bond with Lyra, only a thread, but even so, I could not imagine doing anything to harm her or risk severing it.

My jaw tensed. *I will never trust the queen entirely because of it. To destroy such a bond is believed to cause the same greed and bloodlust that befell the first king.*

"Did your father lose his voice too?"

I shook my head. *His mind. There is always something taken. My father suffered delusions. There were times he recognized us. But the longer he was divided, the less we had him. The crown fell upon my mother's head in his absence.*

"By the gods." For a long pause, Lyra was silent. "If the queen did so much before, there is no telling what she will do now."

She won't touch you.

"I know you want to believe that," Lyra said, "but she tore apart her own husband, Roark."

I own her soul. I leaned closer to Lyra, the tips of my fingers running along her jaw as I spoke. *She made a vow, soul to soul, to never bring harm to you. Should she break it, I will turn her into nothing.*

Lyra's brows raised. "Why would she agree to it?"

She knows of Fadey. She knows we hunt the Wanderer's bones ahead of him and plan to destroy them. Understand, Lyra, I have not forgotten nor will I forget Darkwin. And we will go after him, but the bones are what Fadey needs most. We must find a way to leave here, but the queen is not confident anyone will let you leave once word of Damir's death reaches the clan.

"So what are we to do? Wait until someone kills me in my sleep?"

I could not put off my plan a moment longer. Lyra would either mock me openly, flee from me, or . . . agree. *There is a way to make you untouchable to all Draven folk. By law. It is stronger than a vote of a council.*

"Is this the part where I will get angrier?"

Heat prickled up my neck. *Likely. But it is a legitimate way to keep you safe.*

Lyra folded her arms over her chest. "What is it?"

One breath, two. *Seal our bond.*

"What would that do?"

As I said, it is sacred to my folk. If someone kills one half of a sealed bond, the punishment is execution. If we complete—or seal—our bond, to kill you would mean they die too.

Lyra blinked. "Unless the council agreed with their actions."

Not on this. It would take you doing something horrendous, like murdering the queen, or me, or half the clan.

She arched a brow. "I'm supposed to believe that if people are bonded, they are safe from punishment because their bond is so sacred."

I grinned. *No. Many a ravager is bonded, I'm sure. They are sent to fight, where they die or live if the Norns smile upon them. A law is enforced should anyone slaughter an innocent who is bonded. You are innocent, and the council knows it. They know melders are forced to use soul bones. But you are here now, no longer forced to serve the Jorvans. If anyone were to harm you for merely having melding craft, it would be my right to kill them. They know after Fillip I would not hesitate.*

"If I do this," she began, voice soft, "seal the bond, what exactly does that make me to you?"

For a long, drawn moment I did not make a gesture.

Then, *You'll be my wife.*

13

LYRA

*M*Y WIFE.

Heart in my throat, I could not look away from Roark's hands. Doubtless, I'd misread the word. Surely, his hands moved too furiously, I'd interpreted something else entirely.

"I'm . . . I'm not certain I understood you correctly." Each word was rough over my tongue.

Roark's eyes burned like a trapped flame. *To seal a sjeleven bond would make you my wife, Lyra.*

All gods. I blinked, once, twice. How many knuckles I cracked, I wasn't certain.

Roark's wife.

My hunter. My protector. My lover. My liar.

Could he also be my husband?

My head spun. "I . . . I need a moment."

A bit of my heart cracked at the flicker of hurt on his face, there and gone. Soon enough, Roark was the unflappable, unbreakable

Sentry again. He dipped his chin, and instead of sending me away, he stepped through another door at the back of the bedchamber.

Alone, I collapsed, knees against the edge of the bed. I slid to the woven rug, my face buried in my palms. What in the two hells was I supposed to do? It felt as though with every step I took my life was at risk, every delay returning to Stonegate meant Kael suffered, and every thought always returned to Roark.

Be it as my villain or my savior, my steps continually entwined with his.

From the first sight of the fierce Sentry, the man had burrowed under my skin, a shadowed tattoo on my bones. I let my brow drop to the tops of my knees, desperate to slow my pulse.

Memories of simple moments with the man, before I ever would've dreamed the truth, fluttered through my mind. On the longship that took us from Skalfirth to Stonegate, he'd demanded my compliance for my safety. He'd been an enemy, but also a strange sort of ballast in the chaos.

And the fara wolf in the Phantom Forest sent to tear out my throat, he'd stopped it. The beginning of his betrayal toward his own clan and his first step of loyalty toward me.

I looked around the room, locked in a childish past long gone. I could almost imagine a small, playful Roark practicing how to hold a knife, likely attempting to imitate his elder brother.

My chin trembled.

For what he had suffered, all because that boyish heart saw me as more than forbidden craft, it would've been understandable if he'd slit my throat and been done with me.

Instead, the Sentry of Stonegate, the Death Bringer, kept me upright when fears overtook me; he reunited broken folk when he'd arranged for Hilda's and Edvin's families to join them in the royal keep; he wounded his own soul to defend me.

I sniffed and used the heel of my hand to wipe away tears from the corners of my eyes.

Roark had loved me.

In the truest sense.

Kael loved me, no doubt. We were a family who found each other. We'd yearned for such a connection, clung to it, become a brother and sister in every way save for blood. But Roark loved me despite his instincts, despite the cruelest craft demanding he end me, despite his own desires and loyalties. He had loved me to his own detriment.

And he never stopped.

A pitiful sob broke from my chest, not from pain, but from a twisted sort of delight. My mouth split into a watery smile the tighter I hugged my knees against my body.

Roark chose me over Thane, his own found brother. From the moment the Dark Watch surrounded our makeshift camp, their prince had never backed down, even destroyed one of them, all to keep me breathing.

Roark was no hero, not for me. He was the darkest, most beautiful sort of villain whose sharper edges stirred my soul.

My grin widened. Skul Drek always told me I brightened the night, but with Roark, his darkness was shelter against a blazing sun.

I wiped my eyes once more before rising. My fingers trembled when I clasped the latch on the door.

True enough, Roark had kept secrets, he'd lied, and he'd killed.

But the more I thought on it, the more it all paled beside everything he had done to prove there was no line he would not cross for me. How could I turn away from such a vicious, unbending devotion?

I could not deny it—I wanted Roark Ashwood.

But I wanted *all* of him.

HE LOOKED WEARY.

Seated in a tall chair, his chest still bare, and one boot propped on the stone lip of a smaller inglenook, Roark studied the flames, his chin propped on the claw of his hand. I wasn't certain he even heard me enter the smaller room, a study of sorts connected to his bedchamber.

I leaned one shoulder against the frame of the door. "Is this what you want?"

Roark spun in the chair, startled. One brow lifted with his palm. *What do you mean?*

Slowly, I crossed the space and stood in front of the flame. Heat kissed the backs of my legs, and the constant thrum of my pulse quickened when our gazes locked. "As a servant, I had certain freedoms. Strange, I know. One was being permitted to love and wed freely. No one cared who their servants chose to wed, as long as it was not their sons or daughters. As a prince, you did not have a choice, nor as Sentry. King Damir would've arranged a match for you. So"—I took a small step closer—"is this a match you desire?"

Roark rose to his feet. *I have failed you greatly if you do not already know my answer.*

"No, truly consider it," I said, my voice rough. "I have no plans to wed out of convenience. No matter how I feel about you. I have no plans to be ignored, discarded, or some man's regret five seasons from now."

A low rumble rolled from his throat, a sign of his disapproval for my words, but I held up a palm.

"You've not known me for long. Perhaps the way I thrash in my sleep will aggravate you in the future."

The smallest twitch of a smile teased his lips. *I will hold you in my arms to keep you still.*

"I have a fierce taste for star plums and have no shame stealing them off the plates of others."

I never took a liking to them. I'll gladly hand them over.

"With too much ale, I am quite the fool, embarrassing myself and others. I will endlessly stumble over words and my feet."

Roark tilted his head to one side. *Then I will carry you home.*

I traced a finger along the stones surrounding the hearth. "I can be rather stubborn."

I assure you, I am aware.

"To the point of being hardheaded," I said, chin lifted. "If I do not want to do something, I will dig in my heels so fiercely, you will need to toss me over your shoulder to get me to move."

Roark's eyes darkened. *If that is the consequence, I hope you always stand your ground.*

Gods. I fought my own smile, the burden of reality fading into the darkness for a moment. I stepped closer to his chair. "I've seen your chamber, Ashwood. You're rather . . . disorderly. I like a tidy space."

I make no promises there, he said, his fingers brushing over my palm. *But I swear to always plead for forgiveness.* Roark paused, then tugged on my wrist, forcing me to settle over his lap. His words were spoken against my heart. *On my knees.*

Breath lodged in the back of my throat. With a bit of hesitation, I touched my fingers to the edge of his bottom lip. "There could be another way to keep us both alive, surely."

But none with such a guarantee.

I swallowed. "Why? Why do you want this? I need to know you do not say this, ask this, because you feel you must."

Roark had the decency of considering my words and not speaking straightaway. At long last, he placed his open palm over my heart and: Tap. Tap. Tap.

His words were like smooth satin against my skin.

Because this is mine. The brushes of his fingers were slow, gentle, a whisper. He guided my palm to his chest, patting my hand against his body three times. *And this is yours. It will always be yours. I would not offer this if I was not wholly in love with you, Lyra.*

Gods, I did not know what to say.

Heat spread under my ribs, filling me soul deep.

I loved Roark Ashwood. Secrets and curses, violence and danger, I loved, I craved, I wanted.

A cruel sort of grin spread over my mouth when I levered my thighs in a straddle over his hips. Roark's lips parted and his hands went to my waist when I rocked, just so, over him.

I tilted my head, whispering against his ear. "All of me?"

He nodded, his fingers digging into my waist, no hesitation.

Without warning, I pulled away and stood three paces from him. Roark's eyes were narrow and burned with a new sort of heat.

I held up a palm. "You say you love all of me, for you've had all of me. But I have not had all of you."

Roark arched one brow in a question.

I tugged at the laces of my borrowed tunic, opening the front enough to reveal the cleft of my breasts. "You broke my heart, Roark. That comes with some consequences. You remember my love for torturing men, don't you?"

He swallowed with effort. I watched the movement of it down the length of his corded neck.

I seem to recall a moment or two when you had a man screaming.

I flashed a vicious smirk. "Good. I think you need to pay for the pain you've caused me."

Oh? Roark's face shadowed. *How shall I do that?*

I leaned over the chair, one palm on either arm, caging him. When my lips nearly brushed his, I spoke. "By doing nothing."

Again, he arched a brow.

I nipped at his ear. "You are not allowed to move a damn finger with what comes next. You. Will. Watch."

Lyra. He spoke against my cheek. *What are you doing?*

I pulled back again, opening the front of his tunic a little more so he could nearly see the flush of my nipples. Roark let out a strangled sort of cough but did not rise from the chair.

"You asked me once if I would take all of you, and I agreed. But I didn't know what I was agreeing to at the time. I did not know your depravity, a dark edge whose touch I feel on my skin. How is it fair that you have had all of me, but as I said, I have not had all of you?"

Roark lifted one palm, fingers shaking slightly. *You want . . . ?*

He didn't finish, but I nodded. "Yes. I want you to *watch* what the most vicious piece of your soul is about to do to me."

LYRA

ROARK'S EXPRESSION WAS A TANGLE OF BEWILDERMENT and lascivious heat. I bit down on my lip to keep from recanting my words. Unease splintered in my chest. This was too bold, too much.

Light from the flames darkened, like a shade had been drawn, shadowing the glow.

Roark, unmoving, was slowly draped in silky ribbons of shadows. Fire flickered behind his eyes until the gold faded to a shocking copper crimson. Along the thick scar on his throat, darkness dripped until a shape formed. Broad shoulders, ghostly skin, long fingers with dark fingernails.

Skul Drek stood between me and Roark, his head covered in the dark cowl, his lips pressed tightly.

I shuddered under his watch. This was . . . different. More vicious, more brutal, more possessive.

"Don't move, Roark. You'll watch your darkest pieces have me."

I straightened my spine, holding the burning attention of the monstrous shadow. My fingers opened the front of my tunic so it slid down my arms. Skul Drek tracked the garment, his shoulders lifting with silent breaths.

Through the diaphanous skeins of night, I could make out where Roark remained. His grip on the arms of the chair had tightened, and his jaw clenched enough that every muscle in his face seemed to pulse.

I blinked back to Skul Drek. With slow motions I shouldered out of the tunic and let it pool at my feet, leaving me exposed and naked. Roark hissed through his teeth, but Skul Drek lunged.

I cried out when the force of his darkness pinned me against the wall, arms above my head, the solid thickness of his darkened thigh between my legs. We were not in the mirror realm, so like Roark, Skul Drek did not speak here. But his eyes made a thousand unspoken vows of what was to come.

A touch of fear tingled through me from such heat. Such desire. For a moment I considered that Roark's darker half might devour me in the end.

Skul Drek pressed against me, moving his thigh against my bare center. I gasped and let my head fall back the more friction built between my legs. Heat was followed by a frigid breath. The phantom's mouth moved along my throat, and sharp nicks from his teeth roved down my neck, until his icy breath blew against one breast.

"Gods." I let out a rough pant when I felt him draw in my skin, sucking and nipping the pebbled point.

On the other side of the room, Roark shifted in his seat, a flush to his skin. His mouth was parted, and he panted, but his grip had yet to loosen on the chair.

"Can you . . . ?" I let out a moan when Skul Drek's leg pressed harder against my core. "Can you feel it?"

Roark's eyes snapped up. He gave a jerky nod.

I grinned with a bit of my own wickedness. "Good. Don't move."

In the next moment, a ribbon of misty darkness covered my mouth, silencing me.

Skul Drek tugged on my chin, forcing me to meet his burning gaze. One shadowed finger covered his dark lips. He did not uncover my mouth before spinning me around and flattening my body against the wall.

His hands—or perhaps more of his shadows—reached between my thighs. Cold, sensual touches covered my entire body. My head fell back, throat bared; both peaks of my breasts were pinched and tugged by those chilled fingers.

But as if he had a dozen hands, inky shadows coiled around my waist and slid down my lower belly until they brushed against my drenched core. I shuddered, my knees threatening to give out, but the phantom only caged me against the wall again.

His lips, his tongue, all of it tasted the crook of my neck.

Coils of darkness pinned my palms to the wall. Skul Drek used one hand to tug at my hips, silently urging me to bend forward.

I trembled when I hinged at my waist, palms on the wall, legs spread. From behind, the drip of darkness slid between the globes of my ass. A cry slipped over my lips when he used my own wetness to ease the shadows into me there. The burn of something new, something viciously full, blurred my thoughts until all I could do was feel Skul Drek to my bones.

My body thrashed against the intrusion from all sides, and a muffled scream split under his shadows.

Something crashed behind me.

Roark practically gasped, still seated. He'd kicked over a stool near the inglenook in frustration. His skin was red and flushed, and he looked at his own soul with poisonous venom.

I fell into the touch of Skul Drek, rocking my core against his shadows. I arched my back until both misty palms took each breast, squeezing and molding the shape of me.

The beginnings of release coiled low in my belly, pooling heavy in my core. More light faded, and the heavy mists of the mirror surrounded my ankles.

Good gods, he had pulled me away to the shadows of the realm of souls.

My body was tangled in such need I hardly cared.

Cold surrounded me, and Skul Drek only tightened his hold. When the threads of gold from the tether between us glowed in my sights, I widened my legs. "More!"

"Melder." His rough, rocky rasp danced down my spine now that we were in the mirror.

"Show me what you want," I said in a breathless gasp. "Take me."

A low sort of growl rolled over his lips. Skul Drek dipped his face against my throat, kissing me there. "I will burrow inside you, Melder. Until you are never free of he and we."

By the gods.

A thread of shadows tightened around my throat, pressing enough that I drew in a sharp breath. It was not enough to cut off my air, and the tension sent a wave of pleasure down my spine. Skul Drek claimed me.

I dipped my chin and watched as another thread of darkness glided between my thighs and entered my slit from behind again. Gods, I would not survive. So full, so deep. It felt like a beautiful torture. Shadows touched and tormented every surface of me, inside and out, until I could not breathe.

Warmth returned. Little by little the trance of the mirror faded, by my desire or by Roark forcing his soul to release me, I didn't know. Sensation only deepened the more heat filled the room.

I bit down on the ribbon of darkness over my mouth, whimpering as a fierce, quaking release rolled through me. From the crown of my skull to the soles of my feet, I was engulfed in flames.

Another kick. The same stool flung across the room, and Roark bolted off the chair.

I choked on a gasp when he reached through the darkness of Skul Drek, stepped through the phantom figure, and spun me into his arms.

My body shuddered when copper eyes clashed with gold. When for a moment, for a perfect moment, he became we. It wasn't long until Skul Drek faded into Roark, leaving a faint shadow over his eyes.

My release still muddied my head, but I trapped Roark's face between my palms. "I cannot make out a difference between you." My voice croaked. "You are he and he is you. I see all of you, and I want every dark, cruel, wonderful piece."

Roark crashed his mouth to mine.

He kissed me with such fury, I feared blood would be drawn. Roark gathered me in his arms and drew us down to the woven rug beside the inglenook.

I hooked my legs around his waist and kissed him as though ravenous, as though I would never get enough.

"You're whole," I blurted out between kisses. "You were always whole to me. Every part of you is mine." I gently tapped his face once, twice, three times. "Mine."

Roark's brow furrowed, a glimpse of vulnerability. As though the words meant something deeper. He let out a rough grunt and furiously rid himself of his boots and trousers.

Wildness lived in his expression when he reared over me, gripping my chin to devour me. His tongue, his teeth, his kiss claimed all of me until I swallowed his every breath.

My fingers dug into the damp heat of his bare back, clawing at his flesh like I wanted to peel it off his bones.

Before I realized his movement, Roark pulled away, leaving me breathless. I cried out when he rolled me onto my belly.

Eyes wide, I looked over my shoulder.

His countenance was carved in beautiful darkness, a look of pure need and possessive desire, but beneath it all was the sweetest gleam of devotion.

He wasted no time before he urged me onto my knees and yanked my hips back.

"Roark..."

He gripped my thighs, spreading them. His palms claimed my hips with such force, I was certain marks would be left behind come nightfall.

A tangle of two forces who'd stolen my heart and soul. Skul Drek was there, part of him, burrowed in Roark's blood. Not only had the silent Sentry claimed me, but so had the killer in the shadows.

Both.

One.

Him.

Roark was a man undone. He settled behind me and aligned his swollen cock with my entrance. In a rough thrust, he filled me. My spine bowed from the intrusion. I cried out his name.

He didn't stop. A sort of madness overtook the prince of Dravenmoor. Roark curled his fingers in my hair, pulling my head back as he pounded into my core.

His gasps were rough, raw. Another cold rope of shadows slithered across my cheeks, between my breasts, and down my stomach.

All gods. The ribbon of darkness reached between us, circling the apex of my core while a second slid over my breasts once more, pinching and flicking.

All of him. He was giving me everything.

I would never tire of all that he was. Monster, hunter, protector, lover—I wanted it all.

Roark bit down on the curve of my neck when a second release spread through me like an inferno. I cared little who heard my screams in the royal house. A damn fara wolf could enter the room and it would not be enough to pull me away from this man.

Roark deepened his thrusts, wild, a little vicious, until the heat of his release burst through me with such force I could feel every pulse, every rush.

He collapsed over me, slowly easing out. I fell to my belly, spent and sated. With care, Roark rolled me over, then tugged my damp body beneath his. His fingertips brushed a lock of hair from my brow; he studied my features, traced the edges of my face, like he wanted to recall every flinch, every smirk.

Sweat from his brow dripped onto my chest. He leaned forward and licked it off, pressing two light kisses to the swell of each breast, then kissing my lips with a tender ferocity.

When he pulled back, the light of his golden eyes was returned, but the dark edges of his heart were now mine.

I held one side of his face, my thumb brushing over the ridge of his cheek. "Suffered enough?"

He grinned. *I think, if you need, I could be tortured again.*

I pressed a kiss to his fingertips. "I'll do it."

Roark's face fell. *Be certain.*

"I am. I'll be your wife."

ROARK

I DARED NOT LEAVE THE CHAMBER UNTIL THE MOON WAS highest. Lyra leaned against one post on the bed, a stiletto dagger hugged to her chest.

I lifted one hand. *Windows?*

"Stay clear of them."

Door?

She smirked. "I'm not a fool."

I crossed the space between us and pinched her chin between my fingers, my other hand speaking against her face. *Summon me and I will return. You can always speak to me.*

"Soul to soul?"

You merely need to find the connection. It was how the queen would draw out the creature to do her bidding. I ran my thumb over Lyra's lip, then turned to the door. *I won't be long.*

She tightened her hold on the hilt of the dagger and didn't look away until the door closed between us.

I sensed her fear, but she'd not faltered since agreeing to the sjeleven seal.

The corridors were dim, with only light from sparse tallow candles, and a familiar scent of damp wood and saffron filled every breath. Home, or at least this palace, had once been the refuge of my childhood.

Now it was a pit filled with vipers.

The Draven palace was built like a labyrinth, and done with intention. Should enemies ever breach the borders of the kingdom, most of the township and royal house could hole away in the endless passages and hidden alcoves with rooms unseen. Ram's horns were strategically placed in treetop towers all along the borders, and with their positions, the warning bellow could be heard from one end of the township to the next.

My father, before his soul rend, would hold mock attacks once every season, so folk would know how to maneuver into the royal stronghold with elders and young ones.

As a prince, I was to take cover in the north wing inside a narrow alcove beside the tapestry of the god of war. There, the alcove bloomed into a room in the walls, reinforced with stone and mud, too thick for arrows or blades.

Other sections of the town took up various wings and cellars and the fara wolf keep.

I ought to have confirmed that Brynn and Auki kept the same chambers before trudging all the way to the fara cages. Virki was always near his precious wolves, and the last soul I wanted to know what was about to happen tonight was my uncle.

In the holdings, the air thickened with hints of wet fur, straw bedding, and blood from the hocks of meat fed to the wolves. The ceilings were arched and made of cold stone since the creatures preferred frosts to warm months, but it left passages with fewer servants and guards.

The door was at the end of the corridor nearest to the outer walls.

I knocked once, then stepped back, aggravated that my chest tightened. With what? Nerves? Unease? I was a damn killer, a darkened soul, and the thought of facing childhood playmates left me shifting on my feet.

I knocked again, only to have the door crack open before I could withdraw my fist.

Auki rubbed a palm down his sleep-weary face. He still looked much the same. A stern nose, deep-set eyes, and ears that always stuck out too much for his liking.

When he recognized me, he cleared his throat and dipped his chin. "My prince. Or can I just skip all the damn pretense?"

I waved a hand.

Auki nodded. "Good. Why are you knocking? You always barged your way in before."

Unbidden, my lip curled. Nothing was as it once was. The sooner Draven folk understood that, the better.

I didn't bother speaking—he wouldn't understand me anyway—and shoved past him, searching for Emi.

Auki locked the door at my back and followed my attention to the door I assumed was his sister's. "Take it you're here for Nightlark?"

I dipped my chin in a brisk nod.

Auki didn't make a move. "You know, I've been studying hand speak. Don't know if it's the same as yours, but as soon as Yanson told us what was sacrificed, I figured you'd find a way to talk again. You always did love your voice too much."

I arched my brow.

Auki took a step closer. "Watch."

As though he needed to prove his point, he moved his hands and fingers. The gestures appeared to be fashioning individual symbols. Not exactly the way Thane and I made my words, but similar enough that I was able to see he'd spoken his name.

The barest grin teased my mouth.

I lifted one hand and did the same with less awkwardness, my moves more fluid after seasons of use. *Auki.*

His eyes brightened. "Yes! How did you form the first symbol? It was different. I don't know much, but I can gesture to eat, sleep, those are simple enough; I can warn of an attack. I'll study the way you speak now."

His words struck me like an iron bolt to the chest. All this time, for a dozen full seasons, Auki had been here, my ally, awaiting my return. A friend who'd gotten us into more precarious situations than Gunter, a boy raised to be devoted to the Dark Watch and his kingdom, and he'd always remained loyal to me.

For the first time, realization began to crack through the barbed, jagged walls I'd crafted around the folk of my old life. Auki did not care that I brought the melder here, alive. He did not care that I still claimed a bond to Lyra. None of it had changed the loyalty of a young boy learning to hand speak as best he could because a playmate had lost his voice and he knew they would face each other again one day.

I offered a tight grin, then pointed at Brynn's door.

"Right. Prepare for gnashing teeth."

Hushed arguments followed the moment Auki stepped through the door. A low rumble of a growl came, followed by a hissed curse.

Auki reappeared, back first, his hand out. "Brynn, godsdammit, call her off."

The head of a tall, silver wolf stalked Auki through the door. Òlmr was stunning. Frigid blue eyes, streaks of black in the tuft of her chest, but the rest of her coat was sleek and pale gray.

The wolf had her lips curled, fangs flashing, and was wholly focused on Auki, who scrambled with familiar movements to calm a fara.

Brynn filled the doorway, the long half of her hair braided over her shoulder. She chuckled, observing her brother's attempt to touch Òlmr. Auki's craft had a way with wolves, soothing their minds and hearts. Fitting for a keeper of fara wolves. Brynn held similar talents, but from what I recalled, she was called a soul guider. A craft that could ease burdens until clarity of the mind was restored, a craft that led hearts forward.

Brynn guided the wolves in their training, their battles, their lives.

My old craft, before it was ripped out and replaced with the deledan, had been similar but connected to the guidance of the souls buried in the soil. Much like now, only gentler. It was how I stumbled upon Lyra during the raids. Like whispers of the dead urged me forward until I landed at her feet.

"Next time, you'll learn to knock, Auki." Brynn wore a smug grin that did not shift when she looked my way. "My prince."

Brynn Oakbriar had been in my life since infancy. A woman I'd expected to call my wife when I was a boy, even if we both knew no soul bond would form between us. I would not forget the day she insisted we make our vow that if either of us found a bonded love, we'd defend it for the other with our lives.

She'd always run with the lot of us, always planned to serve the Dark Watch, and like Auki, it was evident she had honored her vow made long ago to a young prince.

"Call him Roark . . . gods"—Auki swatted at the wolf when she snarled again—"he doesn't want pretenses and titles."

Brynn popped one shoulder in a shrug. "What brings you here?"

At long last, Brynn whistled, drawing her fara away from Auki, whose back was pinned to the wall.

Her brother let out a heavy sigh and dragged his fingers through his hair. "Where's Nightlark?"

"Here."

Relief was heady, like a rush of blood from dropping too fast, when Emi appeared behind Brynn. Already securing a belt around her waist, she'd dressed in new clothes, likely Brynn's and too big, but her face was clear of any lingering dirt and sweat, and my cousin's pale hair was braided loosely down her back.

I motioned for Emi to join me. *I have need of you tonight.*

"What's going on? Where's Lyra?"

My chamber. I hesitated before going on. *We need you to witness something.*

Emi's lips parted. "Damn the gods, you're serious?"

I swallowed. *She and I both agree it is the swiftest and best way to keep her safe here. Until we find a way out.*

Emi snorted. "How disappointing you are as a romantic. Sounds very straightforward and dull."

"Wait. Romantic?" Auki snapped his head up. "What's happening?"

Emi didn't respond to him and kept speaking to me. "Tell me you didn't present this as a mere transaction or a duty. Gods, Roark, I told you—"

I waved a hand. *I am not a fool. I spoke the truth of my desire.*

"And she shares the same desire?"

Heat scorched the back of my neck from memories of the twisted, sensual, stunning way I'd claimed Lyra not so long ago.

How all of me had claimed her.

Gods, I had not anticipated that the use of my broken soul would stimulate every surface of my flesh like I stepped too near a blaze. She'd wanted me to suffer, a bit of cruel pleasure handed down for the secrets kept.

I would suffer at her hands over and again if she asked.

"Roark?" Emi tilted her head. "She agreed because she feels the same? You know bonds aren't sturdy if both sides are not devoted."

Auki's mouth parted. "You're sealing your sjeleven bond?"

I frowned at him but spoke to my cousin. *Lyra agreed.*

For a moment, Emi studied my features, as though searching for the lie. Then, little by little, her grin spread. "Did you at least grovel a bit for not telling her the truth sooner?"

I rubbed the back of my neck with one hand and spoke with the other. *Something like that.*

"We can stand as more witnesses." Brynn stepped forward. "You will need us."

Instinct drew me to begin refusals, but Emi placed a hand on my arm. "She's right. Their word is respected, where we are both in disgrace."

I took in the similar features of the twins. Faces from a past I'd yearned to forget. How many moments had I stepped onto battlefields, pleading to meet Salur, so I might be free of my memories from a life ripped away? Those days when I could not even recall why I was shunned by folk I thought cared.

So many seasons I'd simply believed something inside me had grown rotten, depraved, too dangerous to remain in my own clan.

Now those haunts from the past wished to serve me, stand by me. They wished to protect the only bright piece of my soul.

"You need us," Brynn repeated, her voice soft.

I let out a sigh and gestured briskly. *Fine. Someone fetch Gunter. We will also need him.*

"MID BEDDING." GUNTER LEANED AGAINST THE WALL, HIS ARMS folded over his bare chest, his trousers half undone and slipping down his hip bones.

"Don't remind us," Emi hissed. "I never wish to see your ass again."

"Because it is so glorious?" With his hair free from the braid down his skull, the auburn strands fell around his shoulders when he glared at me. "You couldn't have waited a damn bell toll?"

You did not need to come. I would've used another. I gestured over my shoulder when we returned to my chamber door.

Gunter snorted when Emi repeated my words. "Don't tell me you'd actually consider signaling Weaver Flegi. He is terrible with his soul weaves and does not care for the melder. An important thing of note. So I will come with you. Well, I *would've* been coming in much more delightful ways if you'd waited that bell toll."

Brynn rolled her eyes. "I have no doubt Sigrid will still be in your bed when you return. She is moments away from inking your damn name on her breast."

"Envious, Brynnie?"

"Gods, no."

Gunter tightened the laces of his trousers. "I'm not missing this. Can't wait to see the look on Virki's face come dawn."

Where Gunter reveled in my uncle's unease, Virki was the man I trusted the least. If he could betray a sealed bond and his own daughter, it did not take much to imagine what he would do to the melder whose craft he blamed for every wretched twist of fate.

I took care to knock the pattern Lyra and I had predetermined, then stepped into an empty room. The others filtered in behind me, waiting near the doorway while I stepped to the adjacent sitting room.

Inside, the fire in the inglenook had died a bit, the stool I'd kicked during the fiery frustration remained toppled, and there was no Lyra.

Panic grew taut in my chest. I scanned the space, desperate to find her.

Shadows shifted in the corner near an old woven tapestry of the double-headed raven of Dravenmoor.

Lyra peered out, a tinge of red to her cheeks. "Not the most brilliant of hiding places."

In my absence she'd tied her hair off her neck and added a pair of trousers she must've found. Mine, but smaller than I could wear now. Still, they buried Lyra's figure.

I could not recall a more perfect sight.

I went to her side and slipped my fingers through hers, lifting her knuckles to my lips. *Ready?*

With a nod, Lyra followed me into the adjacent room. She cracked one knuckle and took in the crowd meandering about my bedchamber. "Why are they all here?"

We need them to witness.

Emi beamed and hurried over to us. She took hold of Lyra's free hand. "I hear my cousin is horridly unromantic."

Lyra offered me a knowing smirk. "I wouldn't say that."

"I do agree this is the surest way to draw you into the clan as part of the Dravens, not an enemy," Emi said.

"Yes, so I've heard. But are we certain it can't be challenged because everyone on the council despises my craft and believes those gods-awful prophecies?"

A new somberness filled Emi's expression. "To unweave a soul bond is only allowed in certain circumstances."

"Treason." Auki held up one finger. "And abuse of the heart, mind, or body. Especially against one's partner."

Lyra tilted her head, a small grin in the corner of her mouth. "Truly?"

Gunter crossed his arms over his chest. "Why the tone of surprise?"

"It's just that with the exception of a few, from what I've witnessed, I do not think offending your wife's heart is of much concern to most."

"Welcome to Dravenmoor, then," Brynn interjected. "Sealed bonds are cherished. Our women and our men serve side by side, fight side by side."

"Infidelity against a sealed sjeleven bond is another reason one could be unwoven," Auki said. "There are no mistresses, no lovers outside the pair unless agreed upon mutually."

"Virki used betrayal to dissolve his bond with my mother without repercussion," Emi said softly. "For how could a bone crafter be Draven?"

Auki blew out his lips in disgust. "Strange how it took so many seasons for your bone craft to bother him."

True enough. Emi's bone craft presented during her fourth season, but it was several full seasons later that Virki made the accusation of betrayal against his wife.

"More unfortunate is that as his wife's daughter, I still fell to his responsibility," Emi said. "I wish he'd sent me to the wilds with her."

My uncle treated Emi little better than a thrall. A body on which to take out his rage.

"There was no evidence," Emi went on, her voice rough. "Only my craft. Me. The child my mother loved was the cause of her agony."

Brynn placed a hand on Emi's shoulder and squeezed gently.

Lyra did not speak for a long pause, her fingers wringing in front of her body. "Your father was the cause of her agony. Not you."

"I have the wrong craft, Lyra."

"So do I." Lyra held Emi's stare. "House Bien would still be alive if not for my craft. I have spent a great deal of my life not recalling the truth, but I always knew those who loved me were destroyed because of the magic in my blood. But I was told once that I am more than the scars in my eyes. You are more than the craft in your veins."

A bit of heat filled my chest when she gave me a small grin.

I brushed a hand over Lyra's cheek. *There is no true reason for them to disregard this bond, to harm you, or me. Not if they follow our laws.*

"Some may see it as a betrayal, bonding your life to an enemy."

And I care nothing for those worthless opinions.

Her eyes were like frosted glass. "You better mean those words, Roark Ashwood."

I do not want this for strategy, I told her. *I have wanted this from the first moment a girl with silver in her eyes offered a lost boy some water. Never doubt it.*

Her chin trembled, but she grinned. "Well, there were those times you wanted to slit my throat."

I smirked. *Only for a little while.*

"This is a sound move," Emi interrupted. "Are we doing this? Recent nights may not have been so affectionate, but I think you've accepted there is a bond, right, Lyra?"

"Frosted hell, they have trouble acknowledging it?" Gunter scratched his chin.

"While in Stonegate it took some convincing," Emi said.

Gunter looked aghast. "How? I smelled it the instant I saw them."

"What?" Lyra's head canted to the side. "You could sense it?"

"Not sense. Smell." Gunter used his chin to point between the two of us. "Yours, if you'd like to know, has a bit of a sweet scent like honey blooms near the ponds. Smooth against the back of the throat, unlike some that burn something fierce."

I brushed my knuckles down the back of Lyra's arm. *Gunter is a soul weaver, the sort I told you about. Their craft is sensitive to the power of a bond.*

Gunter clapped his hands together. "Let's get to it, then."

Lyra tucked herself a little closer to my side. "You're truly willing to do this, Gunter? No question?"

Levity faded when Gunter spoke again. "I was in the room, Melder." He tipped his head at me. "My father is on the úlfur council. He aided in the split. I followed him. I watched what was done to my truest friend, my prince. I could feel the bond of his soul shadowed, slashed, corrupted. I would rather greet Salur than witness such pain again."

I did not move. Every muscle clenched. All I could recall of those moments were the pain, the fear, the screams, and the smell of blood.

I'd not known Gunter had crouched somewhere in the shadows.

He went to the center of the bedchamber, asked Emi to find a blade, then gestured for me and Lyra to join him. "Now, if you don't mind, I'd like to get on with this, so no one can ever hide this damn bond from you two again."

16

LYRA

MY PULSE WOULDN'T STOP RACING. THE STEADY THUD echoed in my skull when I followed Roark to the center of the room.

Gunter was half dressed, his hair a little wild, and there was a red raised mark on the side of his neck that seemed made by teeth. In this moment, he fit the feral reputation of the Draven clan.

A piece of me did not want to trust him easily, but when Gunter flashed me a grin, for a moment, my heart slowed.

"Melder, you'll stand here." He positioned me in front of his shoulder, facing Roark. "I suppose I ought to stop calling you melder since you're my future queen."

Blood drained from my face, noticeable enough that Brynn and Emi chuckled at our backs.

"Remember? You stole my crown." Brynn twirled a lock of hair around her finger.

I looked over my shoulder. "I . . . I haven't the slightest idea how to be . . . anything like a queen."

Three slow squeezes to my palms drew me back to Roark's piercing regard. He turned one of my hands palm up and spoke. *Nor do I.*

"You were born to royalty."

But have lived apart in the role of Sentry. I never expected to survive Stonegate long enough to inherit my title.

My throat tightened. Roark planned to die as Sentry? No doubt he expected that if ever he slaughtered the king's precious melder, he would be executed. Damir held no qualms about placing Roark on his front lines. If he survived punishment, I had few doubts Roark anticipated falling in battle one day.

To imagine a world where he was not here sent sick waves to my insides.

I returned the pulse of a squeeze to his hand, a silent way of telling him I was glad to be standing here. With him.

"All right, let us begin." Gunter's eyes fluttered closed. He paused for a heartbeat, another, then his eyes snapped open. The blaze of his lavender eyes shifted to a rich shade of indigo. "A drop of blood for aligned minds. May your thoughts and dreams always find a way to unite on the same path."

I jolted when Brynn tapped the hilt of a knife against my arm.

"You'll need to cut your palm," she whispered.

I blinked. "I don't know what I'm doing."

"Didn't even explain the ceremony to her?" Gunter clicked his tongue at Roark and took the knife. "There will be three cuts for each of you. Tell me, Meld . . . Lyra, you're not queasy when it comes to the taste of blood, are you?"

"I . . . don't know."

"I suppose we'll find out together." Gunter leveled the point of the knife against my palm, sliced a shallow cut, then guided my palm to Roark.

I froze. Without looking away, Roark lifted the gash to his lips and licked a drop away. I had no time to think on it before Gunter did the same and I was urged to take a bit of Roark's blood on my tongue.

Where I anticipated the sharp tang, instead there was a bite of heat, like a hidden spice settled onto my tongue.

Gunter cleared his throat and went on. "Another drop for united hearts. May your desires and passions belong to each other always."

Again, Roark's blood fell onto my tongue the same as he took mine. The spice and heat intensified, flowing from my mouth down my throat. I stepped closer to him, some force, some need, urging me to feel him, breathe him in. Roark seemed to feel something much the same. One of his palms drifted from my hands to my waist, to his fingertips touching every divot on my spine.

"For the final draw"—Gunter took my other hand—"the drop for entwined souls. May your love, your life, and your death be bound together into the long halls of Salur."

My fingers trembled when I placed my palm to Roark's lips. When it was my turn, the moment I licked the drop of blood off his skin, a shudder racked my body. I braced against his chest, desperate to touch him. A feeling so fierce, so consuming, enveloped me until it seemed there would be no relief if I did not crack open his chest and nestle inside his ribs.

Somewhere inside me was a heat unlike any I'd felt, not harsh like an unforgiving sun, but gentle, intoxicating. A tug and a stitch, a pull and a jab, it felt as though threads replaced my veins and a loom worked them nearer, tighter, against Roark's body.

Perhaps he felt much the same, for in the next moment,

Roark's hand abandoned my hips and spine and gripped the back of my neck, holding my brow to his. He drew in a long breath, his jaw tense, as though the same need devoured him.

Soft laughter filled the room. Gunter placed a hand on my shoulder and one on Roark's, urging us to part, and I was not certain I could recall a time when I yearned to kill a man so fiercely.

He grinned. "I must secure the weave of your souls, then you can have your way with him. Right now they are completely bared to each other, and it can be *intense*."

I would not call the fire engulfing me intense. It was staggering.

With another long draw through his nose, Gunter pressed one palm against the place over my heart and his other over Roark's. He closed his eyes. "As I weave them together, it helps keep them clear in my craft if you speak your own vows."

Roark's eyes burned like embers. He wasted no time before he had one palm against my cheek. *You brighten the night, you brighten my soul, and you have from my first glance. I swear I will try each day to do the same for you.*

The sting of tears blurred my sight. I covered his palm on my face. "You are my hunter, my protector, my lover. I swear to you, all that I have in my heart will be yours."

Another pull yanked me forward, like a hook beneath my breastbone. The sensation was fierce enough that I let out a rough cough. Gunter did not open his eyes, merely placed the palm that had been on my chest on Roark's, then did the same to me.

"Keep going," he said, his voice so low I almost missed the command. "I am all at once realizing a split soul takes more intricate weaving."

Roark touched his thumb to my lip. *To love you is my honor, my privilege.*

I did not need to look at his palms. His words stunned me, a shock to the heart. I was lost in them, never noticing the shift of the room, the way warm air turned frosted.

"I swear to choose you, Melder. Your soul remains bright over the rest."

All gods. Skul Drek held my burning face in his cold palms.

Between us the threads of gold split and spread, like a dozen ribbons binding every part of me to every shadow of him. The gold sank deeper into my shoulders, my throat, my chest, my middle. From the darkness, I could make out Gunter's glowing shape, moving and adjusting the bonds. Almost the same way I melded bone.

I stepped against Skul Drek, nestling into his darkness. I placed a palm beneath his cowl, touching the icy mist of his face. Here, in the mirror, he was not the same as he'd been in the bed-chamber. He was a phantom, but he was mine.

"I promise that with what we face, there is no one I wish to stand beside more than you," I said. "For you alone, I would give my soul. It was always yours."

Filaments binding me to Skul Drek burned between us. A thousand ropes of golden steel, unbreakable, unmovable. I was his, he was mine. Always.

When the mists of the mirror began to fade, I rose onto my toes and pressed my lips to the cold shadows of his face until warmth replaced the cool air and Roark's tongue brushed with mine, again and again.

Light returned, the gleam of the bond fastening us together faded, but the power remained. A draw unlike any I'd felt before cleaved me to Roark Ashwood. It was not forced, and I knew it.

Strange, but should I choose it, I knew I would be free to walk away. The thought simply made me want to retch.

Roark's fingers dug into my hair, tousling my braid. He kissed me fiercely for another breath, then pulled away, breathing deeply.

My hands rested against the stubble of his face, my brow pressed to his, and I could not stomach the idea of not touching him.

Until a throat cleared, and I realized that we had unknowingly smashed half of Gunter's body between our chests. With a touch of reluctance, I pulled back, but kept one hand laced with Roark's.

"Many thanks." Gunter faced the others, arms open. "I present our newest sjeleven bond. And with such a bond, our newest member of the clan, Lyra."

Emi bounced on her toes, then rushed over to where we stood. Her arms were slim, but she managed to hook one around each of our necks, squeezing me and Roark against her.

"I hoped from the earliest days this would happen." Emi patted Roark's face. "You deserve it, cousin. Perhaps you'll learn to smile a bit more."

Roark only scowled in return.

Eyes wet, Emi took hold of my hand. "You are Draven now, Ly. You are my folk. I love you as I'd love any sister."

A sting built behind my eyes when I embraced her again. Draven. I was not only a melder, not a Jorvan servant. I was now a Draven by bond. To the damn royal house.

Gods, how the twisted Norns spun their webs of fate.

Gunter glanced at our bound hands and wiggled his fingers. "Now let us see."

Roark unfurled his hand from mine and lifted our fingers. My eyes widened. Soft, nearly iridescent bands of gold flashed over our skin, dainty runes that glowed like the first spark of a flame. When the light faded into my skin, a sharp bite followed, but the rune marks still glistened over our flesh.

I shook out my palms, and Roark clenched his fists.

At long last the sting faded, and Gunter barked a laugh. "Took straightaway. Not that I doubted. Good gods, I have never been connected to such a bond. The only trouble came with that damn deledan. Skul Drek seemed to want you only for himself, Lyra."

I arched one brow. "I am his if I am Roark's."

"He saw it differently." Gunter lifted our hands to the others.

Brynn beamed at us. Auki gave a small applause. Emi wiped her eyes with the heel of her palm.

Gunter shook our hands. "Sealed as mates of the soul, in this life and the next."

LYRA

I DID NOT KNOW HOW MANY BELL TOLLS HAD PASSED, NOR did I care much. My arm was slung over Roark's bare chest, tracing the place over his heart, one leg coiled around his beneath the furs and quilts. Naked, sated, sweaty, and blissful.

I never wanted to move.

As though reading my thoughts, Roark brushed his fingers over my cheek. *We will need to face them eventually.*

I nuzzled into the soft down of the pillow. "Tomorrow."

A breathless chuckle followed, but Roark said nothing, merely dragged his fingers up and down my spine, watching the cold gray of dawn slice through the small crack in the shades.

"They're fading." I held his palm in front of my face, inspecting the strange, inked runes from the sealing.

They will, he explained. *But they are always there and can be summoned if needed. They're unique to us.*

"Why do they appear?"

My brother once told me they are written from the hopes of our fallen ancestors. A story they hope our souls will craft while we live.

I studied the runes. Marks of power and strength, of long lives and honor, they were runes of battle and love. I pressed a kiss to the center of his palm and let it fall to the place over my heart.

"What will they do to us, Roark?" My words were soft, the slightest tremble evident, and I hated the vulnerability. If Roark had fears or reservations regarding the rashness of the soul sealing, he did not show it.

With one knuckle, Roark tilted up my chin. He used the same hand to speak against my skin. *By law you are not only a melder, Lyra. You are Draven. To harm you, or me even, goes against everything the clan believes about their craft.*

House Bien belonged to Dravenmoor, body, heart, and soul.

The tip of my finger ran along the stubbled edge of his jaw. "You ought to know, Kael will be furious with us for not waiting for him. He had grand plans of terrifying anyone who desired to make me a wife."

I will beg Darkwin's forgiveness when he is free. His thumb tugged on my bottom lip. *And he will be free.*

I held his stare for a long moment before tilting my chin and kissing him, slow and deep. Roark trapped my face in his palms, adjusting to angle my mouth in the position he wanted. His tongue parted my lips and brushed over mine.

Blood rushed from my head to my lower belly. Gods, I could never tire of the taste of this man.

My husband.

I grinned against his mouth and gripped the roots of his hair. What a strange thought. When Roark entered House Jakobson in Skalfirth, he was a beautiful terror, dark and dangerous. I feared him, loathed him, wanted him, and on that night, I despised my-self for all of it.

How strange it was to recall every moment the sharp, jagged pieces of unfounded hatred peeled away. Those must've been the moments a long-buried bond had slowly restored. Moments when I could see the Sentry as a man with a formidable heart.

Roark was a villain to some, cruel, cold, and vicious. To me, he was gentle, possessive, and my home.

Why are you laughing?

I was lost in his taste and touch and nearly missed his words along my back.

I pulled away, grinning, and raked my fingers through his hair. "I just keep calling you husband in my head and it is fast be-coming my favorite word."

Roark's eyes heated. He dragged me over the top of him and kissed me deeper, harder.

I never wanted to leave the bedchamber. But the longer he held me, the more I believed that, perhaps together, we could face all the darkness that was coming for us.

THE DOORS TO THE GREAT HALL WERE INTRICATELY CARVED with runes and symbols of the gods. In each corner were the ra-vens of Dravenmoor. One head looked up toward the rafters, as if seeking guidance from Salur. The other, more skull-like and deadened, peered down, watching humanity below, a reminder of our own mortality.

It took a bit of cleverness from Roark's mouth and tongue to convince me to step outside the bedchamber, but when the sun was high in the sky, it was impossible to ignore reality.

We needed to face the clan.

Then, somehow, we needed to find a way to be free of their watch to continue our hunt for the Wanderer's bones and Kael.

Already too much time had passed. Fadey and Ingir would be desperate to find me, and if not me, they would hunt the bones ahead of us. Ingir was queen, the voice of Stonegate besides Prince Thane. She could casually allow the false Captain Baldur to search for me, all while claiming *I* was the treasonous melder.

The need to keep a step ahead of their plans grew more frantic by the day.

The small group of Dravens who'd witnessed our soul sealing were another factor in leaving the chamber. Gunter pounded on the door earlier, insisting Virki was already prowling about looking for Emi.

She went nowhere without Brynn and Auki, but it had the úlfur council demanding to greet the melder and see what sort of threat I brought to the clan.

"It's an obvious ruse to get you out in the open," Gunter insisted. "Virki is skilled with that silver tongue of his, always has been. He'll try to spin your life as a threat, but with the sealing, it will be naturally assumed that your loyalty is with your mate and your clan. It will be well."

My insides were coiled in harsh knots, and even surrounded by Emi, the twins, and a feral-looking Gunter, I tasted bile in the back of my throat.

"By the by," Auki muttered, rubbing the still-wrapped wound on his leg from the arrow. "We know who sent the archers against Lyra."

Roark nearly stumbled he stopped so swiftly. His eyes burned. *Who?*

"Brynn might say no man desires her, but she was able to get a few watchers talking over sharp mead this morning."

Brynn tossed her braid off her shoulder, chin lifted. "I never said men did not desire me; they are simply not the men I also desire."

What did you learn? Roark gestured angrily.

When I repeated the question, Auki cleared his throat and barreled on. "Turns out it was Councilman Asmund. You remember him, yes? Lost his son in the raids."

Roark's jaw pulsed.

"He's quiet," Gunter offered with a touch of vitriol in his tone. "Peaceful. Usually a voice of reason on the council. But seasons of hate and grief at the loss of his son clearly have made him a wolf lying in wait."

With a tight fist at one side, Roark spoke with his other hand in swift gestures—a sign he was shouting. *His head is mine.*

"All in due time," Gunter insisted. "Don't go in that room and slaughter everyone. Let them see Lyra, let them know of your bond, then they will have no ability to argue your vengeance."

The way Roark's face deepened in a flush, he was clearly perturbed by the stay of slaughter, but after a long moment he nodded.

Brynn stroked the top of Òlmr's wide head but looked back at me. "Ready?"

"I doubt I ever will be." I tightened my grip on Roark's hand.

With a short nod, he signaled the twins to open the heavy doors.

The hall was crowded. Folk bustled around the long table in the center. Some worked filling ewers with wine and water. Others laughed and plucked flatbreads and aged cheeses off plates before they hurried on.

Dravens flowed through the royal house like it was its own sort of marketplace. Dark Watch warriors tipped back drinking horns before meeting their patrol posts, hair braided off their faces, fur cloaks over the double-headed ravens stitched on their tunics.

Women tended to the young ones who were led through the hall. Some gathered baskets of eggs, loaves of rustic bread, and stacks of linens and wool for the market down the slope.

This was different from the more stoic hall of Stonegate, where Ingir and her ladies avoided Damir and his lovers. Folk in the Draven hall laughed more; they shouted without care for propriety. It felt a great deal like organized chaos, and I was glad for it.

With everyone focused on their own lives, no one looked to us at the doors. No one took note of the way the melder had entered, her hand clasped tightly with the prince's. They did not notice the fading bands on our fingers.

Until Auki somehow stumbled over Gunter's foot and the door clattered against one wall.

I froze.

All eyes seemed to snap in our direction. All voices hushed. I wanted to fall into the cracks of the floorboards.

Roark stepped in front of me. The way his shoulders were strong and back, the way his face was locked in stoic condescension, I could see the prince he'd been born.

Despite knowing folk would not understand his words, Roark spoke all the same. *Where is the queen?*

"The prince asks to see his mother," Emi said.

For a time no one spoke, merely stared. Something heavy and firm brushed against my leg. I shuddered when the great head of the fara wolf came to stand beside me, Auki and Brynn at my other shoulder.

Gunter remained at Roark's shoulder, stiff and nearly daring his clan to speak against the sight of us.

At long last, a man rose from the bench of the long table. His beard was wiry and peppered the same as old Thorian's from back home. He pointed toward a back room. "The queen speaks with the úlfur."

Roark did not wait another moment before pulling me across the hall.

Shards of my heart chipped and cracked away when folk turned their scrutiny to their plates and one woman was so startled at our swift approach, she picked up a tiny girl who shared her features and shielded the child as though we might reach out and steal the babe away.

Before we reached the doors, a man, perhaps a few full seasons my elder, stepped in front of the latch. He spun a knife in one hand. "Standing against the clan, Blackvale?"

Gunter returned a narrow look. "Stand aside, Haukur. Virki isn't here for you to kiss his ass."

The man's lip curled, but he kicked his eyes toward Brynn. "You too, Oakbriar?"

Before Brynn could respond, Gunter shoved Haukur's shoulder. "Step back. Your prince wishes to speak to the queen."

Haukur looked to Roark. Disdain was there beneath the shade of pale green in his eyes. "My prince lost his privileges long ago. Besides, I don't think there'll be much speaking to be had."

The man chuckled at his joke over Roark's stolen voice, but it lasted mere moments. His eyes darkened when Roark stepped nearer, and draped over Haukur's shoulders were the faintest hints of darkness. A cloak of shadows.

By the two hells, Roark was doing something with his craft. Skul Drek was doing something.

Haukur didn't move, didn't blink. His body shuddered and his teeth clenched. A hushed "Stop" broke from his lips.

Roark merely crowded the man even more.

The tips of my fingers prickled, like drawing too near a flame.

Gold surrounded the blade of the knife in Haukur's hand. Broken threads of craft gleamed in my sight. As though I stood half in the mirror and half not, as though Roark's craft called to mine.

Was this the power of a sealed bond? When he summoned more of the darkness of Skul Drek, I wondered if I could drift between the hazy shadows much the same.

I went to Haukur's other side. My palm covered the one he used to grip the hilt of his blade. The man shuddered and winced but managed to look down at me.

"I am glad so many folk use bones in their blades," I said, low and rough.

Haukur whimpered when he watched me hold his curled fingers to the hilt. I would need to open his flesh to meld the bone of the knife to his hand, but the way he watched in horror, perhaps he could see the shine of my craft as well as me.

I spoke with a sweet sort of viciousness, never releasing his fingers. "Your prince seems to be showing you that he speaks well enough. I urge you to keep out of our way. I think I speak for us both when I say that we tire of sods like you who try to stop us. Now, do you wish the prince to keep *speaking* to you?"

Haukur shook his head swiftly.

"Would you like me to meld this blade to your hand, never to be removed lest you cut it off?"

Again he shook his head.

"Then let us pass."

Another hand curled around the back of my neck, spinning me around. Roark's lips were close to mine. I did not know he'd pulled back, too lost in my own furious exhaustion at those who continually cut at Roark's sacrifice.

My husband grinned with such a twisted gleam I could nearly make out the reddish copper of Skul Drek in the gold. *I think you made your point.*

I faced Haukur. The man had slid down the wall to a crouch, the knife thrown on the ground.

I curled my fingers around Roark's tunic. "If one more person speaks of you like you are some traitor, I think I will meld the bones in their necks as one."

The way Roark looked at me, I wasn't certain we would be making it to the queen. I thought he might whisk me from the hall at any moment and take up what we started last night again.

"Well that was frightening and entertaining." Gunter clapped Roark on the shoulder. "But let us get this meet over with. It's time to finally put this damn war against the melder to rest."

ROARK

THERE WAS A NEW SORT OF MALICE IN LYRA. THE WAY SHE threatened Haukur without a pause to consider that she stood inside a hall of Draven folk who did not trust her was reckless.

It was stunning.

I craved more of the shadows in her own eyes.

Haukur would not touch her. At times having a rent soul was a gift more than a curse. With my craft, the frigid bite of my broken soul could touch another. It could slice and draw out pain unseen.

Haukur knew what I was doing, trapping him in the frosted wastes for a moment, cutting at him again and again. But to have Lyra step closer was a move I did not anticipate. Her own craft scorched inside me in a way I'd not felt before, as though our magics had twisted together, a true weave.

I wanted more.

I wanted her.

The wicked, the sweet, the cruel, the fearful. All of it was a new venom in my blood that I hoped would poison me long after I met the gods.

"I don't know where that came from," Emi whispered to Lyra as we entered the council chamber, "but perhaps warn us before you try to meld a man. Gods, do you realize how many of the Dark Watch were in that hall?"

"I know." Lyra nervously tugged on the ends of her hair. "I don't know what came over me. I just . . . hate the words they say about Roark."

"Nightlark, she's woven to his soul," Gunter explained in a rough whisper. "A soul meant to be cruel and wretched. Instincts are going to feel a little different for our melder from now on."

My throat tightened. Lyra would take on some of my darkness?

As though she was feeling my angst over the realization, her palm slipped into mine and pulsed three times. Like she was informing me it was all right with her.

"Words fester like a boil," Emi hurried to say. "Sometimes spreading to others within a clan. There are some who will see Roark as a traitor, forgetting he was a child when a bond took hold. Accept it."

"No," Lyra said, her voice soft and low. "I plan to change it."

Gods, I clenched my teeth to stifle a groan. I needed the woman alone, and soon.

The scrape of wood over the floorboards drew my attention to the table. Members of the úlfur council rose, one by one. Violence was potent, like acid on the tongue.

My hate lingered on the spindly man at the end of the table. A man with a full beard made of knots and braids and golden beads. Malice curdled under my skin when the craft took hold, icy and sharp.

Patience. All I needed was a bit more time of calm, then retribution for attacking my wife would be had.

The queen, at the head of the table, stood last.

"What is this?" Elisabet looked too much like the mother I tried to forget.

She was dressed in a simple blue woolen gown. Instead of the dark kohl over her eyes and lips, she wore a clean face. Her lashes were pale, her cheeks flushed with pink.

I hated her for it.

Once the queen of Dravenmoor had been a loving mother, making swords of branches and battling me in the courtyard until we could not cease laughing. She taught me how to make a plait in my hair and taught me of our lore, our histories, and our sagas.

She was the sort of mother who was gentle toward her sons, proud of their achievements, and loving enough that when she sent me away half alive, I battled for seasons trying to make sense of it. Of what I'd done that was so wrong, my mother tore me apart.

To hate her was simpler. Less painful.

"The melder has finally been brought before the council." Virki leaned over his hands onto the table. "Among a few others."

When Auki took note that Virki would not cease staring at Emi, he took a slight step in front of her.

Still, Emi would be the one to speak for us. The úlfur would not hear Lyra, not yet. When they learned the truth of the bond, they would not have a choice.

I kept my regard pinned to the queen. *We do not come for Lyra to be tried by these bastards. We come with news instead. Glad news.*

Emi forwent my insult, opting to call the council by their title, but finished strong. Like my cousin was readying to stand in front of the both of us when the úlfur, undoubtedly, reacted to the truth.

The queen tapped one finger on the edge of the table. "And what news is this?"

I held out one hand for Lyra's. She didn't hesitate.

Show them, I said against her cheek.

Slowly she lifted her fingers. The fading rune bands were there and matched perfectly.

The first rough gasp echoed in the room.

"All gods." A man whose name I could not recall leaned forward and tossed the hood made of a bear head off his hair. "Are those sjeleven seals?"

More and more the úlfur gawked at our clasped hands; some cursed; some remained silent. None looked at us with such violence as my uncle.

"You made a foolish mistake, nephew. One that will cost you and your little melder your lives."

Lyra stepped into my side but didn't cower under Virki's stare.

I grinned and raised one hand. *I think you'd like to see that.*

"Your prince believes you'd like for that to happen." For the first time, Emi spoke to her father directly. Her voice was steady, her shoulders back, but at her sides her fists were sealed tightly.

Virki jabbed a finger toward his daughter. "You will not speak to me unless I allow it."

"Then you'll speak to me."

Dammit. Lyra stepped forward. I took hold of her wrist, keeping her close, but did not try to stop her.

My uncle's teeth flashed. "Come closer, Melder. We have much to talk about, I'm sure."

Lyra kept a distance from the table but lifted her chin. "You cannot try to end our bond a second time. Much as you tried before, it was restored, and we have made it unbreakable."

"Look at this." Virki chuckled, drawing a few other men to laugh alongside him. "The melder thinks she knows Draven ways."

Lyra's grip tightened on my hand. "I may not be familiar with all of your customs, but I felt my bond from the first moment I saw him." She tilted her head to look at me for a breath. "I am loyal to him, and I am no enemy to you."

Virki went to speak but was silenced when the queen held up her hand.

My mother was not a large woman, but she had always kept a power in her presence, one that was felt, respected. She used it now.

The úlfur went quiet, while Virki's countenance grew a little more murderous.

"I desire to hear from the melder," said the queen.

Despite the queen's word, disquiet rippled over my shoulder. From all angles there were members of the council. Men who'd seen battle, who knew how to kill well enough. Draven warriors who fought in the raids, had been born to despise the corruption of melding craft.

If they made a move for Lyra, I could not stop them on my own. Perhaps the others could get a few swings in. Òlmr would take out a throat or two before a blade cut her open.

They wanted a creature to kill for them. I would remind them of what they made me.

Strange now, summoning the darker soul. Where once I could hardly sense the shift whenever the assassin was needed to attack, now it was as though another layer of my insides unstitched and brought a frosty wind through my pores until darkness stood all around me.

"Finally." Gunter's mouth parted in stun for a bit when the full form of my severed soul took shape. A mere beat of my heart passed before his lips split into a grin. "Didn't get a good look at the Ravines. This close, it's mesmerizing."

Òlmr whimpered and tucked her tail. Brynn's face blanched, and Auki kept eyeing me nervously.

Their reactions did not matter to me. The sight of the unsettled úlfur—even Virki, who took a step back from the edge of the table—brought a warped sort of giddiness.

I grinned, almost sensing the same dark snarl come from the mirrored expression of my soul in the shadows.

One of my hands went to the small of Lyra's back. *Tell them anything. So long as you let them know they are asses.*

She snickered softly but looked to the council. "I do not know what you wish for me to say. I have no desire to be a threat to anyone. I lived simply as a servant for most of my life. You despise me for my craft, but I despise soul bones as fiercely as you."

Another pause, another heated heartbeat. Then Yanson rose. He eyed Gunter for a moment, almost warning his son to remain silent before he spoke. "Lyria—"

"It's Lyra, Yanson," Brynn corrected.

"Apologies. *Lyra*, will you tell us about your time in Stonegate? We know you melded soul bones."

"I did." She swallowed. "I knew nothing of my craft before I was taken to the royal keep, other than being taught to conceal it. Only one person in Skalfirth, my old village, knew what I was."

Buried guilt gnawed at my chest when she explained Darkwin was threatened, all to force her craft to take hold.

The queen looked at me, a little stunned when Emi agreed with the tale, explaining our role in the torture of Lyra's brother. The shadows around me rippled in a wave of anger from her scrutiny. She thought me too cruel, did she?

The queen made me.

"When I understood what King Damir desired with his Berserkirs, we began to plot against him. It was against the king, not his heir. Prince Thane the Bold did not know how deeply his father's corruption had grown."

I knew what Lyra was doing, hopefully giving Thane a chance

to be brought in as an ally. If he did not murder me for my lies first. I could not shake the notion that to defeat Fadey we would need allies within Stonegate.

As fiercely as Lyra needed to free Darkwin, I needed to somehow speak to Thane.

The prince would think me a traitor, he would hate me, no mistake. But Thane was not a fool, and he would not allow the corruption his mother and Fadey desired to go on. He would stand with us, even reluctantly.

There would be no attempt to speak to the prince if war began before we had the chance.

Lyra paused, and I pressed against her spine. *Tell them of the hunt. Most will already know.*

Gammal had spoken to the úlfur about the melder. They would understand the Jorvan's desire to have the Wanderer's bones.

Lyra cleared her throat. "Damir wished to have the Wanderer's bones melded to him."

The council grumbled and grunted. Disdain shifted off my wife to the dead Jorvan king for a moment. A king they did not know was gone.

"What caused you to finally flee?" Yanson pressed.

The queen spoke instead. "My son explained this to me already."

Darkness thickened around me and Lyra from my soul as the tension deepened. The queen couldn't speak of Fadey, or I had few doubts Lyra would be barricaded away to keep her from the melder and Ingir.

I glared at the queen, ready to slice at her soul should she give up the truth too soon.

My mother merely held my stare as she spoke. "Melding craft

is coveted and feared, as we know. My son informed me that the melder had been attacked. He believed the risk was too great to remain, so they fled."

"Fled," Virki said in a growl. "But not to us. Your son was not coming home; he was aiming for the Night Ledges. So much like his brother."

My brow arched. I did not recall when Nivek held any fascination for the Night Ledges.

"Do you blame him for not bringing her to us, Virki?" Yanson asked, interrupting my thoughts. "What am I asking, of course you do. Perhaps you do not recall what a bond is like, but I assure you, there is no god, no army, who would cause me to willingly walk Drifa into danger."

Gunter leaned through the murky shadows, hardly bothered by the mists of the darker soul, and tapped Lyra on the shoulder. "She's my mother."

With a wink he went back to attention, a new look of pride on his features when he regarded his father.

"Royal sjeleven sealings ought to be brought to the council before a weaving," Sampson snapped. "It is an act worthy of council involvement."

"There is no law stating permission from the úlfur must be in place," a frail-looking councilman—Hugo, if I recalled correctly—mumbled from beneath a tattered cowl. A tome bound in pigskin was open in front of him. Histories and Draven law were written in those pages.

Gods, the endless days studying with tutors returned to haunt me with that tome in view.

Hugo opened the front, and pages crinkled and snapped as he riffled through the front few. His hooked finger pointed to a place on one page.

"A true soul bond is a gift from the Norns of fate and the gods themselves. For a bond to seal fully would mean it is accepted by those gods and the souls gone before us. A soul sealing will supersede any tradition, including pomp and ceremony for royal blood."

"Didn't say it was law, Hugo," said Sampson. "Merely said a royal sealing of souls is of note. Puts her in a position to take one of our damn thrones in the future. Shouldn't we ought to know?"

"The úlfur might've been welcomed into such an occasion had you not been vying to take my head all this time." Lyra's voice was harsh, almost reminiscent of the ferocity I felt when I was engulfed in shadows. She turned a narrow glare to each member. "If you had but honored a bond I've learned this clan holds so sacred, I wonder how much blood would not have spilled over the seasons. I wonder how I might've helped stop the soul bones long ago instead of hiding the scars in my eyes. What the world might've been if you'd not let pitiful fear and a seer's words weaken your spines."

Her fist slammed on the table on her final word. Somehow inside my thoughts, I could feel a different meaning behind her words. No mistake, due to our new connections, I knew Lyra hinted more at the pain I would not have endured if they'd accepted a boy's word during the raids, if they'd brought the young melder to our gates so long ago.

Nivek would be alive.

As would my father.

I would have a voice.

I would've had Lyra all this time.

Still, in some ways, the fight to restore the bond that had been shadowed from us seemed to only deepen it now.

For a pause, her words silenced the council. Until Virki

pounded his own fist on the table. "I will not accept this bond. Neither have shown loyalty to Dravenmoor. I do not trust the motives, and I will go so far as to call this secret soul weave treason."

Gunter shoved between us. "You condemn them, then you must condemn me." Yanson shot his son a hardened look, but Gunter was unmoved. "I am the one who wove their souls together. The bond was unmistakable, and I would do it again. If you choose to deny the sanctity of a soul bond, then so be it. Perhaps this is no longer the Dravenmoor in which I was raised."

"And us." Auki followed, and next Brynn. "We witnessed. Will you kill us all?"

"Keeping the melder here is a risk," Sampson interjected. "Should our enemies discover her here, they will come against us. Perhaps it was intentional, and she has convinced our prince she shares in this bond—"

"How does one pretend to have a soul bond, Sampson? Gods." Yanson's temper was growing short. "It is felt on both sides and you know it."

Sampson blustered and stroked his beard out of nerves. "Well, I can't say exactly. But we do not know much about melding craft."

"I could not weave them together if there was no bond," Gunter insisted.

"Sampson speaks poorly about a bond," said the man with those thick braids and knots in his beard. "But his concerns about Jorvans coming for the melder are valid."

My blood heated. Patience for blood was spent.

I tilted my head. Unbidden, I rounded the table, stalking the councilman. His soul was mine now. I stopped in the place across from his seat and leaned between two other úlfur members, my palms flat on the table.

The man eyed me with a touch of trepidation. "Something more you wish to add, my prince?"

Buried soul deep was a quiver in his voice. Something I felt run through the shadows inside, not with my own ears. My lips curved into a vicious sort of grin.

Councilman Asmund. I hear you sent the archers to kill my wife.

ROARK

"Y ou sent the two archers to slaughter the Melder, Asmund," Emi relayed, her voice low.

Asmund's eyes went wide. "Of course not. I've no power over the Dark Watch."

My grin widened. Slivers of darkness peeled off my skin, like a true shadow emerging from under my flesh.

Asmund cried out when the skeins of black wrapped around his wrist, dug into his bones. I closed my eyes, breathing deeply, letting the beast I kept inside taste the guilt on this bastard's soul.

I flashed my teeth when more inky night clawed into Asmund's body, tasting, slicing, hating. The councilman began to sob when the deledan soul engulfed him.

"Roark." Elisabet clapped a hand on the table.

I held up a hand, silencing the queen to a few murmurs of the council. In the next breath, I pulled back the vicious night, commanding the splintered pieces of my soul to retreat.

When the murky shadows no longer blotted out the light of

the room, I spun on the queen. *His guilt burns in his soul. Dark Watchers gave up his name as the one who spoke the order, defying you.*

Emi translated my words to my mother in a brisk whisper. Little by little, the queen's eyes deepened with her own anger. She cast a narrow look at Asmund. "Speak the truth, Asmund, and if you have done this thing, you will be offered a warrior's death so you might greet Salur with honor. Deceive us, and your soul will be marked for the hells. He can sense turmoil in your soul."

For a long breath, Asmund said nothing, merely kept one fist clenched over the table, scanning the úlfur as though they might come to his aid.

Not even Virki spoke for him.

At long last, Asmund let his shoulders slump. "I believed your word to be misguided, my queen. I believed our borders to be vulnerable should Jorvandal attack. I sent the archers. A melder's craft is too dangerous to live among us."

The queen's jaw pulsed, but with a wave of her hand, two Dark Watchers were summoned and Councilman Asmund was led from the chamber, chin high, subtle prayers to the gods to open the gates of Salur to his soul.

I followed his every step, locked in a desperate need to darken his soul, to cut open every bit of flesh before, at last, sending him to the gods.

A hand clapped on my shoulder. Gunter offered a grin. "Let the clan have the honor of disposing of a traitor. It will be done."

A subtle way, no mistake, for my boyhood friend to urge me not to spill more Draven blood.

The council was silent for a long while.

Yanson cleared his throat. "This council was never meant to be made up of traitors. We vowed to always serve the best interests of our folk and follow our queen's word. May Asmund meet the gods in humility for his error." After a few murmurs of prayers from other councilmen, Yanson went on. "As Asmund mentioned, concern for Jorvandal taking back the melder is a legitimate issue. I suggest she is proffered freedom to move about the palace grounds but not to leave the borders of the royal land."

I ground my teeth together. This had been expected. The refusal to allow Lyra to leave the walls was a nuisance but one we'd need to find a way around should we ever find whatever was hidden over the Night Ledges.

"I agree with Yanson," said Kaysar, the twins' father. "She'll be protected here with her clan."

A vein pulsed in my uncle's neck when he spun on the queen. "You accept this bond, Bet? You trust it?"

Coils of darkness wrapped around Lyra on instinct, ready to pull her away should the queen falter on her own vow.

Elisabet considered Virki's protestations for a moment. "I am never one to speak against a bond, but I can see the úlfur is discontent. So we must make our next moves with the majority word. Agreed?"

A few mumbled words of acceptance rolled down the table. Virki's face was a shade of red like a setting sun.

"What does that mean?" Lyra whispered.

They will vote. I gestured the words briskly, jaw set. *We knew this would happen.*

"If they vote our bond is forbidden . . ." She looked to me. "I'll fight if you will."

Unbothered if any of the council saw, I pressed her knuckles to my lips and tucked her against my side.

"From witnesses, we know the prince and the melder fashioned a bond long ago," the queen said. "Even with our . . . efforts to dissolve the connection, it was restored again. A feat believed to be impossible.

"The melder made Berserkirs for the Jorvans, a crime to our

clan. Then again, she stood against them, without their knowledge, and aided the deledan soul in a scheme to find the Wanderer's bones at the risk of her own life. Those are the truths we know. Speak your thoughts on these truths only. I will hear you now."

My chest felt too tight to even take a breath as one by one the council cast votes. Virki and Sampson gave resounding votes against us, but so did four others. I memorized them all, marking their features, embedding the taste of their souls to my own cruelty.

Next, Yanson sighed, attention on the table. "We are a strong clan. We do not fight for glory or prestige. We fight for our folk, for our love." With a clap to the edge of the table, Yanson looked me in the eye. "I stood against the soul rending a dozen full seasons ago and was overruled. Once again, I stand with you, my prince. And you, My Lady Lyra."

Lyra's cheeks filled with a splotchy red, but she gave a jerky nod. Five more after Yanson.

Six stood against us. Six stood with us.

The final word belonged to the queen. Elisabet smoothed her hands down her gown and looked to me. "I have nothing to say, save for who am I to stand in the way of fate?"

Virki's fist clenched over the table. "Elisabet—"

She held up a hand, silencing him again. "My son has taken a wife. And she is now of Dravenmoor."

Those who stood with the queen and Yanson pounded fists over their chest. Those who had been overruled overturned their drinking horns, spilling out the ale or wine onto the floorboards. Nearly as one, they placed the horns on their sides, then pressed fists to their chests much the same.

A symbol of being overruled, but accepting the word of the clan.

All except Virki.

My uncle rounded the table to my mother's side. I shoved Lyra behind me, but Virki stopped his pursuit ten paces away.

He jabbed a finger at my mother. "This will do nothing but put our people at risk. Lives were lost to see to it melding craft never infected Dravenmoor again."

"I'm wholly aware of those who died, Virki." The queen lifted her chin in a touch of defiance. "The woman is part of my household now, and she will be afforded the titles, the protection, and the respect proffered to this house."

It took a moment, but Virki sniffed and nodded. "Very well. As you see to your house, I am within my rights to see to mine. I demand my wife's daughter be returned to my household."

"No." Lyra reached for Emi, who'd gone pale as the frosts.

The queen's face did not flinch. "You still claim her after she left that scar on your throat?"

"I'm sure I'll find uses for her."

I would kill him before he harmed Emi again. The memory of finding my bony cousin outside Stonegate—five of her fingers broken, bruises across her jaw, both eyes so bloody in the whites I could not make out her true color, and gaps of her pale hair missing—was still burned across my brain.

One spot still did not grow new hair, and Emi had learned to braid it in such a way that her scalp was concealed.

Elisabet let her shoulders slouch. "She is of your household, and it is customary for daughters to live in the houses of their birth if they do not have one of their own. Unless, of course, she was positioned elsewhere."

Gods. Was the queen truly relenting to this?

Brynn held up a hand. "There is no lady for the prince's new wife, my queen."

Virki shuddered in unbridled rage. "You would be wise not to speak again, Oakbriar."

"And you would be wise to not threaten my daughter." Kaysar glared at Virki over the lip of his drinking horn.

Kaysar was brutal, but so was Virki. Brynn was taking a fierce risk. When she looked back, I shook my head. My uncle would retaliate against her.

Brynn held my scrutiny and whispered, "A vow to protect your bond with my life. Remember?"

Damn her. She knew exactly what she was doing to protect not only Lyra, but also Emi.

"A lady." The queen hummed as she considered the proposition. "Not all find such a position necessary, but perhaps it would suit the melder since she is unfamiliar with our lands."

"No," Virki snapped. "Emi is of my house, unwed, and I have need of her."

"I would be honored if Emi Nightlark served as my lady," Lyra blurted out. "I am so out of sorts here, and I have few doubts Roark will be taken for meets and . . . and such. It would be of great use to have someone familiar with the territory at my side."

I scoffed. I doubted there would be many meets and councils where I would be wanted, but Lyra knew what she was doing.

"If Nightlark agrees, then it will be done," said the queen.

Virki shot a threatening sort of glance at Emi.

There was no pause before my cousin squared herself against him and said, low and steady, "It would be my honor, my queen. I accept, gratefully."

Elisabet dipped her chin. "Virki, Emi Nightlark is now part of our household."

My uncle turned his ferocity toward his queen. "I do not know when you lost your spine. Not everyone will wait for its return."

Without another word, Virki abandoned the council room and a wave of relief filled my veins.

"Lyra." Elisabet approached.

Lyra stiffened at my side. "Your highness."

Whatever the queen was feeling, she did not show it on her features. Stern. Collected. Unmoved. Almost soulless. "My husband's brother spoke true. You sealed this bond in the shadows, and it has left you wholly unprepared for life as Draven royalty."

I rolled my eyes and looked away but caught the crack in Elisabet's mask. For a moment she looked like the mother who'd scold me when I'd grown too raucous.

She turned back to Lyra. "We will have a feast to bring you forward to the clan. I will expect you to learn our customs and your position as the wife of my son." The queen lowered her voice. "I may have made a vow that I cannot end your life, but I assure you, many here will be waiting to find every fault to use against you. Be wise, and do not let them."

I waved a hand, gesturing for the queen to look at me. *We will not be here long, don't you remember?*

"I suppose we'll see if an opportunity presents itself," Elisabet said once Lyra repeated my words. "But the úlfur ruled she will not leave the borders. As predicted. Be on your guard until then."

Elisabet regarded Lyra once more before mutely abandoning the council room without a backward glance.

My body shook when Gunter gripped my shoulder and one of Lyra's. "Toss me in the molten hell," he said, his voice light. "For a moment I wasn't so certain it'd turn out in our favor."

Lyra let out a shaky chuckle but curled her fingers around my arm. "What do we do now?"

I looked down at her. *Be ready to meld again. We have the Wanderer to hunt.*

LYRA

I DON'T EVEN KNOW HOW TO SEARCH. THIS IS NOT HELPING."
Bright copper eyes locked with mine in the mists. All
around, rot and decay peeled from trees and stone pillars. A
frosted breeze kept raising my skin. I nuzzled deeper into Skul
Drek, the burn from the endless stitches of our bond warming
me from the soul out.

Instead of threats and snarls, I was enrobed in his darkness.

Dravenmoor was far more expansive than the tighter forests
and peaks of Jorvandal. To walk in the rotted mirror realm, there
were fewer places to hide bones of the fallen but more empty
space to wander without much to show for it.

In nearly a week of foraging in the mirror, I'd found burial
mounds for fara wolves whose souls were gamey on my tongue,
like my craft could reach out and taste them without melding.
Another find belonged to a few tiny birds that must've fallen
from their nest not so many months before.

Asmund's bones were added to a small burial ground for Dark Watchers. His execution was swift and public. Elisabet's word traveled to the whole of the clan that the same would be proffered to anyone who brought harm to me, for it would now be treason against the royal household.

I found Draven burial mounds but did not search too far before Skul Drek practically growled at me and urged me to let them rest.

Today, there was even less. Misty, blackened riverbanks and crumbling courtyard gates, but no new bones. No matter how often I closed my eyes and imagined a new land, somewhere in the distance, like back near the Black Fjords or the Red Ravines.

Landscapes were always shifting in the mirror, almost as though I could stand omniscient, but I could not find a single thread with any difference from the fara bones or fallen Dravens.

"If I could see over the Night Ledges . . ." I shook my head and knelt to unstitch the melding I'd done to squirrel and pheasant bones.

To fall into the mirror with Skul Drek shouldn't require melding, according to Gunter. The soul bond between me, Roark, and his shadowed soul ought to pull us to one another. With the sealing so fresh, at times I could only find the tether with my craft as I'd done before.

Small creatures served well enough for now.

I curled my palm around the burning cord between me and my phantom and used it to stand again. When I touched the bond, I let out a hiss through my teeth. Good gods, a rush of blood flooded my lower belly, nearly bringing me back to my knees with a surge of pleasure.

When Skul Drek grunted and yanked me against his iridescent form, no doubt he'd felt the same.

I chuckled and touched the cold shadows of his face. "You felt it too."

His words were a lash, harsh and quick, but his frigid grip tightened around my waist. "Stay your hands, Melder."

My brows raised and at once I let my palms run down his murky chest. "Why?"

Ribbons of shadows pulled my hands away, tethering them behind my back, and in the next breath, my body was enfolded within the cloak of mists of his form.

His gasp caressed my cheek. "Cruel, Melder."

"I'm not cruel," I said, a little breathless. "I just happen to enjoy touching you."

Skul Drek flashed his teeth. "I am he, we are we. A melder's touch burns with pleasure."

"Gods. Sorry." I recoiled and covered my mouth with one palm to hide the laugh stuck in the back of my throat.

Every touch to Skul Drek would be felt by Roark, likely driving him a little mad while we spoke soul to soul. The glow of Emi's form was in the distance, along with Gunter and Brynn. Auki had fara duties with a young pack preparing to bond with new Dravens.

Roark would be suffering silently, perhaps twisted up in frustration, in front of everyone.

Skul Drek narrowed his eyes into bloody slits. "Cruel, Melder."

The laugh squeaked out. "I'm not trying to be, I swear it." I cleared my throat and forced myself to take a step back. "Can you sense the souls like I see the bones?"

"Pieces of the first king and his soul are in the lands, this I sense. But the sight is my melder's alone."

He could feel the power of the Wanderer's soul, but not where it was. I was the one who could see the craft of the soul. Two gifts with the potential to be of use, but we had to find a way to entangle them. Bonded or not, it seemed our crafts remained our own.

"The time is nearly spent." The brush of his shadowed hand ran down my cheek.

Skul Drek or Roark, the man did nothing but fret over the melder's trance that brought me to the mirror. Without the power of soul bones, I did not stumble so fiercely after each meld, but it was disorienting should I remain in the darkness too long.

"Wait. You sense souls." I swallowed with effort and looked in the direction of distant gates, faraway spires. "Can you sense him? Kael? Can we see if his soul is still bright?"

Tears would not fall here, not from my soul, but the vibrance dimmed.

Skul Drek pulled me close. "Lead the way, Melder."

I imagined Stonegate. The smell of evergreens, of the smoke and leather and roasted meats in the market. I imagined Thane's laughter, Yrsa's satin gowns. I tried to draw up the reek of the Stav units, with their rancid trousers and stockings.

"We don't go closer."

My eyes blinked open. The mirror shifted. We stood outside a peeling, cracked, debauched version of the walls around the Jorvan fortress. "What do you mean we don't go closer?"

"The dark one waits for my melder." Skul Drek's lip curled. "Tricks and spells sense your soul. You brighten the night, and they will take it."

This edge of Roark spoke with such venom, such rage, it was odd how I'd come to recognize the shifts in his tone, to tell his loving possessiveness from his bloodlust. The way he spoke of Fadey's presence was harsh and hateful. With me, it was nearly desperate, like he could never get enough and it angered him.

"Do you sense something here at the gates?" I asked.

"Blood spells."

Dammit. "The queen is a blood crafter. She's warded the gates, no doubt. But how can we feel it here?"

"Traps of the soul and the body lie in wait for my melder. The dark one knows my melder comes to me here. He hunts you where the souls speak as well as where the living walk."

Shit. Fadey and Ingir had managed to place spell casts in the mirror?

I looked to the gates again, dark, dreary. I did not know how to get beyond them. "Souls have connections to other souls, do they not?"

His hot eyes narrowed, and Skul Drek curled one of his misty hands around the endless gilded tethers binding us together. "Bonds with the melder only belong to he and we."

"I'm not talking about a soul bond. Good gods, you're rather jealous in this state."

Skul Drek merely growled in response.

"I mean connections. We feel drawn to certain folk. Like Emi says, some souls understand each other. I was just hoping I might feel Kael." I peered up at the hooded face at my side. "You sense souls. Can you find him?"

Skul Drek paused for a long breath, then closed his eyes. I didn't move, didn't speak. Beneath his murky cowl, his features twisted, contorted. When his eyes snapped open again, the copper had deepened to a fierce red. "There is light in the soul you seek."

"Kael's alive?"

Skul Drek tilted his head. "There is light . . . and darkness. There is pain, my melder."

The burn of bile rose in the back of my throat. I hugged my middle. Kael was suffering in his soul. My brother, my friend. The boy who first saw my hair stand on end after sleeping, only to laugh until he nearly retched. The man who loved easily, and was a bit of a rake, but would take a knife for anyone he kept in his heart.

"I must get to him."

"A vow to find a trapped brother remains," Skul Drek breathed next to my ear. "But now time is spent."

True enough. The weariness of the mirror was settling in. But the moment I turned to go, something harsh, like a tangle of barbs, curled around my arm and pulled me toward the gates.

"Melder!" A long, feral hiss sliced through Skul Drek's sharp teeth. His darkness enrobed me, every strand of shadow he could muster laced around my body, limbs, even my throat.

I cried out and reached for him, but whatever blood spell was at the gates fought harder. Something had me in its grasp, something dark.

In the fetid darkness of the mirror, laughter echoed. First it was low, nothing but a whisper in the breeze. But it grew, louder, crueler.

I clung to the skeins of night from Skul Drek, frantically grappling for his hands until I curled my golden palms around the ice of his skin.

"There you are."

A sharp gasp slipped from my lips when I looked over my shoulder. Buried in the mists near the gates, sharp, burning eyes and a cruel, poisonous smile met me there.

Fadey.

A thin, frayed tendril of an ashen rope slithered across the smoky ground of the mirror. My eyes widened. The tether was knotted around my ankle, and across the meadow, where Fadey's ghostly form stood near the crumbling gates, he twirled the other end around his long fingers.

"Lyra. I found you again."

In Stonegate, Fadey insisted that the blood craft of Queen Ingir had tethered us, that he could slip into my mind and thoughts, that he could find me here in the mirror.

Fadey pulled on the weak rope, and my leg jerked painfully behind me.

Skul Drek hissed and clacked his teeth, gathering me in his arms and surrounding me in his shadows. Cold whipped against my cheeks. The blaze of our sealed bond cast out the darkness and blurred the moldy gates of the Jorvan keep.

I felt my body torn away, a rough wrench of my leg snapped the tie of Fadey's haunted rope, and in the next breath, I landed in a heap atop the murky form of my husband's soul.

I leaned into his shadows, desperate for something to numb the wretched pain. My brow pressed against his chest, and in the next moment, a warm palm cupped one side of my face.

Roark looked down at me from the long wooden bench. Somewhere in the trance, I had dropped to my knees.

Tears fell from my lashes. "Fadey . . ." I didn't know what else to say and let my forehead fall to his chest.

Roark nodded and pressed a long kiss to my forehead. His words were formed low, where I could look down and watch the gestures. *No more melding.*

"We must keep hunting. What else are we to do?" I said, a little desperate.

Lyra. I will not risk you, understand? We don't know these spell casts. Until we learn how he's able to find you now, we don't hunt the bones.

My shoulders slumped. I wanted to protest, wanted to argue, but whether it was the exhaustion from the melder's trance or knowing Roark's fear was warranted, I could not muster the words.

"What happened in . . . wherever you go?" Gunter's voice drew my attention.

I leaned deeper against Roark's chest. "Fadey. He . . . he was there. I thought . . . I thought only I could step into the mirror, but he nearly pulled me to him."

Emi's eyes went wide. "What did he do to you?"

I retold the shift toward the gates, the desire to feel if Kael still lived, then of the blood craft guarding the gates.

The wards must've summoned Fadey. Roark spoke in harsh gestures.

"You said there was a rope around you?" Gunter folded his arms over his chest.

"It looked almost like a thread of a bond, like he'd found a way to tie me to him, but it was faded and nowhere near as strong as mine and Roark's."

One of Gunter's brows lifted. "Even weak bonds can only be formed from a connection, be it blood, affection, or through vows."

I held no affection for Fadey, nor his blood, and I certainly had made no vow with him. "He said Ingir crafted a spell from my blood to tether him to my mind and the realm of souls."

Gunter paused for a moment to consider the idea. "Still, even blood craft has limits. One blood cast would not still hold. It would require a deeper connection. I've never heard of blood craft causing a permanent tether, only finding one that can be used again and again."

"How would Ingir's blood craft have found a connection with me? I have no connection to Fadey other than sharing the same craft."

"Then it seems I have more to learn about soul connections and blood craft," Gunter said, rubbing his chin. "And I very much plan to."

We won't be hunting bones until we know more. Roark's jaw pulsed.

"Probably wise," Emi said but offered me a sympathetic look. "We'll find a way to Darkwin and those bones, Ly."

"The Night Ledges," I snapped. "We need to get to whatever is hidden over the Ledges. Which means we must leave here."

"Working on it," Brynn insisted. "We're gathering supplies, but Virki is watching us relentlessly. Like he knows. Honestly, a great deal of the úlfur are watching. Soon I might not be above falsifying deaths to get us out."

"Perhaps we can dress as Jorvan Stav and feign a kidnapping," Gunter chuckled.

Brynn smiled and shoved his shoulder. "We'll tuck that idea next to false deaths."

"Afraid you can't pretend to die until after tonight," said Emi.

Exhausted, frantic with worry for Kael, and burning with rage at Fadey, I still let out a long groan.

Loud and petulant enough that even Roark grinned as he helped me to my feet.

Feasts and celebrations seemed so pointless with all we faced, but tonight was the promised revel where Queen Elisabet would put forth her new melder daughter-in-law for the clan to accept. Or reject, I suppose.

Brynn spoke after a long silence. "I don't understand why Fadey is so obsessed with you if he can now enter the realm of souls. I thought that was why he wanted your bones."

I rubbed my brow, kneading out the tension. "I don't know either. Why does he insist I am this missing piece he needs to find the Wanderer? If we cannot hunt the bones, I'd rather hunt Fadey and make sure a rogue arrow finds his heart. Then the Wanderer can rest and we can too."

"I like this direction, Lyra." Gunter reclined in a chair and kicked his legs off the arm until they were flat on the floor. "We kill the bastard and the Jorvan queen. The end."

Emi chuckled. "I adore this plan, but alas, I do not think Fadey will be a simple kill."

And there is something he knows, Roark offered, a simmer of hate in his eyes. *He's been planning this for seasons—the raids, the hunt for Lyra, the coup with the queen. I want to know why. I agree with Lyra, his obsession with her goes deeper than the Wanderer.*

My heart stuttered. "Was Fadey involved a great deal in the raids?"

Thane always said Fadey was the one who fought the fiercest, insisting he needed to protect and train the hidden melder.

I'd never paused to wonder much if Fadey desired a young, impressionable melder to reach Stonegate. It was always Damir or the Dravens I feared in my mind. "If Fadey suspected your brother ran with me, do you think he had something to do with . . . Nivek?"

The gold of Roark's eyes burned like embers. *I'm starting to wonder.*

"But if Fadey was involved with Nivek's death, he would know about you, Roark," Emi said. "He would know what happened to you that night. Why would he allow you to live in Stonegate with such a secret?"

So sure?

Emi paused. "Well, I suppose I can't say for certain."

"If Fadey knew of Nivek's involvement, it could merely be that he knew the prince hid the melder," Brynn said. "If his obsession is as fierce as it sounds, it might've angered him enough to retaliate. But it doesn't mean he knew of Roark, nor of his bond with Lyra. Vishon and Elisabet kept their second son very concealed from the other kingdoms for this exact reason."

My head ached from unknowns, my heart burned from loss, and my body throbbed from sitting on the floor all morning.

You need to rest and eat, Roark gestured against my palm. I began to protest, but he pressed his fingertips to my lips. *You are no good to Darkwin if you have no strength.*

Since we'd sealed our bond, conversing with Skul Drek was no different from speaking with Roark outside the cold mirror. We were bonded across every realm, but the search for the bones wore me weary, until my legs felt like they would give and I thought I might be able to sleep for days.

Roark did not wait for me to respond before helping me to my feet, taking my hand in his, and guiding me out of the study.

LYRA

THANE WOULDN'T . . . HE WOULDN'T ALLOW KAEL TO BE harmed even if he believes I am the killer of the king, would he?"

Roark's hands stilled on his belt, half unbuckled. He faced me, allowing the belt with the dagger sheathed across his lower back to fall to the floor. He'd practically forced me to sit and eat when we returned. Half the boiled roots and seasoned fish were gone, but the unease toiling inside would not allow for more.

With slow strides, Roark crossed the room to me, lowering to one knee. He took my palms in his hands, a discomfiting grimace on his features.

Thane the Bold was a subject we had not broached much since fleeing Stonegate. Roark told me in the forest that he deserved Thane's hatred, and perhaps it came from knowing the man to his soul, but the thought of it pained him more than anything.

Doubtless, Thane would believe me to be responsible for the death of Damir. The dead Jorvan king had planned to force me to use my craft in melding every Stav Guard of his army. Motive for me to be rid of Damir was there. Queen Ingir would never confess her role, nor give up her accomplice, Fadey.

To Thane's knowledge, I was the only melder alive.

He had witnessed Roark's dark soul emerge, knew he was Skul Drek, the assassin who nearly sent him to Salur.

Part of me avoided talking of the Jorvan prince to spare Roark even the slightest bit of pain; another part was too focused on what moves to make to end Fadey and Ingir and free Kael.

But Roark knew Thane better than anyone here.

"Do you think he would?" I asked again, softer than before.

Roark flipped my palm toward the rafters overhead and spoke gently over my skin, *Loyalty is everything to Thane. He will hate me, but he is not Damir. Any betrayal he feels will not be leveled at anyone but me.*

"And me."

Thane will likely be more inclined to believe I bespelled your soul somehow before he hates you.

A timid grin spread over my lips. "You did, in a way."

Roark traced a finger over my bottom lip. *It is the other way around.*

He kissed me, slow and sweet. I fell into his touch, the unrelenting pull he had on my heart.

Everything.

Even before the soul sealing, Roark had become my safety. Warmth from the fury of a storm, a haven from the darkness in the lands. To not only accept the bond, but nourish it, crave it, he became a beacon in the shadows. He was vicious, cruel, and deadly, but he was my home.

I kissed him harder.

Pain, frustration, fear, joy—all of it pressed against the heat of his mouth. The balance between my love and happiness with this man and the rage against those still out there, lost and at risk, was a narrow line.

For a moment I gave in to the peace of his scent, the pleasure of his touch.

And Roark took it all. He welcomed it.

His palm curled around the back of my head. His teeth scraped over my bottom lip when he ripped his mouth away. I leaned in, chasing his taste, but he pressed his brow against mine for a long, raspy breath.

I let out a small shriek when he lifted me from the chair, urging my legs to wrap around his waist, and crashed his mouth back to mine.

Roark walked us across the room, toward our bed, and tossed me back onto the mattress. A frenzy lived in his eyes, one that hinted that he might need to forget the chaos for a moment as fiercely as me.

Without pause, Roark tore at my gown. I nearly shredded his tunic, ripping it over his head. Clothes were cast aside until our bare skin collided, heated, damp, and flushed.

Roark took his kiss to the lobe of my ear, tugging the skin between his teeth. Next, at my jaw, the tip of his tongue ran across my pulse point.

He dragged the knuckles of one hand down the cleft of my breasts until he covered my heart, and the gentle whirls of his fingers whispered his words. *To see you in pain destroys every piece of me. Let me take it away, even for a moment.*

I stroked the side of his face. "Then brighten the night, husband."

Roark let out a rough breath. *Again. Say it again.*

"You brighten—"

Roark shook his head, his lips, his tongue traveling down my neck.

"Husband."

His gasp skated over the skin near my shoulder until he lifted his head just enough for me to see the sly, vicious grin I loved so much overtake his face.

A deep sort of growl broke from his chest when he joined his mouth back to mine. I cried out his name when two of his fingers brushed over my wet core, teasing me.

He bit down on my neck.

My breaths grew rougher, jagged, when Roark slipped the first finger inside me, then another. He curled the tips, stretching me. His thumb rolled in gentle circles over the sensitive apex of my core.

I was delirious. It was too much. And yet I needed more.

Slowly, I drifted one palm down his stomach. Roark let out a hiss the moment my fingertips curled around his swollen cock, teasing the tip, stroking the pulsing veins.

Already beads of arousal were at the top. I used them to slicken my palm.

Tap. Tap. Tap.

Tap. Tap. Tap.

The short reminders that I belonged to him grew frantic over my heart the longer I stroked him. Roark worked his fingers faster, curling and pinching my core until my body writhed beneath his.

Pleasure drew a fog to my thoughts, stilling my hand on his length. Roark dipped his chin and watched my frozen hand holding him tightly but not moving. A furious, beautiful darkness smoldered in his eyes.

Roark thrust his fingers in deeper. I bucked my hips in the same moment he wrapped his hand over mine around his cock and forced me to move faster. Those eyes held me steady, and those hands robbed me of air in my lungs.

This man owned me, body and soul, and I could hardly form a thought or the desire to take back a sliver of control.

A choked sob rolled from my chest when the burn of release surged through my blood.

My body went limp, but I fought to keep my hand working him. Roark kept his fingers deep inside me, caressing me through the waves of release until I thought the scorch of pleasure would break through my skin.

Our joined grip tightened on his length, and our strokes quickened.

"Roark, come," I said, breathless, desperate to see him lose control much the same. "For me, please."

All at once he stopped and ripped my hand away.

"What are you—"

I swallowed my words when Roark shifted my hips, angling my body up. In one fluid motion, he shoved our pillows beneath me while lifting me higher. I didn't understand what he had planned until he slung both of my legs over his shoulders and dragged his tongue over me.

My jaw tensed and my back arched, pressing my nipples into the chilled air. My hand went to his hair and, unbidden, my thighs clenched around his head.

Gods. All gods. It was too much. I couldn't breathe.

I rocked harder against his face, unable to stop.

More? Through the gaps in his messy hair, his eyes sparked with mischief, one brow arched in his question.

All I could do was nod and fumble through a gasp, "More, Roark. Gods, please."

Our chamber darkened. Wisps of shadows spilled off his shoulders, and I wasn't certain he even noticed. As though my pleas, my cries, drew out all of him.

I moaned against the cool shadows on my skin, touching me

everywhere. My breasts, my throat, my lips. I felt pressure around my neck, not enough to choke off my air, but enough to feel the possession, the claim of his darkest desires.

The way every piece of Roark touched me was a paradox, giving me both the warmest safety and the fear of drawing too near a ledge. Tender and sweet, demanding and dangerous.

Beneath his hands and shadows, his wicked tongue, and his greedy lips, I would tumble over any ledge as long as more of him awaited me at the bottom.

Roark knew how to keep me balanced on the precipice. With his groans and sighs, the tension in his muscles, and his attention to every movement, my husband took a bit of wretched pleasure watching my body twist in the throes of his beautiful torture.

Once more, heat slid down from my skull, landing white-hot in my belly. Far from my control, my hips bucked and thrashed against his mouth. I yanked on his hair, grounding myself to the moment, to the lashes of his tongue on my core.

The sharp edge of his teeth against my soaked entrance pulled a scream of his name. Roark's shoulders moved like he might be laughing when he pulled back moments before I could ride through a second release.

"You bastard," I gritted out and locked my ankles behind his shoulders, desperate for him to begin again.

Roark gripped my legs and yanked them off his body, a new sort of fire in his eyes. Each of his palms pressed against my inner thighs, forcing my legs wide open. Frigid shadows slid along my slit, curling inside and out.

"Gods, Roark . . ." What was I even trying to say?

He grinned with heady viciousness, a true villain, then settled his hips between my thighs. The crown of his length nudged against my entrance, but he held back.

I wanted to scream.

Roark reared over me and covered one nipple with his lips, sucking and licking. One hand covered my other breast, and the second slid around my waist, kneading the globe of my ass, rocking my hips against the tip of his cock.

He was everywhere, and he damn well knew what he was doing. The torment was too fierce. I never wanted it to stop.

The palm on my breast moved over my heart. *You are perfect, wife.*

By the gods, I understood why he wanted to hear the same from me. How strange it was that not so long ago I was convinced I'd never trust the man again and now I was his wife.

Before we had sealed the bond, part of me wondered if I desired it for strategy. No mistake, I craved Roark, loved him, but a husband had not been in my plans. In this moment, I could say without hesitation I would never regret sealing our bond.

Fate be damned, Roark Ashwood was the choice of my heart. My soul.

Without warning, Roark popped his mouth off my nipple and pressed his hips against my center.

My fingernails clawed at his shoulders. "Please. I need you. All of you."

I wanted him to fill me up.

He took my palm and guided it down my stomach, then urged my grasp around his cock. Warm, hard, and thick; a stream of arousal slid out the top. I ran my thumb through it until a small cough spilled from his throat.

Roark shook his head. *Don't make me come. I'll come here.* He cupped my core. *Or here.* Roark kissed me, his tongue deep in my throat. *Choose.*

My brow furrowed, desperate for him. I aligned his cock with my center, and in one swift thrust, he slid inside.

We moaned in unison, both in pleasure and relief, ready to chase our release.

The first thrust was hard and deep. My spine bowed off the bed, my lashes fluttering. The next came slower, pushed deeper, like he planned to split me in two. Delirious and muddled with the sensation of his body and the oaky scent of his skin, I did not notice his command against my cheek for a few breaths.

Scream.

His movements grew rougher, desperate; I could not keep silent even if I desired.

I cried out his name, unbothered if anyone heard, and my body pulsed as I fell apart. Roark hooked one of my legs around his hip and quickened his pace. His breath was hot on my neck. He rocked with enough force that the wood of our bed rapped against the wall, and the ropes holding the mattress groaned.

Roark kissed my pulse point, holding his lips there until his body went still. Warm pulses of his release filled me, over and over. I burrowed my face against him, kissing his head, his cheek, holding him against me.

Roark didn't lift his head but held a palm to my face. *I love you. You are the brightest piece of my soul.*

Tears blurred my vision. I eased his head to my heart, holding his stubbled cheek to my skin. Claimed. Safe. Whole.

LYRA

A FEAST WAS THE LAST EVENT I DESIRED TO ATTEND. There was something dangerous brewing, not only here where the living walked, but also in the mirror. Fadey was growing stronger. How? I didn't know, but we could not stop him, dining at Draven tables.

With a bit of nervous reluctance, I'd dressed in a finely woven wool gown, the hem lined in fur, with a bodice stitched in vibrant threads.

Roark looked the part of a prince. He'd secured his hair off his face with tight braids and beads made of polished bone. His tunic was so black the gleam of the torches did not even catch in the threads, and over his shoulders was a fur cloak, pinned with the double-headed raven.

I'd nearly broken his hand the nearer we got to the great hall. Moments before we entered, Roark paused, insisting one of my plaits had come undone.

There was nothing loose about my braids, but no doubt, he

could see the touch of green rising on my cheeks, feel the sweat on my palms, or perhaps our bond gave up the torment and fear of my soul.

Didn't matter. He gave me a reprieve, and I was grateful for it. The pause gave us time to further discuss the strange tether Fadey had fastened around me during the last visit to the mirror.

"Connections between souls are always burning through craft. They bind us to others," Gunter whispered from his place leaning against the wall opposite us.

"We already went over this. Nothing about Fadey could form a soul connection to me."

Gunter seemed unappeased, like something troubled him but he did not know how to speak it. "I just don't understand it. The moment I knew I was a soul weaver, I studied bonds. How to form them, how to destroy them, how they can be manipulated. All manner of wicked things, mind you. I wish I could've seen it to know how he's managed to keep this tether to you."

"Yes, well, I feel much the same."

Gunter glanced over his shoulder, watching for anyone beyond our small circle. Brynn, Auki, and Emi formed a subtle ring around us, always on guard.

In truth, it was endearing.

Roark had loyal friends before he was exiled. They remained so now, and it warmed my heart knowing that perhaps a touch of the agony he felt over losing Thane might be filled with Gunter, Brynn, and Auki.

When he was satisfied no one was listening in, Gunter faced me. "There are several ways to connect to a soul. A mother's or father's soul will have a connection to their child's. Different than a soul bond, but a connection all the same."

It is how the queen and I are still able to speak soul to soul, Roark gestured.

I nodded, silently urging Gunter to go on.

"Auki and Brynn have a connection as brother and sister. Each tether between them smells similar, so I know they share blood. That is part of my craft, I can find bonds between kin. Wedded souls would have different scents, especially if it is not a true soul bond that unites them as mates into Salur." Gunter sniffed Emi with a touch of dramatics. "Yes, you have several connections, Nightlark. One is almost as gamey as this sod's"—Gunter tilted his chin at Roark—"so I know you share a small bit of blood as cousins. Your other bond is much sweeter."

Emi's mouth tightened and she looked away. Did Gunter speak of a connection to Princess Yrsa, the love Emi left behind in Stonegate?

"If there is no other connection between you, all I can assume is Fadey has a great deal of your blood for the queen to continually use in her spell casts," Gunter said, but it was with reluctance. Like he wasn't certain he believed his own suggestion. "It isn't necessarily bad since the blood is finite. But don't allow them to get more."

Roark ran his knuckles down my arm, a signal we would need to enter, and took hold of my hand.

"Don't let me fall," I whispered.

He grinned and leaned down, pressing a kiss behind my ear.

Inside, the hall was decked in ribbons and fragrant vines. Rafters were wrapped in black satin, and a banner of the Dravenmoor sigil was draped behind the royal dais. Elisabet sat on a high-backed seat with thick pelts and furs over the arms.

Atop her head was a jagged circlet made of onyx steel, and every finger bore a ring of silver or jade. Her eyes were thickly lined in kohl, and her long fingernails had been painted the shade of purple midnight.

A formidable queen.

Voices hushed when we entered, but not as intensely as during our first entrance upon our arrival.

Roark's shoulders were stiff and straight, and he strode forward with a sneer on his lip. I despised how he could not be free, not even among his own clan. Here meant bitterness, torture, and mistrust for my husband.

I did not know if the wounds carved into a young boy's soul would ever truly heal.

Instinct urged me to drop my chin, to look at my feet and avoid every stare, but Emi nudged my ribs gently.

"You are Draven," she whispered. "Royal, a powerful crafter, the wife of the future king. You look down for no one."

Three pulses squeezed my palm. Roark did not look at me, but he was there, steady and sure. Not letting me fall.

I would do the same.

Elisabet rose from her seat and stepped to the edge of the dais. Roark pressed a palm to his chest and lowered his head.

We will greet the queen first, he'd told me earlier as we dressed. *It is symbolic for her to invite us to sit with her. It shows that the queen accepts her heirs.*

I dipped my head in a small bow the same as Roark, waiting. For too many breaths, Elisabet said nothing, she did not move.

I knew of her vow to Roark, but nowhere in the promise to keep me alive had she agreed not to humiliate me by not allowing me a seat at her side. Did I even desire a seat?

If the Norns had not been so vicious in their schemes, I would prefer if Roark and I had slipped away somewhere no one knew us. A simple life, perhaps a small cottage by the sea. Peaceful. Safe.

"Join me." After a dozen heartbeats, the soft, low hum of Elisabet's voice came. "Sit beside me, my son and heir. And . . . my daughter."

A slow build of cheers echoed in the hall. Some horns clanked on the tables. Boots stomped over floorboards.

My heart dropped back into place when I stood. The word *daughter* had been said without emotion, flat and dull, but it was absent the bite of hatred.

Roark studied my face for a breath, a calm smile there to reassure me, but the hunter he was burned behind the ease. A man always on watch, always ready to strike, to slaughter should those he love be threatened.

Emi was seated protectively between Auki and Gunter at the smaller table nearest to the dais. Brynn stroked Òlmr's head, her watch on Virki, who had not bothered to look at the dais. His hooded stare was locked on his daughter.

I bit down on the inside of my cheek to stifle the smirk when Emi tilted her head, never lowering her eyes from her father, and took a methodical, slow drink from a horn. She didn't blink as she wiped her chin with the back of her hand, and there was a bit of delight in my chest when Virki was the one to relent first.

He turned away with a furrowed scowl and offered his scrutiny to one of the men who'd sat at the úlfur council table.

"Melder."

I jolted when Elisabet touched my arm.

Roark frowned, and his hands moved swiftly and furiously. *Address her properly.*

Elisabet studied his ire, then faced me. "It breaks a mother's heart not to hear her son. Would you mind?"

I swallowed, flashing a quick glare at my short-tempered husband. "He does not like me being addressed as Melder, my lady."

Elisabet's lip twitched. "Ah. Forgive me. Habit, you see. Lyra, you are to take Roark's far side. I will take the other. The center is the symbol for the future crown. And you *are* to become king." The queen spoke to Roark with a sharpness, almost scolding him.

We will see was all Roark gestured, but his hand was low to his side, meant for no one to see save me.

He handed me toward my seat and waited for me to settle, then his mother, before taking his place. Almost at once, Roark had a drinking horn in hand and slumped low. With a single glance one could guess that the prince desired to be anywhere but here.

I chuckled and leaned in to whisper. "This reminds me of when we were honored at Stonegate."

I left out the reminder that the honor came from saving Prince Thane after he was attacked by Skul Drek. I did not think Roark had forgiven himself just yet.

He rolled his head to the side, speaking against my cheek boldly. *When we both wanted to fall through the cracks of the floorboards to escape.*

I chuckled, a bit of the tension leaving my chest. "We survived then, Ashwood. We will survive again."

And we did survive, for a time.

Dravens feasted with more vigor than even Jorvans in Skalfirth. In Jarl Jakobson's longhouse, I'd been knocked and shoved from the debauchery. Here, in the royal hall, Skalds sang tales to spritely lyres and drums.

Folk laughed and clapped the tables, stomping their feet to the tunes. More than one drunken fool shouted and tried to throw hands with another for some offense no one else knew until in the end both laughed, pouring more ale.

Gunter had a lovely woman with a heavy chest feeding him on his lap. Auki stood near the table with Emi, speaking and laughing with a few Dravens I guessed were members of the Dark Watch after I noted their blades and cowls.

Brynn had her chin propped on her knuckles, tipping back

her horn with the other hand, watching a young couple kiss at the table across from her.

Folk would come to the dais. Mothers, fathers, children. They greeted their queen and their prince, offering gladness for his return and praising the gods he survived so many seasons behind Jorvan borders.

Roark returned stern nods, watching with a dark suspicion when his people engaged with me. More apprehension lived in their words when they offered a few "My lady"s or even "Lady Melder."

One tiny girl with fiery red braids stood on her toes, her chin barely reaching over the table. After her mother and father had moved back into the crowds, the child slyly slid a broken blade across the table.

The knife was dull, not sharp enough to break skin, but the hilt was lovely. Rune etched, with painted vines around the end, and horridly cracked.

"Mam says . . . she says you stick the bones," she said through a gap in her teeth. The girl kept glancing over her shoulder, like she did not want her parents to return. "Can you stick 'em back together, sùlka?"

Roark sat straighter, intrigued.

I leaned forward. "You want me to fix your blade?"

The girl flashed a wide smile. "Will you? My grandpap made it for me."

She wanted me to meld. Here. In front of everyone. Roark's mouth tightened, but he did not signal me to stop.

I pressed my fingertips to the crack across the bone hilt. The roar of craft thudded between my ears, pulsed in my blood. Each use summoned the magic more swiftly and firmly, like another instinct I could reach in and access as simply as I could smell a bloom.

Along the shards of the crack, glimmers of threads emerged from the bone. Filaments that waved as though underwater. It would not take much time, but the girl ogled my fingers with such awe, I wanted it to last.

The child couldn't see the gilded strings of craft, but she watched the movement of my fingers stitching along her blade. Little by little, the crack sealed until only a faint scar remained where the fissure had split.

She squealed with glee when she inspected the blade.

Dozens of heads turned our way.

"Oh, many thanks, sùlka." The child waved her dull blade and hopped off the dais. "Mam! You was right! She stuck it back together!"

I sent a prayer to the gods to swallow me into the molten hell when a few murmurs followed the girl and looks of stun found me again.

Beneath the table Roark squeezed my thigh, but his expression was shadowed, pinned on the great hall, as though daring anyone to confront me for using my horrid craft.

Elisabet sat back in her chair, sipping her dark wine, a gleam in her eye. One I hoped was more from amusement that my vicious craft had done the unthinkable—fixed a child's toy.

"Well." Emi approached once attention was pulled away from us again, one hand on the high table. "I suppose that was one way to reveal your craft."

"I couldn't say no. She has been the only one unafraid of me."

Emi lowered her voice. "Perhaps our clan can take a lesson from a babe and grow some damn balls around you."

I choked on a gulp of my drink and had to shield the dribble and laughter behind my hand.

When Elisabet stood and pounded the end of her horn on the table, I was glad for it. The attention of the hall shifted to the queen.

"It is no secret why we are here." The queen hesitated. "The Norns often twist paths of fate in unseen ways. We are here to acknowledge and accept that our prince has sealed his soul bond with Lyra of House Bien. The melder."

Silence brought heady disquiet that came from behind and throttled me until it felt as though I could not draw in a deep enough breath.

Then, slowly, fists pounded over chests. A few calls of approval echoed across the hall. Rowdy cheers grew, and stacked on one another, until the room rumbled in celebratory shouts.

My face heated. I leaned nearer to Roark, slipping my fingers through his still digging into my thigh.

Elisabet held up a palm. "For seasons, Jorvans have used melders, forcing them toward corruption. It would be ungrateful of our people to disregard a blessing of the gods that brings the melder to our lands now. Instead of a pawn in their hands, she is now numbered among us."

More cheers.

Gods. There was an unspoken need I had not realized lived inside me. The yearning to be accepted, to have a place in this wretched world. In Skalfirth, I had a home with Thorian, Selena, and Kael. To others, I was nothing.

In Stonegate, I was to be used, corrupted. I could not be Lyra.

Not until the Sentry stood at my side.

Not until the Jorvan prince told me I could be free with them behind the doors.

Only then did I begin to feel like I mattered more than my craft.

To hear the call of acceptance from folk who rather despised my craft meant something. It meant a great deal.

"It is time to make her new house official."

My pulse quickened when Elisabet led a burly man forward.

He had endless black ink decorating his skin, a beard to his navel, and half a dozen piercings in each ear.

"The house sigil is different across the lands, but no less important."

My fingers touched the raised brand behind my ear. Gammal had reshaped the sigil of House Bien long ago. Dravens marked their skin similarly, but more with blessings of their house, runes and symbols for the life their folk hoped they might live.

The choice is yours. Roark gestured low so only I could read the movements of his hands.

I swallowed, then stroked the back of his neck where the faded runes of his house marks remained. "Am I part of your house, Roark Ashwood?"

His eyes flickered like hot coals. *You are part of everything.*

I pressed a quick kiss to the corner of his mouth and rose from my seat. Roark followed, as did Brynn, Emi, and Auki. Gunter scrambled to follow, nearly tossing the voluptuous woman on his lap to the floor.

I fought the urge to roll my eyes. Not only did my husband and his depraved soul prowl around me, now it seemed so, too, did my personal band of Dravens.

"Well, where are we puttin' it, Melder?" The man held a narrow iron stake he would pound into my flesh. His cheeks filled with a bit of red when he looked at Roark.

By the frosted hell. Darkness cloaked Roark's shoulders. The man could hardly hold in his chaos. Did he not recall the risk of constantly dividing his soul?

"Roark." I touched his arm. "Stop."

He speaks down to you.

I scoffed and whispered against his ear. "It's possible some folk don't even know my name. You can't devour their souls for something they don't know."

So you think. His eyes narrowed at the man, but his shoulders lost a bit of the tension.

The inkist had his back turned away and likely missed the moment his prince considered tearing his soul to shreds for not speaking my given name.

I cleared my throat and approached him when his tools were laid out. "I am Lyra."

One of his thick brows rose. "Ikard Willowvane." He sniffed, brisk and wholly unaware of his temperament. "Well, where'll you have it? Aches on the ribs, throat, and belly. I suggest for a lady like you, shoulders, breast—"

Roark grunted, one fist clenched.

I grinned at Ikard. "What about between the shoulders?"

"Suits me. Sit and tug down the dress a bit."

Eyes tight, Roark stepped between Ikard and me, waiting for the man to stand back before he unlaced the back of my gown, just enough so the top of my spine was exposed.

"Your jealousy is going to get folk killed," I murmured.

Not jealous. The corner of his mouth curved when he spoke with one hand. *Protective of what's mine*.

The final tap was soft against my cheek before Roark took his place in front of me.

I would not whimper in front of the entire hall of Dravenmoor.

I. Would. Not. Whimper.

With every notch of the iron and ink against my skin, I repeated the words. Ikard was skilled at his trade, but no amount of gentility with the spike and mallet would ever make new ink comfortable.

It took another bell toll before Ikard stepped back and asked for the prince to inspect his work. Roark's callused fingertips traced the edges of my sore flesh, and he gave a nod of approval.

"Fits you, Ly," Emi said, beaming.

"I would've gone with mischief or something there on the final mark," Gunter offered. "But perhaps your house doesn't have the stomach for any more trouble."

"What are the runes?" I asked.

Honor, wisdom, bravery, and cunning. Roark pressed a kiss to my shoulder, then took hold of my hand, drawing us toward the front of the dais.

Those who observed cheered while others lost themselves in their cups or returned to feasting.

For a moment, this hall, these people, it felt a bit like a . . . home.

The doors banged open. A formidable hush fell across the feast. Two Dark Watch warriors, windblown and weary, shoved into the hall. Heavy steps and long strides had both men to the dais in moments.

"My queen." One man dipped his chin. "Scouts have brought news from the borders."

My heart leapt to my throat.

Elisabet clasped her hands in front of her body. "What's happened?"

The second guard cast a hesitant look toward me and Roark as his companion hurried on.

"The Jorvan king is dead." Gasps echoed against the rafters. The guard swallowed and went on. "Our folk tell us the Jorvandal Stav Guard search for the melder along the ravines, not for use of craft, but because she is the king's killer."

ROARK

THE TWO DARK WATCHERS DIPPED THEIR CHINS AND
stepped back from the dais in the same moment the hall
burst with shouts and inquiries, even a few cheers.

Lyra was frozen where she stood, her skin flushed the same
shade as the irritated redness around her new sigil. Her expression was one I recognized, the look of fright buried beneath a
mask of calm. One she wore when too many found her in a crowd
and left her wanting to fade into the shadows as she'd done all
her life.

I slid my arm around her waist, a cold burn along the scar on
my throat. No mistake, the fear of some voices collided with
the violence in my soul, waking the need to destroy anything—
anyone—to keep Lyra breathing.

And I was not alone.

In front of the dais, Auki took a stance beside Emi, one of his
throwing knives spinning in his grip. Gunter (still eating a slice

of herb bread) sneered at our folk like he was readying to play some sort of bloody game, and Brynn stroked the raised hackles of her fara.

"Is this enough, my queen?" In the back of the hall Sampson stood. At his side, his wife desperately tugged on his arm. He shook her off.

I did not watch Sampson. My attention fell to my uncle, who grinned at the man's side. Sampson had little spine and seemed to crave Virki's regard.

Whatever came through his mouth, I took as the true words of my uncle.

Sampson prowled for the dais but stopped ten paces away. "Is this enough for you to see the melder is nothing but a risk for our clan? A king killer. You wish us to bend the knee?"

His words added a new layer of unease in the chatter, and frantic voices hummed along the tables, against the walls.

I tilted my head, envisioning the ways he would die. A fate like Tomas Grisen with his head spiked atop his own spine? No, perhaps hanging him off the side of a ravine, cutting the rope a little more each day until he died from exposure or the rope split and he fell to the stones below? I could devour his soul, leave him a shell of a man.

"What say you, Bet?" Virki's dark rumble followed, calm as the tension before a storm reached land.

Dark Watchers rose after my uncle, some already touching the blades on their waists in case the queen gave the word.

When Elisabet stepped in front of us, my grip tightened on Lyra's wrist, hard enough to bruise. She didn't pull away.

"What do I say?" My mother's sharp eyes scanned the crowd. "I say my daughter did exactly what was asked of her by her clan."

Unexpected. It took focused effort not to look at the queen

with befuddlement. Lyra stared at the hall, doubtless trying to do the same.

The queen chuckled with a touch of venom. "You must forgive me for keeping such plans concealed. To remove our prince and his soul bond, to prevent bloodshed that would surely come from King Damir's plans, we made calculated moves very swiftly. There was not much time, you see. The Jorvan king left us no more than a day before he planned to meld every soul bone in his possession."

Elisabet hadn't known such a thing until the deledan told her what King Damir had planned, that to meld such a great number of bones would've killed Lyra. *What game was my mother playing?*

"What are you talking about?" Virki stepped forward. "The úlfur knew nothing of this."

The queen didn't flinch as each sweet untruth crossed her lips. "After Lyra was discovered, it became clear a bond had been restored. Our prince would never end the melder, nor would she harm him, so I made the decision to bring the melder to us. Her soul clan. There are times when even our úlfur fall into violent biases. I knew she would need to come here, be seen, be trusted before she would no longer be hunted by our folk."

Stun kept mouths shut and scrutiny on the queen.

"It was discovered that the Jorvan king had much more sinister plans than we thought. With so many melded Berserkirs, Damir was moving to bring battle against our clans—"

"Then we should have met them!" Virki roared. A few grumbles of agreement followed.

The queen merely laughed. "You think so, Virki? Damir had Lyra Bien bound and trapped, ready to force her craft to bind every one of his warriors—including my son—with those corrupted soul bones. How many of you have battled one of Jorvandal's

Berserkirs? How easily do they meet Salur? To save my clan and find time for a new strategy, I ordered my son's wife to do what was needed for her people. Unlike so many of you, it seems, she did not question my word."

Damn the gods. The queen spoke with such finality, such fervor, I nearly believed her deceit to be truth.

Elisabet claimed the battle at Stonegate was her own scheme, all to . . . protect Lyra.

My thoughts were a tangle of affection and mistrust. Had the queen not said from her own tongue that her moves were rarely known by others?

Virki lifted his chin. "I don't believe you, Bet."

"How unsurprising." The queen shook her head as though disappointed.

"You would not have ordered the death of a king without counseling with the úlfur."

"She did." Yanson rose from his place at the front table. Gunter's tiny sister was in her father's arm, playing with the beads in his hair. "Our queen counseled with me and Kaysar, seeing as how we were part of the original plan to bring the melder child to Dravenmoor under Vishon's order. Isn't that right, Kaysar?"

The twins' father tipped back his horn a few places away, then said nothing more but "Aye."

"Gods," Lyra said under her breath.

I felt the same. It was both heartening and unsettling how easily trusted members of the úlfur lied to the whole of the clan.

"Tell me," the queen said, "will you stand against my daughter for being as brave as the god-queen herself and slaughtering corruption?"

"If this is true," Virki went on, "we still face war. Stav Guard will come against us to reach her."

"Then cease arguing with me and ready your wolves, Virki."

The queen beamed at the hall. "Take heart: the heir of Jorvandal, from the word of my son, is more prone to negotiate and find peace than his father. True?"

It took a moment before I realized my mother spoke to me.

I gave a brisk nod. We'd never spoken of Thane. She did not deserve to hear of him since her command nearly forced my bloodlust to slaughter the prince. But she was not wrong about his character. Thane would be king of Jorvandal, and the kingdom would be better for it.

My uncle stepped closer to the dais, but Gunter blocked his approach, a snide sort of grin on my old friend's face.

Virki glowered at the queen, his voice low. "If the council voted upon her death, you would never have followed through, isn't that right?"

"Perhaps."

"You would overrule the council's vote?"

The queen simply leaned forward, holding my uncle's stare. "The benefit of wearing this." She pointed to the circlet on her head. "Do not forget that, Virki."

Elisabet straightened and looked to the hall again. "This news is more cause for celebration. The souls of the fallen are no longer left for Jorvan corruption." A few tentative shouts and cheers followed. "And our Lyra has proven what lengths she will go to protect you, your families, and your loved ones who dine in Salur."

More whoops and hollers followed.

With that, Elisabet came to my side, squeezed my arm, and spoke low, "Leave the hall, go to my chamber. Both of you. We must speak."

Without another word, Elisabet abandoned the feast.

"What in the two hells was that?" Emi said in a low hiss.

Games, cousin. I stepped off the dais and held out a hand for Lyra to take, guiding her off the step.

Emi frowned. "Be sure you play them back."

"I don't know what happened at Stonegate," Brynn said, voice low. "But is the king truly dead?"

Lyra took a breath. "Yes. We knew it would be a matter of time before word spread."

"You killed him?" Gunter's eyes brightened.

"What do you think?"

"Fadey," Auki grumbled. "That bastard is everywhere."

"Yes, and no one in Stonegate knows there is another melder," Lyra was swift to say. "If Jorvans come for me, it is as the scouts said. They come because they believe I killed the king."

"Then we better stop them first if they try," said Brynn.

We must go, I said to Lyra and tugged on her hand.

"We expect to know everything," Gunter called after us, laughing when I left him with nothing but a crude gesture over my shoulder.

THE QUEEN'S CHAMBER WAS WARM FROM A BLAZING FIRE IN her onyx stone inglenook. Dried herbs kept the air fresh with lavender and meadow blooms. More rooms made up her wing, but once, it had been shared.

A lock still bolted my father's study shut.

Guilt for destroying him likely kept her out.

Elisabet stood near the flame, the blaze lighting her sapphire eyes like a poisonous inferno.

"I'm certain you're curious why I told such tales." She looked at Lyra. "It is simple: you will now be both feared and revered within these gates."

Lyra didn't falter under the queen's watch. "Or those who despise me might have more motivation to return me to the Jorvans for their torture."

Elisabet crossed the space between us until she was nearly chest to chest with Lyra. "You have less risk on your head if they believe you are a king killer. The clan cannot know Fadey lives, or battles will begin before we are prepared."

Some know, I gestured lazily and did not face my mother.

When Lyra repeated the words, Elisabet frowned. "Be wary who you tell. We know nothing of Fadey's power, and I do not yet know how to fight such a man who can lie in wait for so many seasons. Not with Ingir, not with Myrdan armies and Stav Guard."

"I agree," said Lyra, her voice soft. "We don't know what Fadey's plans are entirely, but I have reason to believe he is growing stronger with Ingir at his side."

With a touch of reluctance, I retold the experience of Fadey finding Lyra while we searched for bones. Lyra's translation left out pieces of the strange bond he'd coiled around her, but I felt it was more because she was wholly discomfited by the notion that he had the power to do it and not from distrust in the queen.

"Dammit." Elisabet closed her eyes. "For all we know he could be crafting hordes of Berserkirs and—"

I waved a hand, cutting through her words. *He is likely still hidden from Thane, so he cannot craft Berserkirs. Thane believes Lyra is the lone melder.*

The queen scoffed. "Are you so certain the heir of Jorvandal would not side with Ingir and her plans?"

Yes.

"Hmm." Elisabet faced the flames again. "If his character is what you say, it will make what must come next simpler. This hunt for the Wanderer's bones always impacted every kingdom. Even if they do not realize it."

What are you talking about? I penned the question on the corner of a parchment crumpled over a table in the corner.

My mother wheeled on me. "Are you ready to hear it?"

Lyra looked between us. "Hear what?"

"Truths that are not mine to tell." The queen narrowed her eyes and faced me. "You have more power over souls than you know. If you are willing to hear their calls."

A groove formed between my brows. *What secrets are you keeping? Do not waste time.*

The queen went to a small chest against the wall. From inside she removed a linen-wrapped parcel and handed it to Lyra. "When you meld soul bones, tell me, does your craft reveal severed connections from a fallen soul?"

"Severed connections? Do you mean the threads?" Lyra's silver scars brightened when she curled her palms around the parcel. "I see threads and . . . use them to fasten the bones together."

"Yes, those are connections the soul had in life. I need you to meld this, slowly. Just enough to brighten connections that might seem severed. Then he will find them and draw them forward." Elisabet tilted her head toward me.

Draw what forward?

My mother studied my hands, listening to Lyra repeat the question. She lifted her chin. "The souls of the fallen. With Lyra's craft, it will help find the shadowed bonds in the darkness. The bonds that are always there, but you simply don't always see them."

"You want him to summon a soul?"

"Yes." The queen held up one finger. "A certain soul, if you are to gain more insight on your hunt, at least. There is much I don't know about the power of the Wanderer, but there are answers we can gain from the fallen."

Slowly, Lyra unwrapped the parcel. A rounded shard of bone marked in simple runes of the heart. "A soul bone?"

"Not exactly. Remember, meld just enough to brighten the

remnants of the soul in the bone." My mother squared herself to me. "Take us, Roark. Do it again. You have more power than you know."

When I did not move, Elisabet softened her features. "I may never be deserving of your forgiveness, but you must find it within yourself to trust that I am still trying to do all I can to keep you alive." The queen looked at Lyra. "Both of you."

"Why do you protect me now when you wanted me dead before?" Lyra took a stern step in front of me. "I don't understand it. You tore your son apart because he innocently stumbled into a bond with a girl he had never met. Now you vow to keep me safe?"

Elisabet had the decency to hear her out. "When you have lost everything, tell me what you would do, Lyra. We refused to lose another son. His father and I made an impossible choice."

Don't bring the king into this, I interjected, taking a step forward. *He was not able to make those choices.*

After Lyra whispered my response, for the first time since we'd reunited, tears lined the lashes of the queen. I despised them. They dug into my chest, like a blade trying to hack at my ribs to reach my heart.

"You are not ready to believe what I say, but . . ." She hesitated and stepped close to me. "I hope you know your father loved you. Giving his life so you could live was never questioned, save by me."

Lyra blinked rapidly at my side, her fingers digging into my arm.

After the tension of silence settled long enough that it was felt to the bones, Elisabet cleared her throat and stepped back. "This is the only way I know how to help."

"You think Roark can truly summon a soul in the mirror?" Lyra asked.

"I do."

For a drawn breath, the three of us merely stared at one another.

In truth, I did not know how to summon souls, but I could not deny there was a power radiating from the bone in Lyra's hands, something familiar.

I looked at the queen and tilted my head. *Who am I meant to find when we are there?*

When Lyra replied with my query, the queen's grin widened. "Your brother."

LYRA

GOLDEN HEAT COATED MY FLESH, COILING WITH COLD mists. Wood peeled off the rafters. Murky black dripped overhead like cobwebs. The inglenook was deadened and coated in ash.

In front of my face, I held out my palms. Faint threads floated in the darkness. Meld. I was to slowly meld. Not a true soul bone, more like the bones of small creatures I'd used to hunt, for our own answers.

Craft heated over my glowing palms. Familiar warmth radiated from the shard. A presence I'd felt before. Memories from a dream, arms that held me tightly, carrying me away from smoke, blood, and screams.

A bone of the fallen Draven prince. The thrill of truly speaking to a fallen soul hurried my fingers over the surface, snatching wispy threads and weaving them to the outer edge of the opposite shard.

Until a low rumble came from behind.

Skul Drek, cowled and cloaked, curled his haunting arms around my waist, drawing in a breath. Like the scent of my soul kept him locked in with a need for more.

"We ought not be here, Melder," he said in a low, rough rasp. "The dark one hunts your soul."

A shudder ran down my spine. I looked away from the bone and scanned the mists and haunting smoke of the mirror. We were not near Stonegate, but I could not shake the unease of knowing that somehow Fadey might be able to find us here, even behind the walls of an enemy clan.

"Then find the connections we seek and we can leave," I told him and flicked a strand of the delicate gold threads, glittering like fine chains between us.

Gunter's soul weave was no longer thick and gaudy. Now, where Skul Drek shifted, shimmers like spider silk webbed between us. From head to foot, we were joined.

As fragile as it appeared, the strength of it had only burrowed deeper into my bones, my blood.

A smile crept over my lips when I faced the bone again.

"What am I to seek?" Skul Drek dipped his head low, drawing in a rough breath. "All I want is to devour you, Melder."

I did not know if it was the mirror or the heady passion between our souls, but for a moment I considered letting him.

The queen stood stalwart. Elisabet burned like molten amber, the gleam fierce as a sunrise. A tether, weaker than those binding me to my husband, dragged on the murky ground, chained around Elisabet's ankle. The strand wove across the shadows and disappeared somewhere within the cloak of Skul Drek.

Proof of a vow she'd made, soul to soul.

But there were more, darker threads that bound her to Roark, to unseen souls in the distance. Connections. Kin. Lovers. Friendships. As though a veil had been removed from over my eyes, the more I learned of the bonds and of craft to the blood, the bones, the souls of folk, the more I could see them for myself.

The queen was draped in tangles of small bonds. Some weaker than others. Some brighter and shorter.

When he realized we were not alone, Skul Drek hissed at the queen. "Leave us." Robes of cold wrapped around my shoulders, drawing me against him. He dragged his nose against my throat. "I want to taste you again."

By the gods. He was the phantom, the scourge of the kingdoms as Skul Drek, but this was still his damn mother.

I pressed a hand against his chest. "Don't you remember?"

One finger traced the edge of my jaw. "I recall you always, Melder."

I frowned and the pulse of his copper eyes flickered to deep crimson. A sign he was studying me, trying to crack open my skull and uncover my thoughts. "We came here for a purpose."

I held up the bone shard. Elisabet believed my craft could awaken connections to these bones, but Skul Drek would be the one to summon the fallen prince. True enough, one of the unwoven threads reached for the shadows of my phantom husband.

Skul Drek tilted his hooded head. One long, darkened finger touched the end of the filament.

Together we jolted in surprise when the strand burst in its vibrancy and slithered through the mists and rot of the mirror, fading into oblivion.

I was met with a vicious sort of grin when he looked at me again. "There. Now, let me taste you."

I patted his misty chest. "We are not alone and have no answers yet."

"It is a challenge with a rent soul," Elisabet said, a subtle laugh to her tone. "Focus will latch onto one subject. At first, it was to kill for his duty. With your bond, he will only see you. For in our darkest halves is where our obsession lies."

"You speak as though you've had experience," I said. Had she been drawn into the darkness of her king when his soul was torn apart much the same?

Elisabet merely hummed but did not explain deeper.

Teeth bared, shadows deepened around Skul Drek. "Leave us, queenie."

His voice was rough, like grit lined the back of his throat. Darkness, viciousness, cruelty—all of it flared at the slightest word. It seemed should he perceive offense to me, it would flash more swiftly than anything.

I stroked his shadowed face. "Remember, we are here to find your brother?"

Upon mention of the prince, the missing thread flickered against the mists again. A connection from the bone, to the chest of Skul Drek, to the distant nothing.

The craft of Skul Drek could touch souls, steal them, devour them. I never considered he might be able to speak to them.

Craft was ever-expanding. A puzzling piece of lore and unknowns. Powers were unique with soul craft, more so than bone and blood. If it was possible for Skul Drek to summon certain souls—gods, the things we might learn from those who died before us.

Skul Drek closed his eyes, then let out the wicked laugh that once frightened me. Now my hair lifted with anticipation, as though my heart stirred from his villainy.

"Yes," he said. "Princely brothers were lost."

Elisabet shifted on her feet. "You will need to learn how to use your craft if you are ever going to free your wife from those who wish to darken her soul."

"Then give your lessons, queenie. I've souls to take."

"You must remember him." She pointed to the faint thread attached to the bone. "Use the bond your wife has awakened, a bond of brothers, and call to him."

"Hmm. Princely brothers of he and we." He touched the bone shard, closed his eyes again, then the next word came out in a snarl. "Nothing."

"Try harder." A smile lightened Elisabet's features. "Do you recall snapping your wrist as a boy?"

Almost on instinct, Skul Drek jolted away, like he'd been shocked with pain. He bared his teeth. "Rooftops and rain."

"Yes." Elisabet nodded. "You tried to prove you could patch the rooftop of the stables all on your own after Nivek denied you the chance to help with the outer walls."

The more Elisabet spoke, the brighter the thread shone.

"Your brother said you were too young, and you took great offense."

I bit down on my bottom lip. Gods, I could see it. Knowing Roark, his fierceness and damn stubbornness, it was not hard to imagine him insisting he could be like his elder brother. A man I never met, but one Roark had clearly admired.

A small, garbled chuckle slid out. Skul Drek spun on me, eyes narrow, head tilted.

"Mockery." Slowly, he peeled away from me and returned to studying the queen. "Princely brothers taunted he and we. Had to be shown how wrong were the words he spoke."

"What else?" Elisabet pressed.

Another breath, another heartbeat, and the dark, shadowed features of Skul Drek appeared almost . . . wistful. "A fever's rage and stolen cakes."

"As a boy, Roark loved saffron cakes." Elisabet's chin quivered when she looked to me. "The frost of his eighth season he took ill, deathly so. Nivek snuck him a saffron cake every evening. When he recovered, Roark believed the cakes were what healed him and insisted we eat one at every evening meal for at least a full season more."

My heart squeezed. Once, my husband's life had been . . . peaceful. A time when he was not the Death Bringer, when he did not need to bend the knee to greedy kings. When he was merely Roark Ashwood.

An odd warmth flowed on a gust of breeze. The cracking walls seemed a little brighter. The new thread curled inward, as though something on a different end drew closer.

"Never could stomach the damn cakes after that season."

Skul Drek's eyes burned a cruel shade of red when his unyielding regard held tightly to a place in the shadows no more than ten paces away.

A man was there, draped in fading mists. Dozens of shimmering fibers and ribbons of connections rolled off him like the shadows rolled off Skul Drek.

His iridescent flesh was lined with the same gold of the souls in the mirror. Handsome features, bright, and a little sly. A sharp nose and jaw, with thin lips, but those eyes—gold and fierce like Roark's.

His hands were clasped behind his back when he took a step forward. "I do hope it's all been worth it, brother." For a breath, he paused and looked down at me. "Seems it has."

Nivek. The man who saved my life. He was here . . . or his soul was, at least.

My lips parted and closed, words dry as ash on my tongue. What could I say to adequately express anything to the one who'd sacrificed it all for a girl he did not know, a girl his younger brother insisted held his heart?

"Princely brothers," Skul Drek said in a sort of hiss.

Nivek grinned. "As monstrous as ever. You always were a little terror. I wondered if you'd ever have the damn stones to summon me. I've missed our talks where you idolize every word I say."

Skul Drek snapped his teeth in response.

This was . . . strange. Nivek seemed so alive yet hardly there. His voice was low and strong, yet all the while it echoed, as though we were hearing him in a dream.

"Mother." Nivek beamed at Elisabet.

The queen had said nothing, but my chest cracked at the sight of her. Stalwart, formidable, but her brilliant cheeks were stained with a golden flush to hint that tears were spilling beyond the mirror.

Nivek reached out a palm and placed it against her cheek. Elisabet covered it with her own.

"I would do it again," he said, voice low.

A sob split from her throat. She turned her face into his hand and pressed a kiss to her son's gleaming palm.

"Who darkened your soul?" Skul Drek's harsh voice cut through the sweetness of the moment. He glared at Nivek, not out of hate for the fallen prince, more like a building rage for those who'd killed him.

"I don't know, or do not recall. Should you find whoever slit my throat, make it painful. There were those I was forced to part with much too soon."

Two strings I'd not seen before, both tethered to his chest, pulsed in light. My throat tightened. Connection bonds, though one seemed to spread like the delicate web of my own bond with his brother.

"They darkened your soul for taking my melder?"

Nivek stared into the distance, a touch of whimsy on his face, before he faced us again. "I cannot say. I suppose it's possible. But there is something that brings me to pause, a tale I've forgotten. Another reason for bloodshed, perhaps. Either way, I am glad my death was not for nothing." Nivek looked at me again. "The melder. You stand with him, every part of him."

"Yes." I slid a palm around Skul Drek's shadowed arm. Ribbons of cold slipped between my fingers like he was tangling his grip around my hand in return.

Nivek dipped his chin. "Good."

"Thank you for—"

"No need." The prince shook his head. "Simply honor the bond between you. It is the greatest gift one can have, a true love that burns in the soul."

Nivek looked about dreamily. Much the same as with his brother, it seemed souls were distractible, hardly there.

I waved a hand, drawing Nivek to look my way again. "The queen said you might have answers. We, uh, we seek the Wanderer's bones."

"You'd be wise to take care with your words." The prince looked to the darkness at one side. "Do you not sense it? There are threads of craft reaching for you, Melder. Always. Enemies hunt you."

"He's here?" Ice filled my blood. I looked about for any glimpse of Fadey.

"Not yet." Nivek's voice was dark, harsh. "But there are powers seeking you here. We should not talk long lest they find you."

"I will find *them*," Skul Drek bit out. "Their souls will burn."

A shiver danced up my spine.

Skul Drek grumbled. "The first king's soul is hunted by the dark melder *and* my melder."

"The one you sense is another melder," I explained. "He hunts me to meld my bones to his since he believes I have the stronger craft to seek out the Wanderer's lost bones."

"You do. After all, you are the melder fated to destroy our world. Daughter of the god-queen."

Fadey had insinuated a connection to the fabled queen much the same way. "I don't understand."

Nivek smiled with a touch of sadness. "You summon me now because of what I know, yes? You wish me to aid you on this deadly quest?"

"Queenie says answers are in the souls of princely brothers." Skul Drek paced behind me.

"Nivek." I called him by name when his attention fell to somewhere in the distant shadows again. "Your mother believes some of the Wanderer's bones might be over the Night Ledges. At least some connection to him." I spoke soft as a breeze and looked around as though Fadey might be standing behind me. Alone, I went on, my voice low. "She said you would have answers. Did you hide a shard?"

The prince smirked. "Not as you might think. Nor, I daresay, are the bones you seek exactly as you imagine."

"Four bones of the Wanderer," Skul Drek grumbled. "Four pieces lost. The arm, to swing the sword. The ribs, to wear his armor. The—"

"The breast, to have his warrior's heart," Nivek interrupted. "And the skull, for his wisdom. Yes, I know the tale, brother. And I say again, not all is as it seems when it comes to the Wanderer's bones."

Damn the cruel gods. Could anything ever be clear?

"Prophecies were seen and written about the dangers you now face," Nivek said.

"And set the Thief King out to hunt my melder." Shadows around Skul Drek thickened with his disdain for King Damir.

The man would always be the Thief King to my husband.

Nivek did not acknowledge the outburst. "You wish to know what we were told? I shall tell you, then: Gifts of the Wanderer form within the heirs of bone, blood, and soul when a god-queen's daughter finds life of her own. Through death, hate, and war, she unites these crafts once thought broken, forevermore. Heed not this fate and leave the divide, then blood will come and three kingdoms shall not survive."

Cold, worse than the frosted air of the mirror, bit against my flesh. Long, flowing mists curled around my waist, dragging me into the cloak of Skul Drek. He clacked his teeth at the prince, a warning, a bit of rage at the words.

"Those were the words of the seer?" I whispered.

Elisabet hugged her middle. "We interpreted her first words to mean the firstborn heirs of every kingdom would have some connection to ancient craft. But we did not understand how it was possible that war and death were in our futures. Because of this, the clans agreed to meet. Every kingdom in a moment of truce."

I looked at Nivek. He kept glancing to the shadows as though searching for someone. Roark's brother was the firstborn. If he knew the perceived connection, if he hid some piece of the Wanderer over the Night Ledges, did it mean he'd known his life was at risk?

I did not have time to ask before Elisabet went on. "By the time the seer came, every clan had a firstborn heir. Each clan took some pride in believing their child had a destiny of power."

She spoke of Yrsa, the heir of Myrda. Of Prince Thane.

Elisabet moved to stand nearer to Nivek's soul. "But we could not agree on the rest of the seer's words. Other than that they seemed to hint that a new melder would be the cause of the destruction. Most of us believed that it meant uniting all three crafts, for only a melder can bind the bones. But to do so would mean she would become like a reborn Wanderer King with every vein of craft united within her."

In the tales, the Wanderer poisoned his own young ones, his

greed so corrupted he forced his wife's hand to give him the power to meld soul bones, all to save them. For he desired power from the dead; he desired to become indestructible.

"Lyra." Elisabet drew my attention back. "The seer spoke of a daughter, so when a rumor spread of a girl with silver scars in her eyes, born after every other heir, we believed this new melder had the strength of the god-queen. We believed she had the power to unite all the crafts somehow through our heirs. But also the power to destroy our world. Some believed it was the gods' vengeance, at last, falling upon these lands for the curse of the first king. Many voices throughout the kingdoms wanted to stop it from happening."

Dammit. They believed I, a child, had the power to destroy thrones, realms, the very world in which we lived.

"The clans set out to find her, each for their own purposes." Elisabet studied me with intent. "Jorvans sought the girl for selfish reasons. Myrdans, to study the power. And Dravens, to stop whatever battles might be coming."

"Is that how the raids began?"

"No. This was seasons before the raids; you would have been hardly a season old." Elisabet's eyes flashed. "Vishon and I went against the truce, severing alliances. But, like the others, we still hunted the young melder. We planned to shadow her craft, to make the lands forget there ever was a god-queen daughter."

The gleam of Nivek's soul brightened.

A soul shadower. Roark told me his brother had the power to shadow the soul—hiding memories, truths, perhaps even craft.

My pulse raced. Shadows tightened around my limbs; Skul Drek held me steady, a strength in the darkness.

"You wanted to take me, to hide my craft?"

"My king had no intention to kill an innocent child," Elisabet insisted.

The long fingers of Skul Drek gripped the back of my neck. "They came to darken her soul, and princely brothers were darkened all the same."

Nivek chuckled. "What strange ways wickedness speaks."

My husband hissed back.

"But what of the final warning?" I asked. "To leave the crafts divided seems to insinuate that these lands will end. Either way, it seems we are destined for destruction."

Elisabet nodded. "We believed if we found you as an infant and never allowed your craft to take hold, the rest of the prophecy couldn't come to pass."

Something inside me twisted—a nudge, a fear. There was more to the seer's tale, like an unspoken warning whispered in my ear. I simply didn't know what it could be. "When I was a babe, no one found me."

"Some did. With wretched blood casts and hunters in Myrda and Jorvandal, the Jorvan king found you," Elisabet said. "Damir and Fadey tried to gather you but failed. Your folk were wise and ran with you, hiding you away from it all. With you lost to us, and with the Jorvans' depravity and desperation for melding craft, that was when my king made his sacrifice to protect the souls of the fallen."

The king rent his soul in two. He became Skul Drek.

I closed my eyes. "Then the raids came seasons later. Right?"

"Yes." The queen nodded. "When word rose again that the girl had been spotted, it became a battle to reach you first."

"And since the Jorvans used melding craft to corrupt . . ." I could not find the words to finish.

Elisabet did not speak right away. "The úlfur made the decision that it was better to destroy the risk. Fadey had become known for his brutality. The Jorvans would have made you the same."

What was there to say? Damir did try to make me a monster, bound to do his desires by corrupting and twisting souls in the bones of the living and the dead.

But to know so many lives were lost, all in an attempt to erase mine, stacked heavy on my spine.

"Now we face the same trouble," I said, my voice low. "This is why Fadey believes my bones will give him the power. It's not because I fall into a stronger melder's trance. It's because I'm a woman and a seer said I was the one who could unite the craft of the Wanderer King. It's madness."

Skul Drek clicked his long fingernails. "A dark melder will not touch my melder's soul."

"I have no plans to die." I spun toward Nivek. "We must go to this bone you were given as the heir. You were given one, right?"

"I know of the Wanderer's bone that connects to soul craft, yes." Nivek's grin teetered on something wickedly playful.

"We must retrieve it. If I am to unite all the bones to save these realms from falling in needless battles, then so be it. But in truth, I want to find them merely to keep them from Fadey."

"I hid it quite well, but I will say again, not all is as it seems," Nivek said. "Go over the Ledges, to the River Clan. You will learn what you need to know. What comes after will be up to the Norns."

Vague. Not exactly helpful, but with Fadey invading the mirror, it wasn't unwise to speak in such a way.

"Will you tell me where you hid the bone? What it looks like? How large?"

"I cannot say. I hope the bone has grown strong and sturdy after all these seasons. When you find the one who now holds it, tell him I wait for him in Salur. Tell them both. Won't you?"

He left the bone with someone over the Night Ledges? Perhaps two people? "I will tell them, if they even trust us."

"Wise thought. Tell them this and they should trust you: memories are always inked on my heart, my bones, and my soul."

Elisabet studied her son with a touch of uncertainty, as though she wanted to press him for more, but bit her tongue.

Skul Drek trailed a cold finger down my arm. "Time grows short."

The mirror would need to fade. Roark could not remain divided for so long. Already, Nivek wore the same whimsical smile, like his thoughts were drifting elsewhere. "Brother."

It took a nudge from my hand to draw Skul Drek's attention from me to the soul of the prince.

"Remember the tale I have told you tonight. It would be wise to recall that you will need the firstborns of craft. Don't forget them, for they have a part in this fate, and if it fails, they will not survive, much the same as the kingdoms."

"Wait." Panic tightened in my throat. "Are you saying Thane and Yrsa are in danger?"

Nivek took a step back. "Just keep them in mind as you go, Mother." Nivek waited until Elisabet looked to him. "Father misses you and saves a place at his side for when you meet again."

She pressed a hand to her heart, and the faintest glimmer of something golden burned from the second bone in my palm to the queen. Dozens of silky threads from her head to her foot, much the same as mine to her son.

My breath caught.

As the rot and decay of the mirror faded, as the playful gleam of the prince who'd saved me returned to wherever he rested, I knew the truth—the Draven queen carried with her a soul bond.

One that had never broken.

25

LYRA

THREE DAYS SINCE MEETING HIS FALLEN BROTHER, ROARK'S fatigue still left him sleeping like the dead each night.

Each day after the nightly meal, I could see the exhaustion settle in and insisted he let his craft recover. The control needed to hold our souls in the mirror for so great a time made him come damn close to collapsing.

Sleep abandoned me well before dawn. Seated on the edge of the bed, I brushed a lock of his dark hair to the side.

He slept with a furrowed brow, like he might be in pain or still locked in the constant rage of Skul Drek. With my thumb, I rubbed away the tension until he sighed in his sleep.

Pain lived in the gold of his eyes when we emerged from the trance. Roark tried to hide it, naturally, but it was there. An ache, a longing, one I only saw in his features when Thane was mentioned.

Doubtless, Roark—this part of my husband—yearned to speak

to his brother without the rage, the obsession, the bloodlust of the crueler layers of Skul Drek.

I leaned over and gently pressed a kiss to his temple.

In the corridor, Emi was there, braiding the end of her hair. "I feel this is retribution for all those mornings I woke you before first light in Stonegate."

I snickered. "Don't feign like you were sleeping. You, Emi Nightlark, are the only soul I know who greets every sunrise."

"How is he?" she asked when we emerged into the outer courtyard.

"Drained. He has only ever spoken with one soul at a time. But using Nivek's bone helped."

"Gods. To see Nivek again." Emi looked to the sky. "He was always teasing us young ones and playing games. Young as I was when he died, I loved him."

Warmth bloomed in my chest, but beneath it was a fierce ache. Nivek had not deserved to die.

I squeezed Emi's palm. "We're going to find who killed him. They need to pay for taking him from you all."

"Good." Emi held one door open, waiting for me to step into the somber morning light. "Gunter explained how souls weave small bonds on their own and by the time we all meet Salur we have multiple threads, like a tapestry of the connections made in life. But I never thought, well, I never thought Roark could speak to those who'd fallen."

By the look on her face, I had no doubt she thought of her lost mother.

I let my hand fall to her shoulder, uncertain what to say. At times, to say nothing, to merely stand at the side of a broken heart meant more than words.

The courtyard was larger than it seemed, with long, wide walks made of mossy flagstones.

There was a peace here. Trees towered over fragrant shrubs, and vines climbed along stone walls and wooden trellises. It felt like stepping from the harsh world to a land where worries could fade.

When we reached the far edge, my wing of the palace was nothing but dark walls and a distant spire. Emi unlatched an arched gate and led us into the outer wood where trees grew close, rows of sentinels shielding life in the court, and strode down a dirt path.

Dark Watch archers perched in the trees, clad in black and masked from the nose down, but they hardly moved as we strode beneath them. Doubtless more guards stood in the shadows, always observing.

Near a gentle creek was a small clearing separated from the wood by a thin fence. Each post was wrapped in twine with totems—skulls of ravens and hares, and talons—and dried floral vines.

Wooden pails were settled inside the gate, one filled with water and the other with red powder.

Emi dipped her fingers into the water, then the powder, dragging the crimson paste down her features. She signaled me to do the same.

"It is a symbol that we mean no harm to the resting place of the fallen," she explained, her voice soft. "We merely wish to remember."

Mounds adorned the space. Small blossoms coated some, and others were marked with heavy stones, but three near the back were raised and had a small opening covered by wooden doors. Three tombs.

Emi knelt in front of the smallest of the three. She clasped her hands in her lap. I settled next to her, studying the burial mounds.

"Some wish to be burned when they meet Salur. We set them

on the river or on the battlefield with gifts to take to the gods," she whispered. "Then we set the boat or the altar aflame."

I nodded. "We said farewell to folk much the same back home in Skalfirth."

"Others are buried beside us." Emi pointed to the mounds. "The hope is their wisdom and guidance will aid our royal house, our nobles, and the captains of the Dark Watch. Elisabet did not need to do so, but she gave my mother a royal burial after her body was found in the wood a season after her exile. My father raged for days to think his whore of a wife was buried here." She nodded to the largest mound in the center. "Especially after his brother found rest beside her."

King Vishon.

My jaw tightened. Emi's mother's mound had fresh flowers in front of the small door. I doubted a great deal that they were left by her horrid husband.

"I am Virki's blood," Emi said, never looking away from her mother's resting spot. "Gunter even tried to tell him. I was not yet eleven seasons, and I can still recall this stupid, feckless boy who hardly knew how to weave souls shouting at the king's brother that he was hurting his blood daughter."

"He could smell your connection."

"An elder soul weaver said much the same." Emi let her shoulders slump. "I don't know why my father started to despise us so fiercely. I don't know why he did not listen. My mother's craft was remarkable; she could read the true desires of a soul. It was how she always knew when I wanted a tale read or a sweet. She'd grant my soul's desire, as she put it. My mother would climb the trees with me; she taught me the wild ways of the Draven folk."

I laughed softly.

"I loved Virki, admired him. Gods, so much." Emi used the back of her hand to wipe away a stray tear. "I didn't understand how someone who once claimed to cherish me could hurt me in such a way.

"When I fled to Roark, I vowed never to love. I'd seen what had become of my cousin for bonds and what became of me." Emi's voice grew more frantic, heavier. "Then . . . then, Yrsa arrived at the keep and I had my first meeting with the foreign princess. It was as though a fist shot through my chest. I was only sixteen when I saw her for the first time, and Roark, in all his grumbly gestures, had to be the one to explain he believed a soul bond was there. She . . . she robbed my heart straight out from behind all those walls I'd built."

A sob broke from Emi's throat, as though the pain she'd kept buried from leaving Yrsa so abruptly broke free.

When she doubled over, I wrapped my arms around her shoulders, holding her close, letting her rage.

"I love her," Emi said through a sob. "And I betrayed her heart the same as . . . as my heart was betrayed."

"No." I shook her shoulders slightly and pressed a kiss to the top of her head. "No, Emi. You saved me. You saved Roark. You never hurt Yrsa the way your father hurt his family."

"Forgive me. I don't know what came over me." Emi straightened and laughed a little nervously. "Just . . . thoughts of her, of my mother, I think they would've gotten on so well. Yrsa is a royal, but gods, she has a wild spirit. No one loves to swim or climb or take risks in the shadows quite like her. I think that is why she and Thane are such good friends too."

"They are both reckless fools?"

Emi laughed, loud and free. "Yes. I suppose you could say that. I have no doubt, left to their own devices in Stonegate, soon we will hear of the whole ancient keep being scorched to the ground by mistake."

"You will see her again, Emi." I squeezed her hands. "We are finding a way back into Stonegate, for Kael, for Thane, and for Yrsa. Do not doubt for a moment that she is not in our thoughts as one who is in danger."

"I have no doubt the prince and Yrsa are wed." Emi stared at her hands. "I did not want to be the mistress, but I wanted to be there for her. For Thane."

"We don't know what's happened since we left," I told her. "Until we do, you cannot dwell on what might be. She needs you to fight against enemies she does not know are there. Yrsa loves you. She might be hurt, and I understand such hurt, but she will listen to you."

Emi gave me a wan smile. "I hope you're right. Truly."

I helped Emi place new blooms on her mother's burial mound, then King Vishon's, then the third—Nivek's.

"We'll find the truth," I whispered, a burn in my blood, like the prince could truly hear. "We'll stop the bloodshed. You did not allow me to say it before, but thank you. I swear to taunt him a bit in honor of you."

A commotion rose at the end of the wooded path when we reached the courtyard again. Brynn was there, laughing until tears fell to her cheeks. She had her hair braided over her shoulder and wore tattered trousers and a tight top made of linen and leather that revealed a great deal of her middle, and across her belt were pouches that smelled of meat.

Auki tromped down the steps into the courtyard, shouting. "Stop flailing. Gods, are you Draven or not? You need to command, no . . . *command him!*"

Emi and I shared a bemused look, then quickened our steps to the courtyard.

There, we saw a pack of young fara wolves, yapping and nipping at a few fara keepers' belts, where more pouches of meat were at the level of their snouts.

Fara pups struck my upper thigh, but Brynn taught me that in the weeks after a wolf bonds with a soul, that is when their frightening height and strength take hold.

For now, this young pack would remain the size of true wolves while being tamed and trained by the keepers.

Brynn had lost her ability to keep upright, and doubled over, laughing, gasping.

I understood why.

Roark was cornered near the wall, fighting for his life. A fara pup panted and yapped and attempted to howl more than once. The creature jumped, trying to lick the prince's face, then the wolf would land and spin around, its backside curling inward as though he could not contain his delight at the sight of Roark.

Overpowered, all the man could do was try to shove the pup away to get his palms positioned to calm the beast.

Auki kept shouting curses and his disappointment for the prince's lack of skill. Brynn's laughs trailed off, but her face was the shade of a bloody sun and damp with tears. She blew out a shuddering breath, blinking rapidly until she found me and Emi.

"Lyra." She bit down on her bottom lip until her voice steadied. "I think you may have just added to your household."

Dammit. "The wolf is bonding . . ."

"Seems so," she said when I did not go on. "I'd bet my life that your husband finally got his wolf."

A loud grunt escaped Roark's throat when he managed to push the excitable pup. With the help of Auki, he placed his palms over the brow of the panting wolf, and little by little, the creature fell to one side, slumbering, jaws open, like it was smiling.

I bit back a laugh and slipped my arm around Roark's waist. He jumped in surprise but relaxed when he recognized me.

With a quick kiss to my head, he waved one hand in front.
Damn beast won't leave me alone.

"Hmm. I think you might be glad about it."

A flush of red bridged over Roark's face. He didn't speak for a long pause. *I always wanted a fara, but things are different now.*

The wolf pup was bony. Its fur was a midnight shade of black with silver on each paw. One ear was curled and half the size of the other, as though it never grew properly. I knelt beside its sleeping form and stroked its wiry fur.

"Things may be different," I said and looked over my shoulder. "But surely they're not *that* different, are they?"

The smallest smile teased his mouth. *You want an enormous wolf following us everywhere?*

I kept stroking the large head of the pup. "Well, it's not like I can blame the poor thing. I know what it is like to be bonded to you, and it is a coveted experience."

Roark laughed softly. He wanted the wolf—the truth of it was in the way he kept glancing at the beast—but he did not want to inconvenience me with a burly creature bonded to our household, our family, until we went to Salur.

I wanted Roark to be Draven, the clan of his blood. I wanted him to have the wolf he drew in his boyish art as a child. I wanted him to find a bit of the happiness he was robbed of so long ago.

But I could not tell him any of this before a horn blared over the courtyard.

Roark stiffened at once and hurled me to my feet.

From one of the towers near the gates, a Dark Watch warrior called down. "Stav Guard! They've breached the borders! Dravenmoor is under attack!"

26

ROARK

THE PALACE FELL INTO VIOLENT MADNESS.

Dark Watch units swiftly assembled beyond the gates, cowls over their heads, short blades in hand. Ram horns thundered across the courtyard, the sound rippling to the lower townships and villages.

Already the road to the palace was filled with frantic Dravens. Families fled for the safety of the royal house, elders were aided by the young, and children sobbed as their mothers pulled them forward to their assigned wings and safeguards.

Exactly as my father had arranged safety protocols during my childhood.

Between every block of Dark Watch were lines of fara wolves with their bonded warriors.

Brynn and Auki were among the first to leave the courtyard. In haste, Brynn fastened a leather band around Òlmr's neck and sheathed two additional daggers. On command, the wolf would return to Brynn with a second wave of weapons, should she need it.

Auki worked with other keepers and armored the packs with leather across their haunches, spines, and skulls. My uncle barked orders and surrounded himself with half a dozen fara. He tugged the thick woolen hood over his head.

I wheeled on Emi. *Take Lyra—*

"No." Lyra shoved between us, the damn fara pup now awake and following close behind. "Don't even say it. They are here for me—"

Exactly, I interrupted. *In what world would I send my wife to those who wish to harm her?*

Lyra's mouth tightened. "If we are to fight this together— *bonded*—then every fight we face we will be sending each other into battle with those who wish to harm us both. Do not think for a moment that any Jorvan out there will allow you to live should you be captured."

We had no damn time for this argument.

Lyra took my hand and squeezed three times. "Roark, this fight is mine as much as it is yours. They want my life, so let me fight for it. They want yours, so let me fight for you as fiercely as you fight for me."

Gods. I curled my hand behind her head and slammed her mouth to mine. The kiss was fast and heated and came close to painful. All I desired was to lock her away, to never let a blade come near her, but she was not wrong.

Lyra's life had been shredded from these battles for her craft as much as mine had. If anyone deserved a bit of retribution, it was her.

We broke apart, our breaths heavy. My fingers moved quickly against her cheek. *Arrows?*

She nodded. "I won't miss."

Stay as far from them as you can. Consider that every move they make could be a trap.

"This is not where we end, Ashwood." She grinned with a touch of malice. "I'm not nearly done with you."

Together we followed the flood of Draven warriors, farmers, smiths, and any soul able to hold a blade toward the weapon stores kept at the base of the palace. Already lines of men and women were tossing out blades in a hurried manner.

I snatched the first broadsword and ax I could grab. Lyra and Emi were already fitted with quivers filled with bone arrows, hickory bows in their grips. Gunter stood between them, clad in his Dark Watch hood. Yanson stood at his son's back to ensure the two crossed short blades on Gunter's shoulders were secure.

"First battle together." Gunter flashed me a grin. "I've heard such fanciful tales of the Death Bringer. Impress me, old friend, or I'll never let you live down your mortification."

Keep her alive, and I will bathe in all the blood you wish.

"Almost had that one. Something about 'him alive.' No, you pointed at Lyra." Gunter glanced at my wife. "Keep *her* alive. Well, obviously. She's much prettier than you."

Lyra rolled her eyes. "Let us all stay alive."

"Excellent plan." Gunter shook out his hands and clapped his father on the shoulder. "Shall we go kill some Jorvans?"

Without another word, Lyra shoved through, her grip on the bow. "Roark. If Thane is there, we should try to speak to him."

Agreed. If we can.

"And . . . if they have Kael." She closed her eyes. "I don't know what I will do."

I pinched her chin between my fingers, forcing her to look at me. *Kill anyone near him, and we will take him back.*

Her jaw tightened. "Stay alive, Ashwood, or I will find you in the mirror and grant you no peace until you die, all to aggravate you some more."

I chuckled softly and ran my thumb along her bottom lip

before peeling myself from her and rushing toward the ground warriors. Lyra and Emi raced for the slopes and trees with the other archers.

A yap and growl followed me. The fara wolf plodded behind, tail wagging. One palm on the beast's head, I brought him to a halt. There was a stirring in my chest, a strange sort of affection for the creature, and I had no time to focus on it.

I held the beast's golden stare. Not speaking with anything but thought, I told it, *Follow her. If you are with me, you'll know who I mean. Go.*

The wolf sat on its haunches and scratched its mangled ear, its tongue hanging out the side of its mouth.

Damn stupid beast.

I sprinted forward to the front of the line. My folk stepped aside as I passed, some clapping me on the shoulders, others merely roaring cries for bloodshed. Only when I reached the head of the line did I pause.

Perhaps a hundred paces down the hillside, at the edge of the village, no less than fifty Stav Guard stood in lines behind a wall of round shields.

"At your word, Prince."

The queen strode through the crowd. Her hair was tied high on her head and leathers coated her body. In her grip was a dagger, and strapped across her middle were throwing knives. No one could handle a knife like Elisabet Foxglen.

Rumors of the Dark Watch's love of leaving pieces of their victims across the Red Ravines were in part because of my mother. The queen took it as a personal slight should anyone attempt to harm her clan.

She held a love of pinning fingers, eyes, and tongues to trees on Jorvan lands.

I pointed at her. She was the word of Dravenmoor, the queen.

My mother turned to the Dark Watch. "Follow the lead of your prince. No one knows the battle strategies of the Stav Guard better than my son."

Warriors pounded their swords to their chests, a call to arms, of loyalty.

I faced the Stav Guard.

We trained them to stand in a block of shields, to force the enemy to break through. No doubt archers would be in those trees, taking out our armies as we drew nearer. Weakness would be found in the flanks. We needed to encircle them, put them on the defensive, and I needed to do it without losing lives.

This battle was the first where my clan would see me stand with them instead of slaughtering the ravagers sent to face my blade.

It would be the first time they saw Lyra fire Draven arrows.

It was another step in destroying Dravenmoor's mistrust for melding craft.

At my side Gunter clapped a hand on my shoulder. "Plan?"

In the two weeks since the Dark Watch discovered us, Gunter had studied hand speak under Lyra and Emi's tutelage, but he still could pick out only a few basic terms.

I took a knee and dragged a finger in the soil, drawing out the primitive idea. I formed a circle, pointed at each flank of the Dark Watch to aim at their own side of the Stav Guard. The marks and the timing I repeated until captains nodded and passed down the word to their units.

I directed (with Gunter's broken translation) a Dark Watch captain to guide the archers on their shots.

"Let Lyra do as she does," Gunter called after him. "Those bones will find their marks, I've seen it done."

On the final directive, I cut a line down the center. A way to split their ranks, to force them into our net.

Gunter rubbed a hand on the back of his neck. "How do we

break the wall through the middle? There are Stav archers. They'll take us out."

I brushed soil from my fingers and stood. With my thumb I traced the edge of the scar on my throat.

Gunter's mouth split in a cruel grin. "Well, this is the newest favored battle plan. At your word, Death Bringer."

I faced the army below.

One of the captains lowered his shield. "Sentry Ashwood. How good to see you. Jorvandal sends their best wishes for your union with the melder."

They knew Lyra was my wife? How?

"Roark." Gunter drew me back to the moment. "This begins a fight for something bigger than Jorvandal and Dravenmoor. Remember that. You are fighting for your freedom, for hers. They are not your folk anymore."

A muscle throbbed in my jaw against the clench of my teeth.

"Ashwood." The captain shouted again. "A gift for you and your bride from the House of Oleg at Stonegate. You and the melder slaughtered our king, so the royal house felt you both deserved much the same."

From behind the wall of shields the Stav tossed a woman. She landed on her knees, sobbing and clutching a totem tied around her neck with a strip of leather. I knew her but did not recall her face until a bony elder was tossed beside her.

Blood stained his brow, and his silver beard was soaked in it. Injured as he was, the man went to the trembling woman and held her against his thin chest as she sobbed her frantic prayers to the gods.

They were from Skalfirth. I'd seen them the night I took Lyra. They served in Jarl Jakobson's household.

They'd raised Lyra and Darkwin.

I lifted my ax and pointed the blade at the captain, a silent threat. He knew what would become of him should he take the next step. He'd seen me deliver much the same to ravagers and traitors time and again.

The captain used his shield to strike the man's skull. A wet scream ripped from the woman's throat. She wailed and padded at the old man's head, holding her palms over the gash.

When two Stav lowered their shields, blades in hand, I made a frenzied gesture to the Draven archers to take aim. Lyra would not lose another soul she held dear. Men I once led stood down there. Most likely craved a chance to cut the throat of the traitorous Sentry.

Remnants of guilt were there . . . for a moment.

Guilt quickly slid into bloodlust, remorse faded to enmity. Frigid ribbons of night sliced across my throat, my shoulders, my middle. From my hands emerged another set. One step, and the shadowed form of every cruel desire I kept in my soul took shape, one pace ahead of me.

The captain faltered. "You're nothing but a demon, not even mortal. Are you from the molten hell, Ashwood? We Stav always thought as much because of your dirty Draven blood, but we simply couldn't say it to your face."

Darkness reached for the bastard, faster, desperate, yet it was still too slow.

The captain gave his signal. Swords from the two Stav standing over the prisoners dropped on the throats of the man and woman. Her sobs bled into gasps and choking coughs. Until both fell back on the ground.

Dead.

In the woman's hand the totem remained clasped tightly, a plea for protection, for safety.

Her gods abandoned her.

A scream erupted from the trees. Lyra. She'd seen them fall.

No mistake, she wanted to bolt onto the battlefield, but she held her position with the archers in the trees.

Through the heat of our bond, I felt her agony, like a hundred bone needles piercing my heart.

Those who caused it would pay.

Once before, the suffocating, insatiable craving for death had taken me. The night I learned that Tomas Grisen had opened the gates for ravagers to find Lyra.

I'd torn his body apart and spiked his head on the wall of Stonegate.

From the murky shadows the form of the deledan soul rose again. Dark mists pulsed around its shoulders, a sign of fury at the failure, a signal Lyra's heart would break again, and the cost for such a slight would be blood and bone.

The dark soul whirled around, eyes burning with hate.

At my back, boots shuffled when the Dark Watch shifted in unease. In the next heartbeat, shadows broke apart and rushed forward down the slope again. But this was not made of desperation; this was a flood of savagery.

I gave a brisk nod to Gunter. He unsheathed one of the swords on his back and bellowed a roar. Warriors at his back followed.

We ran after the darkness. Half of the Dark Watch veered to opposing sides, aiming at the edges of the Stav Guard shield wall.

Archers shouted from the walls, the trees, the hillsides. Overhead, an arch of fiery arrows burned across the sky, a beacon leading us forward.

The barrage of the Dark Watch shuddered across the damp soil. From the far gates, more chants echoed from hidden units of watchers. Howls and snarls followed. The units of fara keepers and bonded wolves rushed through the trees. More than one cry of pain followed when Stav hidden in the trees, or archers tumbling off their branch perches, fell to the claws and teeth of the packs.

My chest burned as I ran, closer, closer.

Walls of shadows engulfed the Stav. I wanted their souls to be mine.

One breath, two. My dark soul converged like a cloak over the Jorvans. Like a frenzied warrior, a blade of darkness lashed through hearts, through throats. It rammed into chests.

Stav Guard roared commands behind their shields. Men stumbled as darkness engulfed their bodies, leaving them alive but empty. Swords dropped. Shields fell. Stav faltered on their feet the more I craved their destruction.

At long last, the shield wall split.

"Take them! Now!" Ten paces away, Elisabet shouted the remaining Dark Watch forward.

Another wave of burning arrows assaulted the Stav Guard. A collision of steel and blood burst between two sides. I braced, sword and ax at the ready, and leapt into the fray.

My blade struck a Stav's short blade. We locked, and spun, and dodged until I swung the ax against his ribs. He fell. Another came. And another. Battle was euphoric and horrid all at once. The darkest pieces of my soul craved the slide of steel over bone. The other craved to survive.

Never before had I cared if I fell in battle. Now all I desired was to walk free of here, back to Lyra.

Hot, sticky blood splattered across my face. My muscles throbbed, desperate for more.

A man sobbed nearby when Gunter yanked on the Stav's braid, dragging him to the ground. My old friend straddled the Stav and rammed his sword through the man's throat, letting out a bellow of delight as the Stav choked on his own blood.

Another Stav fell forward, a knife from the queen buried in his middle. Elisabet moved like a wraith, there and gone. She leapt over a corpse and had her blade free of the Stav's belly before his body struck the ground.

"The Sentry!" The captain who'd ordered the deaths of Lyra's folk pointed his blade, aimed toward my heart.

He rushed at me, another Stav at his side.

I rolled my ax in my hand, crouched, and met their attack head-on. One slashed for my throat. I ducked and rammed the head of my ax across his chest when he stumbled. The captain was swifter. One edge of his blade caught my arm. I dodged a second strike and spun away. He jabbed. I swung at his limbs.

Our blades locked, drawing our faces near. Blood spilled over his brows. He bared his teeth. "Traitor."

I grinned, tasting the hot drips of metallic blood on my tongue.

He made a move to break away but let out a gasp, mouth open, and went still.

From the captain's pores, dark mists flowed over his body. Inky black spilled from his eyes like poisonous tears. One more heartbeat and the full form of my rotten soul stepped through.

A burn of something golden flashed within me. For a moment, I could feel it knot in my chest, as though I carried a second heartbeat. Little by little, shadows of the darker soul crushed the light until the threads of a living soul were snuffed out.

A wash of cold surged through my insides. The Stav captain fell to his knees, listless and lost. I sent the rest of him to Salur with a swing of my ax, then turned on my heel in the same instant the hiss of an arrow hummed over my shoulder.

A sick thud sounded at my side. The point of the arrow pierced the space between the eyes of a Stav Guard whose sword was raised against me.

I hadn't seen him.

The shot was impeccable. Perfect.

The darker soul and I looked up the hillside. Lyra lowered her bow, a look of beautiful ruthlessness on her features.

A horn blew, followed by calls for retreat. The Stav were pulling back. Dark Watch warriors cheered, blades in the air. But the cry of a name froze my blood.

"Kael! Gods, Kael!" Lyra, as though in a trance, lowered her bow and raced down the hillside.

Emi screamed for her to stop. More than one Dark Watch archer sped after her. Lyra kept calling Darkwin's name, but Kael Darkwin was not there.

All I saw was a Stav Guard holding out his arms, as though beckoning my damn wife straight into them.

27

LYRA

SELENA AND THORIAN WERE GONE. FROM THE TREES, I'D seen them sobbing, yearned to run to them, to shield them.

I could not do any of it. They were innocent and fell to the gods because of their love for a shy girl and a mischievous boy.

The only relief that filled my heart now was knowing that Kael found me. I nearly sobbed at the contentment of his cheerful grin, like a downy bed after a long day. My brother called for me, ran toward me. His arms were open wide. Gods, he looked healthy, safe.

A fierce yank, as though a hook dug into my chest, urged me to run to him. It was a compulsion.

Somewhere in my mind, I thought I might've heard someone cry out my name. Even a burn in my chest; it was as though something yanked on the bonds of my heart. A warning, a plea.

Dread stacked in my chest when more Stav waited at a distance, merely watching me race for my brother. Why did they watch on like this was . . . expected?

Stop. A hiss, a command, a frigid snap of a voice in my soul.

Fear lanced through my veins. Why could I not stop?

The nearer I came to Kael, the crueler his smile became. His features shifted. No longer the handsome edges of a strong jaw and nose; now his chin weakened and a russet beard grew along freckled cheeks.

This was not Kael.

Panic, sharp and cruel, surged through my blood. I stumbled, desperate to stop, but like a lure to a hook, I was snared.

The Stav Guard who stood where Kael had been held a pouch in one palm. Even from ten paces away I could taste the potent herbs of spell casts and the tang of blood. Ingir sent one of her craft spells. I knew it like I knew my brother was not here.

"Lyra!" Now Emi's frantic scream rattled in my skull.

I fell to the ground, scraping at the soil, clawing to get away. Soon, bright, hot agony tore at my flesh, as though whatever craft had summoned me was drawing the blood from my veins.

In the next instant, a wound formed over my palm, open and gushing, but no knife was nearby. All gods, the spell cast was truly pulling my blood toward the Stav. It was ripping it from my own flesh.

"Time to come home, Melder." The Stav Guard laughed.

Shouts from the Dark Watch ordered for arrows, blades, every attention to halt the capture of the melder. No mistake, Roark would abandon the innocent lives in the palace to save mine. A little longer. Hold. Hold.

A snarl and rabid growl came from somewhere over my shoulder. A single heartbeat, and the sound of snapping jaws was overpowered by a shrill cry of a man's horror.

The hook in my veins snapped. I fell forward, gasping. Free.

I spun around, desperate to scramble away, but stopped.

The large paws of the excitable fara pup slashed at the Stav

Guard. The young wolf bit and scratched and tore at the man's throat, face, and hands. In the distance, I took note of Stav archers aiming at the pup.

"Jorvan archers!" I screamed and pointed at the trees.

Fiery Draven arrows rained over the Jorvan forces, sending them back under the cover of the trees. I scrambled for the wolf. A dark, searing rage burned in my skull. They used Kael against me; they taunted me.

For that, this guard would pay too. They all would.

I would see to it that Ingir of House Oleg knew her mistake.

The pup snarled and snapped his jaws. Beneath the beast's attack, the Stav Guard screamed and writhed, desperate to shield his face. Already open gashes marred his skin. I snatched the pouch from the Stav's hand to avoid any further hooks from damn blood spells.

"Dammit!" The moment I touched the pouch, a barb of pain shot through the gaping wound in my palm.

I let it fall to the grass. Another gash opened and crossed with the split wound over my palm, and burning dripped down my wrist.

Teeth clenched, I shoved aside the pain, knelt by the screaming Stav Guard's head, and rammed my fingertips into his open wounds.

He roared his agony.

Craft flooded my blood with such ferocity that I swayed.

Usually when I melded, the threads were golden, dainty, lovely. Be it from the rage, the hatred, or something else, I didn't know, but the threads that burst from the Stav Guard's flesh were boiling red.

I did not care what my craft did to him, I simply began to stitch. Bone split under my fingertips, shifting down his face, around his skull. New shards fastened on his jaw, below the socket of his eye.

The wolf bit down on the man's shoulder, shaking his large head like he might be trying to rip the arm free. The Stav Guard let out a gurgled cry, already his mouth had grown misshapen beneath my touch.

Soon he made no sound at all. His teeth were melded shut, one gnarled, solid barrier to his mouth. I screamed at his manipulated face, ignoring the blood, the wounds. His eyes still had light left in them.

I reached deeper. Craft sought the threads of his bones, shifting and breaking, melding and remaking. Until the small bones of his throat came to light. Narrow threads, thin but strong, were there. I pulled one through a wound in his neck, then wove it back in, searching for the upper bones of his spine.

Stitch after stitch, bones turned molten and joined with others until there was no opening left for him to breathe through. Shards and fragments of his throat were melded across his airway, joined front to back.

The Stav Guard jolted and his chest puffed, desperate for air.

I pulled back my hands, the lust for his death fading the longer I watched his soul flee to the gods.

Bile burned in my throat. The Stav Guard thrashed and trembled, clawing weakly at his neck. Even the pup stepped away, his bloody lips locked in a snarl.

I retched.

Arms encircled me and pulled me against a hard chest. Inside was the beat of a heart I knew so well. Steady. Strong. Mine. Roark was covered in blood, but still he held my cheek to his heart until the body beside me stopped moving at long last.

I tilted my head to see what I had done.

The Stav Guard was destroyed. By the wolf and his melded bones, the man had been slaughtered.

Down the hillside, Jorvan warriors fled toward the distant ravines. Left in their wake, the fallen were sprawled across the lower township, blood staining the stone paths and meadows around the gates. I did not know how many Dravens fell.

Look at me. Roark's gentle words brushed over my cheek.

Blood and gore soaked his skin, but I doubted he minded. Roark brushed damp hair from my face, inspecting my face for wounds.

"I thought he was Kael," I whispered. "It was a blood spell. I couldn't stop."

Roark scanned the pouch beside the dead Stav. He nodded and pressed a kiss to my brow.

I clung to his tunic, desperate to slow the race of my pulse. "I've never . . . never hated so fiercely. I wanted him to s-s-suffer, Roark. I wanted him to hurt. I am as cruel as Fadey."

Roark's arms tightened around my shoulders. He held me for a long moment before tilting my chin. The calming brush of his fingers would always be an anchor in the storm.

We never truly know a heart.

I grinned. "Until we see the darkness inside."

I might like to see yours. Roark tugged on my bottom lip before gesturing against my skin. *Never feel guilt for keeping yourself alive. Never.*

I was not so certain that keeping myself alive was what I had done.

"Lyra." Emi skidded at my side and flung her arms around what little was left to embrace beyond Roark's hold. "By the gods, what was that?"

"Blood craft," I mumbled against Roark's tunic.

"Shit." Emi crept over to the bloodied pouch and sniffed.

"That's horrid. Yrsa always told me the more rancid the smell, the darker the spell cast."

Footsteps drew closer. Òlmr's snout sniffed my face, then moved to the black wolf pup, licking away the blood on his head. The smaller fara swished his tail and nipped at the elder wolf. Brynn and Auki lowered to a crouch, a look of horror written on their similar features at the sight of the Stav.

I turned away, all at once unwilling to watch what tentative bonds of friendship we'd fashioned snap once they realized the truth of what melding craft could do.

"Now, this is more like it." Gunter's voice broke through my fears. He laughed mercilessly and nudged the dead Stav with his boot. He beamed and waved a finger between me and Roark. "I'm not certain which of the two of you have stolen my breath more."

"Pardon?" Auki sniffed. "Did you not see how my three best wolves tore a captain apart?"

"Damn." Gunter huffed. "I do love when you sic the wolves."

"What's with the look, Lyra?" Brynn tilted her head. "You truly should see how Auki calls to the wolves. I've only been able to speak to Òlmr and at times one elder fara together. Three is quite impressive."

She thought I was not impressed with *them*?

I blinked, confused. "I would like to see it . . . sometime."

"Were you harmed? The head, perhaps? You look as though you do not know where you are."

"I just thought, well, you all were raised to despise melders, so I thought if you saw what I'd done . . ."

Gunter snorted and nudged the corpse again. "Lyra, we've been waiting for something as fearsome as this since you arrived. In truth, I'd heard such ruthless tales of melders, I thought you'd be slaughtering the lot of us by the day."

"Auki saw one of our warriors after Melder Fadey got to him

during the raids." Brynn swallowed and looked down at the Stav. "He no longer had a face, and his chest was turned inside out, like his ribs had grown backward. Gunter's not wrong. We know what melders can do."

"Simply glad you did it on our side this time." Gunter gripped Brynn's shoulder. "Any losses?"

"Two wolves, three keepers. Another took an arrow but still lives." Brynn looked toward the palace. "Time will tell how she fares."

"My father said the count of ground warriors is near a dozen. Village folk, we don't know yet. I hear they killed old Aldr on his farm when they crossed the border. But his grandchildren made it to the palace," said Gunter. "Pyres will light the courtyards."

Battles were beginning.

How many more funeral pyres would we face before they were done?

28

LYRA

ROARK TOOK ME TO WHERE THORIAN AND SELENA HAD
fallen. A hate, jagged and harsh, took hold in my heart.

Stonegate, House Oleg, Fadey—whoever was behind their
deaths would pay in blood.

I cried silent tears and washed Selena's neck and her gentle
face where furrows still worried her brow. I placed Draven totems and talismans of luck and safety for her to take into Salur to
chase away the tricksters.

Thorian was my shield as a child, a sturdy fisherman who
would stand one step in front of me, arms crossed, when other
young ones from town would mock my dirty fingers or poorly
hemmed dresses.

Roark found a silver fishing spear in one of the royal holds
and placed it on the mound beside the man. He gestured *Thank
you* to them both. Thanks for what, I could only guess, and I assumed it had everything to do with their love for me.

"They were kind souls," I said, my voice rough. "They were mine, and they did not deserve this."

Roark kept an arm around my shoulders. *Their names will be marked with honor in Dravenmoor.*

The Draven clan did not wash or remove remnants of battle before the funeral pyres ignited.

They believed that to remain clad in battle wear, with the blood still on their skin, honored the fallen souls for their sacrifice. It was proof to the gods that their warriors had fought well and ought to be handed curved horn after curved horn as they joined the revelry in Salur.

Rows of pyres burned through the courtyard. Some Dark Watch sat on the cobbles or in the tall grass while folk who'd been barricaded in the palace served the warriors ale and water.

Healers tended to wounds, but I was left without words for the way the folk of Dravenmoor stood stalwartly to honor their losses.

It was more than in Stonegate. Here, they did not falter until the pyres were nothing but ash.

They would not let their lost ones leave this world alone.

Elisabet walked the lines of her Dark Watch, handing out bread and cheese and skins of water. Roark followed, my hand in his. I did not know what I was expected to say and followed the queen's and prince's lead.

Elisabet kissed the brows of her warriors, thanking them softly for their honor and effort to defend their land. Roark clasped forearms and gave stiff nods until I stopped in front of the captain of the archers.

He was a man made of iron, with a beard split into three braids, and missing one front tooth.

I held out a hand. His face was coated in sweat and smoke. For a breath, the man studied me, then took hold of my palm, squeezing.

"I heard your command," I said, my voice soft. "When I was locked in their spell, I heard you command the archers to stop them."

"You are Draven now." He was brisk and practically grunted his reply.

I would get no more of a response as to why the man defended me, and I was coming to understand that to the clan of Dravenmoor, no more of a reason was needed.

When the pyres died, I leaned against the wall of the palace, away from the crowds, waiting for Roark to finish speaking to Auki about the black wolf who would not stop following him. I chuckled. Even now, the pup sat two paces from my husband, waiting patiently.

Auki was the most fluent with Roark's hand speak, and it was like a new man spoke with his old friend. The mistrust and bitterness had slowly faded the more they could speak and even laugh at times. Gunter and Brynn were not far behind, but they fared better with Roark's parchment writings or Emi's and my translations.

"I live for the day Draven blood will stop spilling for a woman who should not exist."

My body stilled. Virki emerged from behind a post, a massive gray fara wolf at his side. The man was blood-soaked, and it only added to the cruelty in his eyes.

"I would take care with your words. I've discovered I rather enjoy melding mouths shut."

Virki's lip curled. "You think you have a place here, but you do not. My nephew believes in soul bonds so fiercely, but he does not truly want you. He yearns for the bond to strengthen his own craft, which it clearly does. In time, he will come to resent you for all the pain you caused in his life."

His words were a knife to my heart. Cruel words my own mind had said more than once.

I schooled my face into indifference. "Then you do not know your nephew."

"Perhaps I don't any longer. It's been known to happen."

"What is it you want?" I clenched my fists at my sides.

"Vengeance," Virki bit out through his teeth. "You will never know what your life has cost not only me, but every kingdom. You keep us in battles instead of greeting a brighter future."

"I do not make the choices for greedy kings. If battles must be fought in their lust for power, that is on their shoulders."

"Is that what you say to ease your own guilt? The Jorvans know you are now playing the role of a Draven royal. This was merely the beginning of their attempts to retrieve you." The man leaned in, his voice low. "I for one cannot wait until you are placed exactly where you belong—Salur."

I watched him stride away, unsettled and enraged, with a new determination to find the bones of the Wanderer. To rob these corrupted lands of the lust for more power. I could not wait to slit Fadey's throat and prove to these wretched kingdoms that I was no threat to them.

If I could merely survive long enough to do it all.

"HOW DID THEY KNOW WE'D WED?" I LAY OVER THE MATTRESS, scratching behind the pup's ears.

Roark, water still dripping down his bare chest from the hot baths, removed his belt and draped it over the back of a wooden chair instead of placing it in the wardrobe.

When he turned around, he frowned. *The beast does not sleep on the bed.*

I snorted and scratched the wolf even more until his long hind leg flicked like he might be chasing the same scratch.

"How can you say that? He *saved* me, Roark." I kissed the

wolf's snout. "Don't pretend like you're not bonding with him. I see it."

Roark slid over the bed and curled his arms around the sturdy, heavy body of the fara.

The wolf panted and wriggled, like he believed his new bonded might, at last, give him the attention he craved. Instead, Roark shoved the beast across the mattress to the foot of the bed.

He drew me into his arms and held out a palm when the pup tried to return to his place near the pillows. *No*, he gestured swiftly. *She is my wife. Stay there. Be glad your ass is not on the floor.*

A small whine slipped from the wolf, but he obeyed and watched us from the foot of the bed.

I let an arm fall across Roark's stomach, my head on his shoulder. With care he lifted my wrapped hand. The bandages were stained with the slow trickle of blood.

"I'm fine." I curled my palm back.

It hasn't stopped bleeding.

"It was a blood cast," I said with a sigh. "I'm sure the wound will heal differently."

Roark pinched his lips but did not say more. We already had spoken to one of the Draven healers, who'd instantly gone to his herb books looking for protections against blood craft. All we could do was wait.

With his gentle, brutal fingers, Roark drew small circles across my shoulder, saying nothing. We simply sat for a moment in silence.

I do not know whose order brought them, Roark wrote on my skin after a long pause.

I lifted my head. "You speak of Thane?"

He nodded. *Thane is named Bold for a purpose, but this was reckless. Like poking a rabid wolf.*

"I do not believe Thane gave the order," I said. "He wouldn't have killed Sel and Thorian. It had to have been Ingir. They came to take me."

Tension grooved over his brow, but he didn't respond.

"Do you not think so?" I held out my palm. "This felt intentional."

But Fadey and Ingir are not fools. They have made their plans for seasons. You think they would throw them away by sending a unit of Stav Guard against the whole of the Dark Watch?

"So you think it was all a ruse?"

A distraction. Roark tightened his hold on my shoulders and held me closer. *What I know of Stonegate is that the Jorvans are not above sacrificing their own men to get a drop on the enemy.*

To find us. To peek beyond our borders. I traced the hard planes of Roark's chest with one finger. "They know you are the prince of Dravenmoor. Someone sent word to Stonegate that we had wed, and they came."

Yes, a report like that likely spurred the action, Roark agreed. *I would've wanted to do the same if it were reversed. I do think that if it was Thane who ordered this, he wouldn't have done it this way.*

"Meaning?"

He would've sent a warning, or a taunt to get under my skin.

I snorted against his chest. "I can see it. 'Roark, you ass. Not inviting me to your nuptials? True we are, at present, not seeing eye to eye, but I ought to have been there in the first row. I'll never forgive you for this slight. Best, Thane, the better prince.'"

My cheek bounced against his heart when he let out one of his breathy laughs.

After a pause he sobered. *Thane is not like Damir or his mother. He would not risk innocent Stav Guard. He would rather fight beside them, and if he cannot, he pisses and moans.*

True enough. One of my most favored interactions with Thane the Bold was the night we snuck away from our assigned protections and fired arrows into the onslaught of ravagers at the gates.

"Elisabet wouldn't have drawn attention to us, would she?"

It took a moment for Roark to respond, then: *I don't believe so. I hesitate to say it, but she seems sincere in wanting us to destroy the missing bones.*

"You are hesitant to trust her in general. I understand. But do you think you'll ever trust her again?"

He considered my words, mindlessly running his fingers against my skin. *I can understand the desperation to keep me alive after Nivek was lost. But I have a soul bond now. I cannot ever fathom anything that would bring me to willingly break it. She split my father's soul, making him a Skul Drek. To do so, she had to know their bond would weaken.*

"Has ours weakened?"

Roark's mouth tightened for a moment before he went on without acknowledging the truth of our intact bond. *But how would she know it was possible to keep a bond with a split soul? Either way, the distrust is deeper than willingly dividing her soul bond's soul; it is allowing him to be killed.*

"But it was done so you would live. Don't you think your father would want you to survive?"

But his mind—

I clasped his hands before he could finish his gestures. "You told me there were moments when he had a clear thought. Perhaps that night was one."

I did not understand my defense of the queen, but I could not manage to keep my tongue still. As though some deeper piece of my soul yearned for Roark to have some . . . peace, some kindness left from a bloodstained past.

He let out a rough, breathy sigh and gestured slowly. *The point is, I do not understand her true motivations.*

I had not mentioned what I witnessed on the queen when Nivek was summoned, the web of an unbreakable bond. I did not know if I truly trusted Elisabet myself, but the words came all the same. "I do not think her bond was broken."

Roark tilted his head. *Why?*

"I know you see things differently when we speak soul to soul, but I saw endless weaves of a bond across her soul, Roark. I saw it, and it looked so similar to ours."

He rubbed the place over his brow. *But she knew that to rend my soul would break my bond. That was why it was done.*

I propped myself onto one elbow and studied his features. Behind the anger I could almost see a flicker of hope. "Unless she knew a different truth."

You believe Elisabet of Dravenmoor willingly allowed me to keep a soul bond with a melder, knowing it would be considered treason? You think she has been playing a part all this time?

"Why did you not kill Thane?" I asked, my thoughts tumbling in new theories, new possibilities. "You could have taken his soul, and the ravagers would've ended him, but Skul Drek let him live."

Roark winced. Nothing disturbed him more than knowing how close he'd come to killing the prince. *Some of it is a blur since I was not in control entirely, but it was as though, all at once, I recognized him. My hate, my cruelty, could not take him, for he had earned none of it.*

"Your mother had a great deal of control over you in those moments. True, you had regained some, but I believe she could have forced you. What if she . . . didn't want you to lose another brother?"

I stopped when Thane faced me. I could feel him, sense him. Somewhere in the darkness, I managed to pull on the connection between us and stop the slaughter. The queen would have allowed him to die.

I did not know what to say to that.

Roark sat up and propped his elbows on his knees, fists in front of his mouth, considering every word. *If her bond with my father is intact, I don't know what to think anymore. She warned me, no one ever truly knows the queen's next step.*

I pressed a kiss to one of his shoulders. "Perhaps we won't ever know her every plan. Whether she was involved in sending word of our union or not, it doesn't matter. She wants the bones destroyed, same as us. So we must make our own moves. We're running out of time."

Roark peered at me. *And what moves are you thinking, wife?*

"If the Jorvans know of us, if Ingir is making such violent moves against us, I think we must speak to Thane. I don't know how, but he needs to know what is going on in his own kingdom."

Roark lifted one of my palms off his chest and kissed the center. *Agreed. Auki and Brynn have smuggled enough supplies for about a week. We could make our way to the Black Fjords and send word to Stonegate.*

"Don't you think it would only draw out the Stav Guard?"

Not if Thane is the only one to understand the missive.

I furrowed my brow.

Roark offered a sad sort of smile as he spoke. *When we were boys, Thane and I had secret signals we'd write to each other. A code, you could say. If we can get past the Dark Watch, perhaps I can send one. It might intrigue him enough to meet.*

Hope flared like a roaring flame in my chest. "When?"

He shook his head. *The úlfur will be more protective of the borders and of you after the attack. It might still be some time, but I will learn their new rotations and make a plan from there.*

My shoulders slumped a bit in disappointment. It felt like we had no time left. I did not know what Fadey could see in the mirror, if he could only enter with me, or if he'd managed to slip into the trance on his own.

I did not know if he'd heard any hint of our discussion with Nivek.

Roark began to shift so he could face me directly, but he let out a rough grunt when the wolf pup took our nearness as his cue to nuzzle his bony head between us, his tongue lapping at Roark's cheek. He shoved the beast away and pointed to a fur mat in the corner of the room, a silent demand to get off the bed.

The fara tucked his tail, plodded to the mat, and curled onto his lonely new bed with a look of utter dejection.

I snickered and kissed the top of Roark's shoulder. "We have another problem."

Which is?

"You, husband, need to choose a name for your new little wolf."

LYRA

"WHY, IN THE NAME OF ALL THE GODS, WOULD YOU CALL this brute of a fara wolf Kyrre?" Gunter looked disgusted.

"What's wrong with it?" I scratched behind Kyrre's shorter ear.

"It means 'peaceful.'" Gunter raked his fingers through his hair. "Who wants a fara wolf named 'peaceful'?"

Throws them off, Roark gestured three times before Gunter made a signal that he'd understood.

"I still think you should've gone with Myrkr or something a little fearsome."

I chuckled and let Kyrre loose to join the other young wolves in the pen. Brynn had insisted upon a strict training regimen for the pup with the keepers first, then Roark would need to learn how his fara would take to his commands.

"With you, I'd use a whistled tune," Auki had explained. "Specific sounds for commands. Brynn has words she will shout at Òlmr. It becomes like you are both warriors, side by side."

In the days after the attack from the Stav Guard, we'd mourned the fallen, worked with our new fara wolf, witnessed the Dark Watch pike the heads of the fallen Stav Guard at the ravines so any more attempts from Stonegate would be met with a warning, and told the others everything.

From Nivek's words, to Elisabet's strange loyalty in one moment, then her coldness in the next. More and more, I was convinced Roark's mother wore many masks.

Like us, they all agreed that whatever secrets awaited us over the ledges, we had to find them first and soon.

Roark had written a missive to Thane in their coded words and acquired a raven to deliver it. There'd been nothing of a response since.

Truth be told, I wasn't certain Fadey and Ingir had not intercepted the bird through their blood casts.

"I have five days of rations. Brynn and Auki have a little more." Gunter leaned over the gates of the wolf pen, speaking low to both me and Roark. "Ought to be enough to get us over the ledges. If this Jorvan prince has the stones to meet, he'll need to bring his own."

Thane has the stones. He just might come with blades to our throats, Roark used one hand to reply.

"Then I will raise mine to his," Gunter said. "I don't think we ought to include the Jorvan prince."

"Thane is part of this," I insisted. "We told you lot about the seer woman's words. He's an heir and a firstborn. For all we know, he might have a bone shard without realizing it."

"Then let us get our bones first, then make our barters. You cannot convince me the future king of Jorvandal did not know his Stav Guard attacked our gates. He is not your friend anymore, Lyra. Nor yours, Roark."

Gunter was not alone in his concerns. Brynn and Auki remained quiet as they worked with the pups, but discontent about the plan to ally with Thane was written in every shift in their stances, every twist of their mouths, like they might want to argue the notion.

Roark rubbed the healing top of his finger that was missing the tip, the place where the fealty bone was cut off and shattered his loyalty to Thane. I did not need his gestures or his words to know that for the first time, Roark was beginning to believe the brotherhood he'd once had with the Jorvan prince was gone.

"None of this is even a problem if we cannot find a way past the Dark Watch," Emi said, her voice low.

True enough, Roark had been given the new watch rotations. Warriors marked nearly every five paces of the wall through the night and day. Only narrow roads and a few splotches of forest behind the palace might be left out of sight from the Dark Watchers. But all of us getting there unnoticed would be nearly impossible.

"We might need to leave in intervals," Brynn offered.

Dangerous to be beyond the gates without larger numbers, Roark retorted.

After I clarified his words, Brynn shrugged. "True. But I'm not sure we have another way."

Damn the cruel gods.

Every step we took to end this battle over bones seemed to strike a stone wall, forcing us to draw back and start again.

Why had Gammal told such a tale all those seasons ago? What part did the old woman play in my existence? Her words had destroyed my life when my family was slaughtered, then she taught me how to hide. She knew who I was before I was tossed into servitude at House Jakobson.

It was as though she was preparing me for . . . this fight.

I did not know where Gammal fit in all this.

But somewhere low in my belly I knew there was more to the tale. I simply did not know what.

"WHAT IS THIS?" I STUDIED THE DIFFERENT POUCHES LINED up across Emi's bed four days later.

Powders of gray and silver, crushed leaves that reminded me too much of poisonous firevine, and a few vials of muddy liquids.

Emi dropped a leather satchel over her narrow mattress. "Yrsa taught me a few things as she was learning more about her blood craft. These herbs can shield against summoning spells. This can make it more difficult for burning casts to harm the skin. And these"—she lifted one of the silver powders—"are a combination of crushed ice stone and grimfrost bark. Minerals from the stone keep thoughts clear, in case a blood cast tries to manipulate the mind, and the bark allows a mind to be aware of craft."

Impressive. Emi had been wholly unsettled by the blood spell meant to lure me in. When I looked back now, the illusion of Kael had been primitive and easily discernible, but something else within the blood cast had crafted a compulsion I could not ignore.

"Well done, Emi." I helped stack some of the pouches. "This will be incredibly useful."

"Here." She tucked a wrapped bunch of dried purple flowers beneath the clean bandage over my hand. "I've been speaking with the healer, and we both think kalla vine will draw out some of the dark craft from the wound. I hate to say it, but we may need a blood crafter to actually seal it. It's a cursed wound."

I gave her a nod of thanks. Whatever happened to my palm when the blood craft attacked me during the battle had left my skin open and cold around the gash.

In truth, I could not help but wonder if there was more to Ingir's spell cast than we knew.

And when I fell asleep that night, I discovered how horridly right I was.

MY EYES SNAPPED OPEN. BLACK MISTS KISSED MY CHEEKS. I SAT up, strands of my hair stuck to the frosted ground. Smoke and brine danced over my tongue.

Why was I in the mirror?

Last I could recall, I'd fallen asleep with Roark's body curled around mine and Kyrre sneaking onto the bed to nuzzle against me. This mirror . . . it was empty of the beautiful gold of my soul bond. It was empty of Skul Drek.

The glow of my palm was strange. Here, the wound from the blood craft burned in a dark amber shade, not the brilliant gold like my limbs and middle. The ache twisted to a phantom pain, a dull throb.

In the next breath, a glimmer in the darkness fastened to my palm, burning from the blight of the wound. Threads of hateful red slithered through the rot and decay until they ended in a wall of darkness.

Through the shadows a figure materialized.

The heat of his soul was darker than others. His face was sharply angled, his body strong, but his smile was horrid. Cruel and wicked. "Hello, Lyra."

"Fadey." My eyes widened.

His face was different, not quite the same as the mask he wore as Captain Baldur. But there was a familiar fury to his power.

It felt too much like mine.

Plumes of darkness rolled toward Fadey. He used one of the

reddened tethers to work his way through the shadows toward me.

I scrambled to my feet. "How are you here?"

I was not melding. I was not even in the sights of my husband. How did he keep Skul Drek out?

Fadey chuckled. "You won't find him here. As I told you in Stonegate, blood craft is not always the weakest. Challenging as it can be, I've found my way back to your thoughts."

Shit. We were not in the mirror at all. This was in my mind.

"Get out." Panic choked off my rational thought. I clawed at my skull, frantic, terrified, furious.

All Fadey did was laugh. "Damir never truly understood Ingir's potential. You'll need to forgive her for that nasty business." He pointed at the harsh glow of the wound on my palm. "We needed to know where you were. Tell me, how is it in the royal house of Dravenmoor?"

I clawed at the wound. The spell tracked me? They would know when we left, know our moves. I wanted to shred the flesh off my own hand to be rid of it all if we could not cast a blood spell to remove it.

"How are you still finding me?" I took a step to the opposite side when Fadey approached. "You don't have enough of my blood to keep invading my mind."

"You know, I wondered the same thing. The totems and spell casts were long dried up after you fled Stonegate. But Ingir insisted that she had reason to believe we could find a way in, even without your blood. I daresay she's right." Fadey opened his arms wide, beaming. "I've found you again, and here we may speak without shadows listening in."

I bared my teeth. "Skul Drek will never stop hunting you if you touch me."

Fadey lifted his palms. "I have no plans to harm you here. I merely want to talk. Perhaps you will not be so foolishly stubborn if you understand what is at stake."

"You want me dead. Why would I ever listen to you?"

Fadey twirled the gnarled thread connecting us between his fingers. "You can't go anywhere. Might as well."

I tried to yank my hand away, but whatever craft held me here would not relent.

"Stop this game, Lyra," he said in a snarl. "You won't win. This has been too long in the making. Understand, I only wish for all folk to be reunited in one great kingdom as they once were."

"With you as the king."

"I assure you, there are more wretched sorts who rule now."

"Yet you were the king's consort."

"I despised Damir. Any pleasure I brought to that man, I assure you, was so I could serve this greater purpose. From what I've seen of you, the sacrifice of your power will unravel the division of the first kingdom. We've been given a chance from the gods to begin anew, to learn from the mistakes of the first king." Fadey opened his palm to me. "And they've given us the power of the god-queen to restore in a new leader the gifts she broke long ago."

He was mad.

"Even if I was some warped version of the god-queen," I said through my teeth, "I would never give the power of every craft to a man as cruel as you. For you, Fadey, are no better than the Wanderer King and his plague of greed."

Fadey's lip curled. "You do not know everything I have learned about the burden of melding craft. You do not want it. I will be the melder who will shoulder it."

"Ah, well, since you put it so nicely, how can I disagree?" I wrenched back on the tether again. This time there was enough force behind it, and Fadey stumbled.

Whether the connection was growing weaker or I was gaining strength, I didn't know. I pulled again.

He wrapped his fingers around the tattered line between us, his eyes burning with malice. "Think of the lives you will save if you return and face your fate. Think of the pain your hesitation is causing. Poor Darkwin, how he suffers."

"You harm him, I'll destroy you."

"How? Seems the world is against you. As for me, I am merely the stunned captain of the Stav Guard, consoling his bereaved queen at the brutal betrayal of the melder and Sentry." The bastard sneered. "Admittedly, the Death Bringer was an unforeseen problem. I never trusted him, always had a sense there was more to his story, but not even I knew of the second Draven prince. Certainly not what his own folk had done to his soul. We'll handle him soon enough."

"Oh, but I have plans to slit your throat first."

Fadey sneered. "You fight a power you don't understand. You have no idea what this hunt for bones might require you to pay."

"Perhaps I don't, but you made the mistake of telling me the bones are warded from you. Seems I am the only one who has a chance to find them."

"I may not know their resting place, and there may be wardings against me for some, but I do know something you do not. There is more to the hunt for these bones than melding. There are pieces needed to find each one, and you do not know what they are. I do."

"What are you talking about?"

Fadey chuckled. "Did you really think it would be as simple as sensing the bones in your trance? No, there are many pieces to this tale, and all you have is the dark soul of a traitorous prince and craft."

"Yet you still need me."

"Ah, but you already know it is only because you see into the realm of souls in a way I do not."

Tension knotted in my chest, and a prickle lifted on my arms. He was . . . lying. Like a seedling, the thought germinated in my mind, taking root. Fadey was not telling the whole of it. There was more he kept buried on his vicious tongue.

There was more to this hunt than we knew.

"Save your folk, Lyra," Fadey said, his voice fading like an echo down a long corridor. "Darkwin will live, as will your new Draven companions and those simple crafters you left behind in Stonegate. You've already witnessed how those who know you are no longer safe."

My fists tightened and my heart ached for Thorian and Selena. "Don't speak of them."

"You are the restored power of the god-queen. In a sense, I am the restored Wanderer. But I am willing to learn from his mistakes. I simply need you to answer your fate and reunite what the god-queen divided. Wars will cease. Craft will be free. No melders will ever be forced to serve brutal kings again. The land will prosper."

"If it is my fate, then I will find the first veins of craft on my own, and I will see to it that you never touch them."

"You speak with such confidence, but as I told you, there are pieces to this tale, and even if you find them, you will not be able to stomach what must be done to see it through. But I can. Who knows, perhaps the gods blessed me with a darker heart so I might be able to shoulder the burden. You're running out of time, Lyra. Soon the lands will be corrupted even more and lost to endless battles for power. What is one life when it might save thousands?"

Bile burned in my throat. I'd heard the prophecy, the warning of the gods forsaking the land, corrupting their first kingdom should their gifts be left divided.

What was my life if everyone I loved was at risk of losing theirs? The rope between us flickered. It began to fade.

"Until we speak again."

A shroud of darkness encircled me as another raced for Fadey. I fell into the cold mists, sounds of his chilling laughter in my skull when the cracked walls returned to smooth wood and flames chased away the night.

Heavy hands shook me.

My eyes fluttered open. Roark hovered over me, a shadow in his eyes. His brow was damp, and his body nearly collapsed over me when he crushed me to his chest.

Behind me, Kyrre growled and pressed his thick skull to my spine.

You were crying out, Roark gestured after he caught his breath. *Your skin was cold. And this started bleeding again.*

My husband lifted my wounded hand between us. The bandage was soaked, and the blossoms Emi had placed inside were blackened.

My shoulders rose in heavy breaths. Slowly, I told him of the dream—the attack on my mind—and how Fadey seemed to infiltrate my soul and my body with the help of the Jorvan queen.

Roark's arms crushed me to his body again, his pulse as furious as my own. *Damn the bones. He needs to die.*

I pulled back. "We can't reach him. He's not wrong. No one knows he's a melder. There isn't a way to get close to him without drawing him out with the bones."

Roark didn't raise a hand to speak. I did not part my lips. What more was there to say?

Fadey had found us. This would only end if he or we found the power of the first king.

LYRA

I LOOKED OUT THE WINDOW OF MY CHAMBER, MY INSIDES tangled like sharp briars. A darkness burned in my heart. Perhaps it was caused by the bond to a cruel soul, or perhaps since that night the Sentry of Stonegate stole me from my simple life, along the way I'd added to my own villainy.

I loved fiercely—my husband, our misfit band of Dravens, Thane, Yrsa—but I hated in equal measure. Violent hopes for Fadey and Ingir, and even for men like Virki, who still treated Roark and me like a pestilence.

What villains we'd all become.

Once I'd been content to stride through life, head down; my greatest worry was if devilish Pukki would obey my commands or not, and now I craved the deaths of powerful folk, I wanted their suffering.

And I wanted my peace to live a long life with my killer of a husband until we fell into the hall of the gods.

If ever we succeeded and walked free of this alive, what sort of woman would I be in the end?

The door opened and my heart jumped. Elisabet stood in the frame, a dark queen. Her black circlet was surrounded by her braids, and the ebony gown she wore looked like a robe of glossy raven wings.

"I wonder if I might have a private word with you, Lyra." Elisabet grinned. "Walk with me?"

We strode in silence through the courtyard, arm in arm, occasionally nodding and greeting folk and Dark Watch as we went. The queen said nothing once we reached the wood near the burial mounds and did not look my way until we rounded a bend, going deeper into the trees.

My stomach tightened. "Highness. Roark may be looking—"

"My son remains in a meet with Yanson regarding missing blades." Elisabet's vibrant stare shifted to meet mine. "You wouldn't know where a few weapons have gone, would you?"

Dammit. No doubt she knew those missing blades were tucked under Gunter's bed, wrapped in furs, ready for us to flee the moment we could find our opportunity.

Words fumbled on my tongue, a mortifying sort of stammer.

The queen waved her hand as though vanquishing the question and returned to silence again.

Elisabet stepped through a drape of willow branches. Tucked behind the curtain was a meadow within a circle of willows. Heavy branches drooped and created a wall of leaves, only a narrow path carving down one hillside.

Why were we so far from the gates? I looked over my shoulder, but the queen tugged on my arm, drawing my attention.

"I wanted your thoughts on something, Lyra."

"Um, on what? Forgive me, my lady, but should we be this far?"

"We'll be fine. I wanted to ask you about the Jorvan prince

and his betrothed. My son may be biased, not that I blame him, but he was raised to protect the man. He might have confused affection. But you would not be so biased." Elisabet stopped walking and faced me in the center of the clearing. "Is he truly honorable? Or will he fall into the same cruelty as his father?"

I cleared my throat. "Prince Thane was kind to me, and he cares for people. He never used the fealty shard Roark was forced to take. Instead, he earned Roark's loyalty because of his character."

"Hmm. And what were his thoughts on soul bones?"

I popped one shoulder. "Thane was raised with them. He knew Roark did not care for them, but I do not think he thought as little of them as the rest of us."

"And his future bride. The Myrdan?"

What was this all about? "I did not know her as well, but from what I did know, Yrsa is loyal to those she loves." I hoped it remained true should she ever meet Emi again. "She is just and kind and holds honor herself. She trusted Roark with the name of a traitor who tried to have me killed. She did not hesitate, even though the man was a high-ranking Myrdan noble."

Elisabet looked to the distant path. "It is a comfort to hear this, knowing my son sent his missive."

My heart stuttered. "You know?"

"I know many things that go on in my palace, Lyra. My son made his plan, and I don't disagree. But I also made my own."

"Forgive me, my lady, but I don't understand."

"I know you are planning to slip away from Dravenmoor." Elisabet looked back toward the pathway we'd taken. "The additional Dark Watch are presenting a problem, of course. I also understand that my son's missive was received in Jorvandal."

"How?"

"The raven returned. But I could not be certain if the Jorvan prince would respond with a heart for battle or a heart with a desire to be the loyal friend you insist he was."

"Highness, what—"

"I could not find a good enough reason to pull our watchers away after the Jorvans attacked," Elisabet went on, ignoring me. "Even if I could, to have my son suddenly leave Dravenmoor, well, the úlfur would suspect me. I am never so obvious."

I glanced around the willow meadow. "My lady, do you know a way we can slip out?"

"I suppose time will tell." The queen glanced at the sky, then pointed toward the path. "Down there you will find something of use to you. I will keep the guards distracted until my son can follow."

Apprehension lifted the hair on my neck. She wanted me to step into the deep wood alone?

"What? Wait, Queen Elisabet."

The queen did not respond, merely turned on her heel and rushed back up the path from which we'd come.

She left me in the wood.

I could follow her back to the gates, but . . . I looked down the narrow path on the opposite side of the meadow. Was it even wise to go look? I held a level of apprehension for the queen. Then again, her soul was vowed to Roark's. Her word, her actions, they could not bring me harm or she was damned to lose eternity with her king.

I wrung my fingers until three knuckles cracked. Only a glimpse of the path was visible through the shadows after it rounded a bend down the slope.

Elisabet would not send me into an ambush. She'd guided us to Nivek; she'd kept me alive.

She would not kill me.

Still, I unsheathed a small knife from inside my boot before I stepped onto the path.

Through the gaps in the leaves, beams of sunlight brightened the slope more than I thought. The air was fresh and damp, like soil after a soft rain. Nearby, the sound of the gentle flow of water gave up that one of the rivers carving through the kingdom was near.

My pulse quickened. Near a thick, white oak was a leather satchel with a rolled fur mat, prepared and packed. A grin split my lips, and I hurried off the path. A water skin was tied to one side, along with pouches of dried berries and roasted nuts, aged cheeses, and burlap-wrapped bread.

I did not know how Elisabet would smuggle Roark from the palace without notice, but she'd done it well enough here.

A twig snapped. On a nearby branch, a raven fluttered away with a loud caw. I spun around, searching the trees, and only met the gentle sway of leaves and tall grass. One fist tightened around my knife, the other on the pack of supplies.

Gods. I was jolting at every damn noise. I chuckled, a tremble of nerves, but I released the pack and leaned against a tree, one palm to my brow.

Another twig snapped.

This time, before I had a chance to wheel around, a hood fell over my head and sturdy arms caught me around the waist.

I thrashed and kicked and screamed. One of my heels caught my attacker in what felt like the shin.

"Dammit," he bit out. "Hurry with it."

"I'm *trying*," a woman hissed, low and muffled, like she spoke through a door.

I screamed behind his hand, my fists pounding over his skin, desperate to find a scratch, anything, to meld his damn fingers together.

In the next moment his hand lifted, only to return again, now scented like smoke and vinegar.

I coughed and choked against the fumes. Little by little, my body grew heavy. As though a wave of fatigue dug into my bones, I could hardly move my foot to kick anymore.

"There," he said against my ear. "We've got you. No more worries, Lyra. All will be well now."

The voice held a touch of smugness. Almost familiar.

I did not catch sight of my attacker before my mind fell to cold mists of nothing.

ROARK

The pain began in my skull. An annoyance, but in a matter of moments, the heat of the ache dug into my center. Fierce enough I pounded a fist over my chest, drawing Yanson's furrowed brow.

"All right?"

Something was wrong. A tumult of emotion rolled through my thoughts, my heart. To my damn cruel soul. Rage. Fear. Betrayal.

I staggered to the window, leaning over the pane, brow to the cold glass. No one in the courtyard seemed amiss. Folk went about their days, avoiding the additional Dark Watch on guard, but no horns sounded danger.

Nothing.

Lyra.

The moment her name filled my thoughts, ice coated every thread of the unseen bond tethering us as one. Like a shrill cry of fear, soul to soul, I knew something had happened to my wife.

I tore from the room, Yanson shouting my name, his hurried steps scrambling over the floorboards. Skin burned along my scar. Hot rage boiled beneath the surface, and the violence of a nature I fought to tame pounded within me, clawing to be free.

When I shoved through the substantial doors near the front of the palace, I gave in to the darkness.

"Dammit. Would you give me some warning?" Yanson stumbled backward. He was a sturdy man, taller than me and even Gunter, but his pale eyes widened at the sight of the monstrous shadows.

It felt as though the rush of bloodlust, larger than was typical, billowed around the deledan soul until my cruelest desires filled the whole of the courtyard.

Folk screamed when Skul Drek strode through the trees and shrubs five paces ahead of me. In the wake of us both, layers of dark mists coated the blooms until they were painted in black deep enough that the sunlight died.

I did not need to command anything; the most wretched edges of my heart knew what it wanted. To find her.

The form of Skul Drek faded and split. Ribbons of darkness curled over the grounds like dark serpents, scouring the edges of the kingdom, searching for the brightness of her soul.

I shoved through the doors of the wolf keep, the heavy iron on the latches pounded against the walls. Wolves in their pens snarled save one—Kyrre stood on his haunches, his tail swishing side to side, but as though the beast sensed the violence rolling in my veins, his lips curled.

"Roark?" Emi peeked around one of the posts. She sat on the fence watching Brynn and Auki teach a group of young ones how to calm a fara.

Where is Lyra? My hands were frantic and stiff, and I wasn't certain if she'd even understand me.

"I believe she was seen speaking to the queen." Brynn was the one who answered. She leaned over the pen post. "What is it?"

Something is wrong. Where is she?

"He says something is wrong," Emi said.

Yanson entered the keep. "My prince, what is happening? That damn . . . *soul* is tormenting everyone."

"Shit." Emi hopped off the post.

"Why is that shit?" Brynn and Auki directed the young ones to another keeper and made quick work of following when I stormed back toward the entrance. "Why does that matter?"

"It means he felt a threat, soul deep, so the deledan prepares to slaughter."

"*Shit,*" Brynn said on a rough breath.

I had no qualms about peeling my own mother's soul from her blood if she'd done something to my wife.

I unlatched Kyrre's hold when I stalked past. The wolf had already grown since the battle with the Stav. His back haunches reached my mid-thigh. Hackles raised, a low growl emitted from his jaws, and the wolf seemed ready to pounce and attack, the same as me.

Find her. No need to hand speak to a fara wolf. They understood words from their bonded, no matter what language, what dialect.

Kyrre snarled and bolted from the keep, nose to the ground, racing for the distant gates.

The young wolf narrowly avoided crashing into the queen. Elisabet held her gown in one hand, a flush to her face. Her shoulders slumped in relief when she saw me.

"Roark!"

My mother raced across the courtyard, a few Dark Watch warriors falling in behind her. If she was looking for comfort, she would need to look elsewhere.

I gripped the queen's arm, drawing her close. *Where is she?*

Darkness returned, encircling us, our feet, our legs, around our waists. A bit of fear flashed in Elisabet's eyes. She tried to pull her arm away; I only tightened my hold.

"I don't know what you're saying." To her credit, the queen tried to follow my hand gestures. "I was with Lyra in the willow wood. I turned for a moment and they . . . ambushed us. They took her."

Ice chased heat from my blood. *Who?*

My mother did not need assistance to understand. "Jorvans."

"But they left the queen untouched?" To my stun, Emi stood at my shoulder, practically challenging my mother.

Elisabet tightened her mouth. "What brings war the swiftest? A stolen melder, or the queen? They did not want me; they want their melding power back. She will be left alive for now, Roark, but there is no time to waste." The queen faced the courtyard. "The prince will be going to retrieve his wife. They must find this camp before the Jorvans return to Stonegate and Lyra is harmed, or worse."

"You're certain it was Jorvans, Bet?" From the back of the courtyard, Virki stroked the head of his gray wolf.

"Who else, Virki?"

"We ought to be certain before we send our army."

"The Dark Watch will not be going," the queen insisted. "This must be done in haste and stealth. Not a damn war before we know what threat we face." She turned to me, her voice low. "I will not attempt to convince you to send others in your place. Choose who joins you, and get her back."

Low in my gut, a knot of disquiet thickened.

Something was wrong with the queen's report. Elisabet was not one to act rashly. She was calculated and clever. Not to mention, she was not one to keep the Dark Watch behind the gates if a threat was leveled at our clan.

I took a step closer, towering over the woman who once sang me to sleep as a child. My fingers against her cheek, I spoke the threat, slowly. *If you are behind this, I will destroy you.*

After Emi whispered my words, the queen tilted her chin. "I believe they will be headed toward the tip of the Black Fjords, to avoid the ravines. Supplies will be gathered for you and those who ride with you. It's possible you may be gone for quite some time. May the gods keep you safe."

She pressed the heel of her palm to my brow in a blessing, then turned away.

But not before I was certain that the slightest hint of a smile teased the queen's mouth.

TRUE TO HER WORD, THE QUEEN HAD BLADES AND SATCHELS with food and skins of water in the stables within a bell toll.

The rest came from the supplies we'd smuggled on our own in the last days.

Clad in black, I swung a leg over a dark gelding. Uncontrolled shadows draped over my shoulders. When no hint of Lyra remained in Dravenmoor, I contained my hate and drew back the split soul.

But it still burned, growing more desperate, more violent by the moment.

"Lyra has come into her own brutality," Emi said, shoving a knife inside her boot. "She will fight, Roark. We'll find her, then you can finish whatever damage to the Stav she's surely begun."

My teeth ground together, and my fingers tightened on the leather bridle.

There was no question who would join me. Brynn, Auki, Gunter, and Emi sat astride their own charges, cowls over their heads, kohl lined around their eyes and down their cheeks.

Òlmr and Kyrre remained close, ready to run through the wood.

"You were Stav once." Gunter led his stallion to my side. Both his seax blades were crossed over his back. "Where do they camp?"

Find heavy trees. I spoke with one hand and pulled my hood low over my nose with the other. *They use them for protection.*

The others had learned my gestures well enough, but Emi translated all the same. No words should be missed.

"Want us to kill on sight?" Auki asked.

If it means getting Lyra, burn them alive for all I care. I nudged my horse forward, and we disappeared into the darkness of the trees.

LYRA

SOMETHING WEIGHED DOWN MY CHEST. EVERY DRAW OF breath felt burdensome and smelled of pine spice and warm honey. My eyes fluttered, heavy with fatigue. Little by little the weight lifted and the tingle of numbness in my fingertips faded.

I peered through my lashes. Dim light filled a small space covered in dark canvas. A tent. I was in a damn tent.

Blood rushed to my skull, but when I sat up, it felt as though the world tilted on its side. With a groan, I fell back against a burlap pillow, my hand on my stomach to stop the swirl of bile.

"Hush, now." A cool cloth dabbed against my brow. "The herbs leave the mind a bit muddy."

I froze. Through the haze, memories returned with wretched clarity. Elisabet left me in the woods. A satchel of supplies. Then the attack. I remembered nothing more, but it didn't matter.

Someone had taken me from Dravenmoor. From my husband.

And a sinking weight in my belly told me the queen was behind it all.

Muffled voices filled the space, speaking as though underwater. I let my head roll to the side, and the voices drew nearer.

"No marks? On the wrists? Nothing?" A man.

"There's nothing except new runes on her back."

I knew that voice. A woman. I knew her. From where did I know her voice?

I tried to lift my hand to rub the ache behind my eyes, but my arm came to an abrupt halt. Panic lanced through my chest when my other side was bound much the same. I jolted, twisted, tried to break free of the bindings.

A hand fell to my arm. "Lyra, stop. You're safe. You're all right. Stop."

My vision cleared. "Yrsa?"

The Myrdan princess did not look particularly regal. Her black braids were tied high behind her head, and her brown skin was painted in kohl and green shades, meant to aid in disappearing behind trees.

Her smile was one of pity. "Lyra. You're alive." Yrsa sniffed and forced a stronger grin. "You're all right now. We won't let them touch you. We have several Stav with us. They won't get through the watch."

I shook my head. "N-n-no." Simple as the word was, I could not form the sound and it was more a slurred groan than anything.

"Water," Yrsa commanded someone out of my line of sight.

A ladle was pressed to my lips. I choked on the gulp. Gods. There, in front of me, was Prince Thane.

Much like Yrsa, Thane looked ready to rise as the kingdom's assassin. His tunic and trousers were the purest black, and strapped across his chest and shoulder was thick leather lined with knives and daggers and a seax at his waist.

His golden hair was tied in a knot behind his head. That damn cunning smile had not changed. "Lyra Bien." Thane chuckled and helped me sip the water. "It is good to see you alive. I wasn't certain I ever would again."

Relief at familiar faces promptly faded. Thane would believe me to be the killer of his father. Damir's bones had been melded until his skull had caved in. Thane would not know of Fadey. All gods, this was a trap. Likely a moment of healing, all to give me strength before they took my head.

"I d-d-didn't kill him." My voice was a rough rasp, but the water aided in clearer words.

"What was that?"

"The k-king. I didn't kill him."

Thane's eyes shadowed. "Ah. My father. Yes. You know, mere days ago, I might not have believed it. Which is why I am so glad you were able to send your missive and explain. Gods, Lyra what you must've endured. Having your soul controlled in such a way."

Missive?

I shook my head again, but Yrsa moved to the other side of the cot and added a strange, gritty paste to my throat. "This will help clear any remnants of twisted craft. Or so Hilda told us. She looks forward to greeting you again."

I looked down at the bone tonic. Hilda, another bone crafter taken from my village, was still alive. Sincere relief came from knowing, but it did not explain how the prince and princess were here, how they'd found me, and why they'd come.

"This wound, however." Yrsa inspected the wrapped bandage across my palm. "I don't know where it came from, but it was made with dark blood craft. I've already begun an attempt to counter it."

Words burned to ash in my dry mouth. I wanted to scream at them that it was Queen Ingir's work, but I could hardly keep my eyes open.

Thane took hold of my uninjured hand and squeezed. "Do not fret, Ly. We are far enough that Dravens will be at least a day's ride behind us. Soon you'll be safe behind the walls of Stonegate."

I tried to shoot up from the cot, but the bindings held me down, and only a raspy "Please" slipped from my cracked lips.

Yrsa's mouth pinched. "Lyra, rest. You're safe and you'll feel better soon. It won't be long before your soul is free of their horrid chains."

By the gods, what did they mean? I let my head fall back, my eyes clamped shut in frustration, but soon the fatigue, the heavy pressure on my chest drew me into a hazy fog once again.

"We ought to let her sleep" was all I heard from Yrsa before sleep dragged me away.

"THERE YOU ARE. BETTER?" YRSA BEAMED AT ME AGAIN WHEN my eyes fluttered open. She was working a pungent blue paste over the festering blood craft wound. "I think I've managed to stave off the corruption in the flesh. I may not be the most skilled blood crafter, but the infection seems to be subsiding. Another day, perhaps, and whatever spell cast was in your blood will break apart and fade like any other illness normally does."

I swallowed, my throat burned with fire, but slowly I sat up on the cot. "In . . . Ingir."

Yrsa paused her work. "What did you say?"

I pointed at the wound. "Ingir. When you . . . when you attacked."

Yrsa's dark eyes went wide. "What attack?"

They did not know?

The tent flap opened and Thane appeared, a new ewer of water in hand. "She graces us yet again with her presence."

"Thane." Yrsa spun around. "She said the blood curse was from your mother after an attack."

The prince paused, clearly confused. After a long moment he shook his head. "My mother has not left her wing at Stonegate during her mourning. Remember the missive. Lyra, you told us your mind might be muddled from the fading soul craft, that you might not recall even reaching out for our aid." Thane sat at the foot of the cot and leaned his back against one of the thin tent posts. "I'm impressed you were able to have clear enough thoughts to send word at all. I've read of soul crafters who once took over souls during battle. I can't imagine what it was like."

"I didn't send a missive!" My voice found a bit of strength, but it sounded raw, as though I'd swallowed a spoonful of sand.

"You just don't remember."

"Thane." I blew out a long breath, wincing against the ache in my hand when I pushed up in the bed even more. "What missive did I supposedly send?"

The prince removed a folded parchment from his pocket. "You explained it all. I know you did not intend to kill my father, Lyra. Do not hold any guilt. After . . . after I saw the truth, I should've suspected straightaway."

Yrsa held the parchment in front of me, allowing me to read it without untying my wrists.

Prince,

I have little time before the corruption takes me again. My soul is forced to serve our enemy's desires. They plan to come against Stonegate, believing you weak and a coward.

The day of the full moon, I am allowed to walk a path beyond the gates in the willow wood. I will not be of sound mind for long.

I speak true. Why would I plead for the son of the king I slaughtered to bring me back?
You are my only chance.

L

Yrsa folded the parchment when I stared at the top of the tent.

"It is no fault of your own," Yrsa said softly. "Soul craft is mysterious to many of us, so how would we know it could do such a thing?"

"Yes." Thane rose, his jaw tight. "We were all duped."

"No." A tear fell from the corner of my eye. "No, Thane, you're wrong. I am no prisoner of Dravenmoor."

"Lyra, do you think I did not search out if such things were possible? Soul craft can possess other souls, did you know that? They weave them together somehow. Force compliance." Thane's face was flushed. "Who knows how long he had us all locked in his plans."

Hurt and betrayal were speaking.

I wanted to scream. "Thane, you must listen to me. I did not write that missive. I didn't. I am not Roark's prisoner, I am his . . . I am his *wife*."

"Gods, Lyra." Thane spun on me. "We heard all those poisonous lies."

"And sent the Stav Guard to retaliate."

The prince wore a look of sincere befuddlement. "What are you talking about?"

I closed my eyes, feeling the weariness of the fading tonics. It was a heady relief to believe Thane the Bold had nothing to do with the death of Thorian and Selena, but I did not have the time nor the strength to explain it.

The longer I was parted from Roark, the more I felt the rage of his soul.

Whatever affection my husband held for the Jorvan prince would not survive the obsession and bloodlust of his darker soul.

"Try to think clearly, Lyra," Thane insisted with a touch of annoyance. "If the Stav went to battle, I'm sure I would know, for I would be with them."

Reckless, wonderful, bold Thane. He was hurt and angry and had no idea what dangers lived in the walls of his own palace.

"Dravens have hunted your craft for as long as I've lived," Yrsa offered. "Whatever he did to make you believe him, it was not real."

I reached for her hand, exhaustion clouding my mind. "I must return. You don't understand what is happening at Stonegate."

"It's too much too soon." Yrsa moved for a small pouch. The same pine scent I'd breathed in earlier was there. "You need a little more rest, Lyra. It will be clearer in the morning."

"No! Yrsa, please!"

I hardly finished speaking before the blur of empty black stole me away again.

THANE WAS SEATED ON A STOOL IN THE CORNER OF THE TENT when I woke.

More water. More stares. More silence.

Only when he returned to his seat did he speak. "Is he truly Skul Drek? I keep trying to convince myself it was not real. That I did not see what I thought I saw."

In the prince's hand was a rolled bit of parchment. I recognized the writing on the page.

"So you did receive his missive?"

Thane looked at the words. "He taunted me in it, as we always did. Said I was being petulant, and if I wanted the true story, I was to meet him in a week's time near the Black Fjords. I was rather inclined to meet him with every Stav Guard. Until we received your note and my desire shifted to getting you free."

A heart for battle, or a heart to be a hero. Elisabet, what have you done?

My heart cracked on behalf of the prince, for the look of despondency written in every line of his face. Try to hate Roark all he wanted, such pain would not be in his voice if he had not loved him.

"Skul Drek is not what you think." My voice was clearer, stronger. One glance at my wounded palm, and I nearly broke into a smile. The wound was healing. Yrsa's craft was fighting Ingir's.

No mistake, the princess was stronger than she knew.

The prince closed his eyes. "Why did he come to Stonegate? There had to have been a purpose."

"Me," I whispered. "He was to find the lost melder and kill me. In the meantime, he fought against soul bones." I could tell him Roark had little control over his life and the actions of Skul Drek. I could tell him his Sentry never wanted to betray him.

I told him none of it. Thane would not believe a word.

Not yet.

"He didn't kill you," Thane said when I remained silent.

"No." I shook my head. "He didn't. He is not your enemy, Thane."

The prince shook his head and leaned onto his elbows over his knees. "I wish I could believe that, Lyra. You're healing well, so you should know we'll need to be leaving soon."

I LEARNED QUICKLY TO PLAY INTO THEIR HOPES. TO PLAY THE part of the poor melder recovering from a Draven trance.

It worked.

Yrsa wiped away a tear from my cheek and helped me sit up

once she removed the bindings from my wrists. "You mustn't blame yourself. They lied to all of us."

Emi. Yrsa's voice was as harsh as Thane's. She was broken believing Emi betrayed her heart.

I would go mad if I could not find a way to convince them otherwise soon.

"Come." She forced a smile. "I'll help you wash a bit and get some food in you before we set off for Jorvandal. We want to be on our way before nightfall."

"Yrsa, where is Kael?" I ran a cool linen over my dirty cheeks. "How is he?"

She arched a brow. "Your brother?"

"Yes. Is he well? Safe?"

"Lyra, I thought . . . I thought he was with you."

My stomach dropped. "Kael did not come with us."

"I don't know. I have not seen him, and I assumed he was taken with you."

No. No. My eyes clenched. I pressed a hand to my chest. Where was Kael Darkwin? What had they done to him? He lived. He *had* to live.

Something flickered in my chest when the pain grew too much. Like a caress against my heart. A comfort.

My eyes snapped open. Roark.

How many times had Gunter insisted that the bond would be a draw to the other? Craft roared in my head, not to meld, but to find those threads. Heat glided over my fingertips, smooth as fine satin. The burn was a fire after a storm, a lover's touch in the night.

My fingers danced in front of me, hidden from the princess as she gathered a fresh tunic for me to wear.

Unseen, my fingers curled around silky threads. There, crisscrossed beneath my flesh, in my blood, to my soul. I tugged.

Flickers of warmth, like a splash of steaming water, spilled from my chest to my limbs.

Again, I pulled.

The burn of his eyes filled my mind, the villainous cold of his soul, and I tugged them toward me.

When it faded, my spine felt straighter. My pulse slowed. Yrsa smiled and directed me to a corner where I could dress in peace.

"You will not let me leave?" I asked before the princess abandoned the tent.

She dragged her bottom lip over her teeth. "Not yet, Lyra. We . . . just want to be certain you've returned to us fully."

Because they still believed me to be under some sort of Draven control.

I dipped my chin, silently conceding, and stared at the flap of the tent she'd used. A dark tunic stepped in front of the gap. Another guarded the back wall. How many Stav Guards Thane brought with him, I didn't know.

In truth, I didn't understand how he and the princess had slipped away from Stonegate without Ingir and King Hundur stopping them.

It didn't matter. I sat on the edge of the cot, focusing on the tent flap.

He was coming.

No doubt, my husband was hunting me.

"WE MUST GO." THANE RETURNED, A LEATHER STRAP IN HIS hand. He offered me a sheepish sort of glance. "You understand, don't you? We don't want you to get hurt by fleeing. You'll feel clearer when we get back to Stonegate."

"Do you really believe that, Thane?" I hugged my middle. "Do I look confused? Bespelled? In a trance?"

"In truth, you look a little frightening." He held up a hand. "Gods, I don't mean it offensively. I only mean, you look like you might bite if I step too close."

I chuckled flatly. "I won't."

"See, that's what I mean. That doesn't sound like you. We always got on all right, but now you look at me like the enemy, and I simply want it to go back to what it was."

"But it can't." My face softened. "I've seen too much, Thane. Your enemies are not who you think. If you would trust that bit of doubt I see in your eyes, perhaps I could tell you all that has happened. All that will happen if you *do not let me go.*"

Thane parted his mouth to reply, but it was choked off by a shout from one of the Stav Guard beyond the tent.

An arrow hissed overhead and thudded against one of the outer posts. Thane dropped the tether and drew the blade off his belt.

I grinned.

"Lyra." He whirled on me. "Please, by the gods, stay here. I'll see what's going on."

"No need."

"What?"

Passion, fury, violence—all of it sped this way and that across the threads in my heart.

"I already know what is happening," I said, my voice low. "I think you do too. My husband has arrived."

ROARK

THE LENGTH OF A WHOLE NIGHT. THAT WAS HOW MUCH time had passed since I'd last seen Lyra. There was no longer a point in fighting the darkness. Emi and the others kept a wide berth around my horse, avoiding the frigid shadows, as though I might strike should they misstep.

Only Kyrre ran alongside as though nothing was amiss.

At the word of the queen, no one protested our departure, and the farther we rode, the more I was convinced that Elisabet had had a hand in all this. Whether it meant I would soon destroy my own mother, I did not yet know.

We kept a swift pace to the northern edges of the kingdom, aiming toward the Night Ledges. Knolls and forests made up the border of upper Myrda and Dravenmoor. If a Stav camp wanted to keep a steadier pace and avoid the Black Fjords and the Red Ravines, they would remain on foot.

It was a clearer way to allied territory, without the difficult passages of wilder Draven lands where Jorvans could not outpace my clan.

It was reasonable, and Jorvans were logical. Never truly straying from their comfortable paths. The route made sense.

But more than that, there was a cruel inferno roaring through my veins, nearly compelling me forward, an unseen chain dragging me toward a destination I could not see.

Lyra. The small plucks of our bond began when the sun faded behind the trees. They grew stronger, more frantic. Beautiful, resourceful woman. She was guiding us straight to her. Straight to them.

"Roark, smoke ahead." Auki drew his horse to a halt.

We followed. I kicked my leg over my horse, drew my hood low on my brow, and crept for the trees. Hickory smoke burned through the woods. A touch of oil and herbs tangled within.

Faint, but there. All the seasons I'd served as their damn Sentry, I'd insisted the guard eat raw, no flames and no smoke when in the wood this near to Dravenmoor.

Their arrogance would get them killed tonight.

"Òlmr, scout ahead." Brynn tipped her chin toward the edge of the tree line.

The gray wolf tucked her snout, crouched on her haunches, and drifted through the night like a haunt in the darkness. Kyrre stood at my side, hackles raised, teeth bared.

"A camp." Brynn slid off her own gelding and strapped a bow over her shoulder. "She found one not far beyond the trees."

I tilted my head side to side, rolled my shoulders, and took out the bearded ax from a loop on my belt.

Before I ever found a place in Stonegate, I'd been taught to step lightly in the wood, to use the trees to shield the slightest glimpse we approached. Now, with my split soul, I became nothing more than a shadow in the endless night.

Gunter was lithe, and he favored sneaking across raised roots near the bases of tree trunks. His long limbs made it easier to reach for branches and swing over the soil to a new set of roots. Kept his boots from snapping twigs and dead leaves.

Brynn and Auki were hunters. Their steps were as mist across the forest floor. Low, soft, calculated.

Emi took a bow like Brynn, and when the faint flicker of a flame burned through the night, we pressed our backs against opposite sides of a tree.

A small camp. Four tents built for quick disassembly. I counted four Stav Guard in total but six horses. There were more I could not see. Eyes closed, I desired to surround them, trap them, drain the souls from their headless bodies.

It took no coaxing for the deledan to respond to my desires. All around the camp, billows of darkness wove through the trees and hedges, a dark wall to keep the Stav from fleeing.

I knocked my knuckles against the tree, drawing Emi's attention. *Give them a bit of mercy, cousin. Warn them that they are about to meet the gods.*

Emi's grin held little kindness. She drew the bowstring alongside her kohl-marked cheek and let the arrow fly.

Shouts rose inside the tents at once. The few worthless Stav surrounded the front of one tent. One held a bow, the others their blades. Gods, how perfectly foolish this plan of theirs had become. Step over Draven borders, take Lyra, and expect to escape with so few men?

It was too reckless, too bold. Likely something Thane would do with his misplaced sense of honor if he considered he was saving Lyra from the horrors of his traitorous Sentry.

No sooner had the thought fled my mind than a tall, too-familiar figure stepped to the front of the Stav.

More runes were inked on the shorn sides of his scalp, and his dark, golden hair was braided down the center. Thane's pale eyes were like the coldest ice. He scanned the trees, blade in hand.

Damn him.

How many times had I told the fool of a prince to stay out of the fight? He put his neck against the blade too much, and one day it would draw blood that could not be stopped.

I did not want to kill the prince. But I would. If he harmed Lyra, believing her to be the killer of the king, I would send Thane to Salur.

I simply would make it quick.

Emi glanced at me. "What do you want to do?"

"You two were close, yes?" Gunter asked, his voice rough.

I nodded.

"You can use that," he said. "It is what I keep telling you and Lyra. You have the most powerful soul of us all. Use it to command connections."

He believed I could use the deledan to subdue the prince? The same as I forced Elisabet through our connection, perhaps, if any bond of our former regard remained, Thane could hear me.

"Do we take out the guards?" Auki crouched next to me. "It would be done quickly, especially with Òlmr and Kyrre."

Before I could reply, the prince shouted into the night. "Roark! If that is you, then make yourself known, you coward."

I recanted. I would kill him should he call me a coward again. He damn well knew it irked me.

Cover me was all I signaled to Emi. I stood, rolled the ax once in my grip, and strode through the trees.

Shadows followed me, a dark river building in my wake, and movement shifted behind me. No doubt, the others were aimed, ready to attack should I need. Kyrre plodded next to me, a low rumbling growing in his throat.

I stepped from the trees, rolling mists coiled around my legs.

The Stav Guard huddled closer to the prince, ready to pull him back at the first threat, but Thane did not look anywhere but at me.

His jaw pulsed, and there was a new sort of wildness in his eyes I'd not seen before. He took in my approach, the shadows of craft hanging over me like the illusion of a cloak.

Where is she?

"Safe now that she's no longer with you." Thane used the tip of his blade to point at my heart.

Do you wish to die, you ass?

"Only one of us will be dying tonight. Tell me, does that creature you keep inside feel pain? When I gut you and let you breathe as you bleed out, will it feel the same agony?"

I tossed my hood back. Thane shifted, clearly unsettled holding my stare. *Give me back my wife.*

Thane watched every jerky gesture. "She is not yours. And now that she's free of your corruption, I will see to it she has nothing to fear again."

Last warning, Thane.

The prince had the decency to look a little discomfited. Then he turned to the Stav at his back. "Take the Draven bas—"

He had no chance to finish his command before a rush of ice washed over my skin and darkness engulfed the prince from head to foot.

Together we fell away from the blades, tents, and hatred, and into the cruel shadows where souls spoke.

34

SKUL DREK

WHERE WAS MY MELDER?

Danger, threats, rage. My melder was not at my side, and there were wretched souls who took her. Did they try to darken her soul? I would end theirs if they had merely considered it.

"What have you done? Is this Salur? Damn you, now no one will protect her!"

Over my shoulder a glow was there, a man's soul, bright as the flames of the stars. Not my melder.

No.

A hateful sort of grin spread when the soul found me in the darkness and had the decency to cry out in fear. Lovely sounds from a prince so bold.

"All gods." He made an attempt to move away.

I rushed around, stopping a princely soul from fleeing.

"You going to finish what you started, then?"

Brave and bold, this princely soul.

All around, the glimmer and shine of friends and foes kept he and we entangled. Talk would be brief, lest blades begin to open the gates of the gods.

"Where is my melder?" I strummed the boiling threads of gold. The ends faded into the shadows, lost to me.

For now.

"You . . . you can speak? How?"

"Soul to soul. Where is my melder?"

"Soul to soul?" The bold prince ran his hands across the glow of his form and shook his head. "Your melder? No, no, you cannot have Lyra."

"What do you see here?" Brow pressed to his, I forced his attention to the webs of my soul, every piece of it belonging to my melder. "Mine, bold prince. My melder is mine."

"And who are you? Roark? Skul Drek? A demon from the molten hell?"

"I am he, and we are we."

The princely soul shoved back, and only then did the glimmer of a silver thread take shape between our souls. "You almost sound like I imagine he would. This is corrupted craft, twisted. It goes against the gods."

"Or does the bold prince only wish it to be? Would it be easier to sour your heart toward he and we if all you see is a monster?" I pounded a fist to my chest. Darkness plumed around us. "I am he, and we are we."

Why could the princely soul not understand?

Again, I shouted, "I am he, and we are we. We. Are. We."

A wince, one of pain from the heart, burned in the glow of his soul. "If you are the Roark I know, then I never had a brother. Or have you forgotten the night you tried to kill me?"

A hiss slid from between my teeth. I pulled back, frantic, frenzied. Why? Why did the bold soul not trust what could be seen?

Sorrowful words he and we spoke that night, pleading, *pleading*, for a princely soul not to darken. Did it count for nothing?

Fingers in the mists, I tugged at skeins of darkness. "Not all is as it seems, bold prince. Stayed my hand against your soul, did we not?" I wheeled on him, drawing our faces near. "He and we wanted you to live. *Pled* with my melder to corrupt the bones of the fallen and take a soul to save yours. He and we were cursed to protect the souls of the fallen, forced to vow it, but for a princely soul to remain bright, such a vow did not matter."

For a moment, the bold prince looked away, torment deepened the shade of his soul. "Perhaps guilt got the better of you to stop the attack, but—"

"Not all is as it seems." I roared it in his face, tugging at the bonds. "What was no longer is. Bonds do not remain save to my melder."

"Bonds." He studied the ropes of gold. "Are you telling me these are chains?"

"Ah, but these chains are made willingly now, bold prince. Once these were not so willing for he and we. Bonds forced our hand." I knocked my closed fist against the side of my cowl. "Understand?"

"Are you saying you didn't have a choice?"

Teeth clacked. "Yes. Old bonds forced actions. Actions which might not have been done, like attack a princely soul, had the choices of he and we been free."

"Why not tell me the truth about . . . this curse? I would've helped you."

I curled my lip. "Be the bold prince, but do not be the fool."

"Kiss my ass, you sod." The princely soul stiffened, bold as always. "It's disorienting to face you as . . . the assassin who has attacked my folk time and again. And through it all, you were there. My only true friend, my brother, and you shattered it all."

I had no time to soothe royal feelings. "To get my melder."

"Yes. She spoke the same, yet you did not kill her either. Some assassin you are."

I plucked the burning web of my bond. "She has always been mine, bold prince. For my melder did I become he and we."

"I don't understand."

"Does not matter." I stepped nearer. "My melder brightens the night, holds my soul, and holds the heart of he. She lives above all. Never will my melder be harmed from these hands."

"Why would I ever believe a word you say again?"

"Ah, but you already do, bold prince." I plucked the thin strand of silver between us with the black tip of a fingernail from beneath the cloak of mists. "Or this would not be."

Deep breaths rose in the princely soul's chest. "What is it? Get it off."

A laugh, deep and rough, rolled from my throat. I strummed the fragile thread again. "Brothers once. Not of blood, but of bond. You feel the truth. Will you be the fool or be the bold?"

It took a moment, but soon enough the prince reached out a hand and touched the thread between us.

"Why command Lyra to kill my father?"

I bared my teeth. "Thief King did not fall by my melder's hand."

"You hated him."

"To steal the bones of the fallen, I would take one to replace it. Forced chains were made tighter by the actions of the Thief King. But blood did not spill from the word of he and we."

"Who, then? I saw his melded bones, Roark. I saw him."

"Not all is as it seems. Truths must be told if the bold prince will be wise enough to hear them."

He said nothing.

In the silence, heat thrummed through the bonds of my melder. Night brightened, shifted to something more alive.

"Thane," a soft voice said.

"Gods." The bold prince whirled around. "Lyra?"

I drew in sharp air through my teeth. My melder, bright and fierce, stood near the bold prince. I curled darkness around her and pulled her close, drawing my nose against her warmth, breathing in her soul. "I lost you."

"No." Her palms trapped my face. "You can't lose me. Not ever. Through this life and the next."

Need rumbled in the back of my throat. "I want to taste you."

"Well, if you please, wait a bit until I am not privy to such things," the bold prince said. "Ly, I think I have gone to the gods. Nothing makes sense, and yet, I hope it is not Salur." He looked about. "Quite horrid here. Damp and cold and decaying. If this is eternity, I'd rather not."

My melder smiled with affection at the bold prince.

I wanted to devour his soul.

As though she sensed the bite of violence, she faced me. "Let him go. We ought to speak with them all, don't you think?"

"You are there?"

"Yes."

I tightened my hold around her body, and the feel of her drew out the darkest need, the sharpest lust, the demand for more and more of her.

Still, when my melder touched a strand of the bond between us, cold faded against the sharp bite of a fire's glow.

35

LYRA

THERE WAS NO SOUND OF CLASHING BLADES. NOT YET. Alone in the tent, I made quick work of securing boots and a cloak around my shoulders. When I went to run through the door, I was stopped by the princess.

"Lyra." Yrsa's dark eyes held a touch of fear. "We can't go out there."

"I'm not going to sit here and have Thane make a grave mistake, or Roark, should he see no other way to get to me except killing the prince."

"Lyra." Yrsa tugged on my arm.

I shirked her off. "Believe what you wish, but I tell you with clarity, I did not write the missive. You were brought here for a purpose, and I was led to the exact place you found me by the queen of Dravenmoor, Yrsa."

"What?"

"Yes." I let my hands fall to her shoulders, my pulse racing. "Elisabet is the one who took me to the willow wood. She told me

Roark would come after me. We already were planning to leave, and she knew it, but the Draven council was refusing to let me free of the walls, fearing Jorvans would take me back. There are enemies in Stonegate, and we have ways to defeat them. I am not bespelled by soul craft. Now, let me go and stop those two fools from killing each other."

Yrsa's face pinched, but after a few tenuous heartbeats, she returned a brisk nod, took my hand, and together we rushed for the front of the tent.

No blood hung in the air, and no bodies were scattered along the ground, but we seemed to be on the brink of battle.

Arrowpoints were aimed at the heads of two Stav Guard, and two fara wolves—Kyrre and Òlmr—snarled at the other two men. Between the wolves, Brynn and Auki had blades leveled at the hearts of the guards.

Behind them, Thane sat, eyes distant, almost milky. Roark knelt in front of him, the gold of his eyes now shifted to a rich red.

Good gods, Skul Drek had taken the prince.

"Ah, Lyra. Glad to see you unharmed." Gunter flashed a playful grin, never lowering the arrow he held against the Stav Guard. "You're not harmed, right? Because I might as well put this sod out of his misery if you are. You know our dear prince will make it much more painful."

"I'm fine." I went to one of the Stav. Young in his face, terrified, but clearly distraught over the state of his prince. "Thane isn't being harmed. The Sentry—"

"He is *not* the Sentry."

I sighed. "Roark uses soul craft. He's speaking to Thane. If the Dark Watch lowers their blades, will you stay yours?"

The Stav flicked his eyes to me. "Are you mad, Melder Bien?"

I rolled my eyes. Emi held the other Stav Guard still. Her brow was twisted in pain, and I understood why.

Yrsa had not moved from the front flap. Frozen, locked in a tangle of rage and heartbreak, she looked at Emi.

"Yrsa," I said softly. "Let them explain."

Tears lined the princess's lashes. "Whatever there is to explain, it will never excuse such lies."

Emi winced as though she'd been struck.

Gods, I did not have time for this. "I'm going to bring them out."

"Find those connections." Gunter winked. "You'll be all right."

I'd drawn up the bond in the tent, felt the pull to the prince. Now I merely needed to find the crueler threads.

One palm to my chest, the hum of craft was there. Solid. Firm. Flesh on my fingertips glowed in fibrous tendrils. Golden and hot to the touch, filaments spilled off my palms, weaving into a taut rope.

I curled my grip around it, pulling, tugging, drawing the end nearer to me. Each pull and light faded. Smoke burned the back of my throat. A cold breeze flitted my hair about my cheeks.

Murky trees bent and curved. Leaves dripped from the branches like they were made of slime on the banks of swamplands. But in the darkness, the forms of the Stav, of the Dravens, even the two wolves were starlit beams, keeping the shadows at bay.

There, in the center of them all, were Skul Drek and the prince. They were not lashing at each other. Truth be told, Thane looked a little defeated, a little weary.

Skul Drek, the most brutal shards of my husband's soul, stood near the prince. His expression was almost . . . compassionate. Between them lived a glittering silver thread, weak and delicate, but the longer they spoke, the brighter it gleamed.

Brothers without blood. They were the same as Kael and me. If only they would not remain too damn stubborn to see it.

And we had little time to spend bickering about the past.

They would need to accept what had torn us apart, so perhaps we might move on together.

I took the first step forward.

MY VISION HAD HARDLY REFOCUSED ON THE SMALL CAMP BEfore I was crushed against a broad chest. Roark's fingers dug into my hair, tilting my head back. Those furious golden eyes bounced back and forth between mine for a heartbeat, then another, before he slammed his mouth to mine.

There would never come a day when I grew tired of this man's kiss.

I dug my fingernails into the back of his neck, my tongue brushed over his, and I arched against his body.

The rough skin on his palm patted the side of my cheek, once, twice, three times. *Mine.*

I bit down on his bottom lip, consumed with the need for more, a need to nestle beneath his ribs and never break free again.

"My prince, what would you have us do?"

The voice broke through the spell. Brow to Roark's, I breathed him in for a moment.

Behind us, the Stav Guard looked to Thane. The Jorvan prince slowly rose from the dirt, brushing off his trousers. Sweat dampened Thane's brow, he wiped the corner of his lips with the back of his hand, and he gave Roark a strained look.

Yrsa broke through her resentment of Emi and hurried to the prince's side. She gripped his arm. "Are you all right? Did he hurt you?"

Thane swallowed. "I'm fine."

Roark's eyes shadowed. He stood and tucked me behind him, using one hand to address the prince. *I tried to despise you when I first came to Stonegate.*

"After I saved your ass."

You were an enemy and I should've hated you. I didn't. You became my brother.

"Then we see brotherhood differently. You had a fealty bone." Thane glanced at the missing tip of Roark's finger. "A bone I never used, never wishing to take your freedom from you. All the while you kept such secrets from me." The prince ground his teeth together, fists clenched. "You said there are explanations."

Roark dipped his chin.

"Well." Thane took a step closer and held out one hand, a show of a truce. "I'd like to hear them."

Roark hesitated, then, slowly, he clasped Thane's forearm.

Thane wasted no time before slamming his fist into Roark's jaw.

"You are a damn *prince*! And you never said a word!" Thane raged. "Gods. The things we could have done with that twisted soul of yours. The torment we might have leveled against the sods who traipsed those halls. It would've been *glorious*."

He struck at Roark's shoulder again, but one of the Stav pulled the prince back before Kyrre's teeth could sink into the prince's arm.

"Kyrre, no! Down," I shouted at the pup. The wolf pulled back, ears flat, teeth bared.

By the gods. Thane was furious that he didn't know Roark was a prince? That they couldn't play tricks on noble folk at Stonegate with Skul Drek? I fought the urge to roll my eyes. Of course those would be the direst offenses to Thane's nature.

Gunter's arrow was lowered, but he seemed confused about which prince to focus on. No doubt he'd want to retaliate against Thane, but Roark was spitting blood.

Brynn and Auki spoke with Emi, and none of the three seemed disturbed. Almost like they agreed Thane had earned his strike.

"Dammit." The Jorvan prince pulled back, shaking out his hand. "Does that creature in your soul make you made of stone?"

Roark leaned over his knees, one hand on his jaw. I pressed a palm to his back and glared at Thane.

"What?" The prince arched his brows. "The bastard deserved it. Now we can sit peacefully and tell our tales."

Roark straightened, a trickle of blood dripped from his lip, and he glared at Thane. *Feel better?*

Thane lifted his chin. "I do, actually. Thank you for asking. Although I'd feel even better if I could have a go at the other side."

"No." I stepped between them. "We can't waste time. Yrsa, Thane, you both deserve answers, and I hope by the end of them, we don't bid farewell again. I hope you will stand with us."

THE FIRE CRACKLED BETWEEN US. LOGS WERE PLACED IN A CIR-cle, and what an odd gathering it was. Brynn stroked her wolf's head, her glare pinned on one of the Stav Guards. The kohl on Auki's cheeks had smeared into his beard, adding a feral look to his features. It did not help that he kept shaving a branch into a sharp point with his knife.

Gunter had his Dark Watch hood pulled over his head, black streaked through his lips, and he'd eaten something that had stained his teeth to look like blood.

I knew it was a ploy from the Draven folk to frighten their enemies. And it worked. Gunter pestered one of the stiff Stav who sat three paces away, constantly reaching for the guard's knives, asking about the quality compared to Draven blades.

"Ever torn out a man's throat with your teeth, Stav?" Gunter flashed his bloody grin.

Emi's smile was hesitant as she listened to Thane's boisterous tale of his and Yrsa's escape from Stonegate without alerting the whole of the royal house.

Something about Yrsa feigning womanly pains in such a way that her attendants rushed to seek bone tonics, but Thane was there at the window to smuggle her free. They slipped through the tunnel Emi was brought through as a girl, took a few of the more loyal, adventure-starved Stav Guard, and faded into the night.

"Figured it wouldn't be wise to come with a full unit of Stav when we needed to actually cross Dravenmoor's borders, which explains our meager rescue party," Thane said. "We didn't want to alert any Dark Watch scouts, yet here we are all the same."

Emi's smile grew more sincere until she looked at Yrsa and the princess promptly looked away and settled at the side of Prince Thane.

Dejected, Emi took the opposite side of the flames beside Roark.

My husband kept a possessive palm on my thigh but never looked away from Thane across the blaze.

He also didn't wipe the dried blood off his lip.

"Well." Thane folded his arms over his chest. "What do you know that we do not?"

Roark looked at the Stav Guard. *They must swear it on their fealty bones to never speak of what they'll hear.*

The Stav understood Roark well enough to look surprised.

Thane leaned over his knees and tossed a twig into the fire. "They answer to me only. If I hear they have spoken of our conversations to anyone, I'll let you eat their soul."

Roark scowled. *I don't eat souls. Everyone says that.*

"It's more fearsome." Thane waved a hand, dismissing the thought. "Now that we've all agreed to the soul feast, go on. We're listening."

There was little else to do but start at the beginning. Most of the conversation belonged to Thane and Roark, but I would interject with my own thoughts, my own experiences.

We explained it all, from the Unfettered seer's prophecy, to the peace meet where the kingdoms agreed to find the melder babe, to the betrayal of King Damir and King Hundur and the disappearance of House Bien.

The raids and the truth behind them left Yrsa wringing her skirt and Kyrre whimpering, as though he sensed Roark's pain when he described Nivek's death to Thane.

The pup's big head settled on Roark's leg, merely there and steady.

Thane hung his chin when Roark explained the purpose behind his soul rend at the hands of his mother. But a white rage flashed in his slate eyes when it was time to confess the truth of Stonegate.

Thane dragged his hands down his face. "No. It isn't possible. Fadey is . . . Baldur? Lyra, he's been everywhere in the palace. He won't leave my mother's side. Even tried to push mine and Yrsa's wedding forward when King Hundur threatened to return to Myrda, insisting it was too dangerous in Jorvandal. Baldur was livid when we refused."

"You're not wed?" Emi's head snapped up.

Yrsa looked away, but Thane offered Emi a sympathetic smile. "Not yet, Nightlark."

"Wed?" Gunter sniffed the air and pointed to Emi, then across the flames. "But you—*oof.*"

He shot Emi a glare when she kicked his shin.

"Thane, I know it seems outlandish, and I am sorry for the pain it causes you," I said. "But Fadey never left Stonegate. He and the queen have been planning this for seasons."

The prince hesitated. "The Wanderer. They want the bones of

the Wanderer, and you believe . . . all of us have something to do
with it?"

Firstborns are mentioned in the prophecy, Roark explained. *We
believe my brother might have hid his shard in the Unfettered lands for
protection.*

"I don't have a bone of the Wanderer." Thane chuckled. "If I
did, I assure you, I would boast about it often."

"Nor do I," said Yrsa. "I've never heard of such . . ." The princess paused. "Well, that isn't true. My mother would tell me a tale
when I was a young girl about the Wanderer's daughter. She built
a glittering land for herself after her father's destruction, and one
day a granddaughter, born many seasons after the daughter's
death, took up her blade and destroyed the darkness the greed of
the Wanderer had left behind.

"The granddaughter restored the peace and beauty of the
god-queen." Yrsa flushed when she took note of everyone watching her. "It might be nothing. My mother is not bold in front of
my father, but she always told me I could be the girl from the tale.
A warrior queen who defeated darkness."

Your mother would know of the seer's warning. Roark's eyes narrowed. *For all we know, she was preparing you.*

"An eerie thought." Yrsa chuckled nervously and looked at
Thane.

The prince gave her hand a squeeze, then looked to Roark
again. "The only coincidence that could be related is that I know
Fadey encouraged our union. My mother always said the melder
thought it would be wise to keep the firstborns of allied kingdoms together."

"You never told me that," Yrsa said.

"Our fathers had the final word, but mine practically drank
whatever Fadey said."

"And my father drank whatever came from yours."

"It does not solve the problem that two of these supposed firstborns don't have a damn bone," Gunter snapped. "Nor do we, really. We don't know what awaits us over those ledges."

"But you're going, right?" Thane studied me, then Roark. "You're going to find out?"

It is the only move we have to make. Roark spoke slowly. *Fadey is growing stronger and has ways of finding Lyra.*

"The wound is healing," I whispered and showed him my palm. "With Yrsa's help, I think whatever twisted connection they used to track us is breaking."

"Well done, Myrdan," Gunter said, beaming at Yrsa.

The princess shrugged and poked at the fire as if to merely keep her hands busy. "It wasn't all that impressive, and I'm sure there will be a scar. If I had more strength, it would be healed by now."

"Do not downplay your ability," Emi said, a quiver to her tone.

Yrsa held Emi's stare for a heartbeat, then another, before she shook her head and looked away.

Roark pressed a kiss to the center of my palm. *We still must be wary.*

"So here is what we know," Thane said. "Fadey is alive. My mother and that bastard murdered my father, they now control Stonegate, and they did it all to find four missing bones of the Wanderer. Should they be melded to Fadey—wait, can a melder meld themselves?"

I popped a shoulder. "I've never tried."

"There was a rumor that fealty bones would not meld properly if taken from a melder," Emi said.

"He must believe it can be done with Lyra's soul specifically," Yrsa said, avoiding her lover's eyes. "Or he would not be such a snake in the grass."

"Agreed." Thane nodded. "Let us assume it can be done, and he seeks the power of all craft to be lord over the realms of Stìgandr. We know, to him, Lyra is the melder who will give him the power to bind all craft again."

"What we don't know," Brynn said next, "is what awaits us in Unfettered lands, who killed Prince Nivek, and where any of the bones are actually hidden."

"And Kael," I said, my voice rough. "We don't know what they've done to Kael."

Roark lifted my knuckles to his lips and kissed me there.

He said nothing—no false hopes, no assurances that Kael was fine. It was one of the things I loved about the man. He did not shelter me from hard truths, but the blaze in his eyes gave up that he would fight for Kael Darkwin, and if we discovered my fears were true, Roark would kill anyone who'd hurt my brother.

He'd do it slowly.

"Not a promising start," Gunter said in a grumble.

We were silent for a drawn pause. At long last, Thane clapped his palms over his thighs and stood. "Perhaps not promising, but we do have the first step."

Roark arched his brow. *You're in, then?*

"Of course I'm in, you sod. And you knew I would be, so don't act surprised. I'm much too curious to merely go sit and wait. Not to mention, if Fadey believes me and Yrsa are part of a fated plan to make him some sort of god, I have a feeling our necks are at risk of getting slit very soon if we return. I'll take my chances with rogue Dravens."

Gunter barked a laugh. "I can see why our dear prince did not mind you, Jorvan."

Thane held up one finger. "That is a question I have. How is it none of us knew the king and queen of Dravenmoor had a second son?"

"It makes a bit of sense, don't you think?" Yrsa offered. "It kept a target off Roark's back all his life."

"Made it simpler to slip into Stonegate as a random dying Draven boy, that's for certain." Thane's grin was sly. "Tell me, how was it taking orders from everyone when you knew you were a damn royal?"

Roark glared at Thane and scratched his nose with his center finger, causing a few tentative chuckles to break free in the circle.

We ought to rest, Roark spoke to the group. *The Night Ledges will take us two days to reach.*

"Yes." Thane rubbed his chin. "We should leave at first light and keep to the heavy wood. I'm assuming we'll take the pass on the Draven side of the border?"

Obviously, Roark gestured.

"Well, prepare for a steeper route compared to the Myrdan pass. Everyone find a place to sleep." Thane glanced at me and Roark. "I suppose I'll give up my tent to the only two who are wed. By the way, you both ought to know, I'm furious about it. You should've waited until we were all boon companions again."

He did not wait for a response before aiding in arranging mats, furs, and supplies from the camp for the new Dravens.

I snorted and nudged Roark's ribs with my elbow. "I told you he'd feel slighted."

Roark leaned in and pressed a kiss to the corner of my mouth. "Why are you looking at me like that?"

His fingers brushed over the front of my throat, slow, seductive. *I want to taste you, wife.*

LYRA

A SINGLE TALLOW CANDLE IN AN IRON LANTERN ILLUMI-nated the prince's tent. Thane had a wider cot than the one where I was bound. Roark settled Kyrre outside the door to keep watch.

"He already looks like he's grown two heads taller since he bonded to you."

Roark spun on me, ignoring talk of his fara, and dug his fingertips into my hip bones. One palm splayed over my spine and the other slid up my ribs, caressing the side of one breast, until he could speak against my cheek. *Had I not found you when I did, kingdoms would've burned.*

A sigh slid from my throat, his kisses trailing across my neck. "A little excessive since I'm certain this was orchestrated by your mother."

Roark nipped at my pulse point and nodded. *Likely.*

No doubt, Elisabet sent the plea to the prince, convinced he would come to my aid. She'd questioned me regarding Thane before abandoning me, clearly seeking assurance about his character before leaving me to be taken into his hands.

She sent us, Roark gestured, tugging on the laces of the clean top Yrsa had lent me. *She made it seem as though war would begin if we did not leave immediately.*

Roark's teeth scraped across the swell of one breast. I clasped his face in my palms, tugging his lips close. "Then remind me to thank your mother for being devious when we meet again."

I kissed him, frantic and greedy. All teeth, moans, and tongues.

Roark pinned me to the cot, the ropes and thin canvas sling groaning under our weight. His hand palmed my breast, and his fingers slipped beneath the tunic until the tips brushed over my nipple.

"Hmm." I arched my spine. "I thought you wanted a taste."

The vicious smirk twisted over his swollen lips. *As you wish, wife.*

He pulled the tunic over my head and kissed a line down the center of my chest, pausing to draw in each hardened peak between his lips.

I felt wild and uncontrolled. As though if I did not lose myself in this man soon I would split through my own skin. I curled my arms around his head, holding his mouth against me.

Roark's fingers touched and flicked, kneading my breasts. *Let's see how ready you are for me.*

Blood thudded in my skull. He slid his other palm across my middle and dipped beneath the loose trousers. The tip of his finger teased my center, circling and sliding inside just enough to spin my head.

Roark moaned and grinned a little viciously. He mouthed the word *Perfect* against my parted lips and kissed me, deeper and harder.

I panted, desperate for more. He made quick work of peeling the trousers from my legs.

With a touch of copper red in his eyes, Roark knelt at the end of the cot. He dragged his tongue between my thighs, holding me captive to his beautifully cruel kiss. My fingers tangled in his hair, seeking purchase against the storm of his hands, his lips, *him*.

I moaned and bucked, and my thighs tightened around his head as release built and built until tension snapped. I slapped a palm over my mouth to muffle the scream. Tents offered little privacy, and I refused to face Thane or Gunter and their salacious words and winks come dawn.

Roark sloughed off his trousers, reared over me, and filled me in a single thrust.

His mouth brushed against my lips, the taste of me lingering there. I let my tongue trace the bottom edge of his mouth. Overheated, breathless, I rocked against his hips, needing more.

The way Roark loved me—no, cherished me—left my heart feeling like it might pound a hole through my ribs.

His hips moved slowly, making certain each thrust was thorough and brushed against a spot deep inside that locked my head into a beautiful fog. He rolled and glided his cock in and out, nearly removing himself entirely before sliding back in.

"Roark, gods. You're so deep." My head fell back, my throat bared, when he gently bit down on my nipple, his hips rolling against mine with perfect friction and pressure. "I want to feel you everywhere."

I felt delirious, like I could not get enough. Roark seemed to take it as a challenge to break me apart before piecing me together again and again.

He pinched one nipple, rolling it until I could not catch a deep enough breath. He drew the other between his lips and sucked. Hard.

I writhed beneath him with enough frenzy that the cot groaned. For a moment I feared it might break. My breaths were stilted and short. Sweat dampened strands of my hair to my brow.

Roark's eyes were fierce. Darker desires perfectly united with the heart I loved.

Another wave of heat unfurled from the crown of my head to my curled toes, and I broke apart in his arms.

Roark held me close as he bucked his hips harder and ground himself against me, the sounds of our passion between us, until his cock pulsed and he spent his release with a guttural moan. We held each other, breathing heavily.

Slowly, he rolled onto his shoulder, trying to align us both on the narrow space, and cradled my head against him.

Roark pressed soft kisses to my cheek, his fingers following. *I love you. Every piece of you.*

I fell asleep easily, safe in the arms of my hunter, my lover, my husband.

Until, healing wound and all, Fadey invaded my dreams.

ALL AROUND WERE SMOKY SHADOWS AND FROST.

There was an absence in the mirror without the scorching gaze of Skul Drek there to draw me in, to consume me. Then again, I wasn't convinced this was the rotting mirror realm.

"Hello again, Lyra Bien."

The glow of Fadey's soul had darkened even more. Tarnished bronze, as if pieces of his soul were beginning to rot away like the decay of the realm of souls. Between us that damn filament remained, frayed and tattered. It dug into his chest and burrowed into the vibrant web of my soul bond.

I wanted to rip it out.

"This isn't real." I inspected my palm. The dark, poisonous

glow from Ingir's blood craft was nearly faded, once more a brilliant golden sheen across my soul.

Fadey's sneer widened at my frantic attempts to unravel the frayed rope between us. "This is very real, Lyra. I vowed we'd speak again."

A shudder rippled up my arms. I had little desire to know all the gory plans Fadey had. He wanted to use me like a harvest of bones for his own twisted gains. "Your blood spell is gone." I held up my healing palm. "You can't follow us any longer."

"Hmm. Perhaps."

Fadey took a step to one side. I went the opposite way. We circled each other, two wolves on a hunt.

"The way I see it, you remain unable to find all the bones on your own," I said. "Perhaps I will let them rest and end you instead."

He laughed, dark and cruel. "The gods left this power to be found or to poison our land, Lyra. All I've ever desired is to restore the kingdoms, the crafts, as the gods always meant them to be. But it will take a brutality you do not have to finish it."

"Then you do not know what lengths I will go to protect those I love."

"You cannot stop my fate. You cannot stop that you are part of it." He strummed the bond between us. "Look with your own eyes; the gods have joined us. Together we will save these kingdoms from destroying one another with war. I will see to it that your sacrifice will earn you a hallowed place in Salur."

"If I am needed, then perhaps the gods have called me to gather the bones. To protect them from you."

I wanted to wake up. I could not find a way out.

Fadey's eyes were black as scorched tinder when he looked up. "Tell me, did the firstborns find you? It will make it much simpler to gather the bones with the lot of you together."

My heart cinched. He knew we'd reunited with Thane and Yrsa. No. I looked at the fading wound. They must've discovered Thane and Yrsa were gone; they must've used the blood spell to track my movements.

Perhaps it was an assumption we'd reunited, but I had no time to refute his insinuation before Fadey took another step toward me. "You know, our first meeting at Stonegate ended rather abruptly—"

"When I melded your hand to your leg? Tell me, how painful was it to break the bones away?"

A shadow crossed his face, ugly and harsh. "I'm convinced that even with our growing connection, I don't know if the wards against me would've cleared without you if I'd killed you in Stonegate. So that is why I'm here. I will let you go retrieve what is hidden. Then, you will return it to me. After, I swear to you, I will send you to Salur with no pain."

"What an offer. I think I will decline."

"You think I do not know where you're going all because you managed to heal a spell from your blood? It's too late, Lyra. I can sense the truth of it in your mind, you know I will find you before you can use anything against me." One corner of Fadey's mouth curved. "Take care over the Night Ledges. Unfettered clans are not always hospitable."

Heat drained from my face. A dream or the mirror, dread stacked heavy in my belly. "We aren't going to the Night Ledges."

"No point in lying." He tapped the side of his head. "You will bring me the final piece, hidden by the royal house of Dravenmoor. And that *is* the final piece. I know how to claim the rest. You do not."

Damn the gods. Without Nivek's and Roark's actions during the raids, Fadey would have had all of the firstborns and the female melder within grasp. Did Prince Nivek know that by shadowing his bone shard and stealing away the melder, the hunt for the Wanderer would be halted?

For a man like Fadey, such a disruption in his plans would bring out his brutality.

My brow furrowed. "Did you kill the firstborn prince of Dravenmoor?"

Fadey barked a laugh. "How I wish I had gotten to him first. Not only did he take you, but his blood spilled before I could take it for myself."

He wanted Nivek's blood?

"I once thought the hunt was pointless after the firstborn of Dravenmoor died, until I sensed the hidden power still existed, kept from me, but there. What secrets the firstborn of Dravenmoor must have kept."

I flashed my teeth. "And when I find Nivek's shard, I will see to it that you never touch the Wanderer's craft."

Fadey didn't threaten, didn't snarl, didn't shout. He did nothing but widen his smile, as though he knew something I did not. "I figured you would say such things. Never fear, Lyra. I've already seen to it that there will be little choice in the matter. You will do as I ask and bring me whatever you find in the Unfettered lands. You will have no choice." Fadey stepped back. "You were created to be a piece of this fate, Lyra. The sooner you accept it and bend to my will, the less those you love will be harmed."

Fadey's laugh cut across my mind, stirring me from rest as shadows enveloped me.

I woke gasping, Roark's arms holding me close. He cupped one side of my cheek. *Nightmare?*

Furs and blankets across the cot were askew, my hair was in tangles, and my breaths were sharp. The way Roark held me half underneath him, I took a guess that I'd been thrashing. A dream. It'd been a terrible dream.

My shoulders slumped in relief, and I buried my face against the steady thrum of Roark's heartbeat. He stroked my back. *All right?*

I nodded, never lifting my brow from his chest. "I simply want to find what your brother hid and destroy it."

If we destroyed Nivek's shard, Fadey would never have all the pieces. One by one, I would ruin every shard, every burial mound, whatever power held the lost craft of the Wanderer's bloodline.

I would do it as the dark melder chased us until, at last, we turned our blades and destroyed him.

ROARK

FIRST LIGHT CAME FAR TOO QUICKLY. LYRA RUBBED SLEEP from her eyes, weary from all that thrashing during the night. She'd mentioned that her dreams were haunted by Fadey but insisted that we move swiftly, even more desperate to reach Nivek's hidden bone.

There were passes on both Myrdan and Draven lands, narrow canyons with old switchback trade routes that were once used when Unfettered clans still ventured into the lands of Stìgandr often. Centuries before my birth.

All my life Unfettered Folk were the mysterious clans, their laws, culture, and any hint of craft unknown.

No mistake, some sort of power lived in their soils for seers such as the Gammal woman. She'd unraveled lands and crafted wars, all from her words. How she convinced kings and queens of such things, I still did not comprehend.

The journey over the ledges would not be simple, but it was

not so treacherously guarded that we'd be unable to reach the borders. In truth, my unease came more from how we'd be received once we reached the clans.

"Nivek was able to leave his shard. He was the one who arranged for Gammal to take me," Lyra said when I confessed as much. "Whether they will admit it or not, the Unfettered Folk have a part to play in all this. We simply need to find out what."

And it was that unknown that I despised.

Lyra had been hunted for her craft since her first breath—I'd been one of her hunters—and I did not relish the idea of my wife facing a new threat in a new land we did not understand.

Outside, mists rippled over the damp grass like the tides on the fjord. Thane and his Stav worked together wrapping the fur bedrolls and weapons. One of the guards kept looking at the prince, as though discomfited by his royal charge working side by side with him.

Must've been new to the Stav.

Thane did not believe any task beneath him, not when being beyond the gates of the keep did not favor royal lives over low-ranked warriors. Everyone risked greeting the halls of Salur in the wood.

So to the prince, everyone worked together to stay alive.

Gunter leaned against a thick oak, a twig between his teeth. He jutted his chin at Thane and the Stav Guard. "And where were you, my royal sod? We've already secured our packs. Take a lesson from the Jorvan, Roark."

I clapped the side of his neck, grinning. *I spent most of my life as a servant. I plan to take advantage of shouting orders at others instead.*

Gunter squinted, watching my hand speak, but when he chuckled, I assumed he gathered most of the words.

"Gods, you've become a tyrant. You could be, you know.

Threaten those who stand against you by tearing out their souls. You could control the world. Think on it. If this goes sour, I'll be the dark blade who brings your subjects to cower at your feet."

I shoved his shoulder, shaking my head, and went to help Lyra and Emi secure the horses. Emi's braid was not as tightly kept and hung loose over her shoulder. Red lined her eyes, but when I tried to press her on if she was well, my cousin simply shook her head and turned to fasten another satchel to a spotted mare.

By the distance Yrsa kept across the camp, it was not hard to guess what troubled Emi's soul.

No mistake, Yrsa felt betrayed by Emi for keeping my secrets, but Lyra heard me, and Thane found understanding. What kept the princess from doing the same?

I feigned the need to inspect the tents once more, but when I strode near Yrsa, I paused. *The betrayal was mine. Not hers.*

Yrsa had a good heart. I'd known the woman since I'd gone to live in Stonegate. Her friendship with the prince was heartening, and when she loved my cousin, I accepted her—unbeknownst to anyone—as part of my folk too.

She'd even learned my words when she did not need to.

Yrsa's jaw tightened. "Yes, and I am furious with you as well." *But you will not let her explain.*

"Have you ever wondered why Thane and I have never kept secrets from each other?"

I shrugged.

"I caught my father bedding a young servant woman. Barely a woman, really, and she looked terrified. But he was her king. He made me vow never to speak of it to my mother. From then on, he would force me to be what he called his little liar."

For what?

Yrsa's features hardened. "When he took more mistresses,

when he mistreated our folk, he forced me to go with him, forced me to stand nearby, to hear everything he did." She let her eyes close. "Then he would say, 'Now you know this dark truth that will ruin your mother. She is already weakhearted, and to know this might send her to the gods with pain.'"

I'd always thought Hundur was more twisted than even Damir. Deep in the shadows of my soul, I could feel the click of a name added to a list of those whose souls would die.

"I have lied to my mother all my life." Yrsa scoffed bitterly. "Not that she doesn't know. I'm certain she does. But the extortion of breaking her heart with the truth has kept me silent. I despise liars, Roark. Truth was my one condition for all my relationships."

I folded my arms over my chest. *Emi is not your father.*

"But trust is lost."

Because of me. My eyes narrowed. *I am her prince, Yrsa. I was the only soul willing to save her when her father prepared to sell her to a damn brothel in Myrda. To keep my curse hidden was a debt she felt she had to pay.*

Yrsa winced. She knew why Emi had fled Dravenmoor, why she had tried to slit Virki's throat before the traders found her. She had run and not stopped until she reached the Phantom Forest, where she had sent word to me.

I crowded the princess, my gestures slow, almost threatening. *If you wish to blame someone, place it atop the shoulders that deserve it. Mine. Not the woman who loves you, soul deep.*

Without another word, I turned away from the princess.

Emi studied her boots in the dirt, but Lyra stood beside the tall gelding we'd share. A faint grin teased her lips, a secret knowing; she squeezed my palm three times, then took her place just past the withers.

I settled behind her, one arm around her waist. With a simple signal at Thane, he nodded and we tore through the northern wood, the looming slate peaks of the Night Ledges in our view.

WE WERE NEARLY TO THE PASS. TWICE WE'D MADE CAMP FOR the night, and twice Lyra tossed and thrashed in her sleep.

Our mismatched crew spread out across the wide paths honey-combed across the land. Kyrre could not help but pester the horses, nipping at their hooves, and found a bit of enjoyment bothering one of the Stav. The fool kept cursing in pitchy old-language dialect, and the wolf found it delightful.

I never called him off.

Gunter, Auki, and Thane did most of the hunting. Strange how quickly the Jorvan prince got on with my childhood play-mates. Then again, proud as Thane was about his Jorvan blood, he never let something so small as borders change his opinion of others.

Show him their character, and the prince would accept people or not.

Brynn and Emi kept close to me and Lyra, trading tales of childhood and growing up in different lands.

Nights were spent with watch duties while the rest of us slept huddled together for warmth. No flames. Not this near the ledges, not when Jorvans and Myrdans would be tracking their missing royals, no doubt.

On the second night, Yrsa even handed Emi one of the fur mats without recoiling immediately. Still, she had not spoken to my cousin, and the weight of a rejected soul bond was evident in the pulpy circles beneath Emi's eyes.

Time. All there was to do was hope that in time the princess would at least hear her out.

This far north, Dravenmoor was a land of knolls and hillsides topped with frosted evergreens and dark-leafed oaks.

"If Selena were here, she'd force us to don totems to ward off troll folk from stealing us away to their caverns beneath the knolls," Lyra said.

I chuckled. *My father took me hunting here in my eighth season, when his mind was not so divided. He told me the hills and valleys were made from the first pawprint of the gods' fara wolf. The enormous beast howled and shifted the whole of the realms until new, smaller wolves clawed through the cracks of the soil.*

Lyra leaned into me with a sigh, letting her head fall to my shoulder. "You were close with the king?"

I hesitated, speaking against her heart. *For the first seasons of my life, yes. The deledan took him farther away from us as time went on. Near the end, it seemed as though he could only speak with the queen.*

"Is that why you resent her? Because her craft split his soul, but hers was the only one who could still reach him?"

Resentment had built against Elisabet for seasons. From sending me away, using me as a pawn in bloodshed, for the loss of my father. *I grew up in Stonegate never truly understanding my past. But I am beginning to see that as ruthless as her actions have been, they were done to protect what was left of her family. I am not so certain I wouldn't have done the same.*

Lyra tilted her head to look at me. "You already have. Before we even left Stonegate, you have shown there are no lines you will not cross for me, Roark." The silver in her eyes flashed as though a fiercer piece of her craft awakened. "I hope you know, there are no lines I would not cross for you."

I pressed a kiss to her hair and tightened my hold around her waist.

"Roark." Thane materialized beside us, slowing his skittish

horse. "The pass is ahead, but the wolves are snarling. And on this, I trust their instincts more than mine."

Ahead, Kyrre and Òlmr paced frantically, their attention on the bend in the path. *Have bows ready. Keep watch on the trees.*

Thane gave a curt nod and handed a bow to Lyra with a leather quiver. "Plenty of bone arrows there, Ly."

He rode to the front, informing the others.

"Roark," Lyra whispered. "I've dreamed of Fadey these last few nights. In every dream he speaks like he knows where we are, what we're doing."

Dreams can be nothing more than our minds reminding us of our fears.

"But what if they are not dreams?"

My blood quickened. I kicked off the back of the horse and drew my blade. One palm on the neck of the beast, the other out so she could read my every word. *Then remember, there are no lines with me, wife.*

Lyra dismounted and readied her bow. I tilted my head to one side. The searing burn cut through the scar across my throat. Craft, cold and thick, roared in my skull. Before I recalled the truth of my past, I hardly sensed the pull of my darker soul when Dravens had used its power.

When my own cruelty reared its head, the burn was there, a doorway I could unlatch, but I had no power to truly command the split.

Now it was a rush. A frigid tide spilling from navel to nose, pouring out of me like stepping free of my own shadow. Two of the Stav Guard still shouted in stun when the fully shaped form of the deledan poured out of me.

The others hardly noticed.

Thane merely shook his head, muttering about wasted opportunities, and loaded his own bow.

I had hardly taken a step before the first arrow shot into our camp, the point sinking deep into the throat of one of Thane's Stav.

The man coughed, blood spilled over his lips for a few heartbeats, then he fell facedown. Dead.

Shouts broke the silence. More arrows arched toward us in an ambush. At once, my darkness divided into murky rivers of shadows and wove deeper into the trees, hunting any hidden souls. Lyra, Brynn, and Thane fired their arrows into the darkness.

Sick thuds sounded when a point found the heart. Lyra fired at a slower pace, a white gleam to her eyes as she melded her arrows to hidden archers, but every shot brought a man down from the trees.

Stav Guard.

Thane barked commands to cease the moment he recognized the emblem of the white wolf across gambesons of the dead.

The attack did not cease.

Five. Ten. Shadows hunted the trees, finding the taste of souls. They all left a briny layer on my tongue, harsh with hate. It was what first connected the darkness to Lyra; she tasted warm, sweet like nectar.

Around the bend in the path more Stav Guard ran for us, blades at the ready. Gunter bellowed, shouted, and laughed a little maniacally. He swung one sword in each hand, slicing at throats and bellies.

Auki was different. Smooth movements, almost gliding across the clearing like a dancer. The man could cut through a heart, then spin around and ram the point of his knife through a throat.

Brynn shouted short commands at Òlmr while Emi took to slamming her knives into the ribs of Stav Guard, short, quick, deadly strikes. Twice, my cousin pressed her palm against the arm of a Stav to use her bone craft. She despised snapping bones, for the consequence would bring her pain. Still, when the Stav's screams rose over the fight, when his bones bent and cracked, my cousin's lips split into a vicious sort of grin.

When using craft grew too much, Emi slumped.

Before the blade of another raging warrior could strike down Emi, Yrsa stepped in front of her, the princess's knife ending in the man's heart.

I favored my ax in times like this. Killed faster with more brute force. It offered me time to focus on the craft of my soul to chase hiding Stav.

Kyrre! I summoned the fara in my thoughts. *No one gets near her.*

Black fur darted across the path. Stav Guard who aimed for Lyra and her arrows were pummeled to the ground by heavy paws and dripping teeth.

Ice ran down my spine, blood splattered on my face, and my ax lowered to the side. Slowly, my attention went to the curve in the path. My darkness tasted a soul, almost . . . almost familiar, but changed. Parts were harsh and burned against my tongue. But beneath it was a warmth, like Lyra's.

Steel clashed against steel at my back. I looked nowhere but at the broad, hulking form walking through the murky shadows.

I stumbled back when his features—bulky and a little misshapen—came into view.

"You really going to let her kill me, Ashwood? She'd never forgive you."

Ten paces in front of me, Kael Darkwin flashed a cruel, unfamiliar smile right before he drew his blade and lunged for my heart.

38

LYRA

GODS, PLEASE BE ANOTHER TWISTED BLOOD CAST. KAEL, or a man who looked like a twisted version of him, slammed his heavy seax against Roark's ax.

Seasons as the Sentry made Roark Ashwood a deadly opponent. His weapon was smaller, but in one swift motion, Roark had a dagger drawn in his other hand and slashed it over Kael's gambeson.

"Kael!" I screamed, rushing for Roark. "Stop this!"

His gaze found me over Roark's head. Dark, deadened. Those were not the playful, mischievous eyes of the boy I knew. Cruelty, hatred, and violence replaced the light he always carried.

Berserksgangur.

My insides backflipped. Kael was broader than he'd once been. His thighs were bulky, as though stones were stuffed beneath his trousers. His jaw was too square, and his forearms rippled like divots were carved into his bones.

No. Gods, no. Fadey had melded him. Time and again, that bastard had forced soul bones beneath Kael's flesh.

He was a Berserkir.

No mistake, Fadey would've chosen the most corrupt of all soul bones, forcing Kael to blot out the goodness and honor of his soul and turn it into twisted, bloodthirsty impulses.

Another cry tore from my throat. Pain, anguish, guilt—all of it encircled my heart. More Stav kept coming. I turned away from Kael and fired.

Fibers of craft had little time to shape around the bone shafts of the arrows, but still I connected them with the bones of guard after guard.

Blood stained the soil.

I ran forward, desperate to reach the two men who mattered most to me. Each striking to kill the other.

Skul Drek's shadows were frantically attacking. Roark held control of his split soul, using the shadows to carve into the Stav Guard until they wobbled on their feet. Auki, Thane, and Gunter cut them down in the next breath.

More and more, the attack was dying out, but not Kael and Roark. Pounding steps raced beside me.

"Kyrre!" I pointed toward Roark. "Go to him."

I was not bonded to the fara wolf, but he quickened his pace all the same. I didn't flinch when Kyrre leapt onto Kael's back. I wanted the beast to dig into his skin, to give us time to stop him. To save him.

Kael roared in frustration.

He swung his arm, and Kyrre, the swiftly growing wolf pup, was flung to the side. When he landed, he let out a whimper and tried to stand again, but Roark waved one hand and the pup halted.

Kael was too strong for a young wolf.

Roark stumbled against Kael's relentless strikes. My husband was formidable, nearly impossible to best in a fight, but to control so much craft, to take so many souls, and to keep his strikes sure against a Berserkir—Roark was losing.

Kael brought down his sword against Roark's ax. It dropped my husband to his knees.

"Kael, stop! Gods, please!" I skidded in front of them.

My brother's sword was pressed to Roark's throat. Both men breathed in heavy, rough gasps. With an ugly sneer on his face, Kael gripped Roark's hair and forced him to face me, the sword against his pulse.

Inky night surrounded me like a cloak. The touch of Skul Drek curled around my wrists, a tether. A silent warning I was not to take a step closer.

"This is not you, Kael. They've corrupted you."

He laughed. "I'm seeing more clearly than I ever have, Lyra. And you were warned about this. If you have come here unprepared, that is your fault."

"What are you talking about?"

Kael tilted his head but tightened his grip on Roark's hair. "You are to bring what you find over the ledges back to Stonegate. Or"—he pressed the edge of his blade against Roark's throat until a trickle of blood trailed down his skin—"the poor Sentry will die. His life is in your hands, Lyra. Make your choice."

Fadey's promise. He told me in those dreams he would see to it that I had no choice but to bring Nivek's shard to him.

Roark's eyes were hard. He gave a slow shake of his head. One hand at his side was moving with words. *Do not move.*

Over and over, the same command.

Tears burned. I tightened my hold on the bow in my hand. "There are no lines. I told you already."

Coils of darkness knotted around my wrists, my throat, my waist. The hands of Skul Drek tugged me back, choosing me instead of himself, kneeling beneath the blade.

I resisted, heart breaking, and aimed an arrow at the man I'd always called brother.

For a moment, Kael looked befuddled. "You would kill me? After you abandoned me to Stonegate?"

One tear dropped to my cheek. I drew the bowstring taut. "I never wanted to leave you. But I will not let you take him. The Kael I know would never do this."

Could I release the arrow? This was not Kael's doing. This was Fadey, and he knew to use my brother against me was the only leverage he had. But . . . the melder was a fool and did not understand how deep the soul bond, the love, I had with Roark Ashwood had burrowed into me.

He was in my blood, my mind, my heart.

He was my whole soul.

And Kael, the beautiful, joyful man I knew, would never want to live like this. ———

"Lyra." Brynn stepped beside me, one hand rubbing her chest. "I'll stand with whatever you choose, but for your sake, aim for the leg. The side. Try to give him a chance."

At Brynn's voice, something shifted in Kael's focus. For a moment, he looked at the woman as though trying to place her. A flicker of the gentle summer blue of his eyes was there beneath the berserksgangur curse.

It was the distraction we needed.

With Kael's attention on Brynn, Roark spun out of his tepid grip. In the next moment, Skul Drek enrobed my husband. Shadows, thick and cold, wrapped around my brother's bulky throat, choking him. His flesh turned a sickly shade of puce. He swatted at the unyielding grip of Skul Drek's darkness.

Roark's fists were clenched. He looked nowhere but at Kael.

When my brother slumped forward, eyes rolling back in his head, Roark slammed the handle of his ax against Kael's skull.

He fell forward, facedown in the soil, unmoving.

Shadows faded, the heated copper-red of Skul Drek's eyes slipped into Roark's gold. I didn't move, watching as Roark checked the pulse in Kael's neck. My husband lifted his glare to me. He nodded sharply, then gestured for the others to bind Kael before he woke again.

Stav Guard bodies littered the path. One guard wandered aimless, soulless. Yrsa was the one to slit his throat, giving him peace in Salur rather than a life of emptiness.

Thane sat on a boulder and studied Kael. "He's been melded. Fadey really is there."

"Did you not believe them?" Gunter pressed.

"I did, but . . ." Thane shook his head. "Part of me hoped . . . I don't want to have to kill my mother. She has done this, and she will face her end, just like Fadey."

My heart cracked for Thane. He spoke true. Ingir would meet a dark fate if we stopped Fadey.

Roark wore a look of violence when he came to me.

I held his face and inspected the wound on his throat, a little frenzied to calm my fear and assure myself he was alive. He was unharmed.

"They weren't dreams," I whispered against his lips. "Fadey can find me, even with Ingir's blood craft healed. It is like he speaks to me in the mirror the way we do."

Roark's eyes narrowed. His mouth tightened in rage. He said nothing and gave me a fast, hard kiss. A vow that the melder would pay. The possessive nature of Roark Ashwood would take his infiltration of my mind as one of the more grievous sins the dark melder had committed.

A low growl from Òlmr sent a new rush of panic down my spine.

"Is the beast tamed for now?" a smoke-ragged voice called from above.

The dialect was common language, words understood across all the lands. Often tide wanderers, the folk who believed the sea was more their home than any kingdom, would speak it at the docks in Skalfirth to better handle their trade.

Along the dark cliffs of the Night Ledges, shrouded heads peered over. Furs or cowls half covered every face that appeared along the jagged switchbacks of the upper pathways. Spears made of blue asp and onyx stones were in one hand, bronze blades in the other.

Footsteps scraped along the grit and soil of the pathway. Roark had one arm in front of me, his ax in the other hand. I raised an arrow. Thane backed away from Kael's slumped body as four figures emerged among the fallen.

"Saw the beast attack." The figure in the center gestured at Kael's body. Tall, strong, with a slight limp in one leg. I assumed by the tone of voice that the person beneath the mask and hood was a woman. "Why let it live?"

"Don't," I shouted when another figure used the point of a short blade to nudge Kael's hip. "He means a great deal to us."

"He's lost, little one," said the woman. "You wish to risk your lives by bringing him?"

Bringing him? I did not have a chance to respond before Òlmr took a possessive stance in front of Kael, fangs bared. As though Brynn had silently commanded her fara to stand watch.

"I am not leaving him." I lowered my bow, taking a risk. I let it drop to the ground. "Are you of the Unfettered lands? We . . . have need to go there."

The woman chuckled. "Aye, little one. Saw you on your way, so we felt it might be prudent to meet you."

"What in the two hells does she mean?" Gunter muttered at Auki.

The other man said nothing, but simply kept a tight grip on his blade.

I didn't understand their arrival, as though we were expected, when the Unfettered had not raised a blade. They had not attacked.

"Will you take us over the ledges?" I asked.

The woman stepped forward and tugged down her half mask. Her skin was a light shade of brown, and short, dark hair curled over her brow. She looked to be near the age of Elisabet, but swirls of inked runes and patterns of serpents and vines coated her throat and under her jaw.

Tales of her life. Old Gammal told me that Unfettered Folk inked their flesh with their achievements. A grand tapestry of their journey.

"We were sent for you, so yes, we'll take you. Best to see what sort of fate the cruel Norns have planned by entangling our paths." The woman looked down at Kael. "If you insist on taking the creature, he must be bound the whole of the way. No exceptions, no matter what he says. How do you plan to heal him?"

I swallowed. "Remove the corrupted bones. Slowly."

Memories of tearing a Berserkir to pieces thudded in the back of my mind. I would take care with Kael. Little by little instead of all at once. I would unstitch those bones until he was free.

No matter how long it took.

The woman studied Kael. "I suppose we'll see. Come. If you wish to reach our lands before nightfall, you'll want to keep up."

LYRA

THE NIGHT LEDGES ARE MADE OF SLATE AND GRANITE stones. Ancient ash hardened into jagged layers peeks through lighter shards of rock, and over the seasons, folk had carved out switchback roads all along the cliffs. Paths took a sharp veer this way and that up the steep slope that burned the lungs and throbbed in the legs.

The journey was tiresome. Paths were littered with uneven rock and sharp stones, and with the horses, wolves, and us with more aches and bruises from the attack, we maintained a weary pace.

The Unfettered Folk took the head and rear, boxing in the rest of us, but halfway up the steep cliff, I was glad for it.

I studied their steps, mimicking how they avoided slipping and scraping their knees on stones. They moved like the wind across the sea, part of the climb but above it all at once. Lifetimes of traipsing to and from the upper ledges added strength to their bodies and a sure-footed gait I did not share.

Two of Thane's Stav Guard still lived. The other two had fallen with Kael's attack. The men slipped more than once, all the bulky armor over their shoulders adding an uneven weight.

Emi admitted that heights turned her stomach and spun her head. Once we were twenty paces above the canyon floor, she clung to the cliffside with one hand and barely managed to hold tightly to the reins of her horse with the other. Her fingernails dragged along the stone as though she would claw a tunnel straight through it.

Forty paces up, Yrsa let out a huff of irritation, took command of Emi's mare, slipped her fingers through Emi's, and had been whispering soft assurances since.

Roark kept watch on my back, silent and stoic, the warrior alive in his countenance. Always ready to strike.

I looked over my shoulder when we spilled onto a wider switchback for water and rest. The Unfettered were clever and had fashioned a sort of sleigh from twigs and branches. For the first part of the journey, Roark's horse and Thane's dragged Kael's unmoving body behind them.

Until he stirred.

He'd thrashed against the thick bands on his wrists that were secured to another strap around his middle.

Roark stepped in front of my brother, shadows spilling from his pores. Kael's eyes had grown milky and distant, and the red glow of Skul Drek had flashed in Roark. I did not know what the deledan threatened him with, but he'd been scowling and silent since.

Now he walked near the back, his hands bound and tied to the bridle of one horse while Gunter and Auki walked on either side, blades at the ready. Brynn kept near Òlmr, a look of discontent on her face every time she stole a glance at my now-twisted brother.

He understands what will become of him should he try to touch anyone, Roark said against my palm.

I accepted the skin of water he held out. "I know you pulled him away to the realm of souls, which I don't understand. You do not have a bond."

So certain? He cupped a palm around the back of my neck, drawing my mouth close to his, then spoke against my cheek. *You are my wife; he is your brother. Like it or not, fate has shackled him to me as well.*

I could not help it; I laughed.

This Kael, surly and bloodthirsty, likely despised Roark Ashwood having any command over his soul. The true Kael would be giddy that a man he'd always admired was now his kin through me.

"What did you say to him?"

Warned him what would happen should he touch a single soul here. Brutal things you'd be furious I dared even speak. A lot of blood and pain, then a bit of proof what I said was true.

"Roark, what did you do?"

Me? Don't blame me. He turned to offer the water to Thane and the Stav, gesturing over his shoulder. *Blame those darker edges that make you scream, wife.*

Bastard.

I did not know what Roark had done, but Kael kept rubbing a spot over his ribs, just below his heart, as though the bones ached.

As we rose, the air grew thin and crisp, and a heavy cloud cover encircled the upper ledges like a cold swamp. To wade through the mists slowed our steps. When frigid rains fell, the Unfettered did not stop, but merely tugged their fur cowls lower over their brows and trudged on.

Roark shrugged off his own woolen hood and placed it over my head amid my protests. Until the shade of his palms turned a sickly blue, and I forced him to squeeze beside me so we could walk together, siphoning whatever warmth we had left.

By the time stars broke through the murky storm, our feet dragged and our complaints grew silent. What was the point? It felt as though we all knew we kept pressing forward or we stopped and died of cold on the Night Ledges.

A sob nearly spilled out of me when the path flattened and we reached the high peak. More switchbacks descended to a valley below. Distant lanterns speckled the night from a village, shelter, warmth.

The lead Unfettered woman stepped to my side, tossing back her damp hood. "'Tis a simpler journey from the other canyon across the Myrdan border. But you all fared well enough. Even your creature is silent."

Kael kept a distance from the others. His gold curls stuck to his brow, and he pointed his rage nowhere but at the ground.

"You said you saw us." I gave a nod of thanks when the woman handed over the water again. "What do you mean?"

"Our clans are talented in ways your folk are not."

"You do have craft."

"Every soul is blessed by the gods in some sense," she said. "Different abilities do not mean lesser, greater, or dangerous. We do not fear your differing powers, and we certainly don't go boasting about ours. We live simple lives here. Organized in our own ways, but free of power-mad kings and queens."

I took in the Unfettered village. "If you do not bother with our realms, why are you here, helping us?"

"As I said, we do not fear different craft," she said. "We find beauty in all of it, even your dark prince there."

Roark tended to Emi, who could, at last, breathe now that we'd reached wider roads and flat ground. She would need to prepare to descend from the height, but she seemed steadier when Yrsa sat beside her on a boulder.

"His craft is fearsome to many," I admitted. "Not to me."

"What we fear is when gifts of the gods are not used how the gods intended. When greedy folk twist and corrupt." She tilted her head toward Kael. "Such things impact us all. Unfettered may be peaceful folk, but should these corrupters defeat you, they will come to us."

"So you help to avoid future battles."

She smiled. "Wouldn't you? We are bold. Warriors if we must be, but we prefer a life of peace, where we can be free."

"Does no one lead here?"

"We have what is called our Lawspeaker. Like a king in your lands, but he lives in more humility, guiding and serving our clan. He keeps our peace and our laws."

"He sent you?"

"He took counsel from the seemódir. She is an elder who guides us on our fate."

Like Vella falsely claimed to do in Skalfirth. "I knew an Unfettered woman who had been captured and sold. She was a seer and looked after me as a girl."

The woman hummed. "Sold? I do not know any of my folk who would stand for such a thing. They would rather greet the gods. If she remained to look after you, then you must have mattered to her a great deal. Rarely does my clan show much affection to outsiders."

"Again, you are here helping us."

She grinned. "I assure you, little one, I would much rather be warm in my bed right now. But fate has other plans."

The woman said nothing more and led us down the backside of the Night Ledges.

Roark took my hand, keeping close to my side. Thane was in

better spirits without the bitter whip of the canyon winds on our faces and had taken up taunting Auki about his fear of piercing holes in his ears.

Thane tugged on the bones pierced in his lobes. "I'll do it for you, fearsome Dark Watcher. What is your task again? Running with the damn wolves? But, oh, you pale at a small hole in your ear."

Gunter laughed. Even Auki chuckled.

Strange, wonderful, unbelievable—Dravens and Jorvans and Myrdans all walking among Unfettered Folk as allies.

Fadey was horrid and vicious, but did he know how fiercely his greed was uniting enemies?

The moon was high when we reached one of the roads leading to the village. The air was absent of the hint of brine from the long and short seas back home. Instead, each breath was cool and crisp, with the taste of sweet grass and smoke.

Vine-wrapped gates I'd not noticed from above encircled the village. Unfettered lands were made of tall, grassy meadows and slender, crooked trees. The valley was wide and deep, expansive open grounds with a few distant forests.

The woman and her crew led us alongside a dark, winding river. Odd stalks of grass with vibrant blue berries grew in the water instead of on land. Pale petals surrounded the fruit and seemed to glisten in the moonlight.

Throughout the river other people stood knee-deep in the water, harvesting the berries.

"Heila root," the lead woman called over her shoulder. "Our most valuable crop in the River Clan."

My heart jumped. Nivek had spoken of this clan.

"The berries can sustain a man for a month without meat or grain," she went on. "The roots are strong enough to weave into rope, and the blooms can heal the blood, bones, and dire wounds. You may see forms of it in your blood crafted tonics and spells."

"Only blooms under moonlight," said another Unfettered man. "Harvested in the sun, it will wilt."

I had not realized I'd paused to watch the men and women picking the strange stalks until Roark tugged on my hand.

Watchguards lined the gates in narrow towers lit by torchlight. They wore heavy cloaks made of bear and fox pelts. Their faces were smudged like they'd rolled in ash, with black and white paint streaked down their eyes, cheeks, and chins. The guards were armed with spears and blades that reminded me of scythes.

"Keela," a guard shouted down. "You've returned with visitors?"

The woman tossed back her hood. "I found the souls the seemódir saw. Open the gates."

Ropes whipped and went taut. Hinges on the thick doors protested and cracked, but slowly the wooden barrier split.

"Follow me," Keela said.

My pulse quickened and my stomach felt as though stacked stones filled the bottom. I did not let on to anyone that my nerves were raging except to squeeze Roark's hand. No doubt he would not be able to feel his fingers come dawn.

We followed closely, the feel of eyes from the Unfettered guards boiling over my scalp. Then, on my next step, I slammed into something solid, the force of it cracked against my skull.

"Gods." I pressed a palm to my brow, mortified I'd walked into one of the damn walls.

But I hadn't.

Roark reeled around, confused. Nothing was before me. No gate, no wall, no tree. Nothing. I blinked and took a step forward. Again, my body slammed into something solid, something unseen.

What is it? Roark would not release my hand.

"I don't know. I can't go forward."

Brynn strode past with her brother but paused two paces ahead of me. Next, Thane, Emi, and Yrsa.

Even Kael strode past, less like he despised us and more with amused concern on his features. "Trouble, Lyra? We can always return to Stonegate."

Roark glared at Kael. My brother jolted and shook his head, cursing under his breath. Clearly he was battling the viciousness of the soul bones.

The whole of our travel party gathered around me but could continue walking through the gates.

Roark gently pulled on my hand and spoke low between us. *Try again.*

Disquiet rippled over my arms. One step, two—my forehead struck a shield.

I scrambled back. "Roark. I can't go through. What's happening?"

He stepped by my side, pulling me against him, unwilling to move forward without me.

"What is the problem?" Keela materialized through the crowd.

I shook my head. "Something is keeping me out."

The woman returned a narrow look. "You cannot cross our wards? The only soul we've warded from our gates is the destroyer of realms. The one you fight, the one who seeks all folk to bend the knee."

"I-I-I know. Fadey, he cannot step through. That's why he sent my brother to use against me. He believes a bone shard is here, and he desires me to get it for him, but I plan to destroy it."

Keela snorted. "Bone shards. That's what you are after?"

"The Wanderer's." I dragged my fingers through my hair, panic rising. "I can see the souls of bones with my craft. We have reason to believe the power of one of the Wanderer's bones is buried here. Is that why I can't enter? Because I have the same craft as Fadey?"

Another voice, gentler, more aged, broke through the crowd. "The wardings are against his blood, not the power within it, elskan."

I froze.

Roark's arm around my shoulders held me firmer against his side. Another woman, hunched and clad in a long, black silken gown, stepped forward. Unfettered Folk dipped their chins, greeting her as "Seemódir" and stepping aside for her to come to me.

Her knobby fingers were inked in the lovely coils I'd traced so many times, her eyes as kind as I recalled. She beamed down at me, the chip in her front tooth still there. I'd forgotten it.

I blinked through tears. "Gammal. You're alive."

ROARK

THE WOMAN KEPT LOOKING AT LYRA LIKE SHE MIGHT BE near tears, gentle and loving. But when she drew nearer and I stepped in her path, the woman's glare turned so vicious that if I was not determined to keep my wife unharmed, it might've brought me to pause.

"Hmm. You have walked a trying fate, boy." The woman tilted her head side to side, studying me. Memorizing me. "But those steps have been bold and brave. For you, I will always hold affection for how you have protected my elskan. But there is another fate you may yet alter by stepping through these gates."

I'm not going anywhere without her. The woman would not understand me, no mistake, but I would speak it anyway.

To my stun, she laughed. "I have no doubt that if Lyra became a towering tree, you would join its roots."

"You know hand speak?" Lyra asked.

"I know many things." Gammal trapped her face between her wrinkled palms. "Forgive me for using your blood from all those seasons ago. But it was needed to prepare for days as this, elskan. We knew he would strike at us again. He would come looking for what he lost, and I could not risk my people. But I will remove them now so that you might enter."

"What's going on?" Thane spoke, one hand on the hilt of his sword. "You used Lyra's blood to ward her out when she was a child?"

"Well, I could not get to the dark melder, now could I? He was not the one near me. Now, come."

What was she even talking about? Lyra hesitated, then, with her hand still in mine, she took a step after the old woman.

Near one of the posts of the main gate, Gammal stopped. Her spine was crooked and bent, but she knelt as though her knees were spry as a child's. Placed in front of her was a totem hanging over a clay bowl.

"I'll be needing a drop of blood to reverse the ward, elskan."

Lyra knelt beside the woman. "Are you a blood crafter?"

"No." Gammal rested a palm on Lyra's shoulder. "But I have met many who've crossed those ledges. Some have traded their blood casts in return for our hospitality. This, you see, is one such cast I requested when I returned over the Night Ledges. Now, just a drop."

The others gathered close. Yrsa tilted her head. "I've seen blood wardings crafted before."

And? I pressed when she did not go on.

The princess faced me, one brow arched, her voice a low whisper. "Roark, when someone's blood is warded, it will shield against them and . . . their kin."

Shit.

I watched Lyra wince when the seer woman pricked her fingertip. The drop of blood fell to the bottom of the bowl with a hiss, like it boiled against the surface. Across the gates a fleeting shock of white sliced down the wooden walls, gone before I was certain if it had been real.

With Lyra's aid, Gammal rose again. "There. You shouldn't be stopped now."

A rosy flush filled Lyra's cheeks. "Gammal, why does my blood ward against me and Fadey if craft has nothing to do with it?"

She suspected. The tremble of fear, of a desire to fall away into the cracks of the soil, was there in her question. Lyra had been raised sheltered from craft, but she'd learned to be suspicious, untrusting, and press for answers.

I feared the proclivity to yearn for knowledge would serve her too well now.

My palm slid across the small of her back, there for her should she need it. A vow to be the force to hold her upright if she should stumble.

The Unfettered seer looked between us, holding her response inside for a breath, then another. With a heavy sigh, the woman took Lyra's hands in her own. "This dark melder who hunts you is your blood, elskan."

Lyra stumbled backward, her shoulders striking my chest. "No. No, what do you mean, my blood? He . . . he can't be—"

"You are his daughter, elskan." Gammal's voice hardened. "But he is no father."

"SHOULD WE, I DON'T KNOW, MAKE HER SPEAK?" GUNTER, arms folded over his chest, stood at my side, watching Lyra pace near the river's edge.

I shook my head.

"Would it help if we spoke to her?" Emi gnawed on her thumbnail.

Again, I shook my head.

"Fadey." Thane rubbed the back of his neck. "It was well-known that the man was not a stranger to bedding folk, but . . . I think we should speak to her."

I pressed a palm against Thane's chest, stopping the prince from approaching Lyra.

Someone chuckled at our backs.

Darkwin, still bound by his wrists and ankles, sat against a stack of bushels filled with the strange moonlight blooms. "You all wish to pester her. Leave her be. She will speak when she has a moment of solitude to think through what she's learned. Pester her, and she will wear those masks she once hid behind and convince you all she is well inside."

Brynn and the two wolves stood near, ready to ram a blade into Darkwin's skull should the berserksgangur take hold again. The grimace on her features made it appear like proximity to Kael left her in physical pain.

His voice was not the same light, carefree tone I once knew the man to have, but it was not laced in venom. More aggravation than anything else.

Darkwin used his bound hands to point at Lyra. "And when she wishes to speak, it will not be to you lot."

"Think you deserve to speak to her, Darkwin?" Thane rolled his eyes. "You tried to force her back to the bastard who wants to meld her bones to his body."

"I didn't say it would be me." His laugh was dead, flat, and cold when he looked to me. "I'll give you a bit of advice: Don't be a bloodthirsty fool and leap straight to slaughter for what Fadey's done to her. Keep your head, Ashwood."

With all the dark souls melded to Kael, perhaps he could feel the tangle of hate boiling in mine.

No part of me wanted Fadey to take another breath in peace. In truth, what would soothe every piece of my soul would be to know he could not find comfort. I yearned for his steps to ring out such pain that it made him retch. I craved for his screams to lull me to sleep like a sweet tune.

I desired nothing more than to be the one who watched the light leave his eyes, preferably with his own blood staining his skin.

Beneath the hate and rage was a sharp, needling barb. Pain, hurt, betrayal. Emotions that were not my own. Through the threads of our connection, Lyra's pain seeped into my soul.

All at once, Lyra stopped pacing. Her arms hugged her middle, and her shoulders slouched.

No more space, no more waiting.

With the others silent, I went to the river's edge. Hands clasped behind my back, I stood beside Lyra. I did not touch her, did not make a move to speak.

Lyra released a long shudder of a breath. "He doesn't know. Fadey, I mean. He doesn't know, I'm sure of it. The way he speaks of me, of our connection and the bones, he believes Ingir crafted a blood spell to connect us. But she was using a blood bond that was already there."

I did not know what to say. What did it matter if Fadey was unaware that he'd fathered the child he'd been hunting? He was a dead man either way.

"You once saw melding craft as monstrous. You hated Fadey for his brutality. Everything about him lives in me—blood and craft."

I dragged my knuckles down her arm, waiting for her to look at me. *You are insinuating that I will come to think of you as something wicked like Fadey.*

When she blinked, a tear rolled down her cheek. I used my thumb to brush it aside.

"It is not so hard to make the insinuation." Lyra looked down at her palms. "I have felt the darkness in my craft. I've desired to slaughter with it. Perhaps when we find the Wanderer, I will be no better than Fadey."

There is a problem with your logic, I began on her palm. Slowly, I slid my hand up her arm, holding one side of her face. *I have seen the darker edges of your heart. It has only made me want you more. I have also seen Fadey's. It has only made me want to rip out his spine. Listen to me now: you are not the same as him.*

A bit of the weighty shadow brightened in her eyes and, gods, what worlds I would burn to see the light blaze every damn day.

"I want to destroy him." Her voice was low, dangerous.

Then I will drop him at your feet and hand you the blade.

"I feel as though I should take pause, knowing our connection, but it only deepens the desire to end him."

You owe him nothing, and certainly not your empathy and loyalty.

Lyra studied the flow of rippling water for a breath. "I had a father, Horace Bien, and he was kind, strong, firm, and gentle."

She spun on me, practically spitting out her words. "Fadey learned of me, and I have no doubt he fueled the lust for craft to inspire the raids."

I pinched her chin between my fingers, drawing her mouth close. *House Bien fought for you to live. They wanted you to live.*

"I know. And I will. For all of us. Fadey did not just seek House Bien during the raids; he wanted the Wanderer. He wanted us all. His actions killed Nivek and my family, but most of all, his greed nearly ended you."

My fingers tangled in her hair, gripping the roots. *And what do you plan to do about it, wife?*

"No lines for you." She pressed her palms to my chest. "I want to know everything. I want to learn what Nivek needs us to find. I want to discover whatever power the Wanderer left behind. Then, I want to bathe in Fadey's blood."

I grinned against her lips. *This is not the time nor place to seduce me.*

Her laugh was a sound I would die to protect. Cheeks still wet with tears, she kissed me sweetly. "Come on then, Ashwood. We have fate to face."

GAMMAL, KEELA, AND A LINE OF UNFETTERED WATCHMEN LED us through the main roads of the township.

Unlike coastal villages in the Stìgandr realms, the Unfettered Folk depended on routes of trade to distant townships I did not know, or to the passes to our kingdoms.

Homes were made from stone foundations, wooden walls, and thatched rooftops. With the chill, some longhouses had young ones in the windows along with an ewe or a goat kept out of the damp air.

Scents of smoke and spiced lamb tangled with savory herbs and sweat in the main market. Small shacks bustled with folk dressed in furs and thick wool coats and skirts. Unfettered traded silver and jade rings, fishbone hooks, blossoms, speckled eggs that were larger than those I'd seen back home, and colorful threads, wool, and linens.

"You do not trade by sea?" Thane asked the old seer, unable to muffle his curiosity.

"Sea trade is done," said Gammal. With a crooked finger she pointed to distant roads. "The Long Sea curls around the eastern edges of our lands."

Gammal shuddered.

Thane chuckled. "Does that trouble you?"

"Do you know much of the lands beyond your three kingdoms, Prince?"

Thane flushed. "The longer I have been on this strange journey, the more I am horrified to admit I know very little of what lies here beyond the ledges."

"Well, there are troubles here the same as there are troubles where you are from."

"I thought Unfettered lived as they wished. There is no king or queen."

Gammal hummed. "I assure you, the lust for power lives everywhere."

Like the prince, I did not know a great deal of how the distant Unfettered territories worked, but if different clans were scattered across the whole of the territories, no doubt there were those who'd seek power much like Damir and Fadey.

"But back to your question," Gammal said, her voice lighter than before. "There is trade by sea, but the hub is quite a distance, so the journey is only made twice a season. There are many villages along the Elfr River for trade." She opened her hand to the glisten of the river beyond the gates. "That is where our commerce is strongest."

The township was larger than it seemed. Roads webbed to distant gates. Homes were all sizes, but larger farms and longhouses seemed to take up the far edge. Gammal led us near one of the estates with several pens for creatures, stables, and a few workers tilling the soil.

A man—by the rich shade of blue on his coat and the silver on his fingers, I took him for the owner—shouted at a woman who clutched a lanky boy against her body. The boy's limbs were long and awkward, trapped in the seasons before his body determined he could look more like a man. He could not have been older than fourteen, but he was nearly half a head taller than the woman.

The way she shielded him, I suspected her to be his mother.

No doubt the sod who berated her was his father.

One glance and I hated the man.

Strange. I'd witnessed enough shouting and disrespect from pompous men not to be drawn to a halt so viscerally.

But I placed one hand on the post of the fence and simply . . . watched.

The woman was bold, to be sure. Smaller than both the boy and the man, she stood straight, chin lifted between her son and his father. Her hair was a fiery shade and grew down to her waist. The boy's was untamed and like the darkest night.

When the man made an abrupt move, like he might shove the woman, her son stepped in front of her. From where I stood, I could not hear the words spoken, but something about his son caused the bastard to fall back a pace.

He jabbed his finger at the woman once more before turning on his heel and striding away.

"Roark?" Lyra touched my arm. "What is it?"

I shook my head, watching the mother speak to her son. *I don't know. I thought her husband might strike her.*

It was more than that, crueler. A rage took me from behind, there and gone, when the moment faded. I didn't understand it.

Injustices lived in every land. I could not stop them all.

"Ah, you may wish to meet Jordis the Gentle." Gammal stood in front of a rounded house with smoke billowing from the top. She used a wooden walking stick and pointed toward the farm. "Her son is called Sindri the Wild. An interesting boy. Unique. I think you will find his gifts curious, but it is why Brokk has a distaste for the child. Now, hurry on. We have much to discuss."

Lyra took hold of my hand, guiding me toward the hut. Before the boy stepped into the stables, he faced the road. He looked at me straight on. My pulse quickened at my disconcertment.

For half a breath, I could've sworn I was looking right at my brother.

LYRA

GAMMAL'S HUT WAS ROUND AND SPACIOUS ENOUGH THAT we all could fit inside without being shoulder to shoulder. Roark and Brynn commanded the two wolves and two Stav Guard to remain near the door while the rest of us stepped inside.

Auki and Gunter roughly handled Kael onto a chair in the corner. My brother kicked at Auki when he tried to bind his ankles.

"Easy, Berserkir." Gunter gripped Kael's shoulder, giving him a little shake. "You'll play nice, or my prince will crack your skull again. Might be a good thing, to be honest. Knock some sense into your warped mind."

"Gunter." Brynn touched her friend's wrist. "Leave him. I'll keep watch."

Kael scowled at Brynn, his pale eyes tracking her movements, but he stopped thrashing.

Gunter drew in a long breath through his nose and shook his head as though disappointed. "Piss-poor luck, Brynnie."

With that, he settled between Emi and Yrsa. Tension had lessened a bit between the women, but since stepping into the township, they were not speaking much.

Cushions made of fur and wooden stools littered the space, but Gammal sat in a high-backed seat in front of the flame.

The woman pointed to tall ewers with ale for us to take. Gunter and Auki did not waste a moment. Brynn offered one to Kael. He accepted a horn and even returned a grudging nod of thanks her way.

Gammal laced her aged fingers in her lap. "So many paths have crossed in this room, and it has all been, at times, cruelly designed by the Norns who shape our lives. Elskan, you have learned that the dark melder has given you his blood."

I swallowed and knelt to the side of her chair. "You took my blood as a girl, but if you did so, then you already knew we were connected."

"I did not know until I laid eyes on you and saw him looking back at me. A few spells from blood crafters looking for quick coin, and it was clear the blood in your veins belonged to another I once knew. He comes from these lands."

"Fadey is Unfettered?"

"A boy who grew up here. A boy who took pride in his rare craft."

"You have craft in the Unfettered clans?" I asked, my voice soft.

"Our folk are not forgotten from the sagas of craft," Gammal said. "Many are born seers or visionaries. We see power in the blood, and are here to guide it, to free it, to aid it."

I closed my eyes for a breath. "He has found a connection with me. It took blood craft, or so I thought, to link us—"

"I'm certain his blood crafter queen realizes there is a blood bond between you, even if Fadey does not," Gammal said. "It would make it simpler to keep the connection to your thoughts."

Yrsa slouched and nodded. "It's true, Lyra. It would be felt the moment Ingir connected Fadey's blood to yours; she would've known you were his child."

"Clever queen." Thane ground his teeth. "My mother was always slyer than she let on. She's keeping a secret from Fadey, no mistake. Knowledge for her alone ensures that she has a touch of power in case their twisted alliance sours."

"So he will always be able to slip into my thoughts since we're blood bonded?"

"For now." Gammal offered a melancholy smile. "He may try to manipulate you, but he cannot harm you there or the bond he covets between you would snap."

I looked up at Roark. His jaw pulsed in tension. Gingerly, I slipped my fingers through his and squeezed his palm tightly.

"Now, let me tell you of the visions that began this battle. Unfettered Folk visions often teach others or offer guidance."

Gammal cast a swift look at Thane, then Yrsa, then back to me.

A smile teased the corner of my mouth. "You were the one who taught me about craft."

"Yes. But how I also blame myself for putting you in such a dreary place as you are now." Gammal studied her hands. "Many seasons ago, when Fadey was still young, like the other kingdoms in your realms, we Unfettered Folk realized that the use of these corrupted soul bones likely had a darker purpose than the crafting of their warriors."

Gammal opened a hand to Kael. My brother bared his teeth, but for a moment, I thought I might've seen a tinge of heat on his cheeks, like he wanted to curl away and hide from the others.

"Fadey was once honorable. He sacrificed himself to the bonds of Jorvandal. Offered to be the melder of Stonegate so he might learn the truth behind the soul bones." The woman shook her head. "He insisted the gods would not have given him such a craft if he were not meant to do something great on their behalf."

Gammal brushed a lock of her brittle silver hair off her brow. "He ventured into the realms of Stìgandr and lived a full season as a Myrdan man, until he let the silver scars of his eyes be known and he was brought to a young Damir."

From there, Gammal told us of the rise in Fadey's position. When Damir took the throne, for his belief in Fadey's loyalty, the Jorvan king favored the melder. Loved him. Used him. Grew in power and might with Fadey's ambition.

"Fadey melded soul bones. He grew stronger, and practiced his craft with vigor. Soon, he learned from Damir what the hunt truly was about. I've no doubt that he could even sense the power of the Wanderer within the soil of the realms." Gammal studied the flames of the inglenook for a long pause. "For a time Fadey attempted to stop the hunt by lying to the king about what he felt through his craft. But it changed, and eventually he had reason to desire the Wanderer's bones for himself."

"But where do I fit in his plans, then? If this scheme was made before I was born—"

"I didn't say that." Gammal's eyes flashed with a strange sort of heat. Like fury lived beneath the surface of her weathered skin and it was burning. "Again, I was the fool to not see how one of our own had been poisoned by the greed of the Wanderer."

"Then tell us, woman," Gunter said with a bite. "We need to know everything, even if you find it shameful."

Gammal swallowed. "Before his greed corrupted him, Fadey told us of the Jorvan's plans. As the seemódir, I told him of a dream I had, that a daughter of the god-queen could one day have the power to unite such gifts that lived in the blood of the heirs. To be as strong as the first king once was. He took pride in his purpose of protecting the bones . . . until a girl with silver scars in her eyes was spotted."

"He did not know . . . I was his?"

"Without a name of the new melder's mother, I'm certain he took it as the craft merely presenting in a new generation."

"How did his ambition change?"

"Something took hold of Fadey's heart. Something whispered to him that with the power of this melder daughter, the prophecy I spoke of could come to pass. A melder could find the power of the first king, bind it, use it. Rise with it. Instead of protecting her, Fadey hunted her. He used blood crafters, ravagers, and even some of our own folk to hunt this girl."

Auki rubbed the back of his neck. "But if he lived within Stonegate, how could he possibly be Lyra's father?"

Thane offered the man an incredulous look. "Must I explain it to you, Dark Watcher? You see, when a man and woman—"

Auki kicked at Thane's boot. "I understand that part. I didn't realize the melder bedded anyone except . . . well, except the king, as a consort."

"Fadey traveled a great deal," Thane said. "I have no doubt he was not a loyal bedmate."

"True words, Jorvan prince," Gammal said. "Like much of the Stav Guard and Dark Watch, I'm sure, lovers were found in many villages. It is to your benefit, elskan, that he did not realize one such dalliance resulted in the prophesied daughter."

"Female melders are rare, Ly," Emi whispered. "Centuries between their births."

"Yes," Gammal said. "But you brought the visions of uniting the crafts again."

"Uniting? The vision was of my birth tearing kingdoms apart." I bit down on my bottom lip.

The old woman shook her head. "No. It was merely a vision of something we've not yet seen. The interpretation of others made it something wretched."

I did not know what to say to that. If Fadey united the power, no mistake, he would rule with more cruelty than Hundur or Damir.

"When it was obvious Fadey abandoned our clan and hunted the power for himself," Gammal went on, "I went to speak to the kingdom I trusted most. To share with them what I had seen."

The seer's tale my mother and father heard, Roark spoke against my palm.

"But you told the Dravens that you saw the firstborn heirs with the bone shards."

Gammal freed a long sigh. "Gifts of the Wanderer form within the heirs of bone, blood, and soul when a god-queen's daughter finds life of her own. Through death, hate, and war, she unites these crafts once thought broken, forevermore. Heed not this fate and leave the divide, then blood will come and three kingdoms shall not survive."

Yrsa rubbed her hands up her arms, as though warming a chill. "So it was believed that the craft Fadey sensed in the lands meant every heir to each kingdom had something to do with it?"

"Yes. His interpretation has grown rather vicious, I'm afraid," said Gammal. "As you know, he believes he must use Lyra's bones to take the power of her soul, but . . . since my words gave up that the power lives within your firstborn souls, Fadey believes he must take you all to find the true Wanderer King."

Roark closed his eyes. *He plans to kill every firstborn heir?*

"Yes. Because he knows that the daughter of the god-queen's blood is alive, he believes now is the time when the prophecy is completed. Think on it, dark soul," Gammal said gently. "Not only does he believe their souls have some connection to the Wanderer—which in a way he is not wrong about, merely misguided—but he plans to be a king, a tyrant, over all. This will destroy the bloodlines of any who might challenge him."

"And my mother knows?" Thane's face had grown pallid. "She knows he seeks to slaughter me, *meld me* to his bones?"

"Perhaps much like the blood crafter queen has kept Fadey's bond with Lyra hidden, he, too, has kept dark truths from her, Jorvan prince." Gammal leaned forward and patted Thane's knee.

"We don't have any connection to the bones," Yrsa insisted. "I've never seen one, never even been told about this tale."

"But it is no less true. I said Fadey is misguided, but he is not wrong that every heir holds the power of the Wanderer King."

"What do you mean, 'holds the power'?" Thane pressed.

"Three veins of the gods' craft were torn from that first king, scattered among his heirs to make their own lands, palaces, armies, and households. Don't you see? Generations have passed with the bones of the Wanderer within them. The power of the first king has always been there, my elskans."

Thane shook his head. "Like Yrsa, I have never seen the Wanderer's bones."

"All gods." It felt as though the walls of Gammal's hut were closing in on me. "Fadey doesn't need their souls to find the first king. He doesn't realize it, but by taking their bones, he will already have the shards with the Wanderer King's soul."

Gammal's thin lips split in a grin. She leaned back in her chair. "Why is that, elskan?"

"Because the craft of the first king is *inside* them. Because the firstborns are true descendants of the Wanderer King. Like you said, I come from the blood of the god-queen, and they come from the blood of the Wanderer's heirs."

"Yes," Gammal said, her voice firm. "We know from the sagas that the god-queen blessed her three young ones with the purest veins of craft during the Wanderer's downfall. It was what corrupted him with such envy against his own children. Because of this, an unbroken vein has lived on within the three bloodlines, passing on from firstborn to firstborn. Until now, when the firstborns who align with the daughter of the god-queen hold the strongest vein of that ancient craft. Bone." Gammal opened a palm to Thane. Next, Yrsa. "Blood." Finally, she looked to Roark. "And soul."

Roark shook his head. *I am not the firstborn.*

The seer merely returned a pained smile.

"I'm afraid I will disappoint you, dear Gammal," Thane said. "I come from a long, proud line of bone crafters, true. But like my father before me, I have no craft."

"Because it was the Jorvans who began corrupting the power. Gifts of the gods can be taken, sweet prince. And it seems they have taken it from your blood."

Gunter folded his arms over his chest. "Craft faded from your bloodline because of the use of soul bones?"

Thane rubbed the sides of his head. "Seems so."

"But it does not negate that you are a direct line to the Wanderer's eldest son. The keeper of bone craft. And that craft lives within you, burning hotter now that the god-queen's blood is also born."

Thane leaned his elbows onto his knees, fists in front of his mouth, but said nothing more.

"All this is to say," Gammal said, a little weary, "Fadey knew he could restore the power of the first king the moment he learned a girl with silver scars lived. He knew he was not the one with the stronger craft, but he devised his wicked scheme to take the power of the girl fated to carry what he desired. Because of my words, he also turned his sights on every heir."

The truths were monstrous, cruel, evil.

"He would let the girl grow, of course," said Gammal. "Wait for craft to take hold in her blood. Then, he would strike."

Roark's heavy palm covered mine and squeezed three times.

"So my father, Horace of House Bien, knew I was not his daughter?"

"Oh yes. The same as your mother, Gertrude of House Bien, knew she was not your blood mother."

I coughed. "What?"

Gammal stoked the embers in the inglenook before she spoke again. "Your mother was of Myrda, from what we've learned. A young woman who likely thought the formidable melder might love her and their child. When he never returned, we know she went to live in her brother's household. There, unfortunately, the birth sent her to Salur." Gammal's eyes glistened. "House Bien, as I understand it, was kin to your uncle's wife. The mother and father you knew had no young ones and offered to help raise you."

Tears burned. My bond to Roark restored memories, and I could recall it all. Laughter and teasing as my mother chased me to the loft before sleep. My father teaching me to chop kindling and how to fight back against stupid boys who pulled my braids.

And Fadey took House Bien. He took all of them from me.

If Gammal knew about Fadey's plans, why did she not tell my mother and father when she delivered the prophecy? Roark gestured to me.

Gammal held his stare after I relayed the question. "To my shame, we did not realize his darker desires at the time. I went to the soul crafters with the prophecy because they despised the Jorvan's corrupt use of melders. I wish I had known Fadey's intentions, for I might've warned them of traitors at their tables. I thought Fadey would help protect the girl. Alas, the Norns are often finicky when it comes to the fate they reveal."

"What happened after the peace meet?" I asked.

"Fadey grew more determined to find the girl before the Draven clan could hide her behind their walls. He cut ties with the Unfettered, and I believe he began plotting with blood crafters to hunt the girl's blood." Gammal did not look at me; she did not speak to any royal; she looked at Emi. "But there was more I did not foresee. More traitors, more hatred that unraveled so much pain to lead us here."

Emi shifted where she sat. "What are you talking about?"

"It was my understanding that tensions rose among the soul crafters on how to handle the melder daughter should she ever be found. There was a disagreement between brothers. A king desired to conceal the girl behind their walls, shadowing her craft. But his brother wanted her blood to spill. It began to crack brotherly bonds."

Emi's face pinched. "You speak of my father?"

"Yes. But only one other ever discovered how deep your father's disdain for his brother's word had grown. A wife who could read the true desire of a soul. A wife whose craft learned the traitorous schemes of her husband."

"Shit." Gunter paused in lifting a second horn to his mouth and gaped at Emi.

"No." Emi's voice was strained. "That was my mother's craft. What did she learn?"

Gammal paused, her voice gentle. "Dark plans to take a throne for himself, sweet one."

Emi clapped her palms over her mouth. Yrsa shifted around Gunter and sat beside her, her hand on Emi's knee.

Gammal hesitated. "So he banished his sjeleven."

Why did my aunt not speak the truth? Roark spoke with fiery gestures, a flush to his face.

"Ah, I am told mothers will often agree to the direst of terms when true threats are leveled against their young ones," said

Gammal. "Did you know it was an Unfettered spear warrior who found her in the moments before she went to Salur?"

Gammal gestured to Keela.

The woman ran a hand through her dark hair. "I found the soul crafter woman likely a day or two after she'd slipped and fallen down a steep cliff near the ledges. She was fading but pleaded for me to hear her, to vow something with her. She told me of a daughter who lived with her traitorous husband. She told me of the soul vow which bound her to silence regarding his desires. In exchange, he could never kill their girl. I wouldn't make promises to her I could not keep. I could not promise to protect her girl, for I hardly knew the land, hardly knew much about your realms." Keela hesitated. "But I am glad to offer aid to her girl now."

Emi's shoulders shook with silent tears. Roark's jaw was clenched so tightly, I thought he might crack a tooth. I pressed a hand to his shoulder, trying to soothe the vicious soul beneath his skin, and gave a somber look at Emi.

To know her mother might've been tossed out without a word, all to save Emi from Virki's madness, was a horror no daughter should need to shoulder. Virki had harmed Emi, brutalized her, but he'd never killed her. He couldn't kill her.

How I wanted to kill him.

"After her banishment, it is clear he turned his actions against his brother like a viper waiting to strike," Gammal said.

"It was Virki's word that convinced Vishon the only way to protect the souls of the fallen was through a deledan rite," Auki said, low and broken.

Damn the gods. Slowly, Virki had destroyed his brother under the guise of strategy. He'd left Vishon divided, likely convinced that his bond with Elisabet would fade.

What might've happened if the queen had not been devious

in her own right, if Roark's mother had been unable to speak to her king, soul to soul?

Roark shot to his feet, his gestures frantic enough that I had to repeat his words for the others to understand. *He wanted a crown? He wanted to usurp my father?*

A shadow crossed Gammal's features. "It was a planned betrayal that does not end there, dark soul. The firstborn prince of souls was the one who passed word for any traces of the lost melder daughter. He sent word to us regarding the moves of Jorvans and Fadey. After that first peace meet, he found his heart in our lands, you see."

"Prince Nivek?" Gunter eyed Roark. "He did go on those trade journeys a lot. Remember, we always begged him to take us?"

"He trusted us as we trusted him." Gammal looked to the window of her hut for a breath. "The firstborn prince was the one who warned House Bien that if his kingdom came against them in the raids, they would end their child instead of hiding her. Elskan, the firstborn prince and your house were secretly preparing to bring you to me when the raids began. Now, I do not think your brother, dark soul, anticipated that you would have a soul bond with the melder."

Roark returned to his place at my side. I felt him press a gentle kiss to my hair.

"After those raids, he finished what House Bien could not and sent you with the tide wanderer to me. It was then that I suspected the connection to Fadey. When a blood crafter confirmed it through one of their spells, I tried to hide you over the ledges, elskan. But with the fighting, the chaos, we were snatched on the road by thrall traders. I managed to barter for us to take up a place in the young house. I would clean, cook, and keep watch on you until fate took you elsewhere." Gammal wiped a tear from her cheek. "I did not know I would never speak to the firstborn prince again. He saved you all."

"What do you mean?" Yrsa asked.

"Fadey anticipated taking the melder daughter's bones after the raids, and at last, he planned to see his dark scheme through. But with his belief that the blood of the heirs was needed, he made certain each firstborn was accounted for. He planned to take your bones as well."

"We were damn children during the raids," Thane snapped.

"And it mattered little to Fadey." Gammal looked to Roark. "But his plan was thwarted by the soul shadower taking the melder away. Then again, when he was killed."

Roark looked pale. *Fadey killed Nivek?*

"Fadey did not kill your brother, dark soul. Look again to the other traitor who sat at your table."

It took a moment, but I could see the shadow cross his face once he understood.

My uncle? Gods, it was always him. Roark dug his hands through his hair. His face darkened as though he could not draw in a breath.

Emi sobbed silently against Yrsa's shoulder.

"He, too, planned to destroy the melder, then claim his throne. He always planned to destroy the heir of his kingdom."

"He didn't kill Roark, merely encouraged his soul to be split," I said.

"To find you, elskan." Gammal smiled with a hint of despair. "The king's brother still wanted you dead, and if his dark soul nephew had a bond, well, perhaps he would hunt you until they found you."

Most of Virki's hopes had come to pass, but how I reveled in knowing that his wish for Skul Drek to murder me at first sight had been destroyed.

"Thinking that the ability to find the bone of soul craft was lost with the death of Prince Nivek, Fadey intended to disappear," Gammal said. "Until a blood crafter insisted that the power of the soul craft remnant lived on, only hidden. I believe it was the same crafter who sent word that you lived in your fishing village, elskan. I am told Fadey killed her eventually."

I grimaced. "Vella. She was a blood crafter who feigned being a seer in Skalfirth. Captain Baldur—Fadey—did kill her."

Gammal hummed. "Well, it was she who led Fadey to believe the vein of soul had not died off entirely. This is when he sensed the power, but we had already warded our lands against him. I believe to try to break the wards, he aligned with the blood craft queen. He falsified his death and hunted you all in the shadows.

"What you must accept, my elskans, is that the four bones of the Wanderer are here. The arm to lift his sword, the vein of bone craft."

Thane looked ready to retch, and unbidden, one hand ran over his opposite arm.

"The ribs to wear his armor. The vein of blood craft."

Yrsa flinched.

Gammal pointed to me. "His knowledge came from his wife, the god-queen. Her gifts of uniting the craft of the living and the dead make up the skull, for his wisdom."

Dammit. Fadey, my blood father, planned to take not merely my bones. He planned to take my head too.

Roark rapped his knuckles on one of the wooden posts. *We do not have the breastbone, for the heart.*

"We came here because Nivek hid something," Auki said with a touch of hesitation.

"Yes." Gammal's knees cracked when she rose. "The firstborn prince left something you will find of value on your search. Come, I'll show you."

"Roark." I tugged on his hand, pulling him free from the crowd.

Black blood seeped from his scar. His eyes burned like embers. *I am not in control. I do not know who I will harm if I lose it.*

I trapped his face between my palms. "Let me take some of the anger, then. Let me carry it with you. Gods, I am . . . so sorry for what Virki did to your whole house. Nivek saved everyone. He will be honored across the realms, Roark."

I will honor him by slaughtering his killer.

I kissed him, hard and fast. "Then I will drop him at your feet and hand you the blade."

Heat bloomed in my chest, followed promptly by a clawing rage. Palpable and bitter. Roark's eyes closed. His hand went to my waist. More of the suffocating bloodlust swirled against my own stun, my hate, my sorrow.

Only when his breaths returned to a slower, steady pace did I open my eyes. "Better?"

He nodded, but in truth, now he simply seemed more broken. But the shadows had receded, and his skin was not so pallid.

Outside, Gammal and the others stood around a tall man. He was dressed simply, in a pale tunic and trousers, but around his neck was a fine mantle made of bone and jade.

"Elskan, come meet our Lawspeaker."

The man's beard was wiry and long; the end touched his belt when he dipped his chin in a greeting. "Gammal. I heard we had newcomers from across the ledges and came to invite them all to the great hall. We feast as a welcome to you."

I had no desire to feast. I wanted to lash out and bite.

"Weren't you going to show us something, seer?" Brynn asked. She held tightly to Kael's bindings.

"Yes. I still plan to do so. Come, then. To the feast."

"But—" Brynn tried again.

"You all look weary," Gammal interrupted.

"Couldn't possibly be because we've been told a mad melder wants to bleed us out and harvest our bones, now could it?" Thane mumbled to Emi.

Her eyes were red rimmed and tear filled, but she shot the prince a watery smile. As though there was nothing to do but laugh.

Gammal waved us forward. "Come to the feast. Where we shall eat, and perhaps find lost things."

Roark did not speak; he did not look at anyone. His grip on my hand was unyielding. Kyrre plodded at his side and butted his large head under Roark's palm. Absently, my husband stroked his fara, but his bitterness was trained on the road leading to the largest of the longhouses.

Already lanterns were lit, drums pounded in a boisterous beat, and chatter spilled from the doors.

One by one, Gammal, the Lawspeaker, and other Unfettered Folk guided us through the entryway. Gunter remained at our side, occasionally casting curious glances at his prince. My mind a fog, I did not notice the woman walking in through the doors at the same moment.

"Apologies," I muttered when I slammed into her shoulder.

The woman from the farm. In her arms were woven baskets of baked bread. Dirt lined her fingernails, but she'd tied her long hair half off her face and her cheeks were pink from being freshly scrubbed.

It was like looking into a mirror of the past. Once I was the woman who saw to it that the tables were full and the drinking horns were filled.

The woman was half a head shorter than me, dainty freckles dusted her nose, and she had dark, somber eyes.

She dipped her chin at me, then turned to do the same to Roark. She stumbled back. "All gods. How . . ."

Roark's mouth pinched.

"Shit." Gunter covered his nose and mouth with one palm "Soul bond."

"What?" Did he sense a connection with this woman and my damn husband? Could someone have two soul bonds?

"There's a bond." He nodded at the woman. "Smells close to yours, but it's heavier. Darkened. Usually means one half has gone to Salur."

"Forgive me." The woman chuckled nervously. "For a moment, you looked just like my husband. Impossible, since he passed—"

"Twelve seasons ago?" The question came out rough, low. I already knew the truth.

"Yes. How did you know?"

Roark's shoulders stiffened.

I closed my eyes and whispered, "Was his name Nivek?"

ROARK

THE WOMAN'S DARK EYES FLASHED WITH SOMETHING MADE of fire. From docile to vicious in a single heartbeat.

She threw the basket at Gunter and Lyra. "Don't you dare touch him."

Not another word was said and she fled, racing away from the longhouse. I wasted no time and sprinted after her.

Fast as she was, I outpaced her in a dozen breaths. She screamed and kicked when my arms went around her waist, picking her up. Damn the hells, she was feral. The woman knew how to attack, and I had few doubts that come morning my hands and arms would be covered in her marks.

Lyra and Gunter hurried after us.

"Wait." Lyra held out a hand. "Stop. We're not . . . gods, we're not going to hurt anyone."

"You touch him and I'll kill you."

I let out a hiss when she bit my damn hand.

With a grunt I released her. Frustration, annoyance, and

aggravating curiosity took hold. Craft prickled over my throat and skin. Another moment and frigid shadows encircled us all.

She screamed, desperate to flee, but was met with cruel crimson eyes in the darkness.

"Please." Lyra gripped her wrist. "We're not going to hurt you."

"Mother!" A voice cracked from low to pitchy, like it could not determine if it belonged to child or man. Her boy burst from the gates of the farm but stumbled when he took note of the shadows around us.

I gripped his tunic easily and held him in place.

"Please." The woman fell to her knees. "Please, don't . . . don't touch him."

"By the gods, we're not." Lyra stepped in front of her. "This is my husband. He is Nivek's *brother.*"

The woman drew in a quivering breath. She looked to me. "His brother?"

"Meet Prince Roark Ashwood of Dravenmoor, lady," Gunter said. "Our evil shadow monster."

Lyra rammed her elbow into Gunter's ribs. "He's not evil, I assure you."

"Depends on who you ask." Gunter winked.

The boy twisted in my grip. I'd nearly forgotten that I'd stopped him. I released his tunic and held up my palms.

By the time he ran to his mother, most of the murky darkness had dissipated, the hardness of my soul soothed for now.

The woman hurried to her feet, a tight hold on her son's arm. Her eyes shot back and forth between me and Lyra. "You . . . you are the outsiders who the seemódir mentioned." Her attention remained on me. "You are . . . gods, you look so like him."

I took hold of Lyra's palm and spoke, *I want to know who she is. Tell her about us.*

"The prince uses hand speak. He's asking about you. No one in his household, I don't think, knew Nivek had a wife."

She sniffed and used the back of her hand to wipe her eyes. "No. It wasn't known over the ledges. Nivek believed a bond with an Unfettered would not be accepted."

They are soul bonded? I arched one brow.

"You had a sealed bond?"

"I thought it was merely his custom for vows. But when a man from his clan spoke the words, something shifted within me. I felt it. I still feel it, merely . . . distant. He spoke of you." She smiled, a little despondent. "He told me of his younger brother, who followed him everywhere and pleaded to join him on his journeys. He told me he wanted to bring you soon. He wanted you to meet Sindri."

She squeezed her son's hand.

The boy who looked too much like my brother.

My brother's son.

A boy we never knew existed.

"Please." She took a step closer. "I did not learn everything that happened after we lost him. Will you . . . will you tell me?"

At my nod, Lyra spoke the gruesome tale. From her hunted craft, to Nivek's bravery, to the division of my soul. Sindri looked at me then, almost a little impressed.

Lyra told him that through my soul craft we'd spoken to Nivek.

"He said if we are not believed then to tell those he left behind that you are inked on his heart, his bones, and his soul."

Nivek's wife covered her mouth, and tears filled her eyes. "Those were the words he spoke when our bond was sealed. He said them again when Sindri was born."

I touched Lyra's arm. *I want to see her marks from the sealing.*

"Do you have the soul runes?" Lyra held up her hands, and after a pause, the glimmer of runes coated her fingers.

The woman held up her own hands. There, shimmering beneath the dirt on her skin, was the flicker of runes.

I cursed Nivek in my mind, hoping somewhere in Salur his soul could feel my annoyance at his secrets.

I used my chin to point at the woman. *Now her tale. I want to hear everything.*

"Roark wants to know how you met Nivek."

The woman's voice steadied as she described the first time she crossed paths with the foreign prince. She thought him odd, but she'd been a suspicious Unfettered girl who was leery of the craft over the Night Ledges.

She'd met him when they both were only seventeen seasons. He'd taken his first lone trade route since my father no longer could. Nivek intrigued her when he played a rowdy game with young ones, tossing a pigskin ball about the square.

"Gods, when I met his eyes for the first time, it was as though fire dug out my heart and replaced it." She smiled a little wistfully. "He did not explain soul bonds for another season, merely teased me, insisting he was irresistible so that was the reason I felt so strongly."

They'd sealed their bond right after Nivek's eighteenth season. In secret. My brother shadowed our old soul weaver's memory of it. He could not tell our clan the truth.

When she finished, no one spoke. What was there to even say? My brother had a wife. A son. He had a soul bond, and he sacrificed his life so I could keep mine.

As though Lyra could feel my damn thoughts, she took hold of the woman's hand. "Nivek treasured your bond so fiercely, he saved me so his brother could have the same. I am so thankful to him, and we know who took him from you both. They will die for it."

Sindri's mouth tightened. "Let me do it. It is my duty as his son to avenge him."

"Sindri," his mother warned.

"What?" His fists were trembling. "They took him before I could even know him."

You will. I did not think before gesturing the words, knowing he would not understand. *You will know him because you both have a place in Dravenmoor. You are a prince and the heir of your father's kingdom.*

Sindri's golden eyes were not as bright as mine, not as fierce as Nivek's once were, but they gleamed when Lyra explained my words.

"Roark." Gunter leaned in to whisper. "The firstborn heir."

Shit. My lips parted. Nivek's bone would not hold the Wanderer's power because . . . there was already a new firstborn of soul craft when he died.

"What?" Jordis said, a groove between her brows. "Why do you look distressed?"

How could I tell her that my nephew would be hunted, the same as the rest of the heirs?

Gunter did not wait for me to respond. He spoke for Dravenmoor. "You and your son are part of the royal house. You will have the protection of the Dark Watch, and, lady, if I may say so, you may need it in coming days."

Jordis paled. "They want him. I knew it. I've always felt something would come for my son."

Nivek's fears would still be felt through your bond, I told her.

She rubbed a palm over her heart after Lyra explained my theory.

"You will come with us." Lyra took her hand. "Nothing will happen to you or Sindri."

"Don't know who you think you are, coming here and speaking out against our laws, woman." Fifteen paces away the burly man who'd shouted at Jordis earlier stood on the path, a pungent paper smoke between his teeth. "They're not going anywhere. I own them."

"Own them? Unfettered are not owned, I thought." Lyra looked to Jordis.

She studied the soil. "After Nivek's death, I petitioned for help protecting my son. I did not know what was happening. My father and mother had met Salur a season before. Our laws allow protection through debts to be paid."

"That's right." The sod strode closer, blowing a puff of smoke between us. "And lovely Jordis has not paid her debt for her bastard. I've told her ways to see it done swifter."

"And I will forever refuse."

Does he touch you? I spoke briskly, and Lyra recited the question with a dark heat in her tone.

"Ah, I would, but Jordis refuses. I'd wipe her debt clean if she'd spread her thighs a bit."

Sindri made a move for the man. I gripped his shoulder, pulling him back, and shook my head. Where I thought the boy might protest, he steadied.

It was possible he saw the flash of ill intent in my own countenance.

"Her debt is vast," said the man. "Protection for the boy his entire life. Not a small request. She'll be mine until she meets the gods."

I took Lyra's palm, writing my words.

She lifted her chin when I finished. "The Draven prince has an interest in them."

"Oh?" The man tilted his head. "What sort of interest?"

"It doesn't concern you." Lyra spoke like a damn queen. "We'll pay the debt. What is your name so we know who to call upon?"

"Brokk the Sly." Brokk blinked. "You'll pay? For them?"

"You speak to a future king, you sod. Do you think he is not willing to pay for what he wants?" Thane was the one who spoke. "Despite what I'm sure you've heard, Dravens are, at times, diplomatic."

Give me the price, I told him. *Not including the seasons she has worked off her debt.*

"Well, there's the matter of the boy's debt too." Brokk shifted on his feet, looking at Lyra as she finished reciting my demand. "Two mouths to feed under my watch, use of my blades, it's double."

Get me the price by dawn.

"We'll see you at the dawn," Lyra explained.

Brokk flashed a wolfish grin. "As you say, *Highness.*"

His voice dripped with condescension, but his breath shuddered when I crowded him, our brows close. *But if you touch either of them again, I will see to it you pay with your soul.*

I did not wait for his response to Lyra and gestured for Jordis and Sindri to take the path ahead of me back to the longhouse.

"Although I appreciate the sentiment," Jordis whispered in a low hiss, "the debt *is* vast. Brokk is a bastard, but he has many loyal men who would defend him, and he is a skilled warder with blood. That is the arrangement. Sindri will be protected from any harm if he is merely on Brokk's land, behind blood wards."

"We're not leaving you here," Lyra said. "Nivek gave his life defending us, and we will defend his family in turn."

LYRA

ROARK LOOKED LIKE A VILLAIN FROM DARK LEGENDS. HIS black tunic, leather, and boots stood out among the brilliant colors of the Unfettered attire. He leaned back at the table, glaring at the revelry with a dose of heady disdain.

Jordis was there, complying with the commands of Brokk in the hall. She poured ale, avoided Brokk's taunts, and Sindri was not welcome at all. Brokk insisted that the boy had tasks left to complete at his longhouse.

Brokk thought it was a bit of delight, ordering his thralls about in front of a prince who'd yet to take ownership of the debt; I knew his every action was being stitched to the memories of a darker piece of my husband.

A darkness that would not soon forget.

Roark Ashwood was a man who defended his own. He would be a villain on their behalf.

The hall was not as grand as Stonegate or the Draven palace, but it was warm and spiced with herbs. Folk danced, ate, and sang folk songs I did not recognize. Thane and Auki took up conversation with the Lawspeaker.

The man was listening to the Jorvan prince, but when he would reply, Thane's face would flush in a touch of frustration. My heart tightened at the sight of Emi and Yrsa seated down the bench, heads close, whispering.

Gods, I hoped after all this their hearts could still heal. We would need to stand with one another if we were to stop Fadey and Ingir.

"They'll need to die." I turned on the bench to face Roark. "Fadey and Ingir."

That was always my plan. He pressed a kiss to the center of my palm.

"I thought we'd need to destroy the Wanderer's bones and that would be enough to stop him. I thought they were buried. It is no wonder that I could never see them but Skul Drek could sense them."

They are buried. The lore simply never specified that they were buried within the living.

I chuckled and traced the lines of his hand with my thumb. "Sindri is one of the remnants now. Fadey does not know of him, but he knew of the heirs. He must suspect something."

Roark used his other hand to gesture against the tabletop. *He will never get the chance to learn of him.*

"We will need the Dark Watch," I said. Thoughts I could not shake rolled through my mind. "I don't know what becomes of us when we return over the Night Ledges. It feels like there has been a shift in the very soil, as though the land knows a battle rises."

Roark picked at a sliver on the table for a breath. *Thane is trying to convince the Unfettered to join us. Fadey is one of their own, and he has gone against their laws.*

"Do you think they'll stand with us?"

So far, it seems like the Lawspeaker is not interested.

I looked back to where Prince Thane sat. He was tipping back a drinking horn, face as stone. No doubt annoyed the Unfettered Folk were not leaping at the chance to join the cause.

Auki and Gunter plan to ride ahead and send word to the queen.

My stomach backflipped. "It is truly happening. All our lives we have been pawns in this game of twisted lies and betrayal. Now . . . it ends for them, or us."

Roark cupped one side of my face. *This is not where we end. But I plan to gift each royal a remnant of Fadey's bones.*

I snickered. "Is that so?"

It is. Roark's thumb tugged on my bottom lip. *Thane will be welcome to fashion Fadey's arm into a bow. Yrsa might want to make a chair from his ribs. Sindri will make a better knife with the breastbone, and you, wife, you will have his head.*

"I've always dreamed of mounting a skull on my wall."

I thought as much. Roark leaned in to kiss me.

His lips had hardly brushed over mine when a throat cleared. Gammal, gripping her walking stick in hand, beamed at us both. "Pardon. Heard deals with Brokk are being made."

I sat back. "Seems that way. You could've told us Sindri was Nivek's son."

"I believe I told you the boy was unique and you might want to get to know him."

My mouth parted. "Gammal, that's not telling us he is the heir to the Draven throne."

"Well, there were other matters to discuss, elskan." She clicked her tongue, like I was the one being foolish. "By the by, your poor melded brother is asking for you."

The woman gestured toward one of the back doors. There were no additional rooms in the great hall of the Unfettered clans, simply smaller huts and structures for different uses like cooking or bathing.

A small hut ten paces from the hall was lit with a small lantern. Kyrre and Òlmr were both sprawled over the stoop. When Kyrre caught sight of Roark, he shot to his feet, his tongue lolling out one side of his mouth. He nuzzled our hands as we strode past, practically wriggling free of his coat when I scratched behind his bent ear.

Inside the hut, Kael sat against one wall, bare-chested, arms tied out to his sides. Gods, gashes painted his body, all in various marks of healing. Lumps and nodules bulged beneath his skin.

I had no doubt Fadey had melded Kael with a soul bone every day. Perhaps multiple.

His brow dripped with sweat. His breaths were heavy. Jaw tight, he lifted his head. "Ly."

The word, so simple, came out like it was painful.

A fur covered a second entrance. Brynn emerged with a bowl of water and a linen in her hand. She jolted at the sight of us. "Oh, good. You've come."

"What is this?"

Kael grunted and tugged against the bindings around his wrists. Brynn dropped to his side and pressed a palm to his shoulder. "Think through it."

"Godsdammit." Kael's eyes clenched, and he puffed out jagged breaths between his teeth.

Brynn's eyes were glassy. "He has so many corrupted souls fighting his own. The berserksgangur keeps taking hold, but he is beginning to fight it."

Why? Are you guiding him with your craft?

Brynn tugged her bottom lip between her teeth. "Something like that."

Roark stepped in front of me, one hand on the blade strapped to his waist. *The bloodlust only worsens over time. You must be doing something.*

Brynn dipped the cloth into the water and dabbed Kael's brow. He let out a sigh, as though the touch soothed a festering burn on his flesh. "He's fighting, you can see."

"Take one, Ly," Kael gritted out. "Please."

"There are many, elskan." Gammal rested a hand on my shoulder. "But it is the only chance he has."

"You wish me to unmeld them, Kael?"

He turned his head, as though leaning nearer to Brynn, and nodded. "As many . . . as you can."

I knelt beside my brother. He recoiled at first at my touch. Brynn let her hand fall to his shoulder. "It is not simple, but I'll try to take as much as possible. As long as it takes. The pain will leave soon."

Kael closed his eyes. "Do it, pest."

Emotion thickened in my throat. "I'm getting to it, fool."

Roark lowered to one knee at my side, still coiled to strike. My fingertips ran over Kael's chest. So many lumps and divots embedded around his heart.

Damn Fadey had done it with intent; he'd wanted Kael to suffer swiftly.

A nodule on his ribs burned beneath my palms. A soul bone, but not beneath the curve of the ribs, on the outer edge. Smaller, easily gripped. When I touched the spot again, a web of gilded stitching gleamed under the surface of Kael's skin.

Patterns where the threads began and ended. Their origins and tension against his bones.

Craft rushed through me like a rogue wave on the sea. The roar and brine and smoke coated my tongue. The burn bit at the tips of my fingers.

I held out a palm to Roark. "May I have your knife?"

He handed me a small blade from one of the sheaths on his forearm and settled lower on his knee, readying to greet me in the shadows.

Upon the first cut, the mists pulled me away.

KAEL SLEPT BENEATH A FUR QUILT, HIS WRISTS STILL BOUND, A new bandage wrapped around his middle. Fever burned through his flesh. Once, I was told that soul bones yearned to live again. They would fight to keep their existence, leeching on to a new soul.

Bones scattered across Kael flared in poisonous red, black, and green threads when I unstitched the smaller piece from his side. Then another near his hip. I only managed to get a third nearer to his chest before his body shook too violently to continue.

The bones shadowed the brightest pieces of his soul, shadowed the tethers of bonds and connections he'd built through his life.

I thought I'd noticed a strange tether, but more of the darkness from the corrupted bones blotted out the shine before I could be certain.

Doubtless, the rest of his melded pieces would fight to keep him.

I leaned against Roark's shins from where he sat on a bench in the hut. It would take careful planning, careful selection, before I removed the remaining bones.

In truth, I wasn't certain I could take all of them without killing him. Fadey had placed one bone directly over his heart.

Brynn bustled around Kael, gathering the bloody linens and seeing to it that the fur remained over his body. She'd even summoned Òlmr to sleep beside Kael.

By now, I knew Brynn Oakbriar was a genuine soul, a warrior.

But she'd been strange since the pass, almost like she was battling her own fever.

"Brynn," I whispered in a soft voice. "Why don't you go rest?"

"Oh." She smiled, but it was more like a wince than anything. "I'm all right. I can watch over him if you both need to rest. I'm certain that to unmeld is taxing. Looked difficult, at least."

Roark leaned forward, his hands falling over my shoulders. *What is wrong with you, Oakbriar?*

She scowled. "Nothing is wrong with me. Why don't you go sleep, my prince? You look like you're ready to murder half the Unfettered Folk."

I canted my head, studying her fidgety hands. She would reach for Kael, then pull back and tidy up a space that had no need to be tidied. Brynn would wheel around with every moan of pain Kael freed in his sleep.

She was not herself.

"Brynn." I played with the ends of my hair. "You know when I use my craft that I fall into a sort of trance within the realm of souls. Which is why Skul Drek is there too."

She ran a quick hand down Òlmr's head, then looked to me. "Yes. I've witnessed you fall into it."

"Funny thing is, while there, I can see things. Souls. Connections, like Gunter describes. Kael's are utterly tangled because of the soul bones. But they remain, some old, but some looked new."

Brynn's face heated. "What are you saying, Lyra?"

"Nothing." I looked down at the ends of my hair again. "I'm merely, you know, curious if you might've felt anything when you met my brother."

All at once, Roark's spine straightened like a stern rod. *Oakbriar.*

"What?" Brynn picked up one of the clean linens and twisted

it about, as though looking for some sort of use for it. In the end, she merely wrung it between her hands. "It wasn't right away."

Dammit. Roark gestured his curse. His brilliant eyes were wide, stunned. *Truly?*

Brynn's chin quivered. "It was after the Unfettered arrived. When he was sleeping, when the curse of those wretched bones was not taking him. I didn't mean for . . . I didn't want . . ." Her words broke off.

I rose and crossed the room to her. Brynn stood taller and stronger than me, but she practically collapsed against me when I embraced her.

"What cruel gods we have." Brynn sniffed.

"I was told a soul bond does not take the choice from us." I pulled back. "The decision is yours."

Brynn nodded. "I know, and I have fought it. But . . . then he looked at me, like he felt it too. He . . . he started *trying*, Lyra. He started fighting the pull to darkness. I do not even think he knows about soul craft or new bonds, but he is still reaching for it."

Roark crossed the space. *But is it what you want, Oakbriar?*

"When you saw Lyra for the first time, I mean during the raids, what did it feel like?"

Roark glanced at me for a breath, then back to Brynn. *It felt like my soul finally breathed. I felt like she was mine to protect instantly. And I was hers, should she want me.*

Brynn looked down at Kael. "Then I now understand why you risked your life to save her."

All gods. Brynn Oakbriar had found her soul bond.

And he was another life destroyed by Fadey.

Roark cleared his throat, drawing Brynn's attention again. He used one hand to speak. *With my life, Oakbriar.*

She laughed, wet and tearful, but nodded. "I'll hold you to that, you sod. Because there may be a few times when he tries to kill Lyra or something, and you can't slaughter him for it."

Roark let out a breathy chuckle. For the first time since learning all the dreary truths of the past, our present predicaments, and our unknown future, there was a bit of light we could hold on to.

For now.

Dawn brought more unknowns, and I could not help but feel like fate loomed nearer and nearer.

And I did not know who would arise the victor in the end.

44

LYRA

AS PROMISED, AUKI AND GUNTER TOOK TO THE SHARP switchbacks before the sun rose, returning to Draven-moor to report back to the queen. We lingered, packing supplies and readying to face Stonegate. Emi grinned at something Yrsa said in passing before the princess went to load one of the horses with a pouch of bread from Gammal.

"You're speaking." I nudged her with my shoulder.

Emi's cheeks flushed. "We spoke all night. I told her every-thing about Roark. I spoke of Virki. Gods, how did I not see his involvement? He was the one who alerted the úlfur to what Nivek had done."

"No one wants to believe the same person who is supposed to protect them could betray them."

"Yrsa told me how painful it was these last weeks, believing I cared nothing for her. She believed I was lying about everything." Emi paused, a giddy sort of smile playing over her lips. "I told her of the soul bond."

My brows lifted. "And? Does she feel it too?"

"She simply told me she thought that was what love felt like."

"Will you ever seal it?" The trouble was, Yrsa and Thane were still betrothed. They would be expected to have young ones together.

From the lore of sealed bonds, to betray the heart, mind, or body of one's bond, it could corrupt the tether, much like her father's.

Emi sighed. "I don't know if we can. Nothing has changed. She is still a princess, and I am not. We always knew the truth of it. And Thane is as wonderful about it as ever. I think seeing you and Roark has shown the prince how devastatingly deep the bonds can go. For now, I am at ease once again."

"Good, Nightlark. Stay that way."

Emi snickered and gathered another mat, striding over to Yrsa.

"I told you my terms, Highness." In front of the great hall, the Lawspeaker argued with Thane.

"I'm not certain you understand the gravity of what we face. This sod is one of your folk, and he plans to claim every throne, every craft."

The Lawspeaker folded his arms over his chest. "From what I've been told about this power, I suggest you see to it that he does not take off your arm."

Thane looked affronted. "I cannot agree to this trade when you do not offer details of the deal. For all I know, you could be leading me into a position where I sell off my own fingers."

The man's head fell back in a rough laugh. "Ah, Prince of the Jorvans, you are a strange soul. I assure you it could prove equally beneficial for us both."

When the Unfettered Lawspeaker stalked away, Thane approached, a deep frown carved on his face. His typically trimmed beard had grown more stubbled and darker since we'd reunited.

His hair was not neatly braided, and he'd taken a liking to the pelt mantles of the Unfettered. With a wrap of bear fur around his shoulders, he appeared a little ferocious.

"What was all that?" I asked.

"My failed attempts at negotiating with allies. Have you seen these people throw spears? Gods, it's incredible. We could use them."

Roark tugged a strap on one of the fur mats tightly. *And will they not stand against Fadey?*

Thane's jaw worked. "Their Lawspeaker will provide his forces if I agree to aid him with some sort of trade trouble in the Unfettered seaside village. For all I know, he plans to indenture my service as some fishmonger, and I fear I would be forced to leave Jorvandal to the whims of fishing season."

Roark grinned, shook his head, but did not encourage Thane to make any promises in a tentative alliance. We did not know these lands, nor customs, well, and Thane was wise to err on the side of caution.

Are you ready? Roark asked the prince.

Thane's eyes hardened. "I've been ready all night. Yrsa and I gathered all we brought. Do you have enough?"

Roark tossed a leather pouch filled with Draven copper between his hands.

"I follow you, brother." Thane flourished one hand and kept a pace behind the Draven prince.

Unfettered Folk lined the path that wound to the back of the township. Gammal waited at the end of the path in front of Brokk's longhouse. There, a long table, draped in a black cloth with stitched runes, was positioned at the gate.

Brokk sat on one side, smug and clad in a fine lavender top with a strange hat threaded in rich blue and green on the edges. Behind him, Jordis and Sindri stood, hands clasped, heads down.

"Still wish to pay the debt?"

Roark did not lift a hand to speak. He tossed the coins on the table. Thane dropped his offerings next, but then leaned in and sniffed. "You reek of the greed that haunts our lands now. Pity."

Brokk scoffed and unlaced the pouches. "Yet you live in a palace with servants much the same, Prince. Do you think somewhere, someone does not care about them?"

Thane's lip curled. "I do not mistreat those who serve me."

The prince spoke with such venom that for a moment, Brokk's superiority faltered. The man cleared his throat and turned his attention to the coins. After what felt like endless moments, he rummaged through the offerings, inspecting the coin, the silver, and the bangles from Yrsa.

When Brokk closed the pouches again, Roark opened one palm in question.

"What say you, Brokk?" Gammal asked. She spoke to the man with a bite of disgust. The way most of the Unfettered clan avoided Brokk's side of the table, it did not take much to guess that they did not favor the man.

Brokk rose, smoothing his tunic. "We have an agreement. Though out of respect for visiting royalty, I have many items you may wish to trade for this amount instead. I understand you feel some sort of debt to the boy's father, but how will he know if you do not fulfill it? He is dead."

Roark's fist clenched under the table, but his smirk did not fade.

"No? Suit yourself." Brokk went to Jordis. He brushed his knuckles down her cheek. "Farewell, Jordis. The sight of your body will be missed. Your mouth will not."

Roark knocked his knuckles on the table. *Do not touch what I have rightfully purchased.*

Brokk held up his palms in surrender when Thane repeated

the warning. "Apologies. Now, if you'll excuse me, I shall be counting my new royal coin."

The barter was nothing but a conquest for Brokk. A man who took pleasure in the humiliation of others. What did it matter? Relief, heady and bright, gleamed in Jordis's eyes. She embraced Sindri, holding the boy's face and kissing his brow.

Then she went to Roark and Thane. "I will never know how to repay you."

"You have allies in two kingdoms . . . well, we must dethrone my mother first." Thane sighed with a touch of theatrics. "It is bound to be messy business. But if I keep my arm and my head, you will have allies in two kingdoms."

"Three." Yrsa frowned at the prince. "Do we not have a claim in Myrda?"

"Forgive me." Thane dipped his chin. "It would seem you have the protection of all kingdoms. Again, if our bones are not harvested for a rather villainous melder."

Sindri laughed softly. Even Jordis grinned, slow and cautious, like she was not entirely certain how it was done anymore.

Roark stood from the table and lifted my palm, his fingers brushing lightly over the surface. *Will you see that their belongings are loaded? We should be off soon.*

"Where are you going?"

Roark grinned. *There's one more thing I must do before we leave.*

Trepidation stacked in my chest. I'd seen that look in my husband's eyes before, something callous, a little merciless. He left no room for questions before stalking away down the road.

I led Jordis toward the charges, allowing Sindri to tell me all he'd learned of the creatures since working in Brokk's stables.

Now that the chains were removed from his life, the boy chattered a great deal. He had a deep fascination with the fara wolves. Kyrre approached the boy, ears flat at first, but soon enough, the pup nuzzled the boy's hand and panted in delight when Sindri found Kyrre's favorite place on his neck to be scratched.

"He likes you." I chuckled.

Sindri knelt next to Kyrre's belly, using both his hands to scratch the wolf. "I have heard tales of the great wolves of my father's clan. Did he have one?"

"I don't think so. Not every Draven bonds to a fara, but it seems that Kyrre senses the connection to you and your uncle. I expect he will guard you as fiercely as he guards me and Roark."

Sindri hesitated. "Will they . . . accept me, my lady?"

I let out a sigh and knelt by the boy. "My bond with your uncle was meant to be forbidden, much like Nivek believed with your mother. But most have accepted me. I know it is . . . frightening, but you are the firstborn of the heir of Dravenmoor. You are the blood of the clan, and your folk will stand with you."

I peered over my shoulder to the place where Gammal stood in a huddle with Keela and some watchmen. She beamed at me, like she could hear every word spoken.

"Your folk will stand with you, Sindri," I repeated. "On both sides of the Night Ledges."

The boy had unruly hair that waved around his ears. He dressed like the Unfettered, with fur hems and bright stitching. The toes of his leather shoes curled slightly. But the ferociousness of the brilliant Draven eyes and spirit burned in his features.

"I have always felt close to my father," he said. "Even though I do not remember him. Sometimes, well, sometimes I speak to him. I like to think he can hear me."

"He has been close to you. I've seen it, the bond he holds to you, how you are in his thoughts even in Salur."

Sindri twisted one finger in his ear, scratching an itch. "I want to make him proud. I've tried to stand for my mother, protect her, but I don't know how to enter a royal house, Lady. I don't know how to *be* part of a royal house."

"Then it is a good thing you and your mother will not be alone. We will be at your side." I squeezed his shoulder once, then stood to finish gathering our supplies.

One of the doors on the small hut behind the great hall creaked open. Brynn stepped into the sunlight, holding a strap of leather in her grip. Behind her, Kael blinked against the brightness of the sun.

His face seemed bloodless, with deep shadows underneath his eyes, but he was not resisting. He wasn't scowling. There was a touch of green to his countenance, but he moved with a steadier gait, without a single tug on the bindings.

"Kael?" I held my breath, prepared to feel my heart shatter again.

"Lyra." His voice was laced in venom, but a flicker of the light I loved so much had returned to his eyes.

Brynn stepped aside, unsettled.

"Don't . . . go," Kael said under his breath. "Not far."

"I won't," she said.

I leaned close, my voice a whisper. "Did you tell him?"

Brynn shook her head. "He told me that when I stand close, he can think clearer."

"Merely one of those things I can't explain," Kael said. "You took a bone, Ly?"

"Three actually."

Kael twisted until his face pulled in a wince. "Ah. There. I feel lighter in one moment, then like a stone in the next."

"Do you want me to continue removing them?"

"Yes." No hesitation. Certain. Direct. "It is painful, but I do not want to live this way. There is a madness, a hate, that burns inside me. The noise from all these . . . souls is torture."

"I can see why Berserkirs fall into the berserksgangur, then. Perhaps it silences the confusion."

Kael nodded. "But I don't want it. I never wanted to be a monster. I wanted to protect my people, *you*."

My fingers trembled when I touched his arm. "You will, Kael. As long as it takes, I will remove those bones. We must be careful, that's all. Some are precariously placed."

"Oakbriar said as much." Kael gave a quick look at Brynn. "Woman's made of iron, the way she's tolerated me."

I chuckled. "You will not find a more loyal soul than Brynn Oakbriar."

A bit of pink teased Brynn's cheeks. "What is he doing?"

I spun around.

In front of Brokk's gate, Roark stood, unmoving. Simply watching. Brokk stumbled toward the front of his house, his movements like he'd had too much ale. At times he jolted, as though he'd been stung by something sharp.

My eyes widened when Brokk paused at one of the fire pits where boiled dyes cooked in iron kettles to soak into linens. Without a word, the man took a piece of wood and ignited the tip in the flame.

Brokk stepped into his longhouse. Roark didn't move. Only tilted his head to the side.

I went to call out his name, but the words faded on my tongue. Thick, black smoke spiraled from the top of Brokk's thatched roof. Screams from inside the house rose. Servants fled, clutching whatever they'd been able to grab. Wooden walls were set ablaze.

From the doorway, Brokk appeared again, holding the leather pouches of coins and silver used to purchase Jordis's freedom. The man carried them back out, dazed, hardly bothered that his homestead was burning.

On the next glance, Brokk's hand no longer carried the coins.

Where the farmer's grip had been, now a misty coil curled around the pouches. Skul Drek, cowled and ominous, stepped forward as though drifting through Brokk's body.

Roark had his head bent low. By the way his hands moved, he was writing something.

A burst of flames ignited from Brokk's inglenook. More folk fled out of the gates, turning to watch it all burn. Brokk swayed, a little mystified, watching his house go up in flames.

I was frozen, locked on the sight of Skul Drek prowling forward, a wonderfully terrifying phantom.

"This is his craft?" I'd not realized Jordis stood beside me, eyes wide. Sindri stood at her side, a look of concern there until he saw the goats and hogs flee the stables, far from the burning longhouse.

Then the boy sneered.

"He controls and destroys the souls of others if he desires, if they deserve it," I said, a little breathless.

No doubt, Skul Drek had somehow placed Brokk in a bit of a trance, and it was fast fading. Brokk let out a roar of anger, seeming to notice his destroyed estate. No one sought to comfort the sod; most of the Unfettered simply watched, aghast.

By the account of everyone, Brokk put flame to his own home. But from within him emerged a darkness they'd never seen. Some looked on in horror. Others, like Gammal, bore a look of satisfaction.

I watched the flames with dark desire. By the molten hell, the sooner I could put my hands on my husband, the better.

When Skul Drek was five paces away, Roark turned around and strode toward us. His jaw was set. He walked in pace with his darker soul, like a true shadow followed him, drawing nearer with each step.

When he reached us, Skul Drek stepped into Roark from

behind. For a fleeting glance, the coppery red of the phantom stared out at us from Roark's gaze. Coils of shadows remained for a breath, a dark cloak over his shoulders.

Roark walked past Sindri and shoved the coin pouches into the chest of the boy, forcing him to grapple for purchase. A strip of parchment was folded between the two pouches.

The boy gawked at his uncle, holding the payment in his hands. Roark did not look back at his nephew. He stopped by me and brushed a thumb over my cheek. *Now we're ready to leave.*

Gods, this man.

Roark ignored the curious glances of the Unfettered Folk and went to help his cousin and Yrsa with the rest of the horses.

Sindri held the parchment. I did not ask permission and scanned the words over the boy's shoulder.

Sindri looked at me. "Brokk could retaliate."

I looked back at the man. He was on his knees, wailing. I shook my head. "I would like to see him try to challenge your uncle. That is not the half of what he can do."

The boy looked down at Roark's note once more, tracking every symbol.

A prince of Dravenmoor is owned by no one.

45

LYRA

WE TOOK THE SWITCHBACK LEDGES SLOWER THAN
before. More horses and more people joined us on
the return.

Gammal insisted on traveling with us to the summit, determined that more time was needed with her elskan.

Despite the word of the Lawspeaker and Thane's refusal to agree to aid in his mysterious trade trouble without knowing more, two dozen Unfettered Folk joined us up the peaks. Keela, the woman who'd led us over the ledges from Dravenmoor, was the first to offer her blades.

Every Unfettered man or woman brought with them dark, polished spears and a few blades made of bronze and offered to take a stand in whatever battles awaited.

"Perhaps we are shielded by the cliffs," Keela said, dragging her fingers, painted in dark kohl, down her face. "Perhaps your battles would never find us. But Fadey is Unfettered by blood, and I cannot sit by when one of our own disgraces the gods and seeks to place chains on others. Not when our clans take vows to never overrule the voices of many."

"Then how do you stomach men like Brokk?"

Keela frowned. "Our laws are made through debts and repaying them. They are meant to be compassionate and fair to those who seek aid or commit crimes."

"All crimes?"

Keela smirked. "We do not go around embracing rapists or killers, if that is what you're thinking. But our vows of peace make such brutal crimes rare in our lands. Should they happen, they are dealt with painfully and harshly. I did not agree with the bondage of Jordis and Sindri, but there was nothing we could do. Those were the conditions to which she agreed to keep her son protected behind Brokk's blood spells. It is how he earned many of his servants. Women who'd fled cruel husbands; men who'd made gambles with the wrong folk. He is a cruel ass, but Brokk merely took advantage of our laws for his own gains."

"He took advantage of their desperation."

"Yes." Keela swiped her fingers with more fervor, like the thought burned through her. "And many of us hate Brokk for it. We believe the gods rule over us, and we are to live harmoniously in their honor. But, like the gods of battle and war, we should not fear spilling blood either."

"Sounds like we all pick and choose what we think the gods want but in truth just do what we desire."

Keela laughed. "If that is the case"—the woman lifted one of the sleek spears—"then I will do it fighting for a way of life of my choosing."

On the second night we reached the summit, and Kael could hardly walk from the pain of fighting against the draw of the soul bones.

Together Roark, Brynn, and I arranged him in a makeshift shelter inside a narrow cavern on the side of the cliff.

Kael's hair stuck to his feverish brow. He demanded the tethers be added to his wrists halfway up the ledge, and he practically snarled at Roark when he opened my brother's arms to keep him from thrashing.

"You're a coward, Ashwood," Kael gritted out. "Never willing . . . to bond to the bones . . . gods." He clenched his eyes shut and breathed through his nose sharply.

Roark tugged the bands on Kael's wrists tight and came to my side. *Ready?*

I nodded. "The one on his other hip, there. The stitching has it embedded in his true bone, but I think I can get it free without damaging his gait. Brynn, the herbs."

Brynn smiled softly at Kael. "Like we said. It'll help you sleep through it."

Kael's eyes shadowed, and he glared at her, but his voice was gentle. "You won't go?"

"Gods, you're rather needy, Ser Darkwin."

I thought he almost smiled.

"Many women enjoy my pestering."

"Ah, I see." Brynn began adding herb pastes over Kael's chest. He would inhale the fumes, and they would bring fatigue. "Well, you have a choice—keep your many women, or ask me to stay."

I bit down on the inside of my cheek. Perhaps Kael Darkwin had met his match.

Kael let his head fall back. "Stay. Gods, you say *I* am aggravating. Dravens are the demanding ones."

His words slurred, and soon enough his eyes rolled back and he fell into a fitful rest. I followed the burning threads into the shadows.

In the mirrored cave, the air was heavy with brine and smoke. Walls were scorched, like a flame had dragged across the stones. Kael's form burned beneath my fingertips. Soul bones flashed in different shades, desperate to live on.

His body flinched and jerked beneath my palms. The webs of fibrous craft were melded harshly. There was nothing gentle or methodical about Fadey's work. He intended the bones to embed in the body in horrid ways. Kael's back arched when I unthreaded a ribbon of craft and it caught on the bright glow of his true bones.

"Melder." Skul Drek paced at my back, teeth clacking. "It grows to be too much."

His fears were not for Kael. I'd stumbled to the side, fatigue digging into my bones until I could not keep upright.

"I'm almost done."

"Melder." His voice was a low, snapping growl.

I ignored him. Kael jolted again when I found the final thread keeping the jagged shard melded to the curve of his hip. The shadow of Brynn's form was close. Her hand touched him, curling her glowing fingers around his.

Threads from his chest, his middle, spilled around the murky shadows and flickered to where they connected with Brynn.

Much the same as my own, the threads grew thicker the more time passed, the more interactions they had between them. Should they choose to foster the bond, no doubt, soon enough their bodies would be set aglow with a delicate web of a soul bond.

At long last, the final thread snapped.

The soul bone flickered, like a new spark in a flame, but Skul Drek covered the piece with darkness in another breath.

Painful cries rolled through the mirror world. He devoured the fragment, dimming the flashing glow from the soul bone until it was a deadened gray. My phantom lifted the bone and muttered for it to rest now before dropping the piece.

"Too long, Melder." He reached for me, ready to force me from the trance, but when I held out my hand, something stronger yanked me back.

My eyes flashed in panic. The cruel study of Skul Drek flashed bloodred. "Melder!"

His roar of violent rage was the last thing I heard before I was yanked out of the rotting cavern into a deeper, colder darkness.

I LANDED ON MY BACK. THE FORCE WAS HARSH ENOUGH THAT my thoughts spun. All around the mirror was open, no longer shrouded by the cavern walls. Here, trees curved as though they'd been beaten by furious gusts of wind since they were saplings. Leaves dripped in decay and darkness.

"Lyra."

I jolted, the gilded edges of my form flashed to hot white. "Fadey."

Between us the wretched, narrow thread burned like rust over iron. Dreadful and unwanted.

The dark melder sat atop a murky boulder. "I missed you."

My jaw pulsed. All that I knew, all that he'd done, seared through my soul like a molten blade.

Fadey cocked his head and laughed. "You know something? Found something? What is it you've learned?" His fingers plucked the thread between us.

A father's bond to a blood daughter.

No sooner had the thought rushed through my mind than Fadey's eyes narrowed. "What was that thought?"

Shit!

The bastard glanced at the tether between us, his mouth tight. "No. She would've said . . . a kinship bond?"

"Has your lovely blood crafter been keeping secrets from you?"

His glare lifted to me, his shoulders rising in heavy breaths.

"Will you still murder me, Fadey? Knowing I am your blood?" I knew the answer, but the bitter words slipped over my tongue all the same.

Still, for a breath, he hesitated. "This is my fate, Lyra. This . . . *was always my fate!*" His voice bellowed through the darkness. "I can't—won't—stop what I was destined to do. You must understand."

"I understand blood does not make a bond." I yanked on the tendril between us. Agony flooded over me, pain like the strike of a stone to my skull.

I was not the only one.

Fadey doubled over, cursing me. "You cannot break free of me. Give it up, girl."

"You've ruined so many lives. You deserve to fall as fiercely as they deserve to be avenged."

Fadey righted again. "You found what was hidden from me, didn't you? Tell me, did the prince save his own blood? Did he find the bone and bury it away?"

"What little you know," I taunted, flinging words Fadey had once used against me back at him.

"So you will not see reason." Fadey let out a long sigh. "Then you leave me no other decision. Remember, you chose this, Lyra. It did not have to be so painful for him."

I did not know what he meant, until my heart sank.

"Melder." Skul Drek seemed to bleed from the shadows. Furious, dangerous. He encircled me with the desperation of being lost in a storm only to find the blaze of a hearth.

Then, he noticed we were not alone.

Skul Drek did not speak; he did not stand in front of me. To him, there was no need. Someone had taken his melder from him; someone had frightened me; someone had tried to harm me. To my phantom, there was no mercy for such an act.

He clacked his teeth and lunged for Fadey before I could plead with him to stop.

Fadey did not flee. He only laughed and laughed. As though he anticipated this. Skul Drek struck, lashed at the dark melder's soul, but at the first touch, my phantom husband recoiled.

"No!" I rushed for him.

All at once, barbed coils of white threads burst from the center of Skul Drek's chest. The shadows of his shoulders, his cowl, the darkness that made his shape chipped away, tangled in ropes of burning, sharp light.

I reached for him, his cold skin overheated beneath my touch. He was fading.

"What's happening?" I clawed at the tendrils of darkness the more the white thorns spread, encircling him, breaking him. "Stop. *Please.*"

"Melder?" For the first time since I met the assassin in the darkness, fear was in his voice.

"No." I clung to his fading shape. "No. Don't you dare leave me. Roark. Gods."

Skul Drek faded, there, then gone. Nothing more than the mists of the mirror.

All I heard was Fadey's cruel laughter as the shadows retreated from the shelter of the cave.

Until Fadey's laughter morphed into Brynn's screams.

ROARK

LYRA WAS CRYING.

Her sobs were muffled, like she screamed at me from behind a thick door. I rocked. Again. Again. I was shaking. No, someone was shaking me.

"Roark." My wife's voice cracked.

I hated it.

Slowly, I cracked my eyes. Through the haze of dim candlelight, I made out Lyra's tearstained face. Behind her Brynn hugged her middle, Thane looked murderous, and Emi clung to Yrsa's hand like she might snap off her fingers. Even Darkwin, clutching a new wound on his hip, looked despondent.

A wet, hot tongue teased my ear.

Gods. Kyrre, stupid wolf, licked the side of my head.

"Roark." Lyra's fingertips stroked the side of my face. "Roark, look at me."

I reached for her cheek. *What happened?*

Lyra's chin trembled. She shook her head, took my face in her palms, and kissed me. Deep and needy.

Fine enough with me. Answers would come later.

My palm went to the back of her head and I held her against my mouth, tasting her, needing more of her. The possessive nature I kept tamed felt unbalanced. Darkness clawed just beneath the surface.

Lyra broke the kiss but kept her brow to mine. She pressed her palms to my chest. "Fadey did something to you, do you remember?" A tear fell from her lashes to my cheek. "I think he summoned me because he wanted to get to you. He knew you—Skul Drek—would come for me."

Fadey. Vague, uncertain thoughts filtered through my head. A haze shrouded them, but I could draw out the voices the deledan heard. Fadey ripping Lyra from me, the frenzy, the panic. I wanted to destroy him, and I . . . struck.

My brows cinched together. *He burned me.*

Lyra shook her head. "I don't know what he did, but he wrapped you in these bright—ropes, thorns, I don't know—and you . . . faded. Gods, I thought I'd wake to find you . . ." She didn't finish and buried her face against my neck.

"I don't want to point out the obvious, but something is *still* happening to him." Thane's voice was a sharp rasp.

"It's true," Brynn said. "I didn't know what to do. You both fell over and those . . . spread all over him."

I glanced at my palms, my vision clearer. My veins were raised, pulpy, and black.

"Your eyes are awful too," Darkwin offered glumly. He did not mince words, and I didn't know if it was from the soul bones or because he simply didn't have the strength.

Yrsa stepped forward and held out one of the thick bangles

we'd used to purchase Sindri's debt. The piece was wide and polished, so it served as a makeshift mirror.

Looking back was fiery red. Not my eyes. The same dark veins
webbed out from the sockets, down my face, over my throat.

"You said it happened when his darker soul touched Fadey?"
Yrsa asked.

Lyra nodded. "Immediately. Like I said, I think Fadey came to
draw me away with the intent to hurt Roark. What did he do?"

She clung to my palm like she would never release it.

Yrsa knelt beside me and opened a small pouch she'd pulled
from inside the cloak on her shoulders. "I know a cast that can
reveal if any curses or spells were placed on you. I just need a
drop of blood."

The princess pricked my finger. Yrsa never proclaimed to be a
strong blood crafter, but she was one of the most knowledgeable
of the craft. Always reading and learning and memorizing herbs
for casts.

She took the blood and spread it along a strange blue leaf. Eyes
closed, the princess touched the edges until the smear of blood
turned black.

Yrsa's shoulders slumped. "They've cursed you, Roark. Well,
what I'd guess is that Fadey has blood casts around him, so when
you touched him, the curse took hold."

"What sort of curse?" Emi asked.

"I don't know." Yrsa tugged on the end of one braid. "I'm not
skilled with curses, more healing spells. And I don't fully understand your soul craft."

"Can we get it out of him?" Lyra's hold on my palm tightened.

The princess looked a little defeated. "There usually are
counter curses, but I don't know what they've done well enough
to even begin crafting an antidote."

"It's something in your soul," Lyra whispered.

I rubbed a palm over my chest, hate and violence too close. *I feel like I am more him than me. It feels like the darker soul has not settled, but is hovering just below my skin.*

A throat cleared. Jordis. Her long hair was braided now, and she'd lined her eyes with kohl like many of the other Unfettered Folk. "Lyra, Gammal's returned. She may have something for you."

Jordis shot me a sympathetic look, then stepped out of the cavern.

I staggered to my feet, every limb feeling as though it was weighed down by stones. Lyra slid her arm around my waist, allowing me to brace against her as we walked out to the camp.

Sindri looked at me with a touch of horror, his hand on Kyrre's head. The pup whimpered. I let my chin fall, avoiding the scrutiny, the fear of others.

"Elskan." Gammal held a bit of thin parchment in her fingers, her eyes milky and distant. "Sit. Sit."

"Did you see something?"

The old woman swayed. "A soul of shadows burns in chains made from vengeful hate. Freedom is found through the blood of the maker of this cruel fate. Take care, for should the chains not be shed, a dark soul is as good as dead."

A soul of shadows. Me. I was a dark soul. The barbs, the bright tether, it had to mean something had poisoned my soul, and my soul would be the price to pay if we did not find a way to remove it.

Lyra's gaze was burdened. No mistake, she understood the riddle as well as I did.

I slipped my fingers through hers and pressed our knuckles to my lips. The burn of cruelty was there, but somehow I managed to dredge up a touch of tenderness. *This is not our end. Do you believe me?*

She nodded, glassy tears in her eyes. "Don't break that promise, Ashwood."

No lines. I kissed her knuckles again.

"You cannot meld again, Lyra," Darkwin said. "Or unmeld. Not if Fadey keeps finding you."

"At least not until we know more," Emi interjected. "No one knows a deledan rite better than Elisabet."

Lyra brightened. "She might understand what happened."

"Then let us hope your men found the soul queen with haste," Gammal said. Her eyes were clear again, and she wore a sad smile. "For I do not think your enemies will wait much longer."

WE STOOD AT THE IMPASSE OF PATHWAYS THAT FLOWED INTO Dravenmoor.

Gammal reached for Lyra after we finished watering the horses. The old seer pressed a kiss to Lyra's brow. "You have a fate to meet, elskan. From the first inkling of a daughter from the god-queen's blood, I have felt you will change these lands."

"Destroy them," she whispered.

"Destruction does not always mean the end. From the ashes, do new blooms not grow stronger? I do not know what the Norns have in store for you, but trust your heart, elskan. Fight for all you have won, for all those who stand with you here."

I sat atop a horse and took in the sight.

Unfettered Folk, Jorvans, a Myrdan royal, and Dravens. We all stood together, and we all desired to let the Wanderer King rest. Men like Fadey and Damir were the cruel hearts who misinterpreted the lore of restoring the first king's bones.

Such power was never meant for one soul; it was too fierce, too corruptible. Like the god-queen tried to show her greedy husband, the gods' gifts were meant to strengthen every land.

I did not know how Lyra would be the one to restore the power of the Wanderer without the bones, but I knew enough to understand that lore and fables were never direct. Lessons were learned through their tales, and only after did one truly find the meaning behind the words.

"This is where we part." Gammal held Lyra's face. "But I pray to the gods that we meet again."

Jordis and Sindri bid farewell to the Unfettered who would stay behind. My nephew smiled with a bit of shyness when some of the men made him vow he would not become a pompous, spoiled prince.

Lyra settled in front of me, unbothered by the horrid, pulpy veins on my flesh; the tension in my muscles; or the red of my eyes. In truth, she held me a little tighter than before.

Those who remained with the seemódir raised their fists, shouted farewells, and stayed on the edge until the long line of our growing army faded around the sharp path down the Night Ledges.

"ROARK, YOU'RE BURNING." LYRA PULLED BACK ON THE HORSE and turned to inspect my head.

I feel him, I gestured with a shudder. *Trying to get out.*

"Dammit." Lyra kicked her leg over the horse. "Scoot forward. I fear you're about to fall off."

I didn't argue as we maneuvered into new positions on the charge, Lyra holding one of her slender arms around my waist and me slumped over the neck of the mare.

The gnawing at my flesh from something within me was maddening. I could hardly keep focused as we descended the switchbacks. When we emerged from the pass, the bodies of Stav Guard remained where we'd battled them, gray and sunken in the faces.

We left them again.

One palm fell to Lyra's thigh. I spoke to her there. *Lyra. I need you to know that you have always brightened the night inside me. You made my dark existence worth living.*

She covered my hand, squeezing my fingers. "Don't. You're talking of endings, Roark. You told me our bond shattered endings. There are no endings, not with us."

I lifted her palm and pressed a kiss to each fingertip.

No true endings. But we could be separated. Like Nivek and Jordis. Like my mother and father. Soul bond or not, if the gates of Salur called, there would be no stopping them.

"Hold." Brynn led the caravan, but she held up a fist when the two fara wolves raised their hackles. Oakbriar lifted a notched arrow and aimed for the darkness. "Make your name known."

Silence.

Weak, overheated, and locked on the edge of violence; it did not matter. I reached for the hilt of my sword, ready to stand between enemy blades and Lyra.

"Sister. I thought we were closer than this, being twins and all." Auki, hooded and with half of his face shrouded by a mask, stepped onto the path. Four fara wolves surrounded him.

A low, hesitant chuckle rippled down the line.

Brynn lowered her bow. "You did that on purpose. Foolish of you, Auki. Gods, we're all wound in tension. I could've shot you."

Auki tugged the cloth off his nose and winked at his twin. His levity died when he saw me. "Good gods, Roark, what happened?"

"Fadey." Lyra spoke instead. "Change of plans. We need to get back to the queen, see if she knows what was done to the deledan. It has altered Roark's craft somehow."

A shadow crossed Auki's face. "No need. Follow me. The queen has come to you."

47

LYRA

THE DARK WATCH CAMP SETTLED IN THE TREES AND LANDS
not far from the northern tip of the Black Fjords. Tents, fire
pits, and a small barrier of fences to mark the camp's borders
were already in place.

I propped my chin onto Roark's shoulder. "It looks like your
mother moved the Dark Watch not long after we left."

He nodded but didn't unfurl his clenched fists to respond.

Jordis rode alongside us. "What do you think drew them out?"

"I don't know. But if the Dark Watch is on guard and ready for
battle, something happened in our absence."

"Oi. What'd we say, you sods?" Gunter's voice lifted over the
camp. From a crowd of Dark Watchers, the soul weaver shoved
toward the back of the procession.

Three Dark Watch warriors aimed blades at the horses of
Thane and Yrsa. Gunter tugged on one man's shoulder, breaking
his hold. "What'd we say, huh? The Jorvan prince is with us."

The Dark Watcher was young, likely new, and dropped his chin. "Apologies. Saw him and panicked."

"Let them pass. Gods, you call yourself a watcher. We don't panic." Gunter winked up at Yrsa. "Apologies, Princess."

"Are you making eyes at my betrothed?" Thane huffed.

"I might be."

"Get in line, Gunter." Emi rode alongside Yrsa's horse, kicking at her fellow Draven until he laughed and backed away.

"Glad you lot still breathe. Though it seems like our dear prince has seen better days." Gunter quickened his step to our horse. "Lyra, trouble over the ledges? We have not been parted terribly long and already he falls apart."

"Fadey attacked Roark's soul. We need to see the queen."

"Shit." Gunter took hold of the horse's lead and took us to the largest tent in the center of the camp. "Go. I'll see to your things."

Roark slid off the back of the horse, using the creature's neck to steady himself before he reached for my hand.

His grip was tight, possessive, and he looked around at his own people like they were enemies for even glancing my way. Skul Drek did not reason well. Threats, death, depravity—those were always in the forefront of his focus until our soul bond. Now, to him, it seemed no one was worthy of trust, for they would likely turn their darkest desires against his melder.

Elisabet stood over a long tabletop placed on stumps. Maps of the three realms scattered the surface. Yanson, Kaysar, Ofan, and other Dark Watch captains were there with her.

Elisabet's lips parted. "What's happened? Why is the deledan tethered?"

"Tethered?" I stepped back when the queen led Roark to a chair. The prince nearly hissed at her when she tore us apart.

The queen wheeled on me. "What happened?"

I glanced at the captains. "They will know the truth about . . ."

"They already know Fadey lives."

Ofan, the man who spewed his hatred after Roark slaughtered Fillip at the ravines, hung his chin. "Melder Bien, the queen confessed the secrets kept on what truly happened at Stonegate. We know how you fought to stop the bones of the fallen from being used and battled against Melder Fadey. I hope to the gods one day I might earn your forgiveness for misplacing my hatred, for assuming you are like the dark melder."

Roark clacked his teeth at Ofan, much like Skul Drek.

I squeezed his palm and faced Elisabet. "I've no need for apologies. I need to *save* him. Fadey attacked the deledan in the realm of souls."

"How?" The queen's vibrant eyes burned like a new spark of a flame.

"He trapped me, and Skul Drek followed. Fadey attacked him, and he disappeared. When we broke the trance, Roark was like this. What do you mean he is tethered?"

Elisabet cursed and turned back to the prince. "Trapped within him. A rent soul is but a remnant of the whole soul. It is never meant to overpower the body, the mind, the heart. But once it is split, it cannot be forced back into what it was. The remnant will always remain separate. It is a blood craft spell, one with hints of darker curses used against soul crafters in wars of old. The craft is forcing the deledan back into Roark, as though trying to make his soul whole again, and it is poisoning him."

The white glowing barbs. No doubt a binding spell to tether Skul Drek inside Roark's whole soul, forcing a restoration that should never be.

"How do we stop it?"

Elisabet was pale when she faced me. "I can't stop it. Not unless the blood craft is broken. This is Ingir's work. She is clever and cruel. I will take her head."

"No." I stepped in front of the queen. "No. I do not accept that there is nothing we can do for him. I will not watch my husband *die* because his soul is not free."

The queen dragged her fingers through her hair, pacing. "I cannot rend him again. It would take too much from him, likely kill him just the same."

A throat cleared. "Is there a way to slow the poison?"

I startled. Yrsa, Thane, and Emi stood at the flap of the tent.

The princess approached the queen, chin lifted, poised, as regal as I had ever seen her. "Queen Elisabet. Tell me, is there a way to slow the poison?"

The queen looked between Yrsa and Thane, then to Roark. "The fragment of his soul will be trying to get free. It will shadow my son, but if he had other tethers to cling to, it could help him keep in control a little longer. But it would not be permanent."

"Would it be enough?" Thane pressed.

Elisabet's jaw set. "It would be long enough to give me time to kill your mother, Prince Thane."

Thane flinched. "You are trying to test me, Elisabet? See if I am truly loyal to your son? I mean, you did arrange for his fate to cross with mine, hoping he'd betray me in the end." There was a darkness in the prince's tone when he leaned over the table, his eyes on the queen. "Let me assure you, every soul I would go to war for is here. In this camp. The rest, I have resigned, could meet the gods. Some certainly should."

"You would kill your own mother?"

"It is not a desire of mine, no," Thane admitted. "But for them"—the prince gestured at all of us—"I would do many despicable things. They are my family, Queen Elisabet."

"Good." Elisabet's face softened. "Because Roark does not live if your mother survives. It could be a season, two. But he will fall to the poison. No matter how much we slow it."

Thane blew out a breath, but he did not falter. "Then Roark lives. Yrsa, any ideas on how we can give him something to hold on to?"

The princess closed her eyes. I did not know how the blood craft spoke to her; I did not know if instincts played a role, or if there was a shift in her blood. But when Yrsa opened her eyes again, her posture straightened and her voice was sure.

"We need something stronger than the desires of the deledan to pull him out of the haze it is creating."

Roark touched my fingers, drawing my attention. *You brighten the night.*

All gods.

"Me." I spun back to Yrsa. "Create a tether of me, of you, of Emi. Thane. Every one of us Roark Ashwood would die to protect. We are the souls who kept him fighting when he did not have control once before."

Yrsa's grin turned vicious. "Perfect. I know what to do. Everyone who cares for the prince, give me your damn blood."

YRSA HAD HER DARK BRAIDS TIED IN A KNOT ON THE TOP OF her head, her brow was covered with sweat, and she kept shifting her grip on the pestle she ground against spongy, blood-soaked herbs in the mortar.

The line had no shortage of folk, and Gunter and Thane kept pricking fingertips and dropping their offerings into Yrsa's blood craft. Yanson, Kaysar, the twins, Dark Watch warriors, Elisabet. Even Kael. With the help of Brynn, my brother glared at Roark like he despised him but offered two drops of his blood.

"It's because of me," he muttered when he strode past.

"No. Fadey would have been waiting no matter what."

Jordis and Sindri stopped at the mouth of the tent. Elisabet studied them, head tilted, no mistake seeing a bit of her son in the face of the boy. "Who are you?"

Roark scoffed when he slumped in the chair. His fever had lessened, and he seemed less fatigued.

Mother. Meet the hidden bone of the Wanderer. The firstborn of the firstborn. Your true heir to Dravenmoor.

His gestures were as slurred as a drunkard's words. I had to repeat them to his mother.

Blood drained from the queen's face. "Nivek."

I nodded. "This is Jordis, Nivek's wife and sjeleven. And their son, Sindri the Wild."

Elisabet Foxglen was not a woman who ruffled. Never had I seen her uncertain or bothered by the words of others.

The queen went to Jordis first, studying her, like she was memorizing her every feature. "My son's . . . wife?"

Jordis dipped her chin. "Death has only separated us for a time."

Elisabet peered at the boy. "You look like your father, my prince."

The queen dipped her chin in a bow. A signal to all her councilmen, all the Dark Watchers in the tent, that Sindri the Wild of the Unfettered was the heir to their kingdom. Nivek's son, the future king of Dravenmoor.

The boy flushed. "I . . . I might be able to help my uncle, Lady."

Jordis nudged her son. "She is a queen."

"I mean, Queen."

Elisabet's eyes brightened. "How can you help him?"

Sindri shifted back and forth on his feet. "Well, I got the same stuff as my father. I've got soul craft."

"What is your craft?"

Gammal mentioned the boy was interesting. We'd never thought to ask if Nivek's son had craft.

"I, uh, I tell souls what to do. It's not exactly good, I suppose.

And it, uh, it makes me wobbly for a bit. Sometimes I retch if it takes too long."

Yanson chuckled. "Hear that, men? The gods brought us another soul chainer. Haven't had one of those for a few hundred seasons."

"A soul chainer?" Jordis draped an arm around Sindri's bony shoulders.

"It's what we call someone who can command a soul to do something against its will."

"Saw my uncle do it." Sindri flashed Roark a smile. "Convinced old Brokk to burn down his own house."

Elisabet frowned at Roark. "You possessed a man?"

Roark waved her away. *I encouraged an idea.*

The queen faced her grandson. "It's not exactly the same. A deledan can completely take control of a soul, corrupt it. That is what your uncle did, and it is *frowned upon.*"

Roark snorted and reached for my hand, as though it had been too long since he touched me.

"You, if you are a soul chainer, can command a soul for a time. It's dangerous, and in the wrong soul, it could be tempting to make folk do anything you desire."

Sindri nodded. "My mam said the same thing. Wouldn't let me do it to Brokk."

"She was wise to say so," Elisabet said. "But you can learn to use it when the temptation is not there." The queen smiled. "With your clan here, you can learn all about soul craft and how the gifts of the gods should be used to better our people. Now, to help, what are you thinking you wish to do?"

"Well, doesn't he have some piece of a soul inside of him?" Sindri strode to Roark after Elisabet confirmed. "I was thinkin' maybe I could command the soul to not attack him."

My heart leapt to my throat. "Do you think you could, Sindri?"

"I could try. Bet he's a lot stronger than me, but maybe it'll buy some time along with the lady's blood spell."

Yrsa lifted her chin. "It's nearly finished. Anything might help."

Let him, Roark gestured. The red of his eyes flashed.

Sindri stretched his fingers.

"I'm gonna touch you, see if I can find it and all." The boy placed a palm on Roark's arm. He shuddered. "Gods, it's right there. I can . . . I can feel it. You live with this inside you?"

Roark chuckled softly and let his eyes close. Sindri winced, but beneath his finger, Roark's veins pulsed. Wisps of darkness swirled under Roark's skin. The boy coughed. A drop of blood trickled from his nose.

"Sindri," Jordis warned. "Do not harm yourself."

"Little more," he gritted out. "He wants out. Doesn't even know he's hurting his own self. Doesn't know how to stop."

My shoulders slumped. It was brave of the boy to try.

"I'm gonna tell him to be calm," Sindri said, as another drop of blood fell from his nose. "Might help if he's not constantly digging at him."

The veins of Roark's arms, neck, and face bulged for another breath, then faded, lightening for the first time. Roark's eyes remained the fierce bloodred, but he slumped in the chair, his muscles less corded than before.

Sindri coughed again and doubled over. He covered his mouth with one palm.

Jordis pulled him back. "That's all."

The boy drew in a few sharp breaths, but nodded. "Sorry. I tried."

"Thank you, Sindri. I think it helped."

Roark was relaxed in the chair when Yrsa approached. She rolled the crushed herbs and blood inside the mortar over a simple piece of wood. Thane had cut a strip of leather off one of the satchels. The princess tied the wood shard around Roark's neck and tucked it beneath his tunic.

"Keep this against the skin, Roark," she said softly. "This is everyone who stands with you, cares whether you live or die. Use us to pull yourself back should you need it."

He curled his hand around the shard. *Thank you. Does this mean you forgive me?*

Yrsa shoved his shoulder. "It's a start."

Roark's skin no longer burned, and when he stood, he did not stumble. He went to his mother. *What happened to bring the full Watch?*

"Scouts told us Myrdan and Jorvan forces are crossing the fjords. They will be here by morning."

"What?" Thane crossed the tent. "The full Stav?"

Elisabet nodded. "King Hundur has summoned the Shield Riders as well."

Yrsa cursed. From chatter overhead in the Jakobson long-house, I was aware that the Myrdan Shield Riders were skilled horsemen who knew how to kill from above. They were difficult to bring down and used hooked barbs on ropes to snare their victims and drag them behind their charges.

"We've brought two dozen Unfettered spearmen," Jordis offered. "They are fierce fighters."

"Fortunate your scouts caught sight of them," Thane said. "We can be ready."

Elisabet's face hardened. "We sent scouts because we were betrayed. Yanson intercepted a missive to Stonegate scouts, telling them where you all had gone and for what purpose. They come now to intercept you, not knowing the Dark Watch will meet them."

"Who sent the missive?" I asked.

The queen leaned over the table. "Virki has betrayed his clan and stands with Melder Fadey."

48

ROARK

ALREADY THE BLOOD CRAFT SPELL HAD CHASED AWAY
the relentless thrashing under my skin. Calm was there,
but a simmer of something like rage edged each thought, every
movement.

For now, with Sindri's craft and Yrsa's spell, the fever faded
and my limbs felt like my own again.

My mother grew silent when we told her the truth of my uncle's involvement in Nivek's death.

Virki had always feigned the regretful uncle, heartbroken
over being the one who was bound by Draven law and honor to
name the prince as the traitor. He'd always vowed, on his knees,
that he desired a trial for Nivek.

He'd blamed his own crime on the Dark Watch.

When the queen spoke again, she demanded that watch shifts
be put in place, then urged her warriors to rest, eat, and prepare.

"Sindri is being guarded in the tents. The queen does not want
to risk him traveling back to the palace with Jorvans so near, so

he'll be guarded here." Lyra pulled back a thick fur over a mat we'd share. "He's not happy about it."

I chuckled and stripped my tunic over my head. One touch to the talisman left me breathing easier. Lyra studied me when I slipped beside her.

"Your eyes still burn red."

Are they horrid to look at?

She ran a thumb over my lashes. "No. I'm beginning to wonder things about myself, because I might be drawn to the ruthlessness of them. I love your gold, but I don't mind your eyes like this."

I curled my body around hers, my fingers dancing across her chest. *I think I've corrupted you.*

"Hmm. Then you owe me for being a terrible influence, Ashwood." Lyra rolled onto her shoulder and traced the bridge of my nose. "But I'll collect after the battles are done."

She tried to mask it, but there was a quiver to her voice.

We end this, but they do not end us.

Lyra dropped her chin. "I don't understand how Fadey can care for nothing else but power."

Because your heart is not black like his.

"Not once in all my existence has he ever stopped to see me as a person, a daughter, not a tool in his ambition. I cannot fathom such a lust that he hunts living souls, slaughters to hide his own identity, and attacks everyone I love without remorse."

I adjusted on the mat, tucking her body half beneath mine. *I plan to keep my vow, Fadey bound at your feet as I hand you the blade.*

Lyra lifted her head and pressed a sweet kiss to my lips. Her palm brushed over my stubble. "I missed you. I am glad to see you upright again. I cannot tell you how terrified I was that you might not wake from the trance."

I turned my face to kiss her palm. *We have tonight. Let us not waste it with worries of what might be or what could've happened.*

"Oh? What else am I to do when two armies are headed toward us and my blood father wants to tear out everyone's bones?"

I maneuvered us so her back was pressed to my chest. Lyra made a move to protest, but I took the lobe of her ear between my teeth.

Her gasp was the sweetest sound.

She did not open her eyes when I spoke softly to her cheek. *I have some ideas.*

"Roark." Her hips pressed into mine. "You've . . . you've been ill and—"

I covered her mouth with one hand, then let my fingers run down her chin, her throat, until I could speak against her rising chest. *We go into a battle. Whatever the dawn brings, this night will not be spent sleeping when it has been too long since I've heard my wife's moans.*

"Gods," she said in a rough rasp.

One palm slid down the curve of her waist, and my fingertips teased the loose waist of her trousers. Lyra panted. She bucked her hips and tried to roll over to face me.

I only tightened my grip around her waist and shook my head. *No. Stay put.*

Any complaints choked off in her throat when I slid my other arm beneath her head, then reached down the front of her tunic. I palmed one of her full breasts at the same moment my other hand cupped between her thighs.

I was torn in two, and remnants of my soul were bleeding into my heart, but for a moment I was whole—villainy and goodness in alignment, wanting more of this woman.

Never would I get enough of her sounds, her taste, the heat of her body beneath my touch.

I kissed the curve of her neck, thrusting two fingers inside her slit, curling the tips. Lyra gasped and rocked over my hand.

She curled her palms around my forearm and moaned when I pinched her nipple.

"Roark," she said, breathless. "Let me touch you too."

I shook my head and added a third finger.

"Bas . . . bastard." The word ground out in a long groan. Lyra let her head fall back against mine. She rocked and moved over my fingers; she covered my hand on her breast, holding me there.

A whimper slipped through her lips when I quickened the thrusts of my hand. She pressed her hips against the hardness of my length, and it spun my head. Tonight was hers. I wanted her to fall apart in my hands, in my clarity. I wanted to own her cries, her breaths.

Fadey would try to take her from me. He did not see her as the brightest soul. Tonight I would worship her. I would show her every move I made was for her alone. No crown, no craft, no clan.

It was all for Lyra. A woman I was meant to despise, a woman who destroyed me, both edges of my soul, and I never desired to heal from her ruin.

Lyra sobbed and writhed, her movements erratic. She seemed to attempt words, but they slurred into more perfect, beautiful gasps and moans.

She gave in. Her body was mine to command. My fingers pinched and stroked her core, thrusting deeper and deeper until her mouth parted and rough pants rolled over her full lips. Tender attention went to her breasts. I kissed her throat, and my tongue ran over her pulse, nipping her skin there.

All at once, she went taut, her cries of release climbing. I tilted her chin and swallowed the sounds with a furious kiss. My fingers slowed inside her, drawing out every last bit of her pleasure.

Slick with her, I traced the planes of her belly, her ribs.

Lyra's eyes flashed, the silver scars of her craft like a falling star. "You have a cruel soul to not let me touch you."

I grinned. *And you love both edges.*

"No." She dragged her nose along my cheek. "I just love you. Hunter, villain, prince, warrior. To me, all those edges are simply you. That is who I love."

At the dawn—every step, every strike, every death—it would always be for her.

MISTS GATHERED AT THE TOP OF A KNOLL WHEN THE PALE dawn began to break the night. I stood on the edge beside the queen with Kyrre at my side, whimpering. My mother, clad in her leathers for battle, stared at the half a dozen Dark Watch warriors and two fara wolves who urged the boy into one of the smaller tents, concealed from the open fields.

Sindri looked over his shoulder to where Jordis stood, a spear in her grip, her braids tightly woven behind her head. Like the Dark Watch, Nivek's wife had painted jagged streaks of black down her cheeks.

"I am not Draven," she told the queen. "But I stand here in my husband's place and fight for his people."

Sindri was not welcomed to the battlefield. His protests matched his youthful age, the way he looked ready to stomp and kick his feet. In the end he complied. Now he would be shielded in the camp until the Dark Watch found a moment safe enough to get the boy to the palace.

"He looks like Nivek," the queen said.

I nodded.

My mother faced me. "You seem better this morning."

I lifted the totem. *Helps.*

"Roark." Elisabet hesitated. "I do not know what lies in store today, but I must tell you something. Trust me or do not, but I love you. I love your brother. I love my king. I did not have a way to save your life, and your father willingly gave his so you would have a chance to restore what was lost. I never betrayed my bond."

My teeth clamped. *Did you know my bond wouldn't break with the deledan?*

I repeated the question until understanding flashed in the queen's eyes.

"Yes." She stared at the grass. "I thought I would lose my bond when your father volunteered to be rent in two. I did not speak to him for weeks. I could not believe he would ask me to do such a thing. But when it was clear our sons might be at risk should the Jorvans succeed in their plans to continue crafting their vicious warriors, I made my first impossible choice. Perhaps the gods are kinder than I know. Our bond did not break."

You could still speak with him?

My mother grinned. "Yes. When he could not speak to others, he could pull me in through our bond, and we could communicate clearly. I counseled with him there. It was how I knew his desire was to give you the chance to live. The deaths you were commanded to bring to the Jorvans, I admit, came from hatred. I'm sorry for falling into the bitterness over the seasons. I embraced my own darker pieces too fiercely at times. But never truly against Lyra. I knew you would never kill her should she be found. Your soul bond would not allow it."

I did not know what to think. The queen admitted to using my darker soul to slaughter. True, she might've desired for Thane to die when I attacked him, but she knew I would not harm Lyra. She knew, eventually, that we would be reunited. It meant Elisabet Foxglen always anticipated the melder living within her borders.

Since I'd returned, pieces of the past had fallen into place, and I questioned my bitterness more and more.

To know that both my mother and father knew of my infantile bond and gave up everything so I might keep it—the truth was almost too much to carry. The weight of resentment and bitterness I'd shouldered all this time grew heavier with emotion. With a debt to those who'd given me life that I could never repay.

Thank you.

Elisabet returned a small smile. "I would save you again and again. Live today. Be *free*, son. That is how you can thank me."

A horn broke the stillness of the morning.

In the valley below, soupy mists pulled back. My blood quickened. Darkness boiled in my brain.

Rows and rows of Stav Guard units marched through the trees. Shield Riders took the edges, their gilded round shields in position atop their tall, bulky horses.

The whole of the front lines was made of Berserkirs. There were more now than when I'd left. Men clad in tunics with tassels marking their kills. Bones bulged across their shoulders and legs, their thighs thicker than was natural, their necks wide and bulky.

At the head was Fadey.

The melder was clad in black, the white wolf of Stonegate the only contrast on his attire. Unlike the Shield Riders, Stav Guard preferred to attack on foot. They were trained to be swift and brutal—*I'd* trained them. Fadey took his place in front of the Berserkirs. Men he'd corrupted over the seasons. He still wore the face of Baldur the Fox, auburn hair braided down his skull.

Did anyone behind those blades and shields realize who they followed into battle?

Near the back, on the peak of a smaller hill, Hundur was perched atop a fine stallion and next to him was Ingir.

Hate thrashed in my veins. The presence of the blood crafter queen was a signal for the trapped darkness to bleed out again, to break me apart to be free.

I held the talisman. I thought of Lyra's face. The silver in her eyes. The words she whispered before she woke each morning, her silent hopes for how the day might go. It was my most favored part of the morning. My wife, sharing her thoughts with me, admitting she looked forward to seeing them through with me at her side.

"Even though you're still surly, Ashwood." She'd always whisper the final line before kissing my head and leaving our bed.

This morning had been no different, only her voice was hushed, trembling. Fear was there. Still, Lyra spoke of her hopes for the after. We'd all be dining at a weary table tonight, sharing our bloody stories and celebrating that we all survived. Then, she would fall asleep in my arms and she'd wake to a world where, at long last, we were both free.

"So it begins," the queen whispered at my side.

I rolled my shoulders back and looked at my mother. *I will meet you on the battlefield.*

My mother smiled at the old Dark Watch saying. "And I will meet you off it, be it looking down from Salur or at your side with a horn in hand."

The queen took hold of my palm and squeezed.

And I did the same.

49

LYRA

Auki took his sister's hand. "Use Òlmr. Don't get distracted by Darkwin, Brynn. We don't know how he will fare. Choose you, please. Choose you if it goes wrong."

"Hush, Auki," Brynn said, a slight tremble in her voice.

"Thank the gods," said Kael. "It is rather disconcerting to hear how you demand my death before going into battle."

"Would you not say the same if the prince was melded with corrupt bones and might turn on Lyra, Darkwin?"

"I suppose." Kael faced Auki, sturdier since two of his bones had been removed and, no doubt, the bond he did not see was strengthening. He held out an arm for Auki to take. "I swear to you, I will ram a blade through my own skull if I feel the berserksgangur taking hold."

Auki pinned him with a look but took hold of Kael's bulky arm. "Do that, Darkwin. But more, try to survive."

My stomach turned over. I hated this line of talk, hated the thought of losing a single face in our numbers, but I could not turn away.

Brynn frowned at her brother. "Enough. We focus. We fight. We all return."

I closed my eyes. Emi finished securing my hair off my neck. She'd been somber most of the morning. No doubt thoughts of her father plagued her mind. She tapped my shoulder, and I spun around. Without a word, Emi set about painting my face in runes and long lines of kohl.

Next to her, Thane helped Yrsa secure a leather gambeson over her body. "You remember how we've sparred?"

The princess shoved his shoulder. "I am better with knives than you."

"Only because I am ridiculously skilled with the bow."

"The shore of the fjords is taken." A low voice stirred me from my moment of pause. Gunter, his father, and a handful of Dark Watch warriors stepped next to me. A strain burrowed in Gunter's brow. "Fadey burnt their damn longships. He plans to win or die today."

"You're sure?" I straightened.

"It is a message," Yanson said. "Dravenmoor will be his."

"We saw Virki." Gunter's bright eyes shadowed when he looked to Emi. "Took four wolves with him and displays the white wolf on his chest."

The warriors behind us pounded fists against the double-headed ravens over their gambesons, like the truth of Virki's betrayal ached through the threads.

"Make way for the queen!"

The Dark Watch parted like an even darker sea. Elisabet strode through, her hair tied in dark leather, her eyes darkened in powders, and lines of white paint carved through her lips. At her side, Roark followed. Kyrre bounded across the space, nudging my hip until I scratched his thick head.

The wolf sat at my side, tongue flapping.

Across from me, Roark was a prince of beautiful nightmares. The dark strands of his hair were braided off his face, and the runes of protection and strength I'd painted down his forehead were slightly smeared from the heat of the sun.

A slight tug teased the center of my chest. A signal he could still feel the pull of our bond through the rage stirring from his trapped soul.

No lines, I mouthed.

Roark smirked, then turned to where his mother stepped forward.

"For seasons this battle for ancient powers has been fought in small acts of violence, with corruption, but now we end it. Today we fight for not only Dravenmoor, we fight for all lands, all craft. We fight for our lives. There is no fate where we fall today, I refuse to believe it. We owe our blades, our strength, our very lives to those who've gone before us, fighting for a land, for the people they loved. We honor them by living today!"

The Dark Watch pounded their fists over their chests. Unfettered Folk slammed the ends of their spears against the soil, and a breathless sort of chant from their chests followed.

"We take our places in battle," Elisabet went on. "I pray we meet off the field today. But if not, speak of our bravery and honor to those in Salur."

The queen raised her sword.

We did the same, a wave of steel cutting over leather sheaths. Spears, bearded axes, and swords, all pointed toward the somber morning sky.

The next move divided archers and foot warriors for their

first marks. Roark pushed through the bustle and gripped my arm, pulling me against his chest. One palm trapped my face. His scorching red eyes were encircled with dark veins from the poison, but he looked down at me like he wanted to burn my features into his thoughts.

"I will see you soon." My voice croaked.

Roark opened his palm over my heart and tapped my chest three times. *Yours, body and soul.*

"Stay alive, Ashwood."

He kissed me quickly. Then he tore away, like he had to break it or he never would.

"Ready to have some fun, Ly?" Thane shouldered a bow and covered his head with a thick wool hood.

I did the same and fell in next to the prince. The archers were led by Kaysar and another man with a shorn head inked with a wolf skull that looked as though it was devouring him. We took the back road up the knolls at a slow run, crouching in our positions.

"We send the signal," Kaysar insisted. "Lyra Bien."

I jolted from the brisk tone.

He grinned. "This has been your battle since before you were born. Will you begin it, so you might finally end it?"

I blinked, a little stunned, but Thane winked from beneath his hood and handed me one of his arrows. A Dark Watch dipped the point in a pungent oil, then sparked a flame.

I blew out a breath, drawing my bowstring taut against my cheek. Straight ahead, dark rows of Stav Guard awaited their own fates. Was Edvin there? Was Gisli, Hilda's kindhearted husband, forced to fight for Stonegate?

I could not think of it now.

Today, I fought for the whole of the realms. I waited for craft to summon the bone to me. A glitter of dainty ribbons unfurled from the arrow shaft, reaching for the nearest shoulder, thigh, or skull.

Golden threads rippled over the knolls, the mists, until they danced around the neck of a Berserkir on the front line. An opening between his hardened soul bones. In one small spot on the side of his throat, there was room for more.

The moment the threads of craft found their first mark, I let the arrow fly.

A guttural shout of pain echoed over the field when the Berserkir jolted back, the flaming arrow lodged into his neck. Fire licked around his shoulders and chest, devouring him as he fell.

He landed backward, causing the front line to scramble to avoid being set aflame. Stav Guard rumbled and repositioned. Some lifted shields. Others crouched a little deeper.

Fadey looked up to the top knoll. The burn of his rage dug beneath the skin. He pointed his sword toward the place where I'd fired.

When his blade fell, a battle ignited.

The flood of the Dark Watch shuddered across the damp soil. At the castle, horns blared from behind the Shield Riders, warning of our approach. Stav formed tight units. The Dark Watch struck swifter.

"Set those shields ablaze like the molten hell!" Kaysar shouted.

I stood and fired with the archers. Another wave of burning arrows assaulted the flanks where Shield Riders took comfort. Myrdan warriors cried out when burning arrows caught the wood of their shields. Men scrambled to be free of the shields tied to their arms. Some fell from their steeds, the horses fleeing from the inferno.

Screams mingled with the falling warriors. The Dark Watch,

led by the queen and by Roark, collided with the front row of Berserkirs. A collision of steel and blood burst between the two sides.

Thane was ruthless with his shots, calculated, merciless. He killed a man who went for Yrsa before the Stav could even finish lifting his blade. Another breath and the prince had a Shield Rider pinned to a tree, an arrow through his skull.

I hunted for Fadey.

He was a ghost, a haunt. His steps were calculated and carefully placed to keep him shielded. I had few doubts he would keep his presence hidden until he wanted. Shot after shot, we rained down blood on the enemy.

At the final arrow, Kaysar drew a dark seax blade. "Our next move begins now. I will meet you on the battlefield!"

The reply of Salur or drinking horns was returned.

"Lyra." Thane faced me, a new somberness in his tone. "Should I fall out there, I have been honored to know you."

I swallowed the knot in my throat, my short blade in my hand. "And you, Prince."

We ran forward, into the fray.

My sword struck a Stav's blade. We locked, spun, and dodged until I sliced the back of his leg. At my back, another warrior came. And another.

Focus forward. Roark's sparring lessons reeled with the matches between me and Kael. I was no warrior, but I was buried with fury. Rage for my folk who'd died to hide me. Loathing for Nivek's pointless death. Anger for the pain Roark had endured for most of his life.

I cried out when my sword slammed against another Stav. I was shorter but moved swifter than most warriors in their bulky guarders and armor.

I'd use it.

My cuts and stabs went to ribs, to thighs, to the tendons at the backs of knees.

In a matter of moments, my face was splattered in hot, sticky blood, and my muscles throbbed for more.

Auki fought nearby. His graceful motions were a dance of blood. Stav Guard dropped, screaming, when he would strike, then from between the warriors a fara wolf attacked, tearing at their heads and bellies.

Gunter and his father kept close to Emi and Yrsa. The princess spoke true: she was mesmerizing in the way she flung knives. The small blades struck throats and hearts. If her targets did not fall from the strike, Emi came up behind them and snapped their necks with her craft.

Thane slammed his sword against his own army with the same unbridled animosity written on his features. He cursed them. Shouted in their faces. He shoved his sword deep in their chests. Next to him, Brynn cried out, stumbling over a blow from a Stav at her back. Òlmr leapt over a fallen Dark Watch warrior, her paws crushing the Stav into the soil.

Two paces from Brynn, Kael stood, unmoving. There was a twist of pain on his face.

No. The draw to fall into the bloodlust of the Berserkir was there. He watched the fara wolf tear into the Stav. He looked to Brynn, who reached for her fallen sword as another Stav rushed for her.

Kael took aim at Brynn.

"No!" I screamed. "Kael, no!"

His sword sliced through the air.

The edge cut through the Stav Guard aiming for Brynn. The guard stumbled forward, falling half over Brynn's legs.

Kael ripped his blade free of the man's neck and yanked Brynn back to her feet by her hand. Chest to chest, they studied each other, their faces bloodied. For a moment, there was the old Kael in those eyes, looking at the only soul who soothed his.

They broke apart and battled side by side.

I looked for Roark, searched the burn in my chest, desperate to find him. Something tugged in the spot behind my heart and turned me around.

Near the edge of the Berserkir line, I found him.

The Draven prince reminded the Stav Guard he once served why Damir had named him the Death Bringer, why an enemy had become the Sentry of Stonegate. Roark's manipulated eyes shone so vibrantly they seemed to glow. His anger was written in the sharp lines of his face, but it served us well. All my husband's rage was pointed at the warriors who could not be defeated.

Yet the longer they stood against Roark, the more it seemed the trapped soul in his blood snuffed out their every weakness.

Seax blade in hand, Roark fought with a finesse I envied. As if battle were second nature, he chopped at the sturdy bones, again and again, until a Berserkir fell to his knees. From behind, Elisabet and Dark Watchers materialized and slit their throats.

It didn't take me long to realize that Roark and the queen were moving with intention. They aimed for the back knoll. Ingir and Hundur. Doubtless, Roark's binding curse was not only to pain me. It was for this moment. Fadey and Ingir did not want to risk what Skul Drek would do if he was loosed on the Stav Guard.

A scream came from the trees.

I reeled around. Tucked behind the thick oaks, a Shield Rider had Jordis pinned. Jordis was on a direct path to the knoll, spear in hand. Doubtless, the woman was aiming toward Ingir, much the same as Roark, merely from the other side.

I ran for the rider, cutting at thighs and ribs as I sprinted for Nivek's wife. By the time I made it to the tree line, the Shield

Rider was off his charge and had the rim of his shield tucked under Jordis's chin.

She kicked and thrashed.

Blood dripped from the rider, his skull, his hand, his arm. Open wounds.

"Unfettered bitch," he snarled. "What I could do to tame a savage like you."

I let the seax in my hand fall. In the next breath, I clambered up the rider's back, using his straps and leathers for grip and footing.

He shouted in alarm and stumbled. I curled my arms around his throat, clinging to his neck for balance, then pressed two fingers against the gash on his head. Brilliant gold cords of craft dug into his skin, more rapidly than normal. The roar of craft was deafening in my skull. The touch held more heat.

It was as though the power in my blood knew what was at stake and went to battle with me.

The rider screamed when the thin side of his skull cracked and shifted, melting into the hinge of his jaw. I twisted his bones, shrinking his skull with every shift. Jordis kicked the shield off her body.

Her eyes burned. She snatched her spear and thrust the point through the innards of the rider. The man stumbled, his head misshapen enough that his eye sockets had shifted and his nose looked as though it sagged on his face.

Blood fountained over his lips.

He landed on his knees. Jordis's lip curled when she ripped her spear from his belly. I released the rider and let him fall facedown.

My shoulders heaved. I doubled over my knees.

Jordis placed a palm on my shoulder. "You are horrifying."

I grinned. "As are you. Are you going for the Jorvan queen?"

"Roark needs her gone, and I can aim from quite a distance. Elisabet said she would go for Nivek's uncle, his killer, once the queen is gone. Then we all point our blades at Fadey."

I would claim Fadey. It felt as though fate demanded it. "I will keep your path open."

Jordis didn't argue. She simply nodded, and together we raced through the trees.

50

ROARK

DARKNESS CALLED TO ME.

It pounded against my bones, fueled my hate. The talisman was heavy against my chest, but Sindri's craft was fading. The frenzy of the imprisoned monster within clawed and writhed, desperate to find a way out.

I took out the rage with my blade.

Every Stav wore the face of Virki. They fell back, gaping gashes in their throats. My bloodlust turned their features into Damir's. I cut through their chests.

Fadey burned from behind their eyes. I ran at them, bringing them to the ground. Before they could fight back, my ax split their skulls.

I had two objectives in this battle: kill as many of the faces I kept seeing as possible, then find my wife.

Thane battled one of the Stav captains nearby. In Stonegate, the prince was rarely able to use his prowess with a blade because of Damir's protectiveness over his heir. Thane yearned to fight alongside the Stav but was forced behind walls, left to fire his arrows no one knew about from our old tree fort.

Only I knew how formidable he could be. As boys we would spar in secret. As I improved, so did Thane.

This, though, this was a new man I'd not seen before.

The betrayal was written on his bloodied face, but it was his face that gave him an advantage. With each opponent, Thane shouted for them to heed his word to cease fighting. And each Stav who faltered then met the end of Thane's sword.

At my feet a Stav held up his hands, begging for his life. I stepped on his chest, leaned forward just enough for him to meet the cursed shade of my gaze, then rammed my ax into his skull.

I straightened, blood dripping off my chin.

At my next step, a deep, hot spark of pain exploded across my ribs. I stumbled, glancing down where a bolt had rammed into my side. Blood coursed down my tunic. My hand went to the wound, my eyes scanning the field.

Damn.

I wrenched the bolt from my side, ignoring the sharp jab.

Virki was a coward. He stood behind his wolves. "It was never meant to be this way, nephew. If only my brother would have seen reason."

I rolled my ax in my grip.

Virki frowned. "You and I will reconcile in Salur. You will understand when you see what we will become."

My uncle let out a sharp whistle. His wolves lunged. Black and gray met them. Kyrre and Òlmr leapt around me, teeth and claws gnashing at Virki's beasts. Brynn shoved past me, with Darkwin nearby, slashing at another Berserkir. Bloodlust against bloodlust, it seemed an impossible fight.

More fara keepers followed Brynn. The wolves battled, but the keepers reached for their souls. Craft from a fara wolf keeper was soothing and firm, and the beasts found security in the particular touch of a keeper's call.

Virki was a keeper. One of the strongest. But his constant shouts and commands were intercepted again and again by Brynn and the others. Kyrre's jaw latched onto the haunch of one of Virki's wolves and forced my uncle's beast to turn off course.

My uncle roared his frustration and aimed his sword at Brynn.

I didn't have time to think before I raised my ax and blocked a swift strike from Virki's sword. He cut a dagger across my middle.

From the upper knoll where Hundur and Ingir watched, a Shield Rider beside the Myrdan king blew a ram's horn and pointed at me. A line of Myrdan warriors stepped forward, round shields in hand. They came at me without end.

Seasons of being the Death Bringer served me well.

I crouched and moved with careful footing. Exact. Strategic. This many against one took sure strikes and steady motions.

One warrior lowered his shield, bellowed a shout, and lunged. Another came from the other side. I ducked between them. My ax cut at the ankle of one warrior. I straightened and had time to turn and stab the other in the back with my seax.

A third Myrdan cut at the gash across my ribs. A hiss slid through my teeth. The warrior went to strike at my chest. I swung the curved head of my ax, catching him beneath his chin. Virki hid behind his wall of warriors, a vicious grin on his face.

When I was surrounded, my uncle fled.

Comfortable as I was with the blade, too many kept closing in, tighter and tighter.

Somewhere behind me, I heard my mother shouting for Dark Watchers to come to my aid. Battles were slow-moving at times, always caught in another fight, another blade to block. Claws under my skin, hate in my heart, I drew in heavy breaths. Gods, how I wanted them to bleed slowly. How I craved to split in two, to devour their souls.

How I craved their screams, their pain.

My head was falling into the haze of the trapped darkness. I blinked, grasping for the blood craft in the talisman. I fought to see their faces, to see her, to stay lucid. Silver scars. Golden threads. A bright soul.

Blood dripped over my lashes. I rolled my ax in hand and pointed the blade of my sword down in the other. I was resigned to end this here. If I fell, then I fell to thoughts of her.

But I didn't get the chance to strike.

Warriors dropped their blades. Some scraped at their faces, as though trying to dig out something festering in their skin. Others cried out in pain when someone danced around them, touching their shoulders, their arms. Bones cracked and bent. Necks snapped.

More warriors screamed, clawing at their arms and legs.

Darkwin, blood on his lips, kept brushing past the warriors. Before he was forced to be Berserkir, Kael Darkwin was a bone crafter. Under his touch, bones shifted, snapping, twisting, breaking.

He winced. To harm them would harm him; it was the consequence of bone craft. But Kael only grinned a little wider, a little more maniacally, as though the brutality made the bloodlust of the Berserkir rage more.

A Shield Rider stumbled, screaming about knives behind his eyes. An illusion. Blood craft.

"Yrsa!" King Hundur roared from up the slope. "Stupid girl, get out of there."

Princess Yrsa tossed back her hood, her eyes ablaze. She threw more pouches of herbs at the foot of a fleeing Stav Guard. At once, the man stumbled, clawing at his skin in terror from her hallucinogen.

Yrsa claimed not to be skilled with blood craft, but I was beginning to believe those might've been her father's words all
along.

"Tell me, Father," she shouted back. "Did Baldur tell you his
true name? Did he tell you what he's after?"

Hundur glared at his daughter. His fists curled, the hooked
bones Lyra had melded onto his knuckles in Stonegate gleamed
like jagged claws. "I know what we seek. It will only strengthen
our alliance. And you are ruining it all."

"Think so, Hundur?" Thane materialized through the mists.
He wiped his bloody mouth with the back of his sleeve, glaring
at his mother. "Do you know? Do you wish me dead so fiercely,
Mother?"

"What are you talking about?"

"You killed my father," Thane roared. "Now you wish to kill
me. Get off the horse, Mother, and do it, then."

Ingir's brow furrowed. "There are things you do not understand. Your father would be ruthless with the bones. We will restore the first kingdom."

"By slaughtering your children!"

"No."

Thane barked a laugh. "Ah, Fadey didn't tell you. The bones
are within us, Mother! That is how he gathers them. Did you
never stop to wonder why he wanted Yrsa at the palace the moment you decided to kill the king? The bones, Ingir. They are buried within your heirs."

Ingir's face paled. She shook her head. "No, that isn't . . . that
isn't true. It is our blood that will lead the melder to them."

"By spilling our blood!" Thane's voice boomed. "Look at all
you've lost for greed."

A figure slunk closer to Hundur. The king did not turn. He did
not see.

Movement in the trees came from the side of Ingir. Pain shadowed Thane's bright eyes, as though he knew what was about to happen. As though he'd reconciled with it, but the sorrow could not be helped.

Thane's sword lowered. "Will it be worth it to send me to Salur? Perhaps you and Fadey can make a new son."

Ingir shook her head. "You're wrong, Thane. You must be."

"You know, you still have not said that you wouldn't do it."

"You are my *son*." She was frantic. "You must be wrong."

"I'm not, and I do not call you kin any longer." The prince lifted his blade and used the tip to point at me. "But he is my brother, and you poisoned him."

The queen shot her disdain toward me. "You are ensnared by soul craft, and when he is gone, you will be free."

"Is that what Fadey told you? The folk who stand against you, the clans I thought were my enemies, are more kin to me than anyone at Stonegate. Farewell, Mother."

Hundur's cry came first. Emi had moved behind the king like a wraith in the night. One touch to his leg and her craft jerked the bone of his thigh to twist and snap into a sickening angle.

When he doubled over, Emi made quick work of clasping his neck between her palms.

The snap of the Myrdan king's spine seemed to echo across the battle.

Ingir screamed and rammed her heels into the belly of her horse, desperate to flee. When she turned, the point of a spear rammed into her heart. Blood dribbled down Ingir's lips. Her body convulsed, once, twice.

She toppled off the horse in a heap onto the knoll.

Thane closed his eyes. Yrsa was silent, but tears fell onto her cheeks.

Jordis let her hand drop from the throw of her spear. My

brother's wife pressed two fingers to her own brow, then bent to the soil.

Old studies from boyhood drew out a memory of the custom, an old ritual in battle where the one who sent a soul to Salur would point their head, acknowledging they knew they'd done the killing, then touch the earth, a symbol for the soil to now take the body back to dust.

Before Jordis could stand again, some force, some power in my chest doubled me over. As though a fist curled around my lungs and squeezed, I could not draw a deep enough breath.

I had no voice, but my mouth was open in a silent cry. My body shook. Distantly, I thought I could hear Thane's shout of my name. Pain lashed across my scar. Frost lined my veins. Craft roared like a thousand battle cries in my head. I thought my skin might shred off my bones.

In the moments when I thought my bones might flip inside out, a burst of shadows erupted from my scar, my pores, my damn soul.

I stumbled to my knees, surrounded by walls of inky shadows. Mists of frost and night curled over me like a storm rolling over the sea.

I drew in a rough breath through my nose, again and again.

The viciousness I kept beneath my skin was free.

One half of my mouth twisted in a wretched sort of grin. Take them. Take them all.

Swift as the strike of a blade, rivers of inky black shot across the battlefield. The dark skeins of my soul wove in and out of warriors, hunting for those who stood against our melder, our wife.

"Roark!" Thane skidded to a halt, nearly falling off his feet when he reached me. "Are you all right? By the gods, you look frightening. The red is still in your eyes."

My grin widened into more or less a snarl. *Because I am he and we are we. In this moment, we are united in the same purpose. I am nothing but wickedness until they're all dead.*

Thane kept a hand on my shoulder, but his eyes tracked the battlefield. "Well, then, I'd say your twisted soul is making good on that."

True enough, across the field, Stav Guard toppled over, confused when the strike of Skul Drek stole their souls. Dark Watch warriors were there to meet them with their blades.

Gunter whooped nearby and sliced at a fallen Stav whose eyes had gone bleary. Auki, Keela, and Yanson took down the guards the moment I left them as nothing more than shells.

"Roark!" Brynn shouted. "Virki!"

Near the trees, my uncle battled the queen. My mother was two heads shorter than Virki, but she fought with the pain of a broken heart. Virki slashed and cut at the queen, clearly trying to escape into the woods rather than engage.

Elisabet would not let him go.

She struck and jabbed and parried. Virki backpedaled, then slashed at my mother's middle. The point caught the queen across her side. She cried out her agony but struck again.

I scrambled to my feet. Thane close behind.

Virki struck my mother's shoulder. I quickened my pace. For what he'd done to my brother, to my cousin, and to Lyra, Virki would meet the hells.

Fifty paces, twenty. I drew nearer.

My mother made another strike. Virki dodged swiftly enough that she stumbled. My blood froze. Before Elisabet gained her footing, my uncle gripped her hair and plunged his sword into her chest.

No.

"Shit!" Thane's curse near my side rattled in my skull.

Virki ripped the blade from my mother's heart.

Ten paces at his back, I let my ax fly. A wave of violent delight rushed through my veins when the edge buried into the blade of his shoulder. Virki fell forward. He groaned and tried to crawl away, the head of my ax in his flesh.

I stepped onto his spine. Shadows closed in. My uncle let out a sob when coils of black wrapped around his throat. The form of my depravity took hold of Virki's throat and heaved him off the ground. Copper rage met gold hate when the deledan spun my uncle, dangling in his grip, to face me.

I gripped his jaw and mouthed, *Beg me.*

Virki trembled. The ropes of darkness tightened around his throat. His skin turned a sickly shade of blue. His veins popped in his forehead. "P-please."

I flashed my teeth. *No.*

I buried my sword through his stomach. His body spasmed, tethered by my darker soul and impaled by my hand. He coughed and bloody spittle struck my face. Too soon, his suffering ended and Virki went limp.

I unfurled one fist and the shadows released him. Wolves whimpered nearby as the bond to their keeper faded.

I had no time to care and rushed to where Thane cradled my mother's head. Gunter and Yanson knelt beside her. I slid by her side, inspecting the wound. Too deep. Too much blood.

"Roark." Her voice was rough, broken.

Soul bone. We can make you a soul bone. I spoke frantically; Thane did his best to help relay the words.

"No." She smiled. Blood stained her teeth. "No, I . . . I miss . . . miss my king."

I shook my head, one palm on her face. *I don't want to bid farewell again.*

A tear fell from the corner of her eye. "We never will. Remember . . . live. Be . . . be free. I will greet you in . . . Salur, son."

The queen died with a smile.

Yanson pressed a palm to her face. "Save us a curved horn, my queen."

Thane gripped one of my shoulders. The prince said nothing, merely stayed there, a steadiness in the storm.

"Roark." Gunter drew my attention. "This isn't over. Look."

Blood froze. Jordis and Lyra fought beside each other, but through the lines of Stav and Dark Watch, a figure cut through, aiming at Lyra.

He kept a hood over his head, but I'd traveled with Baldur for seasons and I knew his stride, his movements. Fadey moved as Baldur did.

Each breath burned as if torn from my lungs. *She lives*, I gestured in a rush. *Burn it all as long as she lives.*

"Go to the melder! We fight for her now!" Yanson raised his blade. Nearby, Dark Watch roared their agreement.

Possessive shadows cut through the dying battle, searching for my heart. He would not touch her. Smoke from fires at camps, mists from an approaching storm, and shadows from a vengeful soul blotted out everything.

I could not see Lyra. I lost sight of Fadey.

She lives. I repeated the same thought in my head as I led the warriors forward.

Ingir was dead. Virki was dead. Fadey was the last to fall.

And he would. I would not accept anything less.

51

LYRA

Smoke burned my eyes to tears. I swiped the back of my hand over my face, smearing blood and sweat. Jordis killed the Jorvan queen in the same moment that Emi took Hundur. I was drawn to Skul Drek's icy shadows the moment they were freed.

But I'd lost sight of Roark when he rushed after his uncle.

I forced my eyes to stay open, to blink through the burn.

This was the ending. This was the final step in the path of fate. Like a whispered truth, I knew this day ended our world. This day destroyed kingdoms.

Cries of battle were fading. Little by little, the slide of steel against steel weakened. Roars of attack were more grunts of exhaustion and pain. I did not know who had fallen from Dravenmoor. I did not know where to find my husband, so I followed his darkness instead.

Shadows of Skul Drek tore through bodies, striking at souls. Dark Watch warriors would be there to meet them as they fell. A hum of heat tugged at my heart, a call to find him, to bring him to me. The only hint to tell me Roark Ashwood was still alive.

Murky storm clouds mingled with ash and smoke. Soon darkness would call horns of rest, of retreat. If the battle ceased, it would be brought another day. I refused. This ends here. This ends now.

I knew it to my soul.

A blade crashed against my sword. My muscles strained beneath the strike, but it did not last.

All at once, the Stav Guard scrambled backward. His attention was aimed somewhere over my shoulder, his eyes wide in fright. Before I could strike at him, he spun on his heel and bolted toward the knolls.

What was happening?

Another Stav slammed into my shoulder in his own retreat, blood on his lips and fear in his eyes.

My heart stuttered when I heard the laughter. It was almost gleeful and far too young to be on a battlefield.

Gods, no.

Sindri stood at the edge of the field in the direction from which the Stav Guard kept fleeing.

Nivek's son held a dagger in one hand, and the other he held outstretched. His bright eyes flashed as Stav Guard fumbled, crying out in frustration, and it seemed as though the men were fighting against their own blades.

Like something—or someone—was forcing the Stav to turn their own blades against themselves.

Dammit. The boy's craft commanded souls. No doubt he'd done something to his watchguards to leave the camp. No doubt he wanted to avenge his father. No doubt he did not understand how swiftly his body would fatigue from craft.

"Sindri!" Jordis screamed. She was locked in a fight with a

Shield Rider, her panic painfully clear in her eyes. She stumbled backward, and the Rider struck. Jordis blocked the strike, returning her focus to her own fight.

I bolted for the boy, to keep him alive, to keep his mother alive.

Until blinding pain spread across the back of my skull. My head rang, and I fell to my knees.

Somewhere in the haze, I could almost make out the hissing rasp of Skul Drek demanding that I keep my soul bright and lift up my blade.

Where was he?

I blinked against the shock of heat across my skull. My fingertips touched the place just above one ear and came back bloody. I'd been struck.

My body moved as though underwater, slow and sluggish, but I managed to curl my grip around the hilt of my fallen sword and stagger to unsteady feet. I turned halfway around and my blood froze.

Five paces away, Fadey tossed back a dark hood, his face as stone.

His eyes held nothing but disdain for me.

"I tried to warn you, Lyra. I tried to reason with you to avoid this." He opened an arm, a gesture to death and blood and bone. "But you thought you could be victorious. Over me?"

Fadey hardly seemed scathed from the battle and moved like a true warrior, skilled and deadly.

I gripped my sword tighter to hide the tremble in my hands. On impulse, I studied his movements, watched his footing. "You've lost your support. Ingir is dead. Hundur too."

He only sneered. "Saved me some trouble."

I blew out a long breath, crouched lower, and rolled my grip around the hilt of my blade. Across the field, I locked on heated copper eyes. Skul Drek, enrobed in darkness, a plague on the field, found me.

I saw the obsession flare in those eyes before he fell back into the darkness, slicing through the souls of the field, desperate to reach me.

"You're out of time, Fadey. Ingir's spells are undone."

"If you think your creature can touch me, then you are a fool. I came knowing Ingir would greet Salur, Lyra. He can try to take my soul, but he will fail." Fadey clicked his tongue as though disappointed. "Out of respect for our shared blood, I'll make your death quick."

Unseen, hands gripped me from behind. Two Stav Guards grabbed on to my arms, forcing them wide. I kicked and struggled against their hold. Another guard yanked my braid and wrenched me back to the grass.

Fadey stalked closer. His men had my body pinned, my neck exposed. Gods, would he take my head here, display it to the battle? Hunt for Thane, Yrsa, Sindri? The boy was not far, and he did not know what awful danger awaited him.

Would Roark lose himself?

"You are weak," I spat at Fadey when he stood over me, peering down Baldur's nose. "No spine to face me on your own?"

"I grow tired of wasting time. I'd like to get on with it."

"You don't have the bones. You'll win nothing today."

Fadey chuckled. "You cannot convince me you returned from the River Clan empty-handed. I will find the bone of soul craft now that it is beyond the Unfettered wards. When this is over, when I have you and two others, the different veins of craft will lead me to it. I think if fate had been different, I would've liked to know you, Lyra."

The melder raised his sword. I reached for my bond, a chance to bid a final farewell to Roark. *I will wait for you in the shadows.*

Something like a tangle of rage and panic returned through the connection. My chest felt as though it caved inward from the pressure, the tension, the hissing and pleading to keep my soul alive.

Darkness rose, searching for me, hunting me. A wolf howled in the distance. Kyrre. Wherever Roark battled, he was desperately sending anything he could to find me.

Fadey raised his weapon to strike.

It never landed.

The Stav Guards holding me to the ground released me, turning blankly to the battle like they'd all at once forgotten where they were. Above me, Fadey's anger carved into his features. He stared at his sword like he could not grasp what brought it to a halt.

A cough, a groan of pain, drew my attention. And Fadey's.

No. Damn the gods. Sindri stumbled to where we were. Stupid, reckless boy. Blood dripped from his nose, and his skin was pale. He was trying to save me and would destroy himself.

I made quick work of rolling away from Fadey. "Sindri! Run, you must run."

The boy was not yet fourteen, but he'd taken to the battlefield with the bravery of a seasoned warrior. In this moment, he looked like a frightened child, surrounded by blades, by death.

Fadey shook his head, holding his brow as Sindri's compulsion over too many souls faded.

The boy turned, stumbled once, and tried to flee. He didn't get the chance.

Fadey had a grip on the back of Sindri's tunic and yanked the boy backward.

"I felt you. What wicked craft you have. Powerful. But who are you, boy?" The melder laughed and looked over his shoulder.

"Lyra, he looks a little like your dark Draven prince. A relation, perhaps? What have you been *hiding*?"

I let out a scream—not from pain, this was fury, hot and dark. A ferocious cry for all the ways this man, this monster, had stolen from the innocent. For all the ways Fadey had taken those I kept in my heart.

I hurried to my feet and ran at Fadey.

The melder had Sindri by the hair, tilting his head back. The boy was too weak to fight. I forced my legs to push harder, faster. I wasn't going to reach him. Fadey already had his dagger at the boy's throat.

Snarls and growls ripped through the air. I caught a whirl of black fur and gnashing teeth. Kyrre leapt against Fadey's shoulders, carrying the melder to the ground. Sindri cried out, clutching his neck, where blood spilled between his fingers.

The fara wolf scrambled in front of the boy, spine arched and teeth bared. Fadey was back on his feet, one shoulder bleeding from the jagged bite. His blade was lost, three paces away.

A grunt came from behind me. One of the Stav Guard had recovered from Sindri's soul compulsion and had rushed at me. Now an arrow was buried in his chest.

Thane, ten paces away, loaded another arrow into a bloodstained bow.

Together, Yrsa and Emi circled two more Stav. The princess touched one man, and fibrous red light pulsed under her skin. I'd never seen blood craft other than spells, but the magic of Yrsa's blood seemed to burn through her dark skin until the man in her grip had red dripping from his ears, mouth, and eyes.

Emi had switched to wielding her blades, her body likely aching from snapping bones with her craft. She roared her rage with every bloody strike.

Another Stav fell forward. A vacant look coated his features, and coils of shadows billowed off his shoulders. Skul Drek was there, unseen, devouring folk. Another cluster of Stav screamed when Òlmr gnawed on a throat, and spears were flung at the rest. Kael, Brynn, and Auki battled alongside the brutality of the wolves.

But through the smoke, a dark form cut across the battle. His face was coated in dirt, blood, and smeared kohl. Beneath it all, Roark's eyes burned with something violent. He strode toward me, Dark Watch at his back, ax in one hand, and in the other he carried . . . gods, he held Virki's head.

Fadey took in the onslaught, his face cut in rage. For a moment, a breathless instant, we locked gazes. Then, we both lunged—Fadey to his sword and me to him. He reached his blade in the same moment that I swung my own. He held steady against my sword for a few paces, but his fight was outmatched in skill and steel.

Fadey roared his anger and rushed for me, eyes flashing in hatred. I met his pace. No hesitation, no second thoughts.

The rest of the field fell away.

With a strangled cry, I landed a blow against the edge of Fadey's blade. A quick strike, one that tossed us apart nearly as fast. We circled each other. The vibration of the steel prickled up my arms.

The melder's eyes flashed. "We are not them. We do not fight like them."

"Afraid a woman will slaughter you?"

Fadey yanked something pale and narrow from the pocket on his gambeson. "No. I have already won."

Pain unlike I'd known lanced across my middle. A bone. Fadey threw a bone shard against me. Burning craft spiraled around the piece. Threads of dark gold I was certain only I could see rose from the piece and pierced through my leather jerkin, my tunic. They were digging into my skin, drawing the point of the bone into my belly.

I screamed and stumbled backward. Another shard struck my arm. Fadey was melding knife-sharp, jagged bones to my body. Slowly stabbing and shredding my skin. I saw Roark shoving through men, desperate to reach me.

There wasn't time.

I had only one idea how to unfasten the shards of bone melding into my body. *Take me to you!* I screamed over and over in my head.

A tug, like a hook on a reel, snatched hold of my chest. Faster than ever before, I was flung into the murky shadows of the mirror.

"Melder!" Skul Drek hissed near my ear, his frigid hands touching the glow of the cruel shards slowly stitching into me. "Make it stop."

I gripped his hand but looked over his misty shoulder. Surrounded by the blinding glow from endless souls, warriors, wolves, and fallen souls striding toward the distant gates of Salur, Fadey staggered to his feet.

"What have you done, Lyra?" He inspected the dark glow of his palms.

We had no time. I kept one hand on the bone shard half melded to my middle and rose to my feet. "Hold him!"

Fadey's snarl deepened, and he crouched like he might be readying to strike, but in the next heartbeat he grunted and fell back. Dark, slithering shadows pulled taut over Fadey's wrists and throat. He bucked and thrashed, but Skul Drek only tightened his darkness around the melder.

"You think you have me?" Despite the shadows on his wrists, Fadey balled one hand into a tight fist.

I shrieked against the shock of fire burning across my middle.

Without his even touching me, the bone shards dug deeper into my flesh, my soul.

Skul Drek shouted for his melder. Demanded I keep my soul bright. "Release the bones, Melder," he hissed. "Release the bones."

Fadey was powerful. Never did I anticipate his ability of flinging bones like knives with hardly a flinch. He still controlled the threads of his weapons even here. I had to unstitch them.

Hand trembling, I looked down at the bone digging into my stomach. Like serpents the threads wriggled, dragging the point of the bone deeper, deeper. The glow of my body flickered.

Skul Drek hissed and clacked his teeth, and he moved like he was going to abandon the tethers he was keeping around Fadey.

"Hold him," I pleaded, my voice soft.

Those copper red eyes flashed. But in another moment, heat flooded my chest. The glistening threads of our soul bond ignited into an inferno. By the gods, he was offering me his strength through our connection.

I touched one thread of a bone shard and ripped it out of my body. Fire scorched my soul where it severed, like plucking out small, narrow bones, and the pain was blinding. It was no wonder Kael opted to be dosed with heavy sleeping herbs when I unmelded his soul bones.

This was like the cut of a thousand knives.

Still, hand trembling, I reached for the next thread and yanked it free.

Fadey's lip curled. He bucked his hips, watching me unstitch every damn thread of his deadly bone shards.

When the glow of the piece fell into the mists of the ground, I rose, quivering against the pain of the shard in my shoulder, but with a restored, wicked bloodlust flooding through my soul.

Perhaps it was from absorbing the strength of Skul Drek

through our bond, but a depraved need to destroy Fadey flooded my hopes, my thoughts, to the point of obsession.

"I wonder what would happen to you if I took power from the Wanderer's bones?" I tilted my head, sneering at Fadey. "What could I do to you if I summoned it, even for a moment?"

"Then you kill those you love. Their blood is needed, and you'll need to take out their bones." Fadey kicked. He writhed and tugged. He roared in anger when the ropes of darkness would not free his soul.

"No. You're wrong. You always were wrong. If I have the blood of the god-queen, then I can summon all the crafts. Only the Wanderer needed to use melding to take power. But the god-queen, she united all, *shared* craft with all."

With every word spoken, something burned inside me. There was a draw to Fadey's bones, like I might be able to reshape the whole of his body and bones.

"Bold princes stand near, Melder," the graveled rasp of Skul Drek breathed across my neck.

To my side, a mere five arms away, Thane's soul burned like sputtering kindling.

I grinned. The fervor of bone craft was roving off him. Under my scrutiny, the glow of the prince shifted into a shade so brilliant, I shielded my eyes against it.

In all our acquaintance, I'd never felt craft radiating from the prince. But something within my own craft now reached for a tendril of power within him. As though I'd found a new door within my own power and unbolted the latch, awakening something fierce. Something ancient.

I could take Thane's remnant for my own use. The thought burrowed within my heart like a spreading plague.

Threads to unstitch the bit of the Wanderer's claim on bone craft were there in his soul, burning and thrashing.

Beneath my touch, I could unweave them. I could take them for myself. I could leave the prince shredded and bled out of the craft he'd unknowingly carried in his bones.

Or I could use it.

Another thought coated the dark thirst to steal Thane's remnant. No more seriously than asking the prince to pass an ewer of wine, I felt I could reach for the threads spinning in his soul and draw them to me.

My craft could weave his power with mine for something . . . greater.

A uniter of all the gods' magics.

Another flash sparked. I turned and could make out the forms of Yrsa and Emi nearby. They both were crouched, with their feet parted, facing away. Like they stood between me and enemy blades.

Much like Prince Thane, the princess burned brighter, sharper, the longer my attention poured into her soul. Unlike Thane, Yrsa's heirloom craft from the Wanderer sparked in a rich crimson, like fresh blood. Tangled amid the gold of her soul, I could make out the delicate fibers of ancient craft, strands of gossamer webbed around her natural-born blood craft.

Yrsa was wrong. She was a powerful blood crafter. Likely had been all her life. Words of a cruel father, of protective tutors, of the life of a shielded royal, no doubt had led her to think she was of little value save for a marriage alliance with a stronger kingdom.

I reached out my fingertips, and a thick red thread split from the princess, just below her heart. Where her ribs would be.

The tendril was strong and rippled in the darkness like I'd dropped a fraying tapestry beneath the water, flowing and bending on an unseen tide.

Take it. Destroy it.

Or use it.

"Melder." Skul Drek clacked his teeth. His fists tightened, and the coiling shadows binding Fadey appeared strained.

We were running out of time.

I spun toward the edge of the battlefield. The beat of my heart outside the mirror realm must've raced, for the sheen of my soul flickered with urgency.

Between the emerald gleam of two fara souls was the huddled shape of a lanky boy.

Sindri's body was alight with gold, young and strong. Then, like the others, around his heart—where the breastbone might be—was a tangle of flowing threads of craft the rich blue of a peaceful sea. Brine and smoke filled pockets in my lungs, coating my throat with each draw of air.

Soul craft was heady. I lifted one palm, and a blue thread slithered free of Sindri's shine, reaching for me.

Fadey roared his frustration and cursed my soul. He kicked and thrashed. He warned me that the power would consume me.

I listened to none of it and first touched Yrsa's crimson thread.

A bite of pain, like the prick of a thorn, burned over my fingertips. The satin string fastened to me. A stitch waiting to be secured.

Fadey thrashed, new panic in his eyes.

"Melder." Skul Drek used his chin to point at Yrsa's soul.

I startled. Endless faces stood behind the Myrdan princess, haunts and spectrals of the mirror. These were folk long fallen into Salur. The bloodline of those who'd gone before the princess. Her kin.

Thin threads of connections webbed across Yrsa's shoulders, her limbs. Connections she likely did not know were there.

Her folk. Her blood. Her power. They stood by her now.

But with the thread of her power bound to mine, they stood with me. I felt the strength of their souls.

I stood a little straighter, a little stronger.

"You need me, Lyra. You cannot shoulder this alone," Fadey spat, but there was fear in his tone.

Fear that he'd failed.

"Ah, Fadey." I chuckled with a vein of darkness of my own. "Who says I was ever alone?"

I reached for Thane's ancient strand. Like with the princess, a biting thread from the bone craft of the Wanderer in his form coiled around my fingertips in a brilliant white. A new rush of power, of strength. I felt as though I could battle until the gods sank the realms.

Amid the murky shadows, misty faces surrounded the prince. Old kings, queens, warriors. I thought I even caught a glimpse of King Damir's features among them, hopefully a little ashamed for what he'd done to his kingdom. The descendants of bone craft stood by their prince.

By now Jordis's figure was wrapped around Sindri. She'd found her boy, and the wolves defended them both.

Fadey didn't shout or fight when I curled Sindri's blue thread around my fingers, drawing the end into the knot of the others. The melder watched me with hateful resignation.

"You waste such power by not taking it," he said. "All it requires is the desire, the strength to pull it free, and the Wanderer's craft would be yours."

I paused my stitch of Sindri's borrowed thread. "I'll never understand why you desired the Wanderer's power when it destroyed him. It was the tale the god-queen tried to teach her husband—the true power comes from uniting the gods' crafts for all. Together we came against you, and together we'll destroy you."

With the final connection of Sindri's craft, a roar I'd never experienced before broke through my chest, a ram into a crumbling stone wall. I wasn't certain if I cried out; the sound was deadened. All I heard was a storm in my head, as though every sea raged through my blood, my bones, my soul.

I rose, gasping, but bolstered in such a way that I was certain no blade could strike me before I struck back, that fatigue would not reach me before I finished my task, that no craft would unravel mine before I crushed it first.

Skul Drek's eyes deepened to a fiery copper. He flashed his sharp teeth. The obsession and desire deepened and pulsed through our bond.

"Well done, Melder." From behind Sindri, Nivek beamed. The prince's hand was on his boy's shoulder, his other on his wife.

Behind him was a man, handsome and tall. His face was narrower than Roark's, but too much of my husband lived in his features for me not to know this was King Vishon.

The king had his arm around another.

"Elisabet." My heart sank.

"Live and be free," the queen said, her voice an echo. "Love him. We're never far."

Her smile was one of peace, as though she was at last home.

I faced Fadey and pressed the veins of craft to my heart. From my soul I withdrew another line, thin and burning gold. The final connection to bind the three veins of craft together.

Every thread burned over my palms, growing fiercer, stronger. I could see the stitches needed to bind them together, to use the full strength of the gods' gifts—for destruction. As though the threads knew what I desired, I could see the way to meld the strength I'd taken and use it to unravel the enemy of us all. Greed. Bloodlust. Hatred.

"The Wanderer was the first king," I told Fadey. "But the true power of his kingdom could have been great had he not kept it for himself. It was never *his* craft; the power of all magics lived in his queen. Meet the hells, you bastard."

I slammed my palms over Fadey's chest. His cries were a sweet final song, a delight to my twisted soul. The threads of craft pulsed into his soul, chipping at it, breaking it, punishing it for what he'd tried to do here.

I made quick work of weaving the different shades of power. With the thread from Thane, bones snapped and splintered in the distance, the sound echoing through the mirror.

Fadey wailed and writhed, trying to escape my touch.

Heat and the tang of blood burned my nose when I guided Yrsa's thread through his chest. The crimson split, slithering up Fadey's throat, behind his eyes, and down into his belly.

Something hot and wet I could not see here in the realm of souls coated my hands in the realm of the living.

Sindri's thread was crueler. The blue dimmed to a shade so deep it nearly looked black and burst from a single tendril to a cloak of knotted dark yarn, enrobing every glimmering shade of Fadey's soul.

Fadey screamed.

I took hold of the gold thread connected to my own soul. For a moment it coiled between my fingers, the end seeking a place to lay its stitch. I guided the craft string into a place above Fadey's heart, where all the different shades of craft intersected.

There, I wove my string around them all, strengthening their stitches at the seams, ensuring the craft remained unbreakable.

A burst of smoky ash erupted from the fading remnants of Fadey's soul.

His cries were hoarse. Distant. Broken.

"Melder, too much."

A wave of heat cascaded over my body. The things I could do, the power I'd hold, if I only kept each thread knotted like this, mine to command, just as Fadey had said.

I studied the gleaming stitches. What lives I could protect, what power I might have, if I merely claimed these for myself. Thread after thread, I could pull from the ancient craft within the others—

"Melder." A cold finger dragged down my cheek.

I met his copper-red eyes in the haze. Brighter than the threads of the Wanderer's bones, a golden rope was strong, sure.

"Let him rest," he said, his voice a rocky whisper. A voice of understanding.

A light in the darkness, drawing me back.

Friends, folk, and our misfit family were out there, trusting me, trusting us, to end this.

I had my bond. I did not need more.

My shoulders slumped. I let my brow fall to the shoulder of Skul Drek. His long fingers held the back of my head. Embraced in his shadows, I looked down at my palms, at the brilliant threads of the first king.

One by one, I plucked them free of my fingers, releasing them back to the others. One by one, the threads of ancient craft re-settled in the souls of every heir as though it had not been disturbed at all.

I tilted my head, brushing a palm over Skul Drek's jaw. "We'll let the Wanderer rest now."

When he kissed me, the mists faded to the smell of blood, sweat, and death.

Arms held me close. Roark clung to me, his bloody ax still in his hand, as though he would swing at anyone who drew too close. My eyes fluttered open.

My head was against my husband's chest, but my palms were damp and wet with blood.

All around us, Stav Guard, Dark Watch, warriors, and royals stood still, blades lowered.

I swallowed bile when I saw what I'd done.

Baldur's face was gone. Fadey's true features were there. I could see bits of myself in the shape of his jaw, his nose. His eyes were open, his silver scars still alight. But his body was not full. It was sunken in, as though something had melted his bones away and his flesh was draped over it.

It's done. Roark's gesture was slow and gentle over my cheek.

I fell back, energy spent, and leaned against him to keep my head upright at all.

Over. The world reeled in my head. It was over.

ROARK

I HELPED LYRA TO HER FEET AND HAD HER CRUSHED AGAINST my body in the next breath. Her arms wrapped around my waist, holding me tightly. She trembled.

Gods. The relief was suffocating. She was here. Alive. It was done.

I didn't know how long we stood there, clinging to each other, but Yanson was the one to break the silence.

"My prince." Gunter's father clasped my forearm in a traditional greeting. "The battle is Dravenmoor's. You are the overruling voice on this field."

I wanted nothing to do with this battle for a moment longer. I wanted nothing to do with being a voice of authority.

Stav Guard were placed on their knees, with Dark Watch blades leveled at those who'd survived. Thane looked at his folk with unease.

I released Lyra and raised one hand. *Dravenmoor did not fight alone. Thane the Bold will decide where Stonegate's warriors are held. Yrsa of Myrda will speak for the Shield Riders.*

Lyra softly repeated my words.

Yanson dipped his chin. "As you say."

I looked at the body of Fadey. How I'd despised the man during my seasons in Stonegate. He also resented me, always looking at me like he knew the secrets I kept.

I always thought it was his craft I hated, but it was his soul.

I knelt beside him, and a few murmurs filtered through the crowd when I dipped my palms in the blood soaking Fadey's broken chest, the gashes on his throat. I dragged my palms down my face, the hot, sticky blood coating the gore already there.

My chest, my hands, I washed them in Fadey's blood.

A hand fell on my shoulder. Lyra knelt beside me. Tear tracks left long streaks down her face. Without a word, Lyra followed my motions. She closed her eyes and ran Fadey's blood over her cheeks, her arms, her heart.

No one moved. No one gasped in horror. Our armies merely watched us bathe in the blood of our enemy. A taunt to his soul forever. He could not touch us ever again.

When we stood, I gestured to no one specifically, *Take his head. I want it positioned on the wall.*

Gunter stepped forward, a wicked smirk on his face. "Gladly, my prince."

WE SET OUT TO HELP GATHER THE FALLEN. LYRA WATCHED IN silence as Thane and Darkwin helped stack my uncle's body with those for who we would not offer proper farewells.

"You avenged your brother and Emi," Lyra whispered.

My cousin had said nothing about her father's death. She stood near the pile of the dead. Somber. Unmoving.

With slow steps, I went to Emi's side. *I do not regret his death,* I told her. *But he was your father. If you feel sadness for his loss, it would be understood.*

"It's not about him. I feel her, cousin." A small smile tugged at Emi's lips. "My mother rests now. I am no longer threatened by him and feel as though she is at peace, at last."

I dipped my chin. *And how is Yrsa?*

Emi looked back to where the princess stood between a fallen king and queen.

"She only wants to reach her mother. Yrsa and Thane plan to renegotiate the alliances. They wish to include Dravenmoor and the Unfettered lands." Emi chuckled. "It was true, you know."

What?

"What Gammal saw all those seasons ago. Lyra destroyed our lands."

I bristled but paused when Emi shoved my shoulder.

"Let me finish." She shook her head. "She destroyed the lands because it will all be different now. Our kingdoms have danced along these lines of enemies and weak alliances through marital vows and threats of craft. Lyra brought us together, all of us. We are made of stronger things now, bonds that cannot be broken. The lands we knew before no longer exist."

Emi took hold of my hand, pulsed a tight squeeze, then left me to join Yrsa's side.

I looked over the field. Smoke billowed against clouds heavy with unshed rain. White wolf tunics walked beside double-headed ravens as they mourned. For a moment, they were no longer on opposite sides of a battle.

Near one edge, a Shield Rider offered a ladle of water to an Unfettered spearman.

Emi spoke true. The realms of Stìgandr no longer existed.

These lands would be something different. Something more.

By nightfall, Stav Guard had been arranged in half the camp, under the watch of Kaysar and his unit of archers.

Thane spoke with the Stav Captains, working through proper surrenders to ease the disquiet of the Draven armies.

I strode to the edge of the camp where most of the Dark Watch waited near rows of our folk who had not walked off the battlefield.

Sampson fell. He was an ass, but his wife, still in her battle fatigues, silently cried at his side. Ofan fell near the end. As did the twins' mother. I paused to recognize their pain. Auki knelt at her side. Kaysar was unmoving, one hand to his chest, his eyes closed. Òlmr whimpered, her head on her paws. Brynn sobbed quietly . . . against the bulky chest of Kael Darkwin.

He met my stare, dipped his chin, and tightened his hold around Brynn's shoulders.

I clasped Auki's forearm. *Her soul is at rest.*

Auki nodded. "She will see to it that Salur is fully stocked for when we all join her. You know how she enjoyed a good revel."

He laughed, but it came out more like a sob. I gripped his shoulder, then left them to bid their farewells.

Lyra stood in front of the tallest mound. My mother's face had been washed, and my wife kept placing blooms around her head with Jordis and Sindri. Dark Watch stood near their queen. Yanson and Gunter stood among a row of warriors with torches in hand.

No one had washed; no one had undressed from battle. Not until our fallen left the field first.

Send them to Salur, I gestured.

Gunter gave a nod to the men and they split across the field, lighting the mounds of those we'd lost.

Lyra held on to my arm. Sindri took my other side, his fingers scratching Kyrre's big head. Jordis stood next to Lyra, watching as the queen's mound was lit. We were all that was left. So many in my house had lost their lives, fighting for this moment.

Hatred burned somewhere deep inside. The coil of a soul edged in darkness. But stronger tonight was the desire to make their sacrifices worthwhile.

We would live.

We would be free.

LYRA

I STEPPED FROM THE WASHROOM, MUSCLES ACHING, WITH new gashes that would form scars soon enough.

Roark stood in front of the wardrobe, his trousers low on his hips, revealing more than one of his own scars and bruises across his spine and hips. I tried not to stare at the open wounds covering his body. I didn't want to think of how close we came to Salur.

Not tonight.

Not ever.

At the sound of the door, he turned, a half grin on his face. *Wondered if you'd gotten lost.*

I snorted. "I think I could've slept in there. In fact, I might go back."

Really? He abandoned the tunic he'd been selecting in a heap on the floor. *Nothing I could do to convince you to stay?*

He drifted toward me. His arms encircled my waist. I sank against him, my arms going around his neck. "Maybe I could think of a few things."

I kissed him. Together we staggered toward the bed, breathless, weary, invigorated.

With a heated gleam in his eyes, Roark scooped me up and dropped me over the mattress. He tugged the simple shift over my head, baring me to him.

With a low rumble in his chest, Roark reared over me, legs and arms tangled. His mouth trailed the soft curve of my neck. His fingertips traced over the scrapes and gashes littering my body. He kissed the bruises across my breasts, sucking and licking away the pain until I arched my spine, my throat bared, pleading for more of him, his mouth, his touch.

Roark slid his palm between my breasts, speaking there. *Willing to stay yet?*

I moaned when his thumb drifted over the swell of my breast, teasing one hardened nipple. "I might . . . need more convincing."

All at once he pulled away from me.

"What do you think you're doing?" I lifted my head.

Convincing you.

I thought I might scream threats against his life if he did not return until a creeping cold skirted up the inside of my thighs.

Complaints choked off. Ribbons of shadows caressed my legs, then yanked my thighs apart with enough force I cried out in stun.

A frigid breath blew against my core, and I nearly fell apart. Roark held the fractured soul with ease, shifting between his warm, commanding touch and the dangerous frost of Skul Drek.

My eyes rolled back in my head, and I opened myself, letting the dark prince do whatever he wished to me.

Tap. Tap. Tap. Roark moved his hands in the same line down my breastbone, my belly, as his mouth.

I arched my spine, desperate to feel his mouth at the drenched center of my thighs.

He paused, then grinned with a hint of slyness. *Do you know that for you I would burn this world?*

My breath came out in rough gasps as Roark hooked my legs over his shoulders. His vicious tongue, his wicked shadows licked and caressed my soaked core with the perfect suction and pressure.

I lost my thoughts to a bleary fog.

When the rush of release took me, I screamed his name, uncaring if the whole of the clan heard. Roark's rough breaths heated my thighs. He curled an arm around my waist and flipped me onto my stomach.

His teeth scraped against my jawline, his fingers circling across my shoulders, one word: *Knees.*

Limbs trembling, I leveraged onto my hands and knees.

Roark moaned, unashamed, and ran a palm down my spine, giving attention to every divot. Darkness brushed across my cheeks and around my throat, tightening until my body trembled.

Two fingers dragged along my core from behind. Roark hummed in satisfaction, gesturing against my cheek, *So wet for me.*

"Yes." I could barely mumble the word.

Roark kissed my throat, his tongue tracing a small scrape— not from anything fearsome but from a damn branch.

He pressed a palm against my shoulders and bent me forward, lowering me to my elbows. He tugged on my hips, angling them higher. The mattress shifted when he kicked off his trousers.

With slow strokes, Roark teased my core with the tip of his length, nudging the crown in and out until I was practically sobbing for all of him.

This is what pulled me back. His words were slow against my spine. Felt, not heard.

"What do you mean?"

When I could not see through the darkness, this is what pulled me back. A life, a future with you.

Emotion tightened in my chest. My chin quivered. Then Roark's fingers dug into my hips and he slammed into me.

Blood scorched in my veins. Tendrils of darkness tightened around my body, dipping into my core from the front while Roark claimed me from behind. Too much, too perfect. I panted his name. He gripped my jaw, pulled me up, and tilted my head so he could claim my mouth as he pounded into me.

I bucked my hips against his cock. He met my movements with desperate thrusts until I let out a sob of pleasure.

After a moment, he released me. I fell forward again, spreading my knees more, cries muffled in the furs of the bed. The cold sensation of his darkness rolled over my slit, my breasts, my mouth.

I shattered on a strained moan, unable to keep my head upright.

Roark's heavy breaths heated the bare skin of my back until his length thickened and burst hot streams of his release inside me. Once we caught our breaths, Roark pulled out of me and pressed a kiss to the center of my shoulders.

He tucked me into him, cradling my head against the steady thud of his heart. For a moment, all the broken pieces of our lives felt, at long last, whole.

A MONTH AFTER THE BATTLES ENDED, THE DRAVEN PALACE WAS packed with visiting nobles and royals.

The council of the realms was arranged after the funeral pyres had faded. Jorvans and Myrdans returned to their lands to prepare for the meet. It was the first peace meet since King Vishon summoned lands to discuss the new melder.

This one would end much differently.

I studied my palms. Since that moment in the mirror, there were times when I imagined I could see the threads of the Wanderer's craft, tempting me to take more, to want more. To claim it all. No one could but me. I was the one with the gift to bind all the veins of craft.

When the thoughts came, I reached for something deeper. Stronger.

More than my sealed bond, there were now strings attached to a bold Jovan prince; a gentle, vicious princess; and a boy and his mother who'd been welcomed into the clan of Dravenmoor before the sunrise after the battle.

Roark slid his arms around my waist from behind and pressed a kiss to my shoulder. His brilliant eyes met mine in the glass of the mirror. *Ready?*

"No. The idea of dozens of eyes on me at once is making me want to never leave our room."

He grinned and pressed another kiss to the slope of my throat. *No lines, Melder. Say the word and I'll destroy them for making you uneasy.*

I snorted a laugh. "You're a bit of a fiend."

Don't seduce me, wife. We don't have the time.

Roark led me into the corridors. We'd dressed in our fine clothes. Emi and Brynn helped me braid my hair around a jade circlet Roark found in his mother's chamber.

As Roark's wife, I was a Draven princess of sorts, and I had no idea what I was doing. Then again, I wasn't so certain their prince did either. What we knew was that we had a need to agree on new orders for the lands, new treaties, new royals.

The úlfur chamber was filled. Unfettered Folk lined the room, taking in the fine stone of the walls and the iron sconces and tapestries.

Thane was already seated at the table, two Stav Guard on either side. Across from him Yrsa was seated beside Emi and the Myrdan queen.

He spoke with Emi, both looking at their palms, and the prince wore a bright grin as he flexed and extended his fingers.

Mere days after the chaos of the battles had ended, Thane grew feverish, insisting his blood was boiling. It took time, more than one healer, and a drop of his blood for Yrsa to test to realize that bone craft had taken hold in the prince.

Whatever curses had stolen craft from the royal line of Jorvandal had been destroyed after I'd taken the ancient vein to destroy Fadey. Like a dormant seed of power had burst into full bloom at long last, Thane was a bone crafter.

And it appeared that he would be a powerful one.

In the time since, Emi and Kael had taken great pleasure teaching the prince how to recognize the taste, the rush of craft, and how to summon it for his use—be it for brutality or healing.

Jordis kept trying to get Sindri to stop fidgeting in a finely made tunic embroidered with the double-headed raven.

When we entered the room, the úlfur councilmen rose. Their heads were topped in fox head furs or pelts. Runes inked their fingers for wisdom in an official council, and they did not sneer as they had the first time they sat with the melder.

Once Roark and I were seated at the head of the table, Yanson spoke. "We gather as a meet of realms to repair what was broken over the centuries. To find peace and agreements in how our realms move forward. Jorvans, what say you?"

Thane sat straighter. "Jorvandal recognizes the destructive hand it has played in these battles."

I wanted to argue that it was not Thane, but he was the resounding voice, the king of Jorvandal, and the actions of those before him would be his to shoulder.

He shouldered them well.

"I wish it to be known Stonegate will henceforth be an ally to not only the kingdom of Myrda, but also to Dravenmoor." Thane shot a sly sort of grin my way. "As for our Myrdan alliance, our friendship and support will always be yours, but not through marriage."

Murmurs traveled through the Myrdan nobles, and a few of the Jorvans.

We had already expected this.

Thane held up a palm and smiled across the table at Yrsa. "You are one of my truest friends, I love you with all my heart, and I desire nothing but your happiness. If there is to be a marital alliance, let it be with Princess Yrsa and Emi Nightlark of Dravenmoor. I expect to be invited, of course, not like those sods."

He waved a hand at me and Roark, drawing a few laughs from the úlfur.

Yrsa swiped at a rogue tear. "Myrda stands with Jorvandal." She took hold of Emi's hand. "And Dravenmoor. No marital alliance is needed, but one is surely desired."

Emi kissed the top of Yrsa's knuckles.

"What of your tentative alliances with the Unfettered Folk?" Yanson asked Thane.

"Exactly that, tentative. The Lawspeaker of one Unfettered clan has once again reached out as a willing ally, if I aid him in trade agreements near their coast."

Gammal cleared her throat from the back of the room. "Take care which path you choose."

"That's not foreboding at all." Thane chuckled. "Many Unfettered Folk fought with us, so we should keep peaceful trade with them, and it would be diplomatic of me to do the same."

You will keep us informed? Roark gestured over the table.

"Ah, fretting for me already, brother?" Thane winked. "I will tell you every dull detail of my life until your final days if you wish."

I chuckled when Roark scowled and insulted the prince with his silent words.

"We have need to discuss the new ascension of the Draven crown." Yanson opened an arm toward Sindri. "The firstborn of the heir, by our laws, is the future king of the Draven clan."

Sindri sank a bit in his chair.

"As the wife of our fallen prince," Yanson went on, "Jordis the Gentle, you will hold an honored position; you will be a voice of wisdom and honor for our future king. In this, Dravenmoor also holds peace and respect for the Unfettered clans. Blood of their blood lives in Sindri the Wild."

Sindri had fretted the whole of the last week, insisting he did not know how to be royal, did not know how to manage soul craft, and he was only soothed when Roark grew weary of the complaints and dragged his nephew into the mirror.

I would never forget the moment a son was given the chance to summon the thread of his bond to a fallen father.

It was taxing for Roark, and even Nivek's word insisted it was not the way of things to always summon the souls of the fallen. But he told his boy he was always there, guiding him. All he had to do was trust his own heart and heed the words of those who went before him.

Sindri had been more determined in recent days to rise to his birthright.

It helped when Thane, Yrsa, and the úlfur assured the boy that they would be at his side, friends and mentors as he grew.

Roark would serve as the throne in Dravenmoor until the boy came of age, and Gunter vowed to teach the young prince all he would need to know of soul craft.

Brynn and Auki assured Sindri that he could visit the fara

keep anytime he desired, with the hope, perhaps in the coming seasons, that he would bond with his own wolf.

I grinned down the table to where Brynn sat beside Kael. I'd removed half a dozen more soul bones from his body. He had scars across his chin and throat where I'd taken some, but he looked like my Kael again.

His eyes were the same pale blue, bright and joyful.

He laughed with his head tossed back.

He'd even brought his half-siblings from House Jakobson to the Draven palace to meet Brynn and her folk.

Brynn soothed the curse of the berserksgangur that still lived within him. The more I unstitched his bones, the more I knew it always would. Fadey made certain some soul bones could not be removed from Kael's body without killing him.

Kael hadn't been deterred.

"There are stronger bonds to hold to than a lust for battle, Ly," he'd told me and looked to Brynn as she'd greeted Mikkal and Astra Jakobson when they arrived. "I will always have those, and I will always fight to hold them."

"If you can't?"

"Then Brynn and I have an agreement with that fara beast of hers. Quite a way to go, don't you think? The tales I'll tell in Salur of my lover's beast tearing me apart."

There would never be a tale of such things told in the hall of the gods. Kael was too stubborn to fail and leave behind a life he had earned.

"I have something to propose." Yanson drew my thoughts back to the council. "I have thought a great deal of the reason this war was fought. It was all for craft. Each kingdom holds a vein of it, but one united them all." Gunter's father peered over to me. "You restored a soul lost to the shadows, you protected our people when we hunted you, and you had the power of the Wanderer in your hands. You chose to give it back to us all, the way the god-queen always desired. Because you and our prince fight for all of us, for our freedom, for our peace, I propose we claim a high court. A high king and queen."

My skin grew chilled.

He couldn't mean . . .

Roark rose. *What are you saying, Yanson?*

"Yes." I cracked my thumb knuckle beneath the table. "What do you mean?"

"I want the legendary kingdom of the Wanderer King, and I want you both to lead it. Every realm keeps its power, its sovereignty, but I cannot sit at this table without you both as voices of authority. A king and queen of craft."

"I stand with this," Thane said.

"As do I." Yrsa beamed at me.

"Oh, me too." Sindri seemed disinterested and responded because Jordis nudged him. "My uncle would be a fearsome king, eating souls and all. And Lyra can unstitch their bones."

Yanson laughed softly. "What say you? Will you claim a throne? Defenders of the gifts of the gods?"

Roark met my stare, then turned back to Yanson. *Where do we go? Where do we live? Palaces have been claimed. Do you plan to build us one, Yanson?*

We intended to remain in Dravenmoor, part of the royal house, to help Sindri with his burden.

"Wander." Thane laughed. "Become the second Wanderer King. I'll save your old Stav chamber for when you visit."

Yanson faced us. "Remain here if you like, but I hope you accept the title. The king and queen of craft. I hope you lead here, in these new realms you saved for us all."

I wanted to sink into the soil when the whole table rose—úlfur, Jorvans, Myrdans, and Unfettered—to stand with me, with

Roark. To give us a throne we did not expect, a voice we did not crave, and a crown we did not need.

Is this when I destroy them on your behalf? Roark gestured over my hand beneath the table.

"What do you say?" My fingers knotted in my lap.

I say I am yours, body and soul. Be it in a hovel or a palace.

I swallowed and squeezed his palm three times, a response that I wanted him, all of him. The darkest pieces and the brightest. I did not need a crown, nor a throne. But with him, I could face such a burden. Or I could walk away from it and live just as well.

Together, we looked back at the council.

Together, we agreed.

Together, we would face it all.

EPILOGUE

LYRA

I HAD NEVER BEEN SO DEEP INTO THE UPPER KNOLLS OF Myrda. It was lovely and bright, with a rich, salty wind that rolled in off the Long Sea. I leaned out the window of a wooden coach that rattled along the dirt roads like the wheels might spin off.

One arm rested along the edge, my face in the breeze. Next to me, Roark held my hand and looked out the other side.

In the last week, most of Myrda had ventured to the palace in the center knolls for the vows of the princess and her new Draven warrior wife. Gunter had been the one to seal Emi and Yrsa's bond, and the folk of Myrda had been drawn into the rowdy celebrations of Dravenmoor the whole of the night.

I'd reunited with Hilda, Edvin, and their families. Hilda insisted that she never believed I'd killed the Jorvan king, but folk were kept under fierce watch while Fadey and Ingir overtook Stonegate.

Thane's voice had opened the walls and lifted the tension of fear among the crafters within the royal keep.

Months since the battles ended, and the union of Yrsa and Emi was one of the brighter days. More came when Sindri was officially crowned as the heir apparent of Dravenmoor. He would not take the title of king until he came of age, but the boy had found a place in his new clan.

He tended to spend his days with Brynn and Auki and the wolves. Kael found a place within the Dark Watch, trading his Stav Guard white wolf for the double-headed raven seal.

With two remaining soul bones permanently placed over his heart, there were times when his eyes darkened and he would tilt his head to one side, fighting whatever cruel corruption tried to bleed into his soul.

Brynn's touch would pull him back, simple and loving, a guiding light.

Only once had my brother fallen so far into it that he barricaded himself behind a door, and it took an even darker soul to draw him out.

Skul Drek had a way of controlling vicious souls. With Kael, he'd reminded him of his bonds, showing him how weak the darker pieces could be and how fierce his soul bond with Brynn and his connections to me and his half-siblings were growing.

It worked, and he'd yet to fall back into such a dark fog again.

We remained in Dravenmoor. It was no slight to Thane, but Stonegate had been a prison of sorts for us both. Myrda did not feel like home. So we lived in the Draven palace, the king and queen of craft.

To Roark's horror and annoyance, folk desired that we sit on councils. They claimed that our voices held a finality, as though the other royal houses looked to our word more than others'.

In a way, they did. As promised, the heirs of craft held their own sovereignty, but somehow Roark, the Death Bringer, and his wife, the melder, were the royal word of the new realms of Stìgandr.

I found peace at his side, with our black iron crowns atop our heads, or in his arms beside the shore of the Black Fjords, or learning how to scale the damn Red Ravines like a true Draven.

The only time I felt like fleeing was when I returned to Skalfirth to honor Thorian and Selena, and Jarl Jakobson and his wife bent the knee to me.

I refused to sleep in their longhouse and insisted the jarl write to Kael in Dravenmoor with a sincere, apologetic heart for betraying his firstborn. If I was not satisfied, his title of jarl would be stripped.

Roark gestured nothing but allowed a bit of the shadows of his soul to bleed out.

I took some pleasure at the sight of Kael receiving a two-page missive not a week later.

I leaned back against the seat of the coach. Roark was glaring at the Night Ledges.

"Worried for him?"

He let his head roll to the side, facing me. *He shouldn't have gone with so few men.*

"Thane holds his name of 'Bold' for a reason. He'll be all right. He has craft now, and Unfettered Folk are friendly with the realms."

Roark nodded, but I did not think his soul was soothed.

Thane agreed to revisit the trade task the Lawspeaker of the Unfettered clan asked of the prince, determined to create sturdier allies of the clans. The cart came to a halt. Now it was me who looked ready to retch.

Roark touched my hand, a hidden smile on his lips. *I am at your side.*

"Don't let me fall out there, Ashwood."

He kissed me softly and mouthed *Never* before pulling away.

Roark stepped out of the coach first, formidable and beautiful. His dark hair had grown longer since the battle, and he'd added silver beads to the braids on the sides of his head.

He lifted his hand for me to take. In the sunlight, at certain angles, sometimes I could still catch sight of the sealing bands faded into our souls. A perfect union, a match.

I looked up the long lane that led to a longhouse. A small Myrdan farm where goats and pheasants were raised near the shore.

At the front gate a family waited for us. Four young ones, the eldest could not be more than twelve, the youngest maybe two seasons. The mother had soft brown skin with gold piercings all along the shell of her ear.

My attention fell to the father. Broad with a wiry beard that nearly struck his chest. His hair was a shade of the harvest, when the lands turned red and brown.

Roark settled one palm on the small of my back. He did not push me forward; he did nothing but stand stalwart. Always the protector.

"He looks a little like me," I whispered.

My blood uncle. The man who took in his dying sister, who helped her child find a home in House Bien. In recent weeks, I'd spent time in the mirror alongside my phantom husband, searching for connections through blood. I'd found him.

Brolin of House Ekland. The man, we'd since learned, had never stopped searching for his sister's lost girl after he heard of the raids at House Bien.

I was frozen for a breath, two, until Brolin's stoic expression spread into a smile. He waved us forward.

Tears stung behind my eyes. Of all the paths I thought my fate might take me, to be here was never in my imaginings.

I looked at Roark, holding that beautiful gaze that once frightened me. From the first moment he tore back his hood at the gates of Skalfirth, the Sentry of Stonegate, the Death Bringer of Dravenmoor had owned me—heart and soul.

Our bond was born in pain and loss, but to be here, with this man at my side, silent and possessive, I would do it all again.

There were no lines I would not cross.

If I could return to the solitary servant girl throwing star plums at the thief near her cart, I would tell her to take care with her steps. They would be treacherous, dangerous, but in the end, she would gain the fiercest of friendships. She would claim a power that was always there, always within her.

She would see the cruelest edges of an enemy, and they would brighten her darkest night. Always.

GLOSSARY

Berserkir (bare-ser-kerr): Elite warrior of Stonegate.

berserksgangur (bur-serks-gahn-gr): Untamed rage and bloodlust of the Berserkirs.

blood craft: The magical ability to cast spells with runes and blood.

bone craft: The magical ability to manipulate, weaken, and break bones.

craft: Magic.

Dravenmoor: The kingdom of Queen Elisabet. Home of soul crafters.

elskan: An endearment like *darling* or *my dear.*

fara wolf: Trained and bonded wolf used by Dravenmoor.

florin: Currency.

god-queen, the: The Wanderer King's wife.

jarl/jarldom: Similar to a lord, the jarl leads and hails over his/her own territory within a kingdom.

Jorvandal: The kingdom of King Damir. Typically the home of bone crafters.

Jul: A winter holiday.

Lawspeaker: A benevolent Unfettered clan ruler.

melder: A rare magical person born once a generation with the power to meld dead bone to bone to summon the strength of a fallen soul into the living.

Myrda: The kingdom of King Hundur. Holds an alliance with Jorvandal and is typically the home of blood crafters.

Night Ledges: Mountain range dividing the realms of Stìgandr from open territory.

raids, the: The battles that divided the realms into the three kingdoms.

realms of Stìgandr (stee-gander): The continent of the three kingdoms.

Salur: Otherworld, like Valhalla.

seasons: Term to signify years or passing time.

seax: A type of sword.

seemódir: A title for a seer in the Unfettered clans.

ser: Sir, mister.

Shield Riders: Myrdan warriors.

soul bones: Marked bones of the dead used to create Berserkir warriors.

soul craft: The magical ability to manipulate, sever, and control souls of the living and dead.

spear warriors: Unfettered clan fighters.

Stav Guard: The warriors of Stonegate.

Stonegate: Royal keep of King Damir and bone crafters.

súlka: Miss, ma'am.

tagelharpa: A stringed instrument.

thorn blossoms: Used to create a dye to hide silver scars in the eyes.

Unfettered Folk: Clan living over the Night Ledges that serves no kingdom.

Wanderer King: Believed to be the first king of the realms, the father of magical craft.

ACKNOWLEDGMENTS

It is so strange to say farewell to Roark and Lyra's tale (and Skul Drek). I adore them and their passionate love, their vicious world, and their found family I want for myself.

First, thank you to the readers who've gone on this journey with me. I hope you've left it with your souls intact. Wicked Darlings, what would I do without you? You've been with me from the beginning, and I wouldn't be here if not for your love of these worlds.

Thank you to my husband and my four kids. You are my inspiration and support, and I love you all so, so, so much. We all should go on a vacation. What do you think?

To my agent, Katie Shea Boutillier—remember when I first sent you the chaotic first pages of this world? Look how far it's grown, and so much of it has to do with your unmatched championing of my books and career. Thank you for responding to all the panicked emails of "Is everything all right? Is it all going to be okay?" Not only do you remain a unicorn agent, you have also upgraded to "author crash out" fixer. To my editor, Kristine Swartz, and the entire Ace and Berkley team—thank you so, so much for your encouragement and a little bit (maybe a lot) of hand-holding through my first traditionally published series. I tell everyone who will listen that you are the ultimate hype team, and I am so grateful I've been able to work with you on so many books, now and in the future.

To my parents, for supporting all my "saucy" books to your friends and family. (Mom, I promise Dad does *not* need to read every scene of my books.) Dad, thank you for booking the flights to bookish events and slipping into the role of my charitable PR guy and unofficial travel agent. To my sisters, who go on all the authoring adventures with me and keep my books selling and my schedule organized—I couldn't do any of this without you. To my brothers (yes, even you, Landon), for balancing books and helping with our foundation.

To Kaylee and Jasmine—here we are with another book, and your feedback is incredible. Kaylee, I couldn't do it without your keen eye on those beta reads and your helping me realize I didn't write total nonsense. Jasmine, thank you for digging in deep and helping me smooth out all the rough edges and develop the swooniest moments and grittiest battles.

A huge shout-out to Melissa Roehrich for helping me plot out *ahem* one of the spiciest moments I've ever written. You know what scene I mean. Your thoughts gave the inspiration, and all I can say is "Good girl."

Thank you to these characters for living so vibrantly in my head. I love you, and what a journey we've been on together.

May there be many more.

LJ

Set sail with the Ever Seas series by LJ Andrews, where ruthless pirates meet Vikings in a great battle of revenge, and not everything is as it seems . . .

THE
EVER KING

THE
EVER QUEEN

THE
MIST THIEF

THE
STOLEN CROWN

LJ ANDREWS is a *USA Today* and *Sunday Times* bestselling author of fantasy romance. She mystically creates worlds of dark Nordic and Viking myths bound by conflicts that bring together impassioned heroes and heroines. In her non-author moments, she is courageously corralling her four children to the myriad of activities that life involves, along with spending time with her favorite hero, her husband. Add two high-maintenance dogs and a sassy conure to the mix and that sums it up. LJ Andrews thrives spending time in the Rocky Mountains in Utah, where she lives.